The Shadow of the Strongman

(La sombra del Caudillo)

by
Martín Luis Guzmán

The Shadow of
the Strongman

(La sombra del Caudillo)

by
Martín Luis Guzmán

Edited and Translated by Gustavo Pellón

Hackett Publishing Company, Inc.
Indianapolis/Cambridge

20 19 18 17   1 2 3 4 5 6 7

For further information, please address
  Hackett Publishing Company, Inc.
  P.O. Box 44937
  Indianapolis, Indiana 46244-0937

  www.hackettpublishing.com

Cover design by Rick Todhunter and Elizabeth L. Wilson
Interior design by Elizabeth L. Wilson
Composition by Aptara, Inc.

Library of Congress Cataloging-in-Publication Data

Names: Guzmán, Martín Luis, 1887–1976, author. | Pellón, Gustavo, editor,
  translator.
Title: The shadow of the strongman (La sombra del caudillo) / by Martín Luis
  Guzmán ; edited and translated by Gustavo Pellón.
Other titles: Sombra del caudillo. English
Description: Indianapolis : Hackett Publishing Company, Inc., 2017. | Includes
  bibliographical references.
Identifiers: LCCN 2017006028| ISBN 9781624666278 (pbk.) | ISBN
  9781624666285 (cloth)
Subjects: LCSH: Mexico—History—Revolution, 1910–1920—Fiction. |
  GSAFD: Historical fiction.
Classification: LCC PQ7297.G85 S613 2017 | DDC 863/.62—dc23
LC record available at https://lccn.loc.gov/2017006028

∞

Contents

Translator's Preface

La sombra del Caudillo was first published in 1929 in Spain, where Martín Luis Guzmán had fled to from his native Mexico in 1923 and settled to avoid the wrath of Mexican President Álvaro Obregón and Obregón's choice of successor, Plutarco Elías Calles. Instead of Calles, Guzmán supported Adolfo de la Huerta's candidacy to the presidency, which caused Alberto J. Pani, Obregón's secretary of foreign affairs, to warn Guzmán, then his private secretary, to flee for his life.

With this publication of *The Shadow of the Strongman*, English-language readers have access for the first time to an important document of Mexican twentieth-century culture. While the novel was translated into Dutch by J. Slauerhoff and Dr. G. J. Geers as *In de shaduw van den leider* in 1929, into French by Georges Pillement in 1931 as *L'ombre du caudillo*, and into Czech by Zdenek Smid as *Krvavy Dest* in 1937, English-language readers have waited eighty-eight years to read this novel of political intrigue that has gripped generations of Mexican and other Spanish-language readers and inspired an award-winning film adaptation by director Julio Bracho in 1960, which was praised by the Mexican writer, essayist, and political activist José Revueltas and Martín Luis Guzmán. The film, which bears the same title as the novel, was banned for thirty years at the behest of Mexico's Secretariat of National Defense.

I have not been able to discover the reason why *La sombra del Caudillo* was not translated into English earlier, when two other major works of Guzmán were: *El aguila y la serpiente* (*The Eagle and the Serpent* by Harriet de Onís in 1930) and *Las memorias de Pancho Villa* (*Memoirs of Pancho Villa* by Virginia H. Taylor in 1965).

After much thought, I have chosen to translate the title *La sombra del Caudillo* as *The Shadow of the Strongman*. I would like to explain my choice. "Caudillo" is one of those words that are so saturated with cultural meaning that it becomes impossible to find an English equivalent. Though not in common use, it has been officially absorbed into English—proof of its untranslatability. Merriam-Webster's definition is "a Spanish or Latin American military dictator." Apple's Dictionary (OSX) defines "caudillo" as "(in Spanish-speaking regions) a military or political leader," while the Oxford English Dictionary says: "The head or chief of state of a Spanish-speaking country; *spec.* the title (*El Caudillo*) assumed by General Francisco Franco in 1938 as head of the Spanish state, in imitation of Duce and Führer."

For many, if not most, Spanish speakers today, "Caudillo" evokes Franco's dictatorship. Guzmán's novel, however, was published in 1929, when General Franco was serving as Director of the Zaragoza Military Academy and had yet to rebel against the Republic. For the first readers of the novel, the word would not have had the strong connotation of dictatorship that it has acquired since Franco employed it. Spanish coins used to bear Franco's profile and the legend "Francisco Franco Caudillo of Spain by the Grace of God." Using the term "dictator" also seemed inadvisable to me, because by definition, a dictator acquires power by force, and the character in Guzmán's novel is a constitutionally elected president. In 1920s Mexico, the term "caudillo" was used to describe the military men who had led the Revolution to triumph; men like Venustiano Carranza, Francisco Villa, Emiliano Zapata, and Obregón would have been called "caudillos" by their grateful countrymen. Caudillismo, the actual rule of the nation by caudillos, increasingly came to be viewed as a problem by many in Mexico, not least by Martín Luis Guzmán. Unexpectedly, it is Plutarco Elías Calles, a Mexican politician closely associated with caudillismo, who in his final report to the Legislature on September 1, 1928, in a sense, writes the epitaph for caudillos:

> I do not need to remind you how the caudillos—perhaps not always intentionally but always naturally and logically enough— have hampered the appearance, formation and development of other national power options, to which the country could resort in moments of internal and external crisis, and how they sometimes delayed or blocked, even against the will of the caudillo himself—in that same natural and logical way—the peaceful evolutionary development of Mexico as an institutional country, in which men may become, as they should be, mere accidents with no real importance beside the perpetual and august serenity of institutions and laws.[1]

Even as Calles proclaims the end of the era of the caudillo, the word conveys an ambivalence absent in uses of the word "dictator."

Although I retain the term "Caudillo" in the body of my translation, since that is the title that the characters in the novel respectfully use to refer to him, I felt it would not work well for the title of the work. Despite the fact that the word appears in English dictionaries, and historians

---

1. Enrique Krauze, *Mexico: Biography of Power: A History of Modern Mexico, 1810–1996* (New York: HarperCollins, 1997), 427.

writing in English commonly employ it (for example, Jürgen Buchenau in his biography *The Last Caudillo: Álvaro Obregón and the Mexican Revolution*), it is not a word commonly in use by non-specialists and its pronunciation could easily trip up readers unfamiliar with Spanish. The word "strongman" approximates the meaning of "caudillo" and is in common use in English. In addition, the title in Spanish has a beautiful cadence that I feel is approximated by *The Shadow of the Strongman*.

Translating *La sombra del Caudillo* presents many challenges. Chief among them is turning Guzmán's elegant and variable prose into an English version that will do him justice. Guzmán's prose is at times as terse as that of a hard-boiled detective novel, but it easily drifts, without notice, into reveries and descriptions of great poetic beauty and then back again into the direct, unadorned style of a political thriller. The dialogue, also, often presents challenges. A number of the protagonists are characterized largely through the way they speak. The registers of language deployed in the novel range from the nuanced, witty conversations of a cultured man like Axkaná González, whose mindset seems particularly close to that of the author himself, to the high-flown oratory of politicians like Emilio Olivier Fernández, to the colorful ramblings of illiterate peasants who now wear the uniform of generals, like Encarnación Reyes, and the slightly more literate Catarino Ibáñez. Often the humbler the social origin of the character, the more difficult it is to capture the flavor of their folksy speech that is part of the pleasure of reading the novel in Spanish. My approach is to use expressions of an equivalent register in English, always trying to avoid those that are too closely identified with a region of the United States and risk attenuating the Mexican flavor of the novel.

One of the most memorable passages of *La sombra del Caudillo*, and one that caught Carleton Beals' sharp eye in his 1930 review of the novel, is also a crucial moment in the novel's plot. It turns on an inventive use of the verb *madrugar*, to rise early. In common usage throughout the Spanish-speaking world, the verb is intransitive, as is its English equivalent, but it seems that during the military phase of the Mexican Revolution and then in the political struggles that immediately followed, it began to be used as a transitive verb in a very colorful manner. In his review, Beals writes, "'Mexican politics is conjugated with only one verb,' declares the cynical Olivier, 'rise early.' Get the drop on the other fellow, be your weapon a Colt '48, a regiment of troops, or a political convention."[2] "Get the drop

---

2. Carleton Beals, "Mexican Militarism," Foreign Literature reviews, *The Saturday Review of Literature* 6, no. 33 (March 8, 1930): 802.

on the other fellow" is a good rendering of the meaning, but the Spanish word combines the concept of dawn, *madrugada*, with that of beating your opponent to the punch, and the association of this political tactic with dawn acquires special meaning and poignancy for the protagonist of the novel, Ignacio Aguirre, at a late point in the novel when the dawn reminds him of Olivier's warning. This made me realize that although a number of very good phrases, like "get the drop on," are available in English, none use the word "dawn." Below is the Spanish text and my translation:

> —O nosotros le madrugamos bien al Caudillo—decía Olivier—o el Caudillo nos madruga a nosotros; en estos casos triunfan siempre los de la iniciativa. ¿Qué pasa cuando dos buenos tiradores andan acechándose pistola en mano? El que primero dispara, primero mata. Pues bien, la política en México, política de la pistola, sólo conjuga un verbo: madrugar.

> "Either we strike the Caudillo at dawn with all we've got or the Caudillo will strike *us* at dawn," said Olivier; "In these cases, those who take the initiative always win. What happens when two good shots face each other, pistols in hand? Whoever shoots first, kills first. Well then, Mexican politics, the politics of the pistol, has only one axiom: strike at dawn."

Since *madrugar* was used for early morning surprise attacks during the Revolution, I opted for the military equivalent in English, "dawn strike."

The text I translate is the Fondo de Cultura Económica edition of *La sombra del Caudillo*, which is the definitive version revised by Martín Luis Guzmán and published in volume 2 of the *Obras Completas*. In my preparation of the translation and supporting materials in this book, I have benefited from the introduction and notes in Antonio Lorente Medina's critical edition of *La sombra del Caudillo* published by Clásicos Castalia. I have also consulted Rafael Olea Franco's critical edition of *La sombra del Caudillo* published by the Colección Archivos. The works of several historians were of great value: Pedro Castro's *A la sombra de un caudillo: vida y muerte del general Francisco R. Serrano*; Enrique Krauze's *Mexico: Biography of Power*; Gilbert M. Joseph and Jürgen Buchenau's *Mexico's Once and Future Revolution*; Jürgen Buchenau's *The Last Caudillo: Álvaro Obregón and the Mexican Revolution*, and his *Plutarco Elías Calles and the Mexican Revolution*.

My first word of thanks goes to my colleague Randolph Pope who recommended and introduced me to Lucía Guzmán who, at a conference, expressed to him the family's wish to have her grandfather's works translated. I also want to express my gratitude to the Guzmán family, especially to Lucía Guzmán, Ana Luisa Guzmán, and Martín Luis Guzmán Ferrer, for their support and faith in me. I want to thank my colleagues of the University of Virginia's Department of Spanish, Italian, and Portuguese, for their enthusiasm and for their excellent questions when I presented this project at the Tibor Wlassics Faculty Talk. Professor Daniel Chávez of the University of New Hampshire was of great assistance regarding Mexican idiomatic expressions. Likewise, Miguel Valladares-Llata of the University of Virginia Library helped me find valuable bibliographical sources and photographs. I am grateful to my wife, Karen, who read a draft of the translation and made valuable suggestions, and for her support throughout the process of researching and turning *La sombra del Caudillo* into *The Shadow of the Strongman*. Finally, I thank Rick Todhunter of Hackett Publishing Company for his guidance and his editorial suggestions.

Martín Luis Guzmán
Author of *La sombra del Caudillo* (1929)

Chronology of Martín Luis Guzmán's Life[1]

October 6, 1887	Born in Chihuahua, Chihuahua. His mother is Carmen Franco Terrazas de Guzmán, and his father Martín Luis Guzmán y Rendón is a captain in the army. At the end of the year the family moves to Mexico City.
1904	Enters the National Preparatory High School. There he meets the future members of the *Ateneo de la Juventud* (later *Ateneo de México*), which sought to promote intellectual and artistic culture.
1908	Joins the editorial staff of the newspaper *El Imparcial*.
1909 January 7	Enters the National School of Jurisprudence in Mexico City.
July 24	Marries Anita West Villalobos.
August	Appointed chief secretary in the Mexican consulate in Phoenix, Arizona.
1911 January 7	Returns to the National School of Jurisprudence.
	Joins the literary group *El Ateneo de México*. Other members who would also make great contributions to Mexican culture include Alfonso Reyes and José Vasconcelos.
	Takes part in pro-Madero turmoil in Mexico City.
	Attends the National Convention of the Progressive Liberal Party as a delegate.
1913 February	After Madero's assassination, joins other Maderistas in founding the newspaper *El Honor Nacional* to denounce the plots of the supporters of Victoriano Huerta.
May	Leaves Mexico City for the United States, intending to join forces in Coahuila or Sonora fighting Victoriano Huerta. Has to turn back for lack of funds.

---

1. I am indebted to the chronologies in Emilio Abreu Gómez's *Martín Luis Guzmán* and in the Archivos Collection critical edition of *La sombra del Caudillo* edited by Rafael Olea Franco. Antonio Lorente Medina's introduction to his critical edition of *La sombra del Caudillo* has also been very useful.

September	Leaves Mexico City and joins revolutionary forces in Sonora.
November	Joins the general staff of General Ramón F. Iturbe in Culiacán, Sinaloa.
1914	
February	Joins the general staff of General Álvaro Obregón in Nogales, Sonora.
March	Sent by Venustiano Carranza on a mission to Ciudad Juárez, Chihuahua.
March	Joins the general staff of General Francisco Villa.
August	Sent by Villa to accompany Constitutionalist troops as they enter Mexico City and remain there as the envoy of the Division of the North.
September	Carranza orders his arrest together with other Villistas in reprisal for Villa's imprisonment of Obregón in Chihuahua.
October	Freed with other Villistas by order of the Military Convention of Aguascalientes. Travels to Aguascalientes.
November	Villa sends him to Mexico City to serve as advisor to General José Isabel Robles, secretary of war and the navy.
November	Appointed secretary of the National University and Director of the National Library.
	Commissioned a colonel in the Revolutionary Army; Generals Villa and Lucio Blanco confirm his rank.
1915	
January	Chooses exile in Spain with his family to avoid participating in the civil war between Carranza and Obregón on one side, and Villa and Zapata on the other.
	Publishes his first book *La querella de México* (The Mexican Quarrel) in Madrid.
1916	
February	Leaves Madrid with his family and settles in New York City.
Spring	Turns down invitation from the University of Illinois.
October	With the support of Pedro Henríquez Ureña is appointed professorial lecturer of Spanish language and literature at the University of Minnesota.

1918	Directs the Mexican journal *El Gráfico* published in New York and contributes to other Spanish language publications, among them *Revista Universal* (also published in New York).
1919	Returns to Mexico and is appointed chief of the editorial section of *El Heraldo de México*, a daily founded by General Salvador Alvarado.
1920 May	Goes to Mazatlán, Sinaloa, to meet with General Ramón F. Iturbe, who has not joined the uprising led by Obregón against Carranza's government.
May	Boards a U.S. ship to San Diego with Iturbe when the rebellion triumphs and Carranza is assassinated.
June	Returns to Mexico and negotiates the safe return and reinstatement of General Iturbe with the leaders of the rebellion, General Adolfo de la Huerta, and Obregón.
June	Resumes his position as chief of the editorial section of *El Heraldo de México*.
June	Publishes in Mexico City *A orillas del Hudson* (On the Banks of the Hudson).
December	Appointed private secretary of Alberto J. Pani, secretary of foreign affairs in the government of President Obregón.
1921	Representing the secretary of foreign affairs, Guzmán is appointed to the Organizing Committee for the Celebration of the Centenary of Mexican Independence.
March 29	Delivers the funeral oration at the burial of Jesús Urueta at the Rotonda de los Hombres Ilustres del Panteón de Dolores (Rotunda of Illustrious Men at the Dolores Cemetery), in the presence of President Obregón.
1922 March 18	Begins to publish the afternoon daily *El Mundo*.
September	Elected deputy for the sixth District of the City of Mexico, in the thirtieth Legislature of the Congress of the Union.
1923 December	Is forced to leave Mexico by Obregón's government for supporting the candidacy of Adolfo de la Huerta to the presidency. *El Mundo* is confiscated.

1924–mid-1925	Lives in New York City.
Mid-1925– August 1926	Lives in Spain.
August 1926– October 1927	Lives in France, mostly in Paris.
October 1927	Returns to Spain where he works for several Madrid newspapers: *El Debate, Ahora, Luz,* and directs the dailies *El Sol* and *La Voz.*
1928	Publishes *El águila y la serpiente* (The Eagle and the Serpent) in Madrid.
1928–1929	Publishes first version of *La sombra del Caudillo (The Shadow of the Strongman)* in thirty-five installments in the newspapers: *La Opinión* (Los Angeles, California) and *La Prensa* (San Antonio, Texas). Mexico City's *El Universal* publishes thirty-one installments, censoring the conclusion of the novel.
1929	*La sombra del Caudillo (The Shadow of the Strongman)* is published in book form by Espasa-Calpe of Madrid. Plutarco Elías Calles, "Jefe Máximo de la Revolución," bans the novel in Mexico and forbids Espasa-Calpe to distribute in Mexico any works by Martín Luis Guzmán dealing with Mexican topics after 1910.
1931	Compañía Iberoamericana de Publicaciones in Madrid publishes *Aventuras democráticas* (Democratic Adventures), which contains the section titled "Axkaná González en las elecciones", (Axkaná González in the Elections) a series of installments from the newspaper version of *La sombra del Caudillo* that were omitted from the book version.
1932	Publishes *Mina el mozo: héroe de Navarra* (Mina "the Boy": Hero of Navarra).
1933	*Filadelfia, paraíso de conspiradores y otras historias noveladas* (Philadelphia, Paradise of Conspirators and Other Fictionalized Stories) appears in installments in various publications in the United States and Spain.
1936 April	Returns to Mexico with the support of President Lázaro Cárdenas. Resumes his work for *El Universal.*
Months later	Begins to write *Memorias de Pancho Villa* (Memoirs of Pancho Villa).

1938	Publishes *El hombre y sus armas* (Arms and the Man), the first part of *Memorias de Pancho Villa* in book form, which had already been serialized in weekly literary supplements.
1939	Publishes *Campos de batalla* (Battlefields), the second part of *Memorias de Pancho Villa*.
July	Together with Rafael Giménez Siles founds Edición y Distribución Iberoamericana de Publicaciones, S.A. (EDIAPSA), a publishing and bookstore company.
1940	
February 14	Appointed as a corresponding member of the Mexican Academy of Language.
	Publishes *Panoramas políticos* (Political Panoramas) and *La causa del pobre* (The Cause of the Poor), the third and fourth parts of *Memorias de Pancho Villa*.
October 22	Assumes directorship of the magazine *Romance* with the editorial assistance of his son, Guillermo Guzmán West.
1942	
May	Founds the weekly magazine *Tiempo: Semanario de la Vida y la Verdad*.
1943	
October 3	Together with Rafael Giménez Siles, Antonio Ortiz Mena, Eduardo Bustamante, and Eduardo Garduño founds the publishing company Editorial Nueva España.
1944	
February 18	Founds Empresas Editoriales, S.A. with Rafael Giménez Siles to publish works by Mexican authors.
1945	
October 16	Publishes in *Tiempo* the polemical article about religion titled "Semana de idolatría" (A Week of Idolatry). The resulting national controversy leads to a long meeting between Guzmán and President Manuel Ávila Camacho about this topic. On October 23, more than a thousand persons (including cabinet members) attend a banquet to honor Guzmán for his article.
1946	
November	Publishes *Kinchil*, part of his novel titled *Maestros rurales* (Country Teachers), in Colección Lunes, number 25.

1948

March
Becomes editor of a series of volumes titled *El liberalismo mexicano en pensamiento y en acción* (Mexican Liberalism in Thought and Deed), published by Empresas Editoriales.

1949

July 20
With Rafael Giménez Siles founds Compañía General de Ediciones, S.A., dedicated to the publication and republication of important works of literature and history from around the world, with a focus on Mexico.

1951

April 27
At the First Conference of Academies of the Spanish Language held in Mexico City, he delivers the paper "La Real Academia Española y sus filiales las Academias correspondientes" (The Spanish Royal Academy and Its Corresponding Academies). In his paper he argues for the autonomy of the corresponding academies and their parity with the Real Academia Española.

June 16
Appointed to Mexico's United Nations mission with the rank of plenipotentiary ambassador.

June
Compañía General de Ediciones publishes in one volume all five parts of *Memorias de Pancho Villa*.

1952

July 11
Appointed as a full member of the Mexican Academy of Language.

1954

February 19
At his inauguration as a full member of the Mexican Academy of Language, Guzmán delivers the speech "Apuntes sobre una personalidad" (Jottings on a Personality).

October 15
Appointed as a corresponding member of the Spanish Royal Academy.

1957

December 7
Accompanies Adolfo López Mateo, presidential candidate of the Partido Revolucionario Institucional, on his first campaign tour.

1958

May
Accompanies Adolfo López Mateo on his campaign tour of the state of Chihuahua.

August
Compañía General de Ediciones publishes Guzmán's *Muertes históricas* (Historic Deaths).

November 20	President Adolfo Ruiz Cortines presents Guzmán with the National Literary Award.
December	Receives honorary degrees from the Universidad Autónoma del Estado de México and the Universidad de Chihuahua.
December	Compañía General de Ediciones publishes *Otras páginas* (Other Pages), which contains the second editions of Guzmán's *La querella de México* and *A orillas del Hudson*.

1959

February 3	President Adolfo López Mateo presents Guzmán with the Manuel Ávila Camacho Literary Prize.
February 15	President López Mateo appoints Guzmán president of the new Comisión Nacional de los Libros de Texto Gratuitos (National Commission for Free Textbooks).
August and October	Compañía General de Ediciones publishes Guzmán's *Islas Marías, novela y drama* (Mary Islands, Novel and Drama), as well as *Academia*.

1960

January	The National Commission for Free Textbooks, presided by Guzmán, publishes its first free textbooks, which are distributed to children in all primary schools in the country.
February	Guzmán becomes president of the Mexican-Israeli Cultural Institute.

1961

July	Compañía General de Ediciones publishes Guzmán's *Obras Completas*.

1963

September	Empresas Editoriales publishes Guzmán's *Necesidad de cumplir las leyes de Reforma* (The Need to Enforce Reform Laws).
November	Empresas Editoriales publishes Guzmán's *Febrero de 1913*.

1964

	Empresas Editoriales publishes Guzmán's *Crónicas de mi destierro* (Stories from My Exile).
April 24	President Adolfo López Mateo presents Guzmán with the academician's badge of the Mexican Academy of Language.
June 5–7	Accompanies Gustavo Díaz Ordaz, presidential candidate of the Partido Revolucionario Institucional, on his campaign tour of the state of Chihuahua.

1965   Receives the medal for Revolutionary Merit.

1966
November 25   Attends unveiling of the inscription honoring General
                     Francisco Villa on the wall of the Chamber of Deputies.
                     The deputies give Guzmán a standing ovation in recogni-
                     tion of his tireless efforts to have Villa recognized as one of
                     Mexico's heroes.

1968   Receives the Medal for Military Merit.

1970–1976   Is elected and serves as senator for the Federal District.

1976
December 22   Dies in Mexico City at the age of eighty-nine. A public
                     vigil headed by President José López Portillo is held at the
                     Palacio de Bellas Artes.

Chronology of the
Mexican Revolution

October–
November 1910:   Revolutionary movement against Porfirio Díaz initiated by Francisco Madero, uprisings throughout Mexico.

May 25, 1911:   Díaz goes into exile.

November 6, 1911:   Madero elected president.

February 1913:   Part of army rebels in Mexico City.

February 18, 1913:   Victoriano Huerta, commanding general of government troops, joins rebels, forces Madero to resign, and assumes presidency.

February 22, 1913:   Madero shot, presumably on Huerta's orders.

February 1913:   Civil war breaks out. Venustiano Carranza, Francisco "Pancho" Villa, Álvaro Obregón, and Emiliano Zapata lead uprisings against Huerta.

April 1914:   American navy seizes Veracruz to keep Huerta from receiving German arms.

July 1914:   After series of defeats, Huerta goes into exile.

November 1914:   Aguascalientes convention fails to settle differences of Constitutionalist factions.

December 1914:   Civil war breaks out with Carranza and Obregón on one side and Villa and Zapata on the other.

December 1915:   Carranza controls most of Mexico.

1915–1920:   Carranza serves as president.

April 10, 1919:   Zapata assassinated.

April 23, 1920:   Obregón revolts against Carranza.

May 21,1920:   Carranza assassinated.

June 1–
November 30, 1920:   Adolfo de la Huerta serves as interim president.

1920–1924:   Obregón serves as president.

July 28, 1920:   Villa comes to terms with Obregón and retires from politics.

July 20, 1923:   Villa assassinated.

1923–1924	De la Huerta rebellion. Adolfo de la Huerta rebels when Obregón imposes Calles as his successor. The uprising is put down and de la Huerta goes into exile.
1924–1928	Plutarco Elías Calles serves as president.
June 14, 1926	Calles, enforcing the 1917 Constitution, enacts anticlerical legislation, "Calles Law."
1926–1929	Cristero War. Catholic rebellion against the "Calles Law."
1927	Mexican constitution amended to allow reelection. This is controversial because the major slogan of the Mexican Revolution had been "Sufragio efectivo, no reelección" (Valid voting, no reelection).
1927	Generals Arnulfo Gómez and Francisco R. Serrano oppose Obregón's reelection and rebel. Serrano is captured and executed on October 4, Gómez on November 4.
1927	Obregón elected to serve as president for 1928–1932 term.
July 17, 1928:	Obregón assassinated by Catholic radical, José de León Toral.
1928–1930	Congress appoints Emilio Portes Gil to serve as president. This begins the period known as the *Maximato* (1929–1934). The period is named after Calles, who was known as the *Jefe Máximo de la Revolución*, and was, in fact, ruler of Mexico until the election of Lázaro Cárdenas.

Key to Characters in the Novel and Their Historical Models

Novel	History
Caudillo	Álvaro Obregón (1880–1928). President of Mexico 1920–1924.
Hilario Jiménez	Plutarco Elías Calles (1877–1945). President of Mexico 1924–1928. Founder of the National Revolutionary Party, ancestor of today's Institutional Revolutionary Party (PRI).
Ignacio Aguirre	A combination of Adolfo de la Huerta (1881–1955), who rebelled against Obregón in 1923, and General Francisco R. Serrano (1886–1927), who rebelled against Obregón's plan to seek reelection and was killed in Huitzilac, Morelos, on October 3, 1927, on orders from Calles with the approval of Obregón (Castro).
Axkaná González	One of the few totally fictitious characters in the novel.
Emilio Olivier Fernández	Jorge Prieto Laurens, director of the National Co-operatist Party.
Eduardo Correa	Jorge Carregha.
Encarnación Reyes	General Guadalupe Sánchez. He joined the de la Huerta uprising in 1923.
Jacinto López de la Garza	General José Villanueva Garza. He joined the de la Huerta uprising in 1923.
Martín Aispuro	General Joaquín Amaro (1889–1952), secretary of war under Plutarco Elías Calles.
Protasio Leyva	Arnulfo R. Gómez (according to Lorente, General Fox).
Ricalde	Luis N. Morones (1890–1964), a Mexican union boss who served as secretary general of the Regional Confederation of Mexican Workers (*Confederación Regional Obrera Mexicana*, CROM) and as secretary of the economy under President Plutarco Elías Calles, 1924–1928.
López Nieto	Antonio Díaz Soto y Gama, leader of the National Agrarian Party.

Cañizo

Senator Francisco Field Jurado (1881–1924), a member of the Cooperativist Party. He was assassinated for opposing the Bucareli treaty that Obregón needed to obtain U.S. recognition of the Mexican Government.

Manuel Segura

Colonel Hilario Marroquín Montalvo, General Amaro's aide (according to Lorente). He also represents General Claudio Fox who carried out Serrano's execution (according to Castro).

Julián Elizondo

General Juan N. Domínguez Cota (1888–1963), head of military operations in Morelos (according to Castro).

Winter

Alan Francis Winslow (1896–1933), first secretary of the U.S. embassy in Mexico. He saw General Serrano and his friends being held by General Domínguez's troops in Cuernavaca and later investigated the scene of the executions in Huitzilac (Castro).

Sources

Interview in *Diecinueve protagonistas de la literatura mexicana del siglo XX*, edited by Emmanuel Carballo, 73–74. Mexico City: Empresas Editoriales, 1965.

Castro, Pedro. *A la sombra de un caudillo: vida y muerte del general Francisco R. Serrano*. Mexico City: Plaza y Janés, 2005.

Lorente Medina, Antonio. Introduction to his critical edition of *La sombra del Caudillo*. Madrid: Clásicos Castalia, 2002.

Plutarco Elías Calles
Inspiration for Hilario Jiménez.

Álvaro Obregón
Inspiration for el Caudillo.

Francisco Roque Serrano
Inspiration for Aguirre.

Luis Napoleón Morones
Inspiration for Ricalde.

Chamber of Deputies (corner of Donceles and Allende Streets), scene of the Parliamentary Battle.

Book One

Power and Youth

I. Rosario

GENERAL IGNACIO AGUIRRE'S CADILLAC CROSSED THE STREETCAR rails of the Calzada de Chapultepec, and, making a sharp turn, came to a stop next to the sidewalk, a short distance from the Insurgentes stop.

The chauffeur's assistant jumped from his place to open the passenger door. Bright reflections of the early afternoon cityscape—the outlines of houses, trees on the avenue, blue sky covered at intervals by large, white cumulus clouds—slid across the dark bluish window as the door opened.

Several minutes elapsed.

Inside the car, General Ignacio Aguirre, minister of war, and his inseparable, irreplaceable, intimate friend, Representative Axkaná, continued to talk with the characteristic animation of young Mexican politicians. The slight tone of detachment in which Aguirre spoke immediately distinguished him as one of the important public officials in Mexico. The nuances of his speech marked him as a man of authority even when he wasn't giving orders. Axkaná, on the contrary, let his words flow, sketched out theories, and explored generalizations. Though his gestures made him appear feeble, his arguments were stronger than his colleague's; he was clearly not a powerful man himself but an advisor to such men. Aguirre was the military politician; Axkaná the civilian politician. The former acted at critical moments in public affairs; the latter believed he guided those events, or at least explained them.

At times, the din of the trolley cars—swift in their race along the avenue—echoed inside the car. Then the two friends, their voices straining, revealed other, subtler aspects of their different personalities. Aguirre seemed tired, impatient. Axkaná displayed a rare mastery of word and gesture, without losing his quiet, pensive air.

Both reduced the theme of their conversation to brief conclusions.

Aguirre said:

"Then we agree you'll convince Olivier I can't accept the nomination to the presidency of the Republic..."

"Of course."

"And he and everyone should support Jiménez, who is the Caudillo's candidate..."

"That too."

As Axkaná put out his hand, Aguirre insisted:

"Using the same line of reasoning you just used?"

"The same."

The hands clasped.

"For sure?"

"For sure."

"See you tonight, then."

"See you tonight."

And Axkaná jumped nimbly out of the car.

His slim figure emerged, golden and splendid, into the afternoon's enveloping glow. On one side he was bathed by the sun, on the other his body's reflection danced on the surface of the impeccably polished car. His warm face shone above his dark blue suit; his eyes were the same green as the light that descended from the tree branches. The slight tilt of his hat over his right eyebrow gave him a faint military air that seemed inherited. But the bulge of the pistol at his hip unmistakably marked him as a civilian.

Facing the car, he took a step back to allow the chauffeur's assistant to close the door. Then, drawing closer again, he opened the door once more and, putting his head into the car, said:

"I remind you again of the recommendation I made this morning."

"This morning?"

"Come now, don't pretend."

"Oh, yes! About Rosario."

"Yes, about Rosario... I feel sorry for her."

"Sorry? Why? Don't be a child!"

"Because she's totally defenseless and you're going to drag her through the mud."

"Please, I'm not mud!"

"Of course you're not, but the mud will come later."

Aguirre reflected for a second, then said:

"Look, I promise you one thing: I, for my part, will do nothing to bring about what you fear. Now, if 'things' just happen, I wash my hands."

"'Things' won't just happen."

"Very well. Then my promise is enough."

"I don't think so."

"Yes, my friend, yes. In this case I really promise you."

"Really, how?"

"Really… I give you my word of honor."

"Honor."

The two friends were silent for an instant and held each other's gaze. The same fatigue that, shortly before, was noticeable in Ignacio Aguirre's voice now passed a veil over his dark pupils. Axkaná's intense, clear eyes suddenly gave Aguirre a penetrating, inquiring look.

Axkaná was the first to speak:

"Fine," he smiled. "I'll settle for that. Although, to call a spade a spade, among politicians, 'honor' is hardly a guarantee."

Aguirre tried to reply, but there wasn't time. Axkaná, his smile turning into laughter, had already slammed the door and was heading for the Ford taxis lined up on the other side of the street.

The Cadillac then got moving, advanced to the corner of Avenida Veracruz, and turning there, sped along in the direction of the horse track.

As the speed increased, Aguirre kept thinking of the way Axkaná had looked at him. He remembered Axkaná's last words, his smile, and then, almost imperceptibly, his thoughts turned to Rosario. Or rather: both memories merged, woven together inseparably. Aguirre felt the memories move inside each other, and, allowing himself to be affected simultaneously by them, he gradually sank into a state of strange imagination and confused intentions.

At that very same time, under the towering treetops of the Calzada de Insurgentes, Rosario awaited the moment of her meeting with Aguirre. Since this was a custom that had been going on for more than a month now, the brilliant light of siesta-time felt free to do as it pleased with Rosario. The light pursued Rosario as she strolled along; it acted as if she were another feature of the landscape, included her in the play of humid brilliance and transparent radiance. She was, for instance, lit from above by the fiery glow of her red umbrella as she passed through sunlit areas. And later, as she passed the shady spots, she was dappled with golden glitter, covered by tiny disks of gold that rained from the branches of the trees. The shards of light, like liquid jewelry, fell first on the bright red umbrella, then slid to the pale green of her dress, and finally puddled—aglow and shimmering—on the ground where her foot had just stepped. From time to time one of those luminous drops touched her shoulder until it dripped, backwards, down her naked arm, moving in time to the rhythm of her steps. Other drops stuck to her ankle, illuminating its suppleness in the fleeting moment when her foot was about to lift from the ground. Yet if Rosario turned her face, other drops of light were caught, trembling intensely, in the black curls of her hair.

A star came to rest on her forehead as she turned to look at Aguirre's Cadillac, which was now approaching. Her umbrella, sprinkled all over with similar stars, created a background for her beautiful head, turning her, for a moment, into a Virgin in a niche. Giving her a golden-pink glow, the luminous aura enhanced the oval of her face, enriched the darkness of her eyelashes, the outline of her eyebrows, the contours of her lips, the freshness of her complexion.

Ignacio Aguirre observed her from afar: she radiated light and beauty. And as he drew near, he felt a vital force, something impulsive, impetuous, that his body somehow communicated to the Cadillac: the automobile expressed this with a series of quick, nervous jolts to the brakes. The driver, who knew his master, sped on and, like a horseman bringing a virile horse to a dramatic halt at the end of a race, suddenly stopped the car in exactly the right spot. The car's body shook, the axles vibrated, and the screeching wheels left black and pungent tire tracks on the road.

Youthful, eager, smiling, Aguirre opened the door. His manner did not indicate he was about to get out but rather that he wanted to invite Rosario in.

"Are you getting in," he said, "or do I get out?"

By way of an answer, Rosario lifted her head and leaned it on the shaft of her umbrella. Her pose was clearly taunting. The star on her forehead came to rest on her breast.

"You get out, of course. When are you going to stop asking me the same thing?"

"The day you agree to get in."

And Aguirre stretched his leg out onto the running board.

"Is that so? That will never happen."

He jumped to the ground and held out his hand. Rosario accepted it in the very feminine, suggestive way in which she liked to shake hands: with a graceful twist, her head and bust facing in slightly opposite directions, twisting her wrist and lifting her shoulder so as to show the dimples in her elbow as the hand surrendered.

Aguirre, as he squeezed her fingers with a slightly brutal force, asked, stressing each syllable:

"Never, you say?"

The rude pressure of the hand was offset by the caressing softness of the voice. Aguirre knew from experience the amorous effects of such contrasts.

"Never!" she repeated, also stressing both syllables. Without blinking she held Aguirre's gaze, which hit her full in the face.

But the mute challenge ended quickly, because Aguirre, as always when he looked into Rosario's eyes, fled swiftly from them to avoid getting dizzy. As a good soldier, he knew the only reason to enter into amorous battles is to win them—otherwise, victory lies in retreat. In Rosario's case, furthermore, all retreats were roads to glory. Rosario had just turned twenty: her bust was shapely, her legs well-turned and her head was endowed with a grace and elegance of movement that enhanced, with a remarkable active radiance, the beauty of her features. Her eyes were large, brilliant and dark; her hair black; her mouth precisely drawn and sensual; her hands and feet small and agile. To behold her was to feel that all the yearnings of adult vigor and all the desires of youth were suddenly churned up like a sea in a storm—at least, that is what Aguirre felt. When she spoke, her speech—a little common, a bit timid—revealed a lively and promising (though somewhat lacking) intelligence and a candid spirit enhanced by her well-groomed body and her good taste in clothes. When she smiled, the fineness of her smile fully indicated what the qualities of her spirit might have been with greater cultivation.

"Very well," agreed Aguirre, "then, it's never. We'll have to settle for strolling under the trees of the boulevards as we have up to now."

Rosario, who had closed her umbrella, began to walk toward the Colonia del Valle, as was their custom.

"We'll have to settle for the boulevards!... And don't you think that's enough?"

But Aguirre did not answer right away. Under Rosario's bare arm, the red cloth of the umbrella had just come into such an intimate contact with her skin—so white, soft, and smooth there—that the need to be part of that touch began to torment the young minister obsessively. Accordingly, he came closer to Rosario in order to better reply to her question, and spoke. But his words were unconnected to his thoughts, just as his thoughts were unconnected to his feelings.

And thus, they walked and talked for a long while.

At Rosario's side, Ignacio Aguirre did not in any sense appear inferior, neither in terms of his good looks nor his manners. He was not handsome, but his build combined slimness and vigor in an extraordinary way, and this favored him. His bearing was decidedly masculine, and the grace, directness, and ease in his manner compensated for the deficiencies of his incomplete education. His athletic, muscular build was evident beneath the cloth of the civilian suit, although to a lesser degree than when he wore his more form-fitting uniform. And even in his face, which in itself was imperfect, there was something that made the whole of his features not only pleasant, but even attractive. Was it the smoothness of the line from his temples to his chin? Was it the meeting of his forehead and nose at the double brushstroke of his eyebrows? Was it the fleshiness of his lips that enhanced the fading, curving lines toward the corners of his mouth? His matte complexion, and the even shadow of his cleanly shaven chin and upper lip, compensated for his unhealthy color, in the same way that he compensated for his incipient near-sightedness by making a particular gesture when trying to see into the distance.

As they walked and talked, Rosario, shorter than him, did not see his face as much as his shoulder, arm, chest, and waist. That is

to say she felt attracted, perhaps without realizing it, by the principal source of Aguirre's physical charm. And sometimes, too, as
she spoke to him or listened, Rosario gave herself over to imagining the masculine movements of her friend's legs under the capri-
ciously moving pleats of his pants. Aguirre's legs were vigorous and
full of energy.

II. The Magic of Ajusco

They had walked, inattentively, from the last houses of Colonia del Valle to the flat land bordering the Piedad River. The Cadillac, meanwhile, took a countless number of turns around the block and came to stop, in readiness, at the end of the last passable street.

Now Aguirre was leading Rosario by the arm. The clouds frequently covered the sun and, at intervals, changed the light into shade and the shade into light. The afternoon, though still young, aged prematurely, renounced its brilliance, and hid itself behind a garb of halftones and shades.

Contact with the nakedness of Rosario's arm encouraged Aguirre's cynical womanizing. Giving his words a feigned naturalness, the minister unexpectedly asked:

"Why don't you make up your mind, honestly and bravely, to be my girlfriend?"

"What cheek! And you have the nerve to ask me?"

"Nerve? There's no need to exaggerate: new laws, new customs. As you can imagine, we revolutionaries legalized divorce for a reason!"

"Yes, of course! I'm sure. But not so that you revolutionaries could have both mistresses and wives at the same time."

These words, which she said in an almost angry tone, seemed about to leave a mark in her gaze and expression. But her annoyance did not last long. Seconds later, Rosario's manner, in marked contrast, revealed there was only one truth: she surrendered her bare arm to his hand, and he caressed rather than held it.

"You're right," Aguirre concluded, certain that the double meaning of his phrase would be understood. "As long as we continue to be friends in this delicious way, what would we gain by being lovers?"

Rosario pretended not to hear and changed the subject.

Their words, always turning on one theme, made detours every so often only to return shortly, reinforced by the new slant, to the only subject that interested them. He was skilled at this, she even more. Rosario too liked to hold herself aloof, or to pretend to be aloof, thereby allowing the reality of her body to be more present to Aguirre.

To seem aloof this afternoon, Rosario turned her attention to the spectacle of the mountains. The huge mass of Ajusco rose before her at the end of the valley, high above the distant forests and villages. While Aguirre spoke, Rosario gazed into the distance.... Ajusco was crowned with storm clouds and wrapped in gloomy, violet shadows that even from afar tinged, with an unreal, dark cast of night, the region of light where Rosario and Aguirre stood. And during the longer and longer spells when the sun was covered, the stormy deity of the mountain was sole master of the landscape: the sky became tarnished, the end of the valley and environs were shrouded in darkness, and the clouds, recently snow white, dulled to a dim opacity.

For a long time, Rosario, silent, did not take her eyes from the distant mountain. Aguirre tried to imitate her, he too stopped talking, but not given to contemplation, he almost immediately resumed speaking.

"What is it about Ajusco," he said, "that you never tire of looking at it?"

Still gazing at the mountain, Rosario answered:

"I look at it because I like it."

"That's a fine answer! I gather that you like it. But, why do you like it so much?"

"Because I do."

"A woman's answer."

"Am I not a woman? Well, that's precisely why I like Ajusco, because I am a woman."

"More than the two volcanoes?"

"More."

"I don't believe it."

"Because you're a man."

"That has nothing to do with it. How can you prefer that black, rough hill to the beauty of the two volcanoes? Just look at them and compare."

Rosario smiled with an air of pity. She said slowly:

"You, my dear General, like volcanoes because they have the soul and appearance of women. I don't. I like Ajusco, and I like it for the opposite reason: because of all the things I know, it is the manliest."

"All?"

"All."

"Without a single exception?"

"None."

"In other words, according to you Ajusco is manlier than I am."

Aguirre's was a smiling petulance; Rosario's disapproval was noisy.

"My, how conceited!... To compare yourself with Ajusco!"

And then, as a challenge, she added:

"If you were Ajusco..."

But she left the sentence unfinished. Guessing, Aguirre repeated the words to get her to finish her thought:

"If I were Ajusco..."

Rosario recovered just in time.

"No," she muttered, "nothing. I don't know what I was going to say."

Aguirre then whispered in her ear. Rosario heard words that she also felt, words that were sonorous and warm, words that brushed her ear with a double reality. She felt her heart tremble in a strange way; she felt her face on fire, and while she wanted to object that Aguirre's other hand, by way of stressing his words, was now also caressing her arm, she could not understand why the desire to allow him to do so was greater. The view of Ajusco, grave and manly, was momentarily confused in her consciousness with the rough sensation on her forehead caused by the cloth that covered her companion's shoulder.

Did two minutes elapse? An hour? Standing in the middle of the field, they were unaware of the rhythm of external time.

A flash of lightning and then thunder suddenly brought Rosario back to the reality of the afternoon and the open air. Two drops, hard as stones, hit her face. Above, the invisible spirit of Ajusco, hurling over her and over the whole valley the whirlwinds of its enormous black plume, tinged everything with its stormy ink. The white cumulus clouds of the early afternoon were now a single leaden purple cloud, whose curls unrolled toward the earth in thick, almost-black curtains. The two drops had been followed immediately by two others, three others, and after these innumerable ones. Water suddenly controlled the essence of everything; the valley disappeared under a waterfall.

Instinctively, Aguirre and Rosario began to run toward the car. But since it was far, it was certain they would be soaked by the time they got there; the rain seemed to stretch out across the distance even as they ran. To protect herself a bit, Rosario opened her bright red umbrella; it soon turned dark cherry. Passing through the umbrella, the water was sifted into mist.

Aguirre did not seem to care much if he got wet or not. He ran laughing beside his companion. Meanwhile, his consciousness plunged down three river beds: the novelty of the sensation—the water slipping between his hand and Rosario's naked arm; a vehement wish—that the cloudburst would become stronger as they got closer to the car; and the physical, pleasant, and immediate exertion—as he helped her jump over puddles, for which he sometimes had to lift her totally, clasping her by the waist.

They reached the Cadillac, then radiating liquid dust: the torrential rain, as it broke against the roof and sides, was pulverized. The chauffeur's assistant had come to open the door and, despite the downpour, stood there, cap in hand. Rosario saw, fleetingly, that tiny streams rushed down either side of his nose.

"I'll close the umbrella," said Aguirre. "You get in."

And his peremptory tone, as he grabbed the umbrella with his other hand, was followed by the pushing of his arm.

Rosario weakly tried to resist. Like a blow to the head or a dizzy spell, the sudden onset of the rain had thrown her inner strength off balance.

"No," she barely said, "I'm not getting in."

Aguirre leaned toward her:

"Yes, do get in," he whispered in her ear. "I give you my word of honor nothing will happen."

And, almost lifting her, he made her go in through the door.

Inside the small confines of the car, Rosario had the sensation that Aguirre was physically a much larger man than she had previously realized. She felt small, tiny. In front, on the other side of the glass, she could see the chauffeur and his assistant: motionless, their backs and heads erect.

Following Rosario's gaze, and thinking he understood it,
Aguirre leaned forward and drew the curtain across the glass. He
did it reflexively; he was thinking about something else. The word
"honor," which he had just somehow pronounced, still rang in his
ears, and the memory of the word, said in this way, was beginning
to produce a deep uneasiness in him. For a moment, he almost
came to believe he had not said it, or if he had, Rosario had not
heard it.

He allowed several minutes to elapse in silence, an embarrassing silence. Then, without looking at his lady friend, he observed:

"The cloudburst won't last long; then you can get out."

She was smoothing her hair and looking out intently. The
downpour was becoming denser as it continued. Under the shadow
of the water curtains, night seemed to be falling.

After a while Rosario also spoke:

"No, I don't want us to wait here."

Aguirre gave an order for the car to move and, as if he had
to do so before his order was carried out, drew the rest of the curtains.

Partial darkness enveloped them.

"If you think this is too dark," said Aguirre, "I can turn on the
light."

"No, no. We're fine like this."

Her arm and his hand brushed against each other.

"How awful," he exclaimed, "you're freezing!"

After which he took his overcoat from the seat and put it
around Rosario's shoulders.

"Thank you," she said.

"Do you feel better now?"

"Yes, much better."

Rolling softly, the car sheltered them from the floods of water
that hit against its leather rooftop and windows. And that gentle
rolling helped soothe the internal upheaval Rosario felt. Several
minutes passed. The calming effect was increased by the touch of
Aguirre's coat—a warm touch that rustled and gave off a masculine
fragrance.

Aguirre's right arm, which had been protected from the rain
by Rosario's umbrella, was relatively dry. He casually slipped it
behind Rosario's neck in order to raise the coat's collar. But,

having done this, he left it there. Then it seemed to him that the coat was not sufficiently closed, and in order to adjust it, he used his other hand. And then, as if suddenly seized by an impulse not his own (even though such impulses were totally familiar to him), he took Rosario's chin, drew her toward him, and kissed her on the mouth. The kiss was moist with rain and youth.

Rosario's reproach sounded weak and soft.

"And you gave me your word of honor!"

To which Aguirre replied even more softly:

"And I'll give it to you again. If you order me, I'll get out of the car immediately."

Rosario's head was resting on her friend's athletic chest. "She order him...?" She chose to keep her head where it was.

III. Three Friends

THE DAY AFTER HIS ADVENTURE WITH ROSARIO, AGUIRRE LEFT HIS office at the War Ministry resolved, as ever, to enjoy himself. Though there were several reasons for his feeling this way, there was one above all: the conclusion he thought he'd reached when talking with Axkaná González about the fundamentals of conduct. "If it is fair," he had summed up, "to accept or inflict present sorrows in view of future satisfactions or joys, it must also be fair to seek out today's pleasures in exchange for tomorrow's sufferings. Some may choose the former, others may choose the latter, and perhaps in the end we will all come out even."

Even the mere formulation of such a philosophy, more suitable than any other to the impulses of the young minister of war, produced in him a deep and almost new joy. It brought to mind forgotten delights from the days before the Revolution. And for that same reason, many hours later, he was approachable and generous with every petitioner who dared accost him as he walked from the elevator door to the floorboard of his automobile, Axkaná always by his side.

Once on the street, the warm caress of the midday air, made even milder by the cushioned ride of the automobile, flooded him with especially pleasant sensations.

After skirting the Zócalo, the Cadillac entered Avenida Madero and advanced slowly, so slowly that its very essence—as a machine made for speed—was dissolving into soft lethargy.

The clock had just struck two. The deserted avenue seemed to be on hold. The stores were closed; the sidewalks empty; the polished sheet of asphalt, uncluttered by cars, shimmered in the sun. Only a few of the sinful women who exhibited themselves there at the hour of the *paseo* were still circling—tedious, dawdling, and tireless—in their Ford taxis. The colorful passing of their dresses seemed to break up the unity of the light, underscoring the transparency of the air. It was the dazzling midday light, already enriched and slightly tempered by the remote intimations of the afternoon.

It was Axkaná, not Aguirre, who was aware of these slight atmospheric nuances. Impervious to all that was merely aesthetic, Aguirre took pleasure in the parade of the women, who smiled when they saw him, beckoned to him and, if necessary, leaned halfway out of the cars in order to keep communicating with him at a distance. One of them, whose car came so close to theirs as to almost brush against it, threw one of the pastries she had been eating at the minister's hands and laughed uproariously at her own mischief. Her fine, crystalline laugh snaked for several seconds down the street and was lost in the metallic gleam of the store windows.

Axkaná asked, "Who is she?"

"Adela."

"Adela?"

"Yes, Adela."

And Aguirre waved his hand against the rear window of the car, in order to prolong his connection with the girl whose Ford was driving away. He immediately added:

"Yes, it's Adela Infante, the one from Medellín."

"Obviously, I don't know her," replied Axkaná, wishing to move on, since the subject basically didn't interest him.

But Aguirre, very fond of certain topics, did not let it go:

"Yes, yes, of course you know her! And she definitely knows you. She's that girl who used to work in the Ministry of Finance, who always wore her hair loose after she took a bath. Her hair is beautiful (it's the most beautiful thing about her, apart from her laugh); so quite soon the Section head and the Department head were tangled up in it, then the senior administrator and the undersecretary, then the personal secretary and then the minister. Finally, unless I'm wrong, all of us in the government eventually got tangled up there..."

The passing of another Ford, with another woman inside, made Aguirre interrupt himself. Soon he added:

"The fact is we met Adela at the Gunpowder Factory the evening of the party General Frutos gave to celebrate the Caudillo's birthday. Now I see you never gave her a second thought. I did. One night..."

Once again the minister's talk was interrupted. The Cadillac had stopped; the door had opened, and in had jumped another of General Ignacio Aguirre's favorite friends: the noisy and agile Remigio Tarabana. Standing inside the car, bending at the waist so as not to hit his head against the ceiling, Tarabana shook his walking stick and exclaimed:

"You two have kept me waiting for an hour! One hour! I really think that's too much."

Despite his use of the plural, his words were directed only at the minister of war, as were the emphatic gestures he made. For further emphasis, he unceremoniously set himself in the free space between the two friends, took off his straw hat and, when he had fanned himself with it until his arm was exhausted, placed it on the head of his bamboo stick. Meanwhile, he continued:

"Didn't you ask me to meet you at one thirty? Yes, of course you did, but only in order to make me wait, as usual! And to think that not a few of us idiots still believe you!"

He had taken out an extremely white handkerchief, which he shook to spread out its fresh folds, and then wiped his neck and face with it. His dark fingers contrasted with the whiteness of the linen and displayed the luster of a beautiful blue cabochon set in the subtle gleam of platinum. That discreet and manly blend of harmonious colors and sparkles was characteristically Tarabana. It matched his aristocratic facial features, his precise and faultless manners, and the cut and style of the gray suit that fit so well it made him look slender (although he was not).

Aguirre managed to reply to Tarabana's reproaches while still enjoying the entertainment of the women passing in the Fords. Gesticulating to those outside the car as he spoke to those inside, he asked:

"And why should I care you had to wait?"

In his reply, Tarabana affected that air of mock scolding that bold protégés adopt with those who are powerful but benevolent. The tone of his words clearly belied what he said:

"Don't be rude, Ignacio. Learn to be polite.... And above all, when are you going to act in a manner befitting your position? It's scandalous for a minister of your importance to be flirting like this in the middle of Plateros Street and in broad daylight with disgusting parasites."

Aguirre's reply was half threatening and half smiling:

"Look, *Jijo*, I have told you..."

"*Jijo*" was Tarabana's nickname, given to him by his friends. It played on the similarities between his name—Remigio—and the unflattering epithet *hijo de puta*.

"What have you told me?"

"That the person who can scold me has yet to be born..."

Tarabana laughed heartily, ironically. But immediately, in order to shield himself, he performed the deft maneuver that never failed to work with Aguirre: he provided evidence of his usefulness.

"Fine, fine!" he exclaimed, taking his hat from the cane and replacing it on his head. "Behave as you wish; you're free to do so. In the end, I don't care about that, I care about this."

He paused briefly. Then continued:

"The 'El Aguila' deal is now settled. Tonight or tomorrow they will hand over half the money. One thing, though, the directives have to be very broad, very substantial, as I told you from the start.... Otherwise, nothing doing."

Axkaná, who knew well how such encounters always ended, had not paid the least attention to the argument between his two friends, but he joined the conversation as soon as it turned to business.

Confronting Tarabana, he said, "One of these days, you're going to compromise Ignacio. It's right (or wrong, but in the end, probably inevitable) to attempt some discreet operations with prudence. But, Tarabana, the truth is you just don't stop, you don't protect yourself, and you certainly don't protect those who are ultimately responsible. Every day it's directives, directives, and more directives."

His tone, though admonitory and forceful, was also affectionate and calm. Nonetheless, Tarabana, quite forgetting his manners, lost his temper:

"*I'm* compromising Ignacio? *I* don't look to protect those who are ultimately responsible? I really don't know where they get that you're intelligent. I want you to know that so far, I've never slipped up, and I also want you to get this straight: I'm not the one who is after Ignacio to do this, but the other way around. It is Ignacio who is after me. You hear that? *He* is after *me*. Now, that he is more than justified in doing so, that's another matter. He'd be

very stupid if he wasted his opportunities and exposed himself to
being left out in the street the next time there's a power struggle or
if the Caudillo gets rid of him for one reason or another. But, let
me tell you again: what good is all your philosophy, and all the
books they say you read? Do you think the money this one spends
comes out of nowhere? Then where do you think Ignacio gets
everything he squanders on his friends, including you and me? Do
you think people just give it to him?"

"Enough!" Aguirre cut him off, effortlessly putting into those
two syllables the whole power of his authority. "Axaná knows I'm
no child and I don't need anyone to take care of me."

Axaná, imperturbable, kept silent. The partly enigmatic,
partly incredulous smile with which he had received Tarabana's
outburst grew. When he had spoken before, his green eyes had
lit up with a rich expressive glow, more expressive than his own
words. Now his smile was enough to convey that the importance
of what he had said was in the advice his phrases contained, not in
the incident they provoked.

Aguirre continued speaking, now in a more serene and
friendly tone:

"It's your fault, *Jijo*. I warned you once not to discuss business
in front of Axaná, in order to avoid his sermons."

The Cadillac had passed the little Guardiola garden and,
tempted by the wide Avenida Juárez, began to shake off its sleepy
pace and pick up speed. Axaná saw the green foliage of the Alameda
turn transparent in the glare of the sun, and further on, he felt as if
from one world—that of quiet inactivity under the light—the car
was entering another—that of the explosion of sound and movement. There was a shattering din of voices. The evening newspapers were out! The voices of children and adults multiplied and
zigzagged around the statue of Charles IV, while noisy, frenzied
crowds of men and boys flew from the streets adjacent to Bucareli
onto the avenue. Most of the boys ran toward the center of the city,
others down Reforma, and others down Balderas or Humboldt.
Some, with incomparable daring, jumped onto cars and buses,
boarded streetcars, got off, were lost in the portals of buildings,
reappeared.

One boy—he must have been eight or nine—grimy face,
sharp eyes, his mouth twisted in the paroxysm of shouting, peered

suddenly over the window of the Cadillac: "*El Gráfico* is out, boss! *El Mundo!*" There he was, light and winged like Mercury. Without knowing why, Axkaná bought six newspapers, three of each, from the boy. When the car sped off, the paperboy jumped to the pavement ready to board another car approaching on the opposite side. He had left prints of his dirty fingers on the car glass—but when he jumped, the newspapers under his little arm seemed like wings.

Aguirre and Tarabana, now whispering, continued their financial conversation. Axkaná absentmindedly read the headlines; then, as the papers fell from his hands, he began to look outside. The car glided swiftly between the rows of trees on Reforma and seemed to draw to itself the gilded statue of the Angel of Independence. Fringed by the sun, the Angel, looking radiant and huge against the mantle of a remote cloud, appeared to fly above, thanks to the fleeing automobile below.

Axkaná's soul was associative, dreamy; for a moment, it also flew, and its flight, inspired by the view, was a bit whimsical and fanciful, a bit sad like the gray stain of Chapultepec Castle over the splendid pyramid of green.

IV. Banquet in Chapultepec Forest

The group of politicians whom Ignacio Aguirre had invited that day to eat at the Restaurante de Chapultepec received their host with a greeting that was nothing short of boisterous.

This was because Aguirre, who knew how to enhance his prestige by making himself desired, made his admirers and supporters wait for more than an hour on that occasion. And that is precisely why they redoubled their expressions of enthusiasm when they saw that the young minister of war had finally arrived; it was the only way they could preserve the high opinion they had of themselves, since they were deputies or councilmen, senators or generals, governors, high-ranking public officials.

There was a great deal of rattling of iron chairs among the garden's little tables, and the rising of many manly silhouettes against the shady hedges of the large kiosk built between the trees. Innumerable feet crunched sand as the exclamations, the applause, and the laughter went on for a long time.

The glasses of aperitifs induced all to sit, and calm was finally restored. The minister installed himself in what could be considered the place of honor, between Encarnación Reyes and Emilio Olivier Fernández. Reyes was a divisional general and chief of military operations in the state of Puebla. Olivier, the most extraordinary of the political agitators at that moment, was the chair of the Progressive Radical Bloc in the Chamber of Deputies, founder and leader of his party, ex-mayor of Mexico City, and ex-governor.

Not far from Reyes and Olivier, on either side, Tarabana and Axkaná found places. Their orders were taken by waiters who, in their solicitousness, bent over until their faces touched the backs of the chairs.

Aguirre did not have to mention what they should serve him. He started joking with Encarnación and answered Olivier Fernández in phrases denoting special political caution. As he did so, José, the favorite waiter of important politicians, went, on his own initiative, to get a bottle of Hennessy Extra. He quickly uncorked the bottle, filled a glass to the brim, and placed it before the minister of war.

All of the ambitious waiters and bartenders in Mexico City knew about Aguirre's habit of always drinking from a new bottle. And it lent a very masculine aura to the young general's fondness for drinking. It was also understood that Aguirre, like all big drinkers of his type, would look at the tiny glass in front of him with false detachment. For Ignacio Aguirre could only be satisfied by a whole bottle, one he'd drain little by little. It was impossible for him to expand his hedonistic horizons without such abundance.

This time he kept at his jokes with Encarnación and his chat with Olivier for a good while, as if, in effect, there were no cognac in the world, and if in the end he deigned to extend his arm toward the glass and bring it to his lips, it seemed a mere concession to his friends, not something he wanted. Had he been alone, he would have acted in the same way—but then it would have been out of a sense of private rather than public etiquette.

After he drank, the minister asked the chief of operations in Puebla:

"And come to think of it, Encarnación, since when do you come to Mexico City without my permission, and furthermore, dare to do so without first presenting yourself at the Ministry of War?"

His voice, jovial and frank, was louder than before, interrupting the other conversations and making everyone turn to hear.

Encarnación knew the question was not the reproach of a bureaucrat, but rather the verbal sparring of a comrade-in-arms, the playful remark of a superior—a superior who was his friend—offering an official acknowledgment of his right to misbehave. He too wanted, therefore, to display his capacity for wit, and he began by smiling. He smiled in such a way that his face, with its dark complexion, slightly slanted eyes, sparse mustache, and beardless chin, lit up with an ambiguous glow. For Axkaná, who saw him from the side, that smile seemed to fluctuate for a second—like all of Encarnación's smiles—between imbecility and awkwardness, and the next second, between cunning and vulgarity. Sitting across at a nearby table, Deputy Juan Manuel Mijares, Axkaná's intimate friend, thought he saw a similar look on the face of Puebla's chief of military operations. But the vast majority of young politicians present did not share that opinion, to judge from the favorably predisposed silence with which they all prepared to hear the clever reply of the general from Puebla. The latter, as Aguirre served him a cognac after serving himself, kept smiling, smiling. At last, conscious of the partiality with which everyone anticipated his words, and enjoying it, he said suddenly:

"Hell, why look for you at the Ministry, Aguirre, when I know I'm gonna find you in a tavern?"

With this he threw back his chest, while his hand, making a wide sweep around the narrow, felt brim of the hat he was wearing, groped in vain for the great circle of his usual charro sombrero.

Aguirre laughed sincerely at the joke and the satisfied mob of young politicians joined him in uproarious laughter. Tarabana and Mijares also laughed; even Axkaná laughed, although distantly, as if distracted. Could anyone doubt that Divisional General Encarnación Reyes was a man of wit, or that his wit both proclaimed and confirmed his talent?

Because, as everyone claimed, Encarnación had never been to school and did not know how to read or write. Nor did he have any intellectual background beyond his military intuition, to which he owed his career as a soldier, and his civilian foresight, to which he owed his career as a politician. His laughter was coarse and unrestrained; he was wholly uncultured, primitive and uncouth. But Encarnación's presence caused a shiver among the young politicians who, imagining their own future successes, increased the intensity of their expressions of admiration for him—one of their great men, one of the formidable and necessary leaders of their cause. Thus Encarnación's quip was met with repeated laughter and aperitifs; laughter and tequila; laughter and cognac. Inspired by his jest, coarse, vulgar, rude jokes—the first clear signs of euphoria—ran from table to table.

When it was announced that lunch was served, they all took the last sips from their glasses and rose noisily, heading toward the great dining hall. Then a kind of spontaneous procession formed: Aguirre, Encarnación, and Olivier, leading; then Eduardo Correa (mayor of the city) with Agustín J. Domínguez (governor of Jalisco) and various Jalisco deputies; and then around Axkaná, around Mijares, the principal members of the Progressive Radical Bloc of the Chamber, and last of all, slightly in disarray, the rest.

Emilio Olivier Fernández, a great politician in his own way, expected the banquet would yield excellent results for the plan he was developing.

That is why he sat Encarnación Reyes to the right of Aguirre—who was in the place of honor, equidistant from both heads of the table—and for the same reason chose for himself the first chair to the left. The governor of Jalisco, his faithful collaborator in all sorts of political endeavors, he placed to the right of Encarnación. Eduardo Correa, Juan Manuel Mijares, and the other leaders who had his absolute trust were strategically scattered about so they could keep the mood of those present within the appropriate range.

At present, he wanted to convince Ignacio Aguirre of the deep enthusiasm with which the "Progressive Radicals and other like-minded factions" promoted Aguirre's candidacy to the Presidency of the Republic, in opposition to the other candidate, General Hilario Jiménez; and, even more, Fernández wanted to make Aguirre feel that his popularity was already evidence of an indissoluble alliance—"founded in the nature of things"—between Aguirre and his political supporters. Fernández had made good use of his six years as revolutionary, ruler, and agitator; though he was barely over thirty, he had already acquired a mastery of the mysterious workings of Mexican politics and the masses.

Facing Aguirre, between Tarabana and Axkaná, was General Jacinto López de la Garza, Encarnación's personal intellectual advisor and chief of his general staff.

López de la Garza belonged to the category of revolutionary and political military men who, years before, had abandoned their law books for the promising and glorious fields of the Revolution. Instead of fighting, he'd made a successful career by managing the heads of illiterate generals and social reformers devoid of any learning. Now, to the benefit of the Progressive Radical group to which he belonged, he ruled the brain of the Chief of Operations in the state of Puebla. He ruled it so well that, under his influence, Encarnación Reyes had become Olivier Fernández's armed fist, the general ready to support with bullets whatever the Progressive Radicals built with words. To make this patently clear was another purpose of the banquet. Olivier Fernández wanted to advertise that, if the need arose, Encarnación Reyes would throw himself and all his troops into the fight for the Progressive Radicals and for General Ignacio Aguirre. Cleverly disguised allusions followed in succession without a break, as a parade of delicacies and wines made its way around. De la Garza, a master in the art of insinuation (some of his "comments" were barely smiles, questions, and exclamations that managed to fix on the most hidden thoughts, without actually touching them), made the most of each of his whispered dialogues with Tarabana or Axkaná, then only to say, out loud, something to suggest that he was talking about "it"— the next struggle for Power. From time to time he would direct somewhat enigmatic words to Encarnación, who, compliant to his mentor, would answer in the only possible way.

Thus López de la Garza would ask unexpectedly:

"But isn't it true we're making preparations, my General?"

To which Encarnación would answer:

"Yeah, 'course we are!"

Or, for instance, raising his glass, López de la Garza would exclaim:

"Here's to the next one, my General, our victory!"

And Encarnación, smiling knowingly, as he continued to drink, would answer evasively:

"Darn lawyers! Always spillin' the beans."

At such moments of confidential outbursts, glasses clinked, eyes glowed, faith was strengthened. Olivier used such outbursts to support his own efforts: he leaned toward Aguirre to whisper observations almost in his ear; he addressed Encarnación mysteriously, and he spoke at the top of his voice to those who ate farthest away. Then, from the glimmer of the crystal, the deep tonalities of the wines, and among the colors of the petals spread over the tablecloths, there seemed to rise visions of future battles with their enemies—a fatal struggle, a bloody, cruel fight to the death, like the matador's with the bull, like the hunter's with the beast. But far from casting a shadow over the present joy, such visions enhanced it, heightened it, made it more intense and dominant with every passing minute.

From one end to the other of the double row of guests, the feeling of hostility toward their opponents flowed then with an unstoppable force. Although taking infinite shapes, as if it were stirred deep inside by secret commanding voices, the instinct to fight and conquer manifested itself, in all of them. Aguirre, wrapped in silence, and perhaps opposing the others in thought, perceived from time to time that, as far as feelings went, he too followed the same course as his friends. He was not swept up by the warmth of seeing himself surrounded and feted by a multitude of supporters, but he did feel the indecipherable impetus, the unknown virus that generated and gave force to the enthusiasm of that partisanship. Olivier Fernández thought he could sense the machinery preparing the campaign and entertained the fantasy that the campaign was in his hands. Encarnación lived several lives in a single moment; the taste and the aroma of the wine evoked memories of his wild and terrible days; he felt nostalgia for fighting, fleeing, killing, and risking his neck.

It was the same for the others; all felt the same vibration, even Axkaná. The latter, as an actor and spectator, tried to penetrate the essence of those emotions that also affected him. Seeing how the others burned, as he himself did, he wanted to gather together the passionate expressions of those around him, and to read in them, as in the written letters of a language, the national truth that might be hidden beneath all of this.

V. Leaders of the Party

THE BANQUET OVER, AXKANÁ EXPLAINED ONCE AGAIN TO EMILIO Olivier Fernández why Aguirre refused to enter the next electoral contest.

It was a lively conversation with precise phrases, amid the buzzing of the departing automobiles and with evident indifference toward the landscapes of Chapultepec Forest. In the soft twilight, the Forest looked even more beautiful than it usually did. Axkaná and Olivier had entered the tree-lined lanes on the far side of the small plaza in front of the restaurant and talked as they walked. The leader of the Radicals was already a bit impatient and was saying, in a voice both experienced and youthful:

"But let's talk plainly, Axkaná. Has Aguirre made a commitment not to run?"

"He has made no commitment."

"Oh! Then I repeat: he's playing hard to get, which would be fine by me if he did it only with others, not with me."

"That's not it either."

"Then he's fooling all of us."

And when he said "all of us," the young Progressive Radical stressed the words by striking the trunk of a nearby tree with his walking stick. It was a way to vent the anger that was already winning him over, and justifiably so. Because in his entire—brief but extremely intense—career as a politician, it was the first time Olivier had run into a potential presidential candidate who for months had stubbornly refused to acknowledge the obviousness of his candidacy, an absurd and inexplicable attitude.

With his customarily placid tone of voice, Axkaná tried to transmit to the leader his own conviction.

"I assure you," he said, "that Aguirre, at least in this case, is sincere. He realizes he can be the candidate; he has no doubt that if he were to insist, his victory would be assured, because he himself says that Hilario Jiménez, without popular support, is no good even as the candidate of the *imposicionistas*. But he also knows if he accepts, it will lead directly to a rupture with the Caudillo, to a collision with him, to open warfare against the very man who, up to now, has been his supporter and his chief, and that's entirely a different matter. The mere mention of such a stance is repugnant to him due to his friendship and gratitude. We need to respect his scruples."

"Gratitude! In politics, there is no such thing as being grateful for anything, because no one gives anything. A favor or service is always done because it suits you. A politician, consciously, never acts against his interest. What's there to be grateful for?"

His aphorisms sounded conclusive. Axkaná stopped him:

"As you wish, but the fact is Aguirre doesn't think that way, and in this case we're talking about Aguirre."

Olivier did not hear him:

"Above all," he continued, "why doesn't Aguirre tell me? Why isn't he frank with me? Twice I've gone to propose the matter directly, offering the support of all the groups we control, and on both occasions—listen to me!—on both, the only thing he's done is procrastinate. People, of course, get tired and become undisciplined. Some are going over to the Hilaristas because they're afraid it will be too late if they wait, and I can't stop them because I'm lacking the only argument that would convince them."

He was silent for brief seconds. Axkaná, silent too, was gazing into the distance. The leader continued:

"You'll agree there's still time for Aguirre to say yes unequivocally."

"He has said no unequivocally."

"That's not true."

"What do you mean it's not true?!"

"It's as plain as day. In politics, instinct is the only guide, and my instinct tells me Aguirre isn't sincere when he rejects his candidacy. I know, furthermore, he'll accept it soon, although not soon enough to keep his present denials, false though they are, from weakening us. And that's what exasperates me most."

Axkaná did not believe in instinct, but in reason. Even so, he did not fail to grasp that Olivier Fernández's prophecies were correct. When all was said and done, Aguirre would accept. He, however, because he was less instinctive, and because he was more generous, got to the very heart of things. He understood that although Aguirre would accept later, he was now being sincere when he refused.

"In any case," he concluded, "don't think there's any deceit involved; I guarantee it."

Almost all the cars, crammed full of generals and politicians, had left. Only Olivier's and Aguirre's cars remained in the small plaza. The young minister was still engaged in pleasant conversation with Encarnación Reyes, as they walked arm in arm and back and forth from the garden hedge to the foot of the steps. Others, Remigio Tarabana, General Agustín J. Domínguez, General López de la Garza, and Eduardo Correa, also talked near the cars and with sudden, loud bursts of laughter.

When Axkaná and Olivier came to join them, Aguirre had Encarnación get into his Cadillac. He invited the rest to form two groups—one with him, the other with Olivier—and everyone left.

That night, Aguirre and his seven companions ended up at Calle de la Magnolia, at the house of some of Olivier Fernández's lady friends.

The vitality of the young chief of the Progressive Radicals was superabundant to the degree that he needed all sorts of nocturnal outlets to keep his spirit tolerably in balance in the daytime. Without this release, his aggressive temperament and his ever-burning compulsion for action threatened to disrupt whatever they encountered. Olivier Fernández needed dissolute habits as much as others need rest. But at present other motives impelled him. Olivier knew Aguirre well; he knew that only wine and the effusiveness of drunkenness could move Aguirre, could bare his soul, and that evening he wanted to force Aguirre to make a political confession.

The girls greeted them with an extravagant display of joy. At their head was *La Mora*, who cruised daily through Calle San Francisco with her head wrapped in a colorful kerchief, against whose red, green, blue, and yellow hues her warm dark complexion and her eyes, two black spots, stood out. *La Mora* was small and flexible and when she walked, her shoulders, waist, and ankles played in such a manner as to turn her pure harmonious form into pure harmony of movement. She rightly deserved to reign among her friends, although had she not existed, any of the other girls would have deserved to don the crown she wore so well.

They were ushered into the dining room, and the girls and men all sat at the round table and made ready to enjoy, for hours, the calm dissipation of which Olivier Fernández was so fond. Beer bottles were set in rows on the oilcloth that covered the table. In front of Ignacio Aguirre the girls placed a bottle of cognac. They brought wineglasses, tumblers, and ashtrays that would have seemed rather common anywhere else, but which here were imbued with new glamour, thanks to *La Mora*. Because her dynamic presence at once seemed to endow men and things with a share of her harmony and rare prestige. Was it an illusion? As she distributed bottles and glasses, the light, trained on the center of the table by a lampshade that came down almost to the oilcloth, seemed to overflow its course in order to follow her arm and her hand, and meanwhile *La Mora*'s dark eyes—two black spots in the half-light—glimmered and glowed and her body went from one place to another, leaving perfumes like rhythms, rhythms like perfumes. When she finally came to sit between Aguirre and Encarnación, it struck Axkaná that there was no separation between her person and her surroundings.

Shortly after he began to drink, Olivier Fernández began to discourse on politics. The rest followed him. Therefore, the girls devoted themselves to listening with deep interest, although perhaps they did not understand well the matter discussed. Amid the whirlwind of sometimes incomprehensible phrases, they peered with fascination into the abyss of ideas and passions that kept the souls of these friends of theirs aflame and which were capable of setting them against each other until they were torn to bits. The girls admired the men as much as if they were aviators or bullfighters, and although they believed the men to be generous and rich, spendthrifts like bandits of legend, deep down that wasn't what attracted the girls the most. They were enthralled instead to hear the men sketch out their future plans, because then they felt they were breathing in the essence of authentic bravery at its very source. These men were reckless beings, daring spirits, susceptible, as they themselves were, to giving themselves totally in a flash, for the sake of a whim, for an ideal.

Encarnación Reyes, kindled by the cognac, by *La Mora's* perfume, and by all he heard, soon came to feel as if he were enveloped by the heated atmosphere and excitement of a political rally or a session in Congress. The men played the role of congressmen; the women were the public. This impression was reinforced by the fact that Olivier Fernández could not say four words in a row without assuming the attitude and tone of an orator. His whole life was in politics; his soul in the Chamber of Deputies. At that moment he was trying to remember, with Aguirre and López de la Garza, what happened to them in Tampico, four years before, when they were campaigning for the Caudillo. But instead of trying to recall the events quietly to himself, as anyone else would have done, Olivier felt the irresistible urge to stand and climb onto an imaginary podium. The stream of words gushed from his mouth as they would have in the Chamber, except that here they flowed only before the small circle at the table scattered with bottles and glasses, before the rows of pairs of eyes partly hidden in the shadows. The light did not reach above his waist. But higher up, in the region where the light faded into soft shadows, his arms moved, his face gestured. And you didn't need to see him in order to fall under the spell of his eloquence, because there and everywhere, Olivier Fernández was a great orator. *La Mora* and her friends listened to him in ecstasy; they surrendered meekly to the divine magic of the word that bypasses intelligence to reach the soul and thus convinces and captivates.

The empty bottles gradually accumulated on the sticky oilcloth; there was less than half a bottle of the Hennessy Extra left for Encarnación and Aguirre. At one point, the minister of war remembered that he too was a good speaker when he wanted to be, and thought he too should rise to answer Olivier Fernández with another speech. Although inferior to that of the leader of the Progressive Radicals, his oratory, in fact, was not bad. It reflected the athletic vigor of his muscles; it prevailed convincingly, like his ample chest, like the vigorous curve of his shoulders, like the dominating bearing of his stature. But when they heard him, unlike when they heard Olivier, *La Mora* and her companions did not feel that the word was a thing of magic, but simply an accessory to the body's physical expression.

López de la Garza spoke in turn, and then Domínguez, the governor, and then Tarabana, and then Correa, the mayor of the capital. Even Encarnación tried once or twice to string together phrases in the manner of his military and political comrades. Thus, even as dawn approached, the furor continued, unabated in Olivier Fernández, waning in the others.

Empty bottles blackened the table. Now fading, Encarnación only listened, while one of his bronze hands caressed *La Mora*'s black curls. The warmth of that hair gradually captured all his senses, all his faculties. For all that, Aguirre, always alert, had not pronounced, despite the rising optimism alcohol produced in him, the revelatory words that Olivier awaited in the depth of his own drunkenness. That is why Olivier, always loath to surrender, continued to produce clause after clause of beautiful sentences, by now almost only for himself.

As in the beginning, Axkaná continued in full command of his faculties: sober, serene, strong. Not for an instant had he ceased to observe, nor had he stirred from his place, and only one feeling seemed to gradually win him over. Now, as everything around him was winding down, his admiration for *La Mora* grew. Seated at the other end of the table, she smiled at him; warm and caressing threads of luminous attraction flowed from her eyes and fixed on his green ones. Then Axkaná understood, better than ever, the souls of his friends. He understood why they did not consider their lives complete—even though, as ministers, generals, or governors, they were masters of the political destiny of a whole nation—without the daily brush with the lowest debauchery. They lived, or could live, as princes; they had, or could have, as their mistresses the most beautiful women that money could buy. But none of that had enough zest for them. They needed something else: the harsh and abrupt immersion in the impurest of pleasures.

Without intending to, Axkaná yielded gladly and reciprocated *La Mora*'s smile. Now the threads of mysterious attraction flowed from his green eyes and kindled their light in her black pupils.

Book Two

Aguirre and Jiménez

I. A Political Clarification

Weeks and months went by, followed by days of intense activity for generals, governors, and other dignitaries interested in contributing—or giving the impression that they were contributing—to the election of the future president. The number of trips multiplied, interviews were held, enthusiastic emissaries were dispatched bearing secret deals.

And it wasn't that all those figures, or even most of them, had very clear or very firm ideas about the advisability of following a given course. At bottom—personal advantages aside—only a few felt the need for one over another to be the Caudillo's successor. But since both candidacies were already decided—since both, although no one knew why, were proclaimed at all times and in all places as the antagonists of an inevitable encounter—the members of the groups acknowledged the need to take a stand. "Ignacio Aguirre or Hilario Jiménez?" That had been the word on the street for two years. (Not the voice of the nation: the word on the street, the sly voice of the common folk, that stirred up ambitions and passions by dint of rushing to predict them.) And once an unknown hand had cast the die in this democratic process, the throng of sincere friends and false supporters surged around General Jiménez and General Aguirre.

Not all of them acted in the same way. Barring the occasional exception, civilian politicians brought to their candidate, together with their ostensible support, their open opposition to the rival candidate. They were, or hoped to become, governors, deputies, councilmen, and thus felt it was up to them to proclaim the virtues of their group at the expense of the group that opposed them. They broadcast their attitude, exposing themselves, of course, to the reprisals and hatred of their enemies. Not so the military politicians. These, because their troops would later become the sole winning argument, practiced—except in the rarest of cases—the restraint that was indispensable to the triumph of arms when the moment of truth came. That is to say, the nature of their role compelled military politicians to behave with duplicity and allowed them to entertain either candidate until the last moment. Most of them deceived both sides by deed or appearance. Remaining half-hidden in the shadows, they appeared murky, vacillating, suspicious.

Their method was extremely simple. They went to visit Ignacio Aguirre—the interview was usually held at the office of the young minister of war—and once alone with him they whispered in his ear, or practically did. The language they all employed—brigade chiefs, military commanders, chiefs of operations—was always one and the same, if not in actual words, then in their import. They all paid their respects with a uniformity of cadence that was truly military.

They would declare to Aguirre, "Comrade, you know," or, "My General, you know you can count on me for absolutely anything you want, for sure, no ifs, ands, or buts. I'm one of those who support you with my hand on my heart, not one of those phonies and traitors. And if some gossip comes to you and says that I'm talking to General Jiménez or that I'm on his side, don't give it a second thought, don't take it seriously, because if I do so it's only to keep others from suspecting me. You know we all have to play both sides when it comes to these things."

And then they went (if they had not already done so) to see Hilario Jiménez at the Secretariat of the Interior and repeated more or less the same words.

Thus, Jiménez and Aguirre, despite their experience in these matters, both felt that practically the whole army was theirs. General Jiménez would say to his closest supporters: "The army, to a man, belongs to us." And General Aguirre would think to himself: "If I wanted to be president, it would be mine for the taking."

One of those mornings, Aguirre took advantage of his working session with the Caudillo to have the conversation that he felt was overdue. He and the president had gone out to the terrace of Chapultepec Castle after reviewing a large number of documents.

The young minister of war wore his hat, held his walking stick, and had his portfolio under his arm. The Caudillo, also wearing a hat—in his case because of his habit of only baring his head indoors—took him in with a look that was at once serious and cheerful, impenetrable and ironic. They had both finished walking from one end of the terrace to the other three or four times. The rhythm of their steps floated briefly over them and then drifted like the daylight into the shadows of the richly furnished rooms. And now, leaning on the parapet, they both talked.

Far beneath their feet, like a sea viewed from a promontory, the foliage of the forest moved in enormous green waves. Seen from above, the tops of the giant trees acquired a new and awesome reality. Lower and farther away spread the panorama of the fields, the streets, the houses, and the line, smaller yet magnificent, of the Paseo de la Reforma, leading to the city, crowned with towers and domes. The morning light elevated and suspended, deepened and widened the vast expanse observed from that height.

Aguirre had immediately felt touched by the majesty of nature and of history; this always happened to him whenever he looked out from that magnificent overlook. The essence of the forest, the mountain, the clouds, resonated in his spirit with arpeggios of vague memories. Porfirio Díaz? 1847? But it was also, as always, a fleeting, glittering feeling, because Aguirre's spiritual sensibility was stunted by the roar and violence of his revolutionary apprenticeship.

Mindful only of political problems, he said to the Caudillo:

"I wanted to say two words about the electoral situation."

The Caudillo had the imperious eyes of a tiger, eyes whose golden glints matched the somewhat fiery disorder of his gray mustache. But when they looked at Aguirre, they never lacked (not even during critical moments in combat) the soft expression of affection. Aguirre was well used to having the Caudillo look at him in that manner, and it moved him so deeply that perhaps it was the root, more than anything else, of the feelings of unswerving devotion that bound him to his chief. However, this time he noticed that just as soon as he mentioned the topic of the election, his words arrested the Caudillo's customary look. Now, when the Caudillo answered, only spurious, ironic glimmers remained in his eyes; he became opaque, impenetrable.

"I'm listening," he said.

But even these seemingly neutral words did not leave the president's lips without being accompanied by the nervous gesture—a

trace of old wounds—that revealed he was more than merely willing to listen; he was ready to defend and attack.

"I just want to make one or two things clear," continued the
young minister, "to make sure both you and I are on guard against
insidious gossip."

"All right, all right, let's see."

As he spoke Aguirre felt that for the first time in ten years
an invisible curtain was being drawn between his voice and the
Caudillo. With each passing second, the Caudillo seemed to
become more severe, more hermetic, more distant.

Unable to shake off this impression, Aguirre continued:

"In the last few days, one by one, almost all the troop commanders have come to visit me."

"I've been told..."

"... And most of them, or rather all, have offered me their
support in case I accept the candidacy..."

"Hmm."

"I..."

"Yes, that's it. What do *you* think?"

"... I answered, as you can imagine, that I don't consider
myself worthy, nor is it my ambition..."

"Fine.... And that is what you believe? That's what matters."

The question was wrapped in the deeply ironic tone that
Aguirre had often heard the Caudillo use when addressing others,
but never when talking to him. So now the tone of the Caudillo's
voice disconcerted and wounded him, just as his chief's look and
expression had. Something inside him broke as he replied:

"If I didn't believe it, my General, I wouldn't say it."

"What?... I think..."

But the president did not finish the thought. He turned his
face, lowered it a little toward the sea of green treetops, where the
breeze undulated, and settled his gaze there for a few brief seconds.
Then, as if he were starting from scratch, he said:

"Right! I see you don't understand me..."

Were the affectionate look and tone going to reappear? Aguirre expected and believed they would. He even thought for a
moment that everything pointed that way. But in the next moment,
that faint hope was swept away by a rising tide of irony and suspicion.

"What I'm asking you, Aguirre," the Caudillo continued, "isn't whether you in fact believe what you're saying to me. I'm asking if you in fact believe what you told your supporters. Two very different things. Do I make myself clear?"

"Supporters" was pronounced slowly, "Do I make myself clear?" in the tone of easy, commanding confidence that the Caudillo used to remind his listeners that he was the victor of a thousand battles. It was a hard and cutting tone that made Aguirre feel, for the first time in his life, that being his chief's subordinate demeaned him. He would have given anything then to win back what had just vanished, what he had unwittingly lost! The better to master the inner whirlwind that threatened to overwhelm him, Aguirre joined the spontaneous eloquence of his sincerity to the cunning eloquence of rhetorical emphasis:

"Yes, my General, now I do understand," he said. "But I protest with total frankness, with that frankness you know and have always known so well, that the two things you separate in this case are one and the same. Speaking with my supporters I thought exactly what I am saying today: that I don't feel entitled to succeed you in your office, nor am I tempted by any such ambition. This is what I have explained to all the generals, whom I have advised, you must believe me, to transfer the support they offer me to General Jiménez."

The minister and the president scrutinized each other. The veil of fatigue that never left the pupils of the former, contrasted strangely with the intense glow emitted by those of the latter.

After a pause, the Caudillo observed:

"I could understand the issue of your unworthiness if this didn't involve General Jiménez at all. Because I know well that you, perhaps for reasons worthy of consideration, believe that you surpass your rival in many respects. How can I explain then that you would consider his candidacy more acceptable than your own?"

"First of all, my General, because it's public knowledge that he does aspire to the presidency…"

"And second?"

"Second, because… because it's possible and even probable that you'll look kindly on his ambition."

The Caudillo replied quickly:

"It wouldn't be me, but the people.... But let's come back to you. Is it possible you're fooling yourself when you say you have no aspirations?"

And when he asked this, the Caudillo's smile, his expression, and his gestures were so glacial that Aguirre answered as if he were speaking, not from where he stood, but from a great distance, from the depths of the forest whose foliage, under the sun, seemed like watered silk, from the remote zone of the bluish hills:

"No, my General, I don't believe I'm fooling myself."

And he understood that his effort had been in vain.

Minutes later, Aguirre's car ran wildly down the ramp, sank into the mass of green, and was, for a moment, a submarine of the forest. Likewise, still stunned by the unexpected consequences of the interview, Aguirre sank to the very bottom of his reflections. He tried to understand how it was possible that the Caudillo, his friend and chief of more than ten years, could not bring himself to believe a single word he had said.

II. A Candidate for President

THE CAR RAN TOWARD THE CITY WITH ALL OF THE THROBBING VIGOR of its forty-horsepower engine.

Aguirre was pensive. His idle retinas barely perceived the lines, like vapor trails, that the ornaments of the Paseo de la Reforma seemed to trace on the car windows. The lions at the entrance of Chapultepec Park passed by and he did not see them, then the stone markers of the Independence Column, the little palm garden. And thus, in a few seconds, his inattentive gaze merged the sight of the Seville Fountain next to the mass of trees, with that of the Cuauhtémoc traffic circle.

Here, slowing down, the driver turned to his master for orders. Aguirre pointed to the left. His gesture was minimal—a product of his deep contemplation—but it was quick and precise. Interpreted by the driver, it meant: "To Rosas Moreno," in other words: "To Rosario's house." The car headed there.

If instead of left, Aguirre had pointed right, his mute order would have meant: "To Calle Durango," or better yet: "To Calle de Niza." Because Aguirre at that time lived in the three houses: in Durango, with his wife; in Rosas Moreno, with Rosario; and in Niza, with that Arévalo woman: Paquita Arévalo, a young and beautiful actress from Madrid who, like many others in Mexico, had traded the art of the stage for the more lucrative and no less conspicuous art of being a minister's mistress.

For Ignacio Aguirre at that moment, the most natural choice among his three homes was Rosario's. That is what his daily habits and his inner turmoil called for, and both needs were so visceral that going there was less an act of volition than a sort of mechanical obedience, as unavoidable as if he were on rails.

It was common knowledge that Aguirre almost never set foot in the house of his legitimate wife. This was not out of a lack of affection or out of cruelty, but owing to more recondite spiritual complexes: a certain secret disapproval of himself; a certain respect for ways of living that were superior to his will, though not his feelings. Aguirre usually reached Paquita's house at dawn. That was the time when his ravaged body (which refused to surrender) and the qualms of his spirit (still alert in spite of everything) were in conflict, demanding great and beautiful inducements embodied in mindless flesh: narcotics in the shape of a woman who totally lacked a woman's soul—or, at least, the best part of a soul. And since this wonder was personified beyond expectations by the Spanish actress, who was as beautiful as the sun and as dumb as a rock, Aguirre went to her when he needed to be soothed and to dull his senses. On the other hand, Rosario's home was good for peaceful or sad hours. He thought of it as a halfway point between his home, from which his shame kept him, and the life of dissipation, to which his whole being impelled him. It was a welcoming refuge, sedative and amorous, and at the same time a diminutive paradise that did not exclude the charm, for him indispensable, of what is reprehensible and produces delight.

Hours later, from the balmy softness of that refuge, Aguirre sent for Axkaná. He wanted to inform him of his conversation with the Caudillo and ask his advice.

Axkaná found him in bed and in the talkative mood that was typical of Aguirre whenever he had to make any critical decision. He seemed to have been talking for a long time and, judging by the indentation at the edge of the bed, it was evident that his interlocutor had been sitting there and she had just left. That mark, and the indiscreet noise of an inner door, as Axkaná was admitted to the house, betrayed someone's flight: Rosario's. Axkaná thought he heard the fleeting remnant of a laugh, and tried to catch it with his imaginative sensibility. But he was unable to: Aguirre's continuous, flowing phrases impeded him.

The minister was saying to him, "Tomorrow I'll need all my circumspection, all my intelligence. That's why, as you can see, I'm going to bed early. I intend to rest for fifteen hours straight..."

Axkaná drew up a chair. Interrupting himself, Aguirre stopped him:

"Sit here on the bed so you are in the light."

And he pointed, perhaps unwittingly, to the place that had recently been occupied by the body that had just left. Axkaná sat there.

Aguirre continued:

"I'll get up at eleven with a clear head, with a sound body, and ready to hear and sense everything well. What I mean is that then I'll know for sure what to expect…"

Before Axaná could even ask a question, Aguirre immediately launched into a detailed account of his conversation that morning at the terrace of Chapultepec Castle; as he did so, the flow of his speech became increasingly agitated. The mere memory of the Caudillo's words seemed to inflame him; he repeated again and again everything the Caudillo had said: analyzed it, discussed it. Such was his vehemence that it struck Axaná as something new. This did not seem to be the merely vice-prone and immoral, merely intelligent and cynical Aguirre of the day before. Today's Aguirre even seemed naive, sensitive even to the clash between what is noble with what is ignoble. Even the veil of fatigue that always dimmed his eyes was gone, for now his gaze issued with the same brilliance as his gestures, not dulling but sharpening his words.

Furthermore, the extraordinary agitation in his voice seemed even greater in contrast with the soft atmosphere that surrounded him, an atmosphere not suited to a man of action, but to a man of pleasure. The floor lamp next to the bed shed a soft light on him; shining on his silk pajamas, it added new luster to his handsome athletic chest. From the ceiling lamp, which was not on, came the tinkling of tiny crystal tubes barely visible in the half-light, quite in harmony with the blue satin of the furniture, which emerged as bright spots beyond the direct radius of the light. From the next room—through whose door Rosario had just fled—drifted a slight whisper of sound and a faint yet saturating perfume. They were the sounds of a woman, the perfume of a woman, the warm half-darkness where the palpable, enveloping presence of a woman hovered.

For Axaná, who had a deep knowledge of Mexico's political world, Aguirre's news was of no importance. That the president had not believed the protests with which his minister rejected the future presidency was almost a matter of common sense. That was to be expected. What did surprise him was that his friend, hurt by that skepticism, would yield to passion. Axaná would have expected diffident disappointment, not this almost sentimental release that in a way fit in so well with the luminous watered silk that bathed Aguirre here.

By way of conclusion, Aguirre now said:

"For ten years I've been by his side, ten years of absolute discipline, obedience, submission, ten years in which his political will has always been mine, ten years of fighting for the same ideas (always his), of defending the same interests (above all his), and carrying out deeds that bind you infinitely and eternally, of executing common enemies; of employing accusations, denials, and betrayals to remove opponents and rivals who stood in my way only because they stood in his.... And after all this, what? What was it all for? For him to give more credit to a rumor, an intrigue, a dubious report than to my frank, loyal word, my honest, sincere decision spoken by myself in simple words."

Axkaná listened, mesmerized by Aguirre's eloquence. The latter thought he was expressing the tragedy that his chief considered him false, but that was not how Axkaná saw things. He saw in his friend the tragedy of a politician ensnared by the environment of immorality and lies that he himself has created; the tragedy of a once sincere politician, who, having renounced in good faith the aspirations others attribute to him, still fails to open his eyes to the circumstances that will force him to defend, soon and to the death, the very thing he is rejecting. In other words, Axkaná thought the same as the Caudillo. Except that while the latter, a great master of the political game, used to judging the ambitions of others in terms of his own, suspected Aguirre of deceit, Axkaná knew his friend's sincerity was absolute. For him the whole misunderstanding lay in Aguirre's failure to match his desires to the mysterious workings of politics. Bent on resisting, the minister of war was unable to realize the magnitude of the wave that was raising him up.

In any case, Axkaná did not want to clarify the situation. First because, in his present mood, Aguirre would have considered the true explanation of what was happening to him to be absurd, and then also because, being sure that Aguirre would eventually accept the candidacy, Axkaná, for several reasons, did not want to influence that decision. He only said:

"Politically, the Caudillo is right. He judges your case in reference to what any one of his generals would do, what he himself would do. If he were in your place, wouldn't he be striving to be president? That's exactly why he assumes that you're doing and will do the same thing."

"Politically! It's not a political issue between him and me; it's a point of friendship and comradeship."

Axkaná replied:

"That too is an error. In the field of political relations, friendship does not figure, does not survive. From those below toward those above, there can be mutual interest, support, loyalty; from those above to those below, there can be affectionate protection or utilitarian esteem. But simple friendship, an affective feeling that joins equals? Impossible. That can only be among the lowly, the nameless, political troops. If no common interest unites them, chiefs and leaders are always envious competitors, rivals, potential or actual enemies. That's why the day after they embrace and pat each other on the back, the closest politicians destroy and kill each other. In politics, the most bitter, the cruelest enemies, often start as the most intimate of friends."

Once he started in that vein, Axkaná was likely to go on endlessly; Aguirre knew it. Nervous, he quickly checked him:

"Fine, fine. That isn't relevant; you're just theorizing."

"On the contrary, it is perfectly relevant. It tells you why the Caudillo, your chief, your friend up to now, is about to stop being one. In his eyes, his interests and yours no longer coincide. He thinks you stand in the way of his wish to make Hilario Jiménez president. And, of course, he's preparing to crush you."

"But that brings us back to what I was saying: why should the Caudillo believe that, when it isn't true? You know I unconditionally accept Jiménez as his successor."

"Yes, I do, of course, but I know it because I believe it. Since he doesn't believe it, he doesn't know it."

"He doesn't believe it because he doesn't want to."

Axkaná would have liked to reply: "You're also wrong about that. Despite all your resolve today, before long, you will be Hilario Jiménez's opponent." But that is what he would not bring himself to say. He, therefore, had to skirt the issue:

"The Caudillo doesn't believe it," he said, "because he imagines you're doing what he would do in your place: feigning for as long as possible, to keep from losing the advantages of your ministerial rank."

Suddenly, Aguirre's agitation was replaced by perfect serenity.

"Fine," he concluded with great calm, "in that case, I'll resign tomorrow."

"To resign now would not fix anything. The Caudillo would only believe that you feel you're already strong enough."

"In other words, it's not possible for him to see the truth. Isn't that it?"

And as he said this, Aguirre rose from the bed, stretched his arm, and rang the bell.

"I wouldn't go that far," Axkaná replied.

The head of the maid appeared timidly at the door to the adjoining room. The minister ordered:

"Two glasses and bring the cognac closer."

And the two friends were silent.

Moments later the maid reappeared. She placed a plate and glasses on the night table. From another piece of furniture, she brought the cognac decanter.

"Turn on the light," Aguirre then ordered.

The light bulbs on the ceiling lamp shone. The maid left noiselessly.

While Aguirre, in silence, slowly filled the two glasses, the murmur of voices was heard from the other room. One was the maid's, the other, Axkaná recognized as Rosario's. Aguirre took one glass and offered the other to his friend. He emptied his, filled it again, drank again, and he poured so much that a few drops fell on the silk and lace bedspread, leaving dark stains.

"In conclusion," Aguirre asked at last, "what advice do you have for me?"

Axkaná, whose glass was still full, was looking at the liquid against the light. He reflected for a moment. Then he said:

"I only see one course of action: for you to talk to Hilario Jiménez and to show that you support him. If you get him to believe you, he'll convince the Caudillo."

"And if he doesn't believe me?"

"If he doesn't believe you? . . ."

Axkaná moistened his lips with the cognac and again raised the glass. Once more, he was looking at it against the rays of the recently lit lamp, whose somewhat bluish light gave to the air of the room the tonalities of Venetian crystal, turning the topaz of the cognac into gold.

"If he doesn't believe you?" Axkaná repeated, and once more brought the glass to his lips.

Ultimately he found the way to respond without answering the question, of expressing opinions without giving advice.

III. The Rivals

The next day, Hilario Jiménez and Ignacio Aguirre met for the last time. When they were alone and face-to-face, both politicians had the feeling that this was the moment that had to come sooner or later. Both were generals, both ministers—one of the Interior, the other of War—and they were both being singled out, by some indecipherable hidden power, to collide with each other on the road of new ambitions.

The minister of the interior received his cabinet colleague with a cold gesture—with the coldness he had shown him for months, and making even less of an effort to conceal it than at other times. Because, although Jiménez seemed devious, he was direct, and though he seemed false, he was loyal. Even as Aguirre shook Jiménez's hand, which he'd barely extended, Jiménez's appearance became more baleful; his look darkened under the deformed curve of his bulbous eyelids.

"I've come," Aguirre began, coming right to the point, "to lay the cards on the table. Comrades-in-arms have the duty to get along, or, if not, at least to know why they've broken with each other and are fighting. Do you agree?"

Aguirre sat on the sofa facing the balconies. After the first words, Jiménez went to lock the door to his private office, then the other door, and he immediately came to sit, his profile outlined against the light of the street that made a hazy plane out of the fabric of the curtains. During all these movements, his tall, muscular body—although already declining into his sorely tested fortysome years—confirmed something Aguirre had always thought: that from behind, Jiménez gave a more accurate idea of how he was than from the front. Because then (without the misleading expression of his face) what stood out was his vigorous muscular build. His four limbs looked stronger, firmer, agile, and his whole body acquired a certain air of confidence, the aptitude to bring to fruition even the smallest endeavors with precision, with energy. And that was him to a T—more so, of course, than the deformed spirit his sinister features seemed to betray—since it squared well with the essence of his intimate being: his ever-resolute will, his intelligence (practical and with very few ideas), and his character (aloof, slow, and proof against the stings and scruples that can lead one astray or hold one back).

When Jiménez sat down, Aguirre continued:

"I know well enough I can speak plainly with you. That's why I begin by telling you that I understand my situation perfectly. I realize I have many supporters and I'm not unaware that with their help, I could take on the fight for the presidency. But having said that, I can also tell you that the possibility of becoming president does not entice me. Therefore, don't be surprised that I won't fight for my candidacy, as anyone else in my situation would do. Instead, I intend to leave the field totally to you, and even, insofar as I am able, to convince my supporters to back you."

Aguirre paused. Perhaps he wanted to give Jiménez a chance to reply; perhaps he was studying the effect of his conciliatory words. But the minister of the interior only listened. He had crossed his legs that now, folded one over the other, suddenly seemed weaker. Coming from deep within his eyes, which were harder to see in profile than from the front, his gaze was fixed on his knees. Aguirre continued:

"If you have any serious reason to believe that what I'm telling you isn't true, I'd like to hear it."

Jiménez then turned to face him and came directly to the point. Looking at his rival head on and with concentrated hardness, he declared tersely:

"I have many reasons."

"Tell me."

"It would take too long."

"Tell me the main ones."

Both felt that their tone was new. They did not speak like friends or enemies, like acquaintances or strangers. The measured restraint in their tone—a neutral and false softness, irritated and indifferent at the same time—placed them on the brink of separation, at the end of a friendship that dies because it has run its course. Although they had been comrades for years, partners in fatigue, excess, and triumph, they already spoke like two men whose previous affection, at length confronted by uncontrollable political passions, discovers in itself the efficacious means to turn into hatred.

Jiménez reflected for a few seconds and finally said:

"The first reason I have for not believing you is that I can't see the cause that makes you reject a candidacy that, according to what you, yourself, say, is being offered to you from all sides."

Aguirre addressed the point:

"There are several causes, but you only need to know this one: At present I don't aspire to become president because I know for a fact that the Caudillo supports you and not me, and even though I understand that his supporting you is not an insurmountable obstacle, I prefer to desist out of affection. To oppose you is to oppose the Caudillo, to disown him, to reject him, and I want you to know that is precisely what I will not do for any ambition great or small."

Aguirre's voice vibrated with more than enough sincerity to dispel anyone's doubts. But presidential candidate Hilario Jiménez was not anyone. In the thrall of suspicion, his soul, contrary to what could be expected, became murkier even as Aguirre's became more transparent. Turning hypocrite for a moment, he even ventured an idea that he could only express with the tinseled words of a political cliché:

"And your duty to your country?"

But the magnitude of the lie was such that it could not fit into the absolute frankness of the dialogue. Aguirre pushed it aside with a gesture he could not repress and that broke his rather solemn attitude as he answered.

"Hilario, we're talking heart to heart, not with phrases made to fool people. Neither you nor I hear the call of our country. Leaving aside three or four fools and three or four dreamers, what we hear is the call of groups of opportunists looking for someone to hang their hats on, in other words, three or four bands of political schemers.... Duty to your country!..."

But Jiménez, who was already returning to the ground of sincerity, replied:

"Frankness deserves frankness. I don't agree with that, or don't agree totally. My experiences in these matters have taught me that under the personal self-interest to which our political maneuvering can be reduced, nevertheless, there's always something of the nation, something of the country's interests. And I'll add that if there are political agitators (and I admit there are) at present, I see fewer of them on my side. Emilio Olivier Fernández, for example, and all his Progressive Radicals are political agitators; Axkaná, with his Revolutionary Student League is a political intriguer.... But they're not on my side; the masses, the workers, the peasants are on my side."

Jiménez said this with a certain cold and offensive enthusiasm. For a moment Aguirre thought his temper would get the better of him; the accusation against Axkaná had hurt him deeply. Nevertheless, he was able to contain his anger and answer very calmly.

"You're wrong about Axkaná González, with me he's not a politician, he's a friend. Of all, he's the only one who hasn't advised me to accept the candidacy. But in the end, none of that matters right now, nor does it matter that you imagine that 'the masses' are behind you, just because two dozen scoundrels who exploit the labor organizations and the name of the peasants assure you this is the case.... No, don't interrupt me. If I came to tell you the truth, it's only fair for you to listen to the truth.... I mean there's no reason for you and me to fool ourselves; we know how the game is played from the inside. I repeat that my supporters, except a few, are political agitators, and that your supporters, also except a few, are political agitators.... Now, if you believe that only my supporters are political agitators, so much the better for what I want to show you. If you believe that, it'll be easier for you to understand why my duty to my country does not obligate me to accept the candidacy, because it's not 'the masses' who are nominating me, but political agitators.... Is there any other reason you don't believe me?"

"If you won't be a candidate, why don't you make an official announcement?"

"Because, as of now, no political party has made an official offer either. As soon as one does, rest assured that I will."

Jiménez, a reluctant debater, said little. He kept silent, went back to looking at his knees. Despite everything, it was evident that his ideas about Aguirre's intentions had not changed. After a brief pause, the latter persisted:

"What doubts remain?"

Jiménez reflected. Then said slowly:

"I know you've been working on the army."

"Whoever said that is lying!"

"They don't say you're doing it yourself; others do it in your name."

"If so, they're doing it without my authorization, even without my knowledge."

"The fact is they do it."

"And even if it were true, what's the point if I neither authorize those efforts nor plan to benefit from them?"

"The point is I can see who my opponent is.... And I figure there's no use regretting it now."

"In other words, you give more credit to gossip than to my honest and spontaneous declaration?"

Jiménez, feeling he had won the last point, went on to say with complete naturalness:

"Frankly, Aguirre, your coming to see me, you who are so rebellious and arrogant, also makes me wonder. If you wanted to fool me, what better way to do it? The more I think about it, the less I can make out what your goal is."

"You can't? Well, it's very clear or at least easy to explain. In short, yesterday I spoke to the Caudillo in order to put an end to this misunderstanding. Since he didn't want to believe me, I immediately decided the only solution was to come and convince you of the truth so that you can later make him see it. Satisfied?"

Aguirre paused. Without saying anything, Jiménez was expressing something; there was a certain nuance to his silence. Aguirre guessed that his adversary already knew about the previous day's interview in Chapultepec. He concluded in this manner:

"But I find all my efforts are useless. It seems there's an attempt to push me down the road I don't want to walk. I'm telling the truth and no one believes me."

Now there was a long pause. Both rivals remained motionless. Jiménez was looking toward the door of his private office, and Aguirre's gaze, crossing that of his opponent, fixed on Jiménez, who was silhouetted against the sunlit surface of one of the balconies. The absolute certainty that everything had been said floated in the air. Aguirre made to get up. Then Jiménez added:

"I'm not pushing you to do anything at all. Nor do I refuse to reach an agreement. But the evidence on the table can only be destroyed by evidence that will surpass it. Do you understand? If you provide that evidence, I'm ready to accept it as good."

The minister of the interior said the last words extraordinarily slowly, with an almost solemn air. Aguirre accepted in the same tone:

"You can have any evidence you want, so long as it doesn't humiliate me."

"Fine. First of all, remove Encarnación Reyes as commander of troops in Puebla and replace him with the general I choose."

"If the president orders me to do both things, of course. I would have done it already without any need to negotiate. He commands the troops; I only obey."

"Yes, I understand, but we're talking about something very different. I know the president can order Encarnación to give up his command, but it's also possible that instead of obeying the order, Encarnación would rise up in arms, and with him, probably, Ortiz in Oaxaca, and Figueroa in Jalisco. That's why I am asking you to do something different; I want Encarnación to know that you yourself agree to his removal. That's the only way you can prove you're my supporter and not my adversary."

Aguirre felt an enormous surge of anger, but he contained it. He only said:

"Anything else?"

Jiménez continued impassively:

"Yes. For the Progressive Radical Party to nominate me as their candidate, and if they don't do it soon (we can set a prudent deadline), you will let me deal with Olivier Fernández, Axkaná, and the other leaders in my own way..."

Aguirre stood up. Fury flooded his chest, buzzed in his ears. Nonetheless, his exterior appearance somehow remained serene.

It was melancholy rather than anger that made him say:

"In sum, you're asking me to hand over my friends, to sell them to you in exchange for some cordiality."

"I don't know," the other replied. "I only see that a movement against me is being organized in your name, and I'm asking you to destroy it, if it's true that you're with me."

"What you ask is far more than I can do.... We'll let things take their course."

Still sitting, Jiménez added:

"Maybe there's another way..."

"What?"

"For you to remove yourself."

"Yes, to run away."

"Not run away, just make a public statement that you concede to me."

"And abandon my supporters, betray them."

"If you're not their leader, you're not betraying them by conceding."

Aguirre was already on his way to the door when he again stopped and offered a last guarantee.

"If it's enough for you, I'll resign immediately as minister of war."

"That's nothing. If you resign your supporters will feel stronger. No, that's not enough for me."

"Fine. In that case we were friends up to now."

And as he opened the door, Aguirre heard Hilario Jiménez correct him from his seat:

"Not up to now. It's been months since we stopped being friends."

Book Three
Catarino Ibáñez

I. Transaction

Inexorably, Ignacio Aguirre's fate continued to be spun out in the Chamber of Deputies. Everyone there knew that the minister of war was refusing the candidacy, but for all of them, friends and foes alike, it was just a pretense, a ruse employed by the presumptive candidate of the Progressive Radicals to gain greater advantages from the start. Thus, his most enthusiastic supporters were neither disheartened nor impatient; they rejoiced. They assumed that Aguirre was working on the army, laying out the remaining threads of the military plot that would later lead them, Mexican-fashion, to victory. And if the lack of absolute certainty made the less fervent supporters indecisive, in the end it increased the ferment of enthusiasm. Because it made the supporters of Hilario Jiménez's candidacy redouble their efforts to win converts among the undecided, and that, in turn, made it essential for Aguirre's friends, in order to close ranks, to stress even more the apparent reasons or the true grounds for their confidence in victory.

Nevertheless, Olivier Fernández and the other leaders of the Progressive Radical bloc did not think it would be an easy task or a smooth road. They had to counteract the reality of Hilarismo, a dynamic and tangible reality, with the mere possibility of Aguirrismo, an impalpable and vague possibility. They had to combat the proactive and personal work of the opposing candidate, with no weapons other than the continued inaction of their own candidate. In other words, they had to confront a body with a shadow. And if outwardly this did not weaken them yet, inwardly it was beginning to erode their faith, making them feel exposed to a play of forces that did not come from them, but from others.

One afternoon, Emilio Olivier Fernández had the ominous realization that the situation was slipping through his fingers. In the course of the morning, he had confirmed the defection of four deputies—four of the most reliable, if not the most effective, ones.

As he analyzed the occurrence later, he concluded that although it mattered little in the face of the overwhelming force of the Radical bloc, the circumstances provided sufficient cause for alarm. Because all four defections were typical. In the case of one of the deputies, a colonel, the government had given him a regiment on condition that his replacement would join the Hilarista group in the Chamber. The other, for a similar commitment, was promised a diplomatic post. And the other two, without much ceremony, sold out for money: one for five thousand pesos that the Secretariat of the Interior gave him, and the other for seven thousand from the Ministry of Foreign Affairs.

What more did one need to understand how far the Caudillo would be willing to go in order to help General Hilario Jiménez, and consequently, how difficult the electoral fight would be in Congress? Olivier was in a better position than most to appreciate it; he knew deputies and senators in depth; he knew how fragile, how false and corruptible the personalities of almost every one of them were. In short, after considering the matter for a bit, he came, with his characteristic cynicism, to repeat what the Caudillo himself told him in a very different situation two years before: "In Mexico, Olivier, there is no majority of deputies or senators that can resist the caresses of the Secretary of the Treasury."

Always quick to make decisions, Olivier Fernández resolved to attempt right away the switching of sides that the circumstances required: a switch so abrupt that his faction, thanks to the element of surprise, would be able to keep its predominance intact. It all hinged on taking full advantage, and without delay, of the situation he himself had created. He needed to employ the faculty he most valued among those he possessed, a faculty as paramount in politics as in war: he had to turn the adverse consequences of the previous plan into the useful elements of the new one. Now it was time to undertake an enormous stock market transaction in the political field. Like someone who has been inflating the value of a stock in order to then let it drop and realize greater profits, all Olivier had to do was to abandon Ignacio Aguirre, or rather to go over to Hilario Jiménez. When all was said and done, he had an irrefutable argument to explain his conduct afterward: Aguirre's refusal to accept the candidacy. And as far as justifying his ambitious aspirations in Jiménez's eyes, the enormous magnitude of the maneuver he was about to propose to him was reason enough.

That night Olivier telegraphed Agustín J. Domínguez, governor of Jalisco, to come immediately to Mexico, and thirty-six hours later he was holding a secret meeting with Domínguez and Eduardo Correa, the mayor of the city. There Olivier set forth his fears, his ideas, and his plan, and with regard to the latter, entered into all kinds of details about the most direct methods to achieve it.

"In sum, as you can see," he concluded, "this is an extremely bold step, so bold, I have not wanted to take it *motu propio*, but only with the understanding that I'm backed by the opinion of the party's principal leaders. Do you agree?"

Among all the leaders of the Progressive Radicals, Correa and Domínguez were Olivier's most trusted men; they followed him blindly; they were simply his instruments. Both granted the approval he requested as "principal leaders of the party" and they immediately helped to finish up the plan at hand.

What most claimed the attention of the three young politicians were two things: first, the review of the proposals they would make to General Hilario Jiménez; second, the selection of the cunning and subtle intermediary who would get both sides talking.

When Jiménez heard them, a day later, Olivier's proposals seemed extremely simple, at first. They were as follows:

"The National Progressive Radical Party and affiliated parties and clubs undertake to support the candidacy of General Hilario Jiménez to the Presidency, so long as the candidate guarantees to those parties the following four points: First, two thirds of the total number of seats in the future Federal Congress; second, the control of local and municipal governments wherever Progressive Radicals or their affiliates are presently in control; third, the mayoralty of Mexico City; and fourth, half the portfolios of the future cabinet."

Hilario Jiménez was suddenly disconcerted. Confronted with such demands, his head, which was not very firm, somehow conjectured that such a proposal had to be founded on something solid. But since he also glimpsed the dangers of challenging the conditions that were imposed on him, in order to buy time, he replied:

"I accept the pact in principle, but with the prerequisite that Olivier and his people give some tangible proof of the sincerity of their motives."

The answer did not please Olivier very much, first, because it forced him to give something away, and then, because it left Jiménez free to retract. But on further careful appraisal of the situation, Olivier and his advisors concluded that the accord, if it were carried out, was worth something in the way of concessions. It was then agreed that the "tangible proof of sincerity" requested by Jiménez would consist of the following: that the Progressive Radical Party of the State of Mexico would proclaim him candidate to the Presidency of the Republic at the convention that was about to meet in Toluca. And since their offer was well received, Olivier and his two assistants took the necessary measures at once. In other words, they gave General Catarino Ibáñez, governor of the State of Mexico, instructions about the course that the convention being planned was to follow.

General Catarino Ibáñez was delighted by Olivier's orders. He was delighted not so much because, as a Progressive Radical, he was obedient to his chiefs, but because of the weight they lifted from his shoulders. Because, despite his tactic of protesting his secret support of Aguirre on one side and Jiménez on the other, he was already quite committed when it came to electoral matters, and his commitments tended precisely toward Jiménez.

That being the case, his orders for the execution of the new directive produced immediate results. The state's political leadership was set in motion, announcements circulated, and it rained bulletins, manifestos, and programs, and three days after all this started the work was cemented by five or six politicians in each town: to the great jubilation of the Hilaristas, the selection of delegates to the Toluca democratic assembly began everywhere.

General Ibáñez's work was all the more effective because he used his own methods to carry it out. In his old job delivering milk, he had learned the art of doing business with other people's money: he would tell his boss that not all the clients paid him on time. And since that system had rendered him such magnificent results in the private, commercial sphere, he now employed a very similar one in the high spheres of public life. His supreme civic virtue consisted in knowing how to translate everything to his profit. Thus, in the present case, he came and went between Toluca and Mexico City pretending to execute the will of Olivier, but he actually behaved as if he were fulfilling his own promises: he asked Jiménez for direct orders and gave him advice.

Matters had reached this point, two days before the meeting of the convention, when Olivier received from Jiménez an urgent message to come see him that night. Olivier came to the meeting with the deep-seated delight of the victor. He guessed that the candidate, now convinced by all that was being done in Toluca, was rushing to conclude the agreement with a view to obtaining greater advantages. But once he was before Jiménez, Olivier discovered this was not the case. Jiménez, contrary to what Olivier expected, had changed his mind, and his attitude and his tone were such that seeing him was enough for the leader of the Progressive Radicals to go from extreme joy to extreme displeasure. Jiménez's first words sounded like concluding remarks:

"You know," the candidate declared, "that I always keep my promises, and that's why I never offer to do the impossible. I have thoroughly studied your proposals, which at first seemed to be acceptable; today I see they're not and I reject them."

Since Olivier's original terms reflected the most he had hoped to gain, he was in a position to agree to lesser terms. For a second he felt he should try. But that very instant, looking Jiménez in the face, he realized it would be useless. Behind the candidate's words lay something more than his personal decision, something more than his spirit: without a doubt, the will of the Caudillo. Olivier then opted to show that he was sure of his power and even somewhat indifferent. He only said:

"And the convention the day after tomorrow, General?"

"The convention," answered Jiménez, "is not a done deal. Just as you were pushing it in my favor, you can make it vote for another person."

"Yes. That's also true."

Now the problem was to redirect the Toluca convention. That is where Olivier and Eduardo Correa headed the next morning.

They found the city plastered with Hilarista posters and the governor and all his minions saturated with the most acute Hilarismo. The proclamation of Jiménez's candidacy by the assembly the next day was taken for granted.

Catarino Ibáñez, of course, judged that twisting the democratic slant of his convention was an impossible deed.

"I for one won't try to do it," he said, "Didn't you ask me for an Hilarista convention? Well, you're looking at it. I know my job: the delegations are Hilarista to the bone."

Olivier argued that, if it came to that, the assembly could be dissolved. But Catarino objected:

"Dissolve it?... No way! As we speak, Toluca's bursting with delegates from every town. The bands have already been hired, and first thing tomorrow the Indians from the haciendas are coming to the demonstration; almost all have been paid."

"Well, then we lose all that."

"But look here, Olivier, do I also lose my political reputation? At this stage of the game I'm already in up to my neck. What excuse or reason do I give now to explain that nothing of what I said goes?"

In the end, after a great deal of discussion, Catarino's point of view prevailed. Finally, he suggested, with the aplomb of a general and governor:

"In order to get a different outcome, I can think of only one solution. Let's see what you think, Olivier: you and some friends from Mexico come tomorrow to make speeches. As for me, you already know, I'll help any way I can, except for speaking. And we'll see what we can do. But make no mistake about it, and I'll say it again, the convention is Hilarista to the marrow..."

II. Convention

Next morning, two hours before the convention began, Emilio Olivier Fernández and a large group of party leaders arrived in Toluca. Among them were Eduardo Correa, Francisco Cifuentes N., Juan Manuel Mijares, López de la Garza, and Axkaná. As they jumped from their cars, the governor greeted them with a flood of exclamations and friendly smiles.

Catarino was apparently well prepared for the solemn ceremonies of the day. Now he was wearing a splendid suit of khaki gabardine—with dark buttons made of woven leather—that gave him an air that was at once jovial, rough, and prosperous. The shade of the cloth went with his shoes, and that of the buttons with the coppery hue of his face and hands.

When the greetings were done, Catarino affectionately put his arm around Olivier's shoulders, as he said:

"Looks like I've got good news for you. Last night I was talking to the leading party members of some towns; first thing today I met with others, and from all our chats I get the feeling that it won't be impossible to get the assembly to go in a different direction than you first ordered.... I mean, without a blot on my personal reputation.... Whole thing now is up to you and your buddies: it all hangs on what kind of speeches you make."

Axkaná, who was then seeing Catarino Ibáñez for the first time, observed him with care. For now, the general's exterior aspect told him nothing. It was like that of so many other soldiers of the Revolution, transformed, as if by magic, into governors or ministers: illiterate, certifiably uncultured, and now holding the highest positions of public trust. But looking more deeply, Catarino's manner began first to awaken Axkaná's curiosity and then his distrust. Axkaná detected something unquestionably false in the honey with which Ibáñez sought to sweeten each of his words, and that impression of duplicity was reaffirmed as the dialogue between the governor and the boss of the Progressives advanced.

Now Catarino was saying:

"Makes no sense for us to show up at the theater right now, Olivier. The convention kicks off at eleven, and it's hardly going on nine. If you like, we could spend some of this time visiting my stable and my cows."

But Olivier replied that the stable would have to wait:

"The important thing now is to speak separately to the heads of the delegations, to tell them they're not supposed to vote for Jiménez anymore, but for Aguirre.... And later, we'll be glad to see your cows and whatever you want."

"Later on! Come on Olivier, later on we won't have time. It'll be ten-thirty and we'll still be looking for the delegations. Anyway, ain't I telling you I already talked to the most reliable bosses? What else is there to do? In an hour, when people gather in the theater, you can make a deal with the rest. Right now, it would just be wasting time for nothing.... Now, if what's really going on here is that you don't give a hoot about seeing my dairy business, then I just won't say another word: we'll do what you want."

It was evident to Axkaná that Ibáñez was tugging at the heartstrings. Olivier answered:

"How odd of you to think that, Catarino. You know very well I'm as interested in your things as in mine."

"Well, if that's true, don't deny me this pleasure I've been waiting months for. You won't believe my milking shed! Every time I made an improvement, I said to myself: 'When Olivier sees this, boy is he gonna envy how rich I am...'"

And Catarino Ibáñez laughed at what he had just said, expressively tightening his arm around his friend's shoulder. After such an embrace, Olivier had to surrender.

"All right," he said, "since it matters so much to you, let's do it. Let's go meet your cows."

And Olivier also felt he needed to underscore his words with an affectionate gesture. He raised his hand to Catarino's jacket and ran his thumb and index finger down the border of one of the lapels.

The governor's dairy was certainly marvelous—marvelous from the point of view of the commercial ambitions of a former door-to-door milkman. Ibáñez had poured the dreams of his indigent youth into it, and later, with the new aspirations that experience breeds, he had eventually surpassed them. He had discovered—who knows how—an Englishman from Jersey who ran the place for him with great skill, which is to say, according to the major advances of the dairy industry. The whole facility was perfect, or close to it. The sheds, the dairy, the corrals all exuded efficient and wise prosperity. Cleanliness reigned overall; the animals and the machinery were fit for a parlor.

"More than a milking shed, this looks like an automobile showroom," said one of the young politicians as he entered.

And the phrase, because of its aptness, made the rounds for an hour and a quarter, and kicked off the laudatory exclamations with which Olivier and his friends greeted the miracles Ibáñez showed them. They admired everything, and meanwhile, just as Catarino expected, they envied, for a moment, the deep satisfaction of being owners of all they saw.

In the sheds, between the double rows of blond or cinnamon-colored cows, of black-and-white spotted cows, of rosy cows, the governor stopped again and again to show his favorite jewels. When they got to a cow that occupied a roomier and more luminous place than the others, he made a special stop.

"This one," he said, "is the best there is in the whole world. Just lookin' at her you can tell. She cost me... wanna bet you'll be shocked when you hear what she cost me?"

He was principally addressing Olivier. And then he added, turning to the Englishman from Jersey who followed them at a respectful distance:

"Let's see, Mr. Gorey, tell these gentlemen what this here cow cost us."

Mr. Gorey advanced two steps:

"Two thousand pounds sterling. About twenty-two thousand Mexican pesos."

Ibáñez let his friends savor the amount and continued:

"She's *Charhar*"—he meant "Shorthorn"—"and is the great granddaughter of Granny, the famous cow that won the prize at the London Exposition of 1900. Like her great-grandmother, a month after calving, she produces thirty-one liters of milk a day and more than a kilo of pure butter..."

"Three and a half percent butterfat content," the Englishman stated with technical precision.

Correa could not resist the temptation of asking a question: "And how many cows like this do you have, General?"

"Like her, none; but about fifteen or twenty that come close to her. And I have other very fine ones—no less than forty—*Charbar, Yersay,* and *Holstan,*" by which he meant "Jersey" and "Holstein."

In the adjacent shed the object of their admiration was a magnificent Guernsey bull. It was perhaps less elegant of line than the Jersey bull next to it, but greater in size and of more opulent vigor. Under his fine skin, of an almost orange luster, you could sense the beating of endless procreative forces, fecund, inexhaustible youth.

"This here is it," exclaimed Catarino. "Now we really got to the best of the best. Tell you the truth, this animal's worth so much and costs me so much, I just can't bring myself to tell you."

And Catarino bathed the bull in an almost ecstatic gaze. The beast sleepily chewed its cud and swept the ground with the light curls of its tail, which ended in a tassel.

"You look very rich to me, Catarino," observed Olivier.

"Rich? No way! This is all I got. Here's all my savings."

Finally, the young men admired the less spectacular, although no less well-endowed, nor less luxurious, dependencies of the dairy: the milking shed, the butter and cheese factory, and pretty close to eleven, they returned to the city.

In the car, Olivier, for a few seconds, contributed to Ibáñez's happiness with these words:

"Now, Catarino, confess how much your whole dairy is worth."

"The truth, the honest truth?" The governor vacillated, half smiling and half mysterious. Immediately he added: "Olivier, not much more than four hundred thousand pesos, I can assure you. I already told you: this is all I have."

At the site of the convention, the arrival of the governor and his friends was greeted with murmurs bordering on applause. All the representatives of Progressive Radicalism in the State of Mexico were there, ever disposed to hear and obey the commanding voices of their leaders. They did not know that the top bosses were already somewhat in disagreement regarding the fundamental question. They assumed them to be of one mind and unanimous. They imagined them intent only in proclaiming with brilliance the watchword they had secretly sent to the lower ranks.

A voice boldly set off the series of "vivas":

"Viva don Catarino Ibáñez!"

"Viva!"

"Viva Olivier!"

"Viva!"

And at once, two or three voices clashed in their enthusiastic cry:

"Viva Hilario Jiménez!"

"Viva!"

At this point, the applause that still lingered from the two earlier "vivas" was joined by a new, long, and deafening volley of applause.

It was a dense crowd. Ibáñez and the Mexico City politicians made their way through it to reach the platform. As he walked, Axkaná felt the warmth of the groups that pressed together on either side to let them pass, and thanks to his greater height, he towered over the sea of heads. The auditorium was crammed to the last corner; in the gallery, the delegates crowded against the railing. Suddenly, Axkaná felt moved, although he did not know why. While all applauded and cheered, he felt that there was something very touching about that political assembly of some thousand men whose flesh was barely covered with rough *manta* cloth, something also in the way the large wheels of their palm sombreros waved at the end of some arms, something in the clapping of dark hands—barely visible against the blue of the hand-woven *cambaya* smocks, or standing out against the yellowish white of peasant shirts and pants. Their bronze faces, framed by their matted black hair, somehow expressed the joyful inkling of a possible hope. "Yes," thought Axkaná, "this is the hope politicians exploit and betray."

Ibáñez, his friends from Mexico, and the board of the local party occupied the seats behind the table. They were done now with the registration of credentials and other prerequisites. A secretary approached to say something to the governor. The latter, rising, declared the convention was officially open and announced he was yielding the chairman's seat to Emilio Olivier Fernández, president of the Progressive Radical Party of the Republic. He was interrupted by applause. Later when they had changed places, Ibáñez noted that before proceeding to the discussion and consideration of the candidacies, the platform of the local party would be read for ratification, and some formalities would be dealt with.

These tasks advanced quickly. Moments after they had started, Ibáñez and Olivier summoned one of the vice presidents, gave him the bell, and headed for one of the corners of the stage. There they went back to their topic. Olivier wanted to speak right away to the most influential members of the delegations. Catarino argued that it was best to hold off until they got to the candidacy for the presidency, after the candidacies of the deputies and senators had been discussed and approved.

"Otherwise," he said, "we run the risk the delegates will get mixed up and make a mess of the whole thing."

But so much resistance was beginning to get on Olivier's nerves. He said in the tone that forecast his explosions:

"Look, Catarino, I'm your friend, and you know it, but if you think you're going to manipulate me as it suits you, you're wrong. It's fine for you to protect your reputation, as you say, but not at the expense of the general interests of the party. I'm telling you once more that we need to come out of here with Ignacio Aguirre as our candidate, not Hilario Jiménez, and I assure you we're going to do that now, cost what may. Don't be insubordinate, because governor and all, I'll keep you in line."

And with a hand he signaled for Correa, Mijares, Cifuentes, and the other leaders to come closer. Catarino, who knew and feared Olivier, gave ground.

"Olivier, don't get me wrong, I'm not against your orders as president! I'm only giving my opinion about the best way to keep things on track. You're set on talking to the heads of the delegations? Right, you got it."

Distracted by the reading of the documents and by the votes, the assembly did not suspect what was going on at the other side of the platform. It also did not notice, a few minutes later, that several delegates congregated there and with mysterious expressions on their faces talked or argued with the governor and the leaders.

"What order," Ibáñez asked the first delegates who approached, "did I give you last night? Come on, you Maximino, tell them."

"Well, ya said that now we're supposed to work for my General Aguirre and not for my General Jiménez anymore."

"And are you working that way? Yes or no?"

"Yes, Governor."

Catarino then turned to Olivier.

"Convinced?"

"I had no doubt," the leader answered, "nor is that important. What I want to know is if the delegations are well briefed so the change will be made without upheavals or surprises. Are we new at this kind of thing? Let's see, Maximino, how are your people?"

"Mine? ... Well, I kinda think mine, and I think others too, are beginning to come around, but not what you'd call convinced yet, they're not there yet. Since the push for Hilario was so strong, now we have to kinda go easy. See, you gotta figure that when we gave out the money for expenses, we told 'em it came straight from my General Jiménez. Truth is, I expect a lot from the speeches, just like his excellency the governor was tellin' us this mornin'."

Olivier interrupted him:

"Speeches don't have much impact in these matters. The key here is for the delegates to have precise instructions and to obey them.... Right now you're going to pass on to your respective delegations this last-minute resolution that the central board of the party has taken: when the presidential candidates are proposed, you have to reject Jiménez and choose General Ignacio Aguirre by acclamation. You understand?"

While Olivier was speaking in this manner to the *mangoneadores*—the towns' political operators—Catarino, smiling, did not take his eyes off them. The delegates listened and stared at the floor.

The same thing happened with the rest of the groups that came right afterward. Olivier, each time more energetically, helped by Correa and Mijares, itemized the steps they had to take. The three of them did not beat around the bush. The delegates listened in silence. Catarino did not blink.

But then, when they left the group, the heads of the delegations, instead of going immediately to join their people, stayed to talk things over. They talked to the candidates for deputy and for senator, and once they got back to their places, their return caused commotions and muttering.

When it came time for the speeches about the presidential candidates, Olivier and his leaders remembered what Catarino told them the day before: "the assembly is Hilarista to the marrow." The warm oratory of Correa, Cifuentes, Mijares, and others penetrated the audience less than if it had been made of granite. Every time the name Ignacio Aguirre rang, the silence was dense. On the other hand, as soon as the name Hilario Jiménez was mentioned, be it in censure or in mockery, a thick, long, and thunderous applause would burst out. Olivier suffered the cruelest of his defeats there. Despite his enormous gifts as an orator, he ran out of breath when faced with the two or three would-be orators who asked for the floor to launch into a vilification of Ignacio Aguirre.

It was two hours of absurd, one-sided, and at the same time stormy debate. Finally, when the matter was going to be put to a vote, Olivier called Catarino aside. He understood it was a lost cause, he realized the governor had defected. Feigning he was not fully aware how matters stood, he said:

"As you can see, Catarino, I haven't done anything to hurt your political credibility. In return, the least you can do, in this case, is to help save my political credibility also, because, otherwise, as you see, this whole mess is going to end very badly. There is absolutely no way I can allow a faction of my own party to defeat me in a matter of such importance. Can you take care of it?"

"I'll take care of it, Olivier."

"Perfect. Then here's what we can do: we've got to get the convention to leave the nomination of the presidential candidate pending, alleging we haven't been able to consider sufficiently the citizens who've been proposed. Agreed?"

Ibáñez wanted to honor his commitment to Jiménez, avoiding, if possible, a conflict with Olivier. The latter's proposition seemed to him ideal, because that way, even as he rendered Olivier a significant service, it left him free to sell it to Jiménez as a triumph over Aguirre.

"Fair is fair," he agreed immediately. "You saved me earlier, now I save you."

No sooner said than done. He summoned the heads of the delegations back to the corner and explained to all of them, now coming from him, "the new turn of events." A motion to delay was going to be presented, he said, a motion that would postpone the nomination of the presidential candidate, and it was essential, it was an order from him, for that motion to be approved unanimously.

"Understand?"

Shortly after the assembly ratified that accord, the clock struck two. The delegates now could only think of the barbecue they had been promised after the street demonstration, and which was going to be served in the garden of a beautiful confiscated house. Humble and docile, they all got ready to leave. They left with the clumsy softness of a herd, with barely mumbled rejoicing. As they chatted, their consonants softened, and their trembling laughter seemed fated to fall to the ground as soon as it was born. Axkaná walked among them. Once again he did not know why, but the feeling of tenderness he had felt not long before was turning into a feeling of compassion. It was a kind of compassion similar to what he felt before orphan children.

III. Demonstration

THE CHEERS OF THE DEMONSTRATORS AND THE BAD CHORDS OF THE street musicians added to the provincialism of Toluca's streets. Its wonderfully clear sunlight shattered as it glimmered on banners and trombones. Its clean, transparent air was roiled by an uproar so alien to its purity. Windows and balconies opened and closed; curious people peered out of house doors or stopped at the edge of the sidewalks to see the parade.

Despite their hunger, the foot soldiers of democracy accomplished their mission well. As before, they were unaware of the true nature of the events in which they had played a part during the assembly. With mechanical enthusiasm, they continued to cry out "Long live!" and "Death to!" as they'd been told to by their bosses. They broke out in synchrony:

"Viva Hilario Jiménez!... Viva!"

"Muera Ignacio Aguirre!... Muera!"

Their cries, reverberating from corner to corner, gave birth to the spirit of the crowd and fed it; gave birth to something intangible, something encompassing that made the slogan-covered banners flutter as if with a life of their own.

Sometimes those leading the cheers, insufficiently familiar with the names of their heroes, mixed them up:

"Viva Ignacio Jiménez!" they shouted.

Or rather:

"Muera Hilario Aguirre!"

Catarino Ibáñez and Emilio Olivier marched at the head of the column. The most notable members of their respective retinues followed, a step behind. Catarino glowed, his gabardine suit radiating gubernatorial splendor, the emanations of a politician who is now unstoppable. From time to time, when he was greeted from sidewalks or doors, he practiced the aesthetics of his most exquisite bows. He leaned forward rigidly, as he raised his hand to his hat, and as the brim curved slightly under the pressure of his fingers—the brim of a hat that was neither military nor civilian, but of a mixed nature—his posture, from behind, emphasized the outline of his pistol at the level of his belt.

To Catarino's right, Olivier walked with easy grace. So as to soften the reversal he'd suffered a little earlier at the theater, he tried to lend a casual air to his participation in the demonstration. But this outward display was nothing but clever pretense for public consumption. Inside, with each new step, the leader felt a growing rage for the sly trick Catarino had just played on him. "You betrayed me," he thought, "but how dearly you'll pay for it!" His resentment became greater whenever Catarino, between the clashing of cymbals and the bass drum, shared his impressions of that political event. Because then, in order to reply to the governor in friendly words, Olivier had to curb his burgeoning ire, he had to wrench himself from the passion that utterly possessed him. It happened, furthermore, that at those very moments, the democratic crowd, as if it guessed what was transpiring in the heart of their supreme leader, yelled with a *non sequitur* that was as cruel as it was inopportune:

"Viva Catarino Ibáñez!... Viva!"

"Viva Olivier!... Viva!"

Axkaná was also among the first in the parade and among those who stood out the most. As he saw it, the force of the demonstration did not flow from the demonstrators to the spectators, but the other way. More than the event itself, he was interested in the effect the event had on those who watched it, or better yet, the contrast between effects. Because he had noted immediately that when the humble people by the doors and by the stream looked at the parade, they seemed to be witnessing an event that, though familiar, was always beyond their intelligence, as if they beheld a phenomenon whose cause was unknown and remote, like lightning, or rain. On the other hand, the people on balconies—and those in carriages, and in cars, and on horses with fancy Sunday tack—only looked at the demonstrators with a hint of incredulity or clear signs of scorn. In their view (as their disdainful attitude proclaimed), the rudimentary civic function that was evolving before their eyes had nothing to do with them. Therefore, if they deigned to look on, it was only from the height of another spiritual plane. What these people were witnessing was not something worthy

of their interest—much less their participation—not even for the
sake of their fortunes, or their freedoms, or their lives. At most
it was a kind of circus parade: a grotesque procession of paint-
smeared clowns and beasts that had escaped from their cages.

"Take a good look," Axkaná said to Mijares. "Notice the
smiles of the 'respectable people.' They're so lacking in a sense
of citizenship they can't even realize it's their fault, not ours, that
Mexican politics is what it is. I wonder which is greater, their fool-
ishness or their cowardice."

Meanwhile, as it passed, the civic procession grew. No longer
were the legions of Indians, brought just for the occasion from the
nearby haciendas, in the majority. Now, mixed with them—flank-
ing, enveloping, following them—were the masses of Toluca. The
blue of the *cambaya* cloth worn by workers was now beginning to
cover the whiteness of the peasant's *manta*, yellowish in the sun.
The murmur of bare feet was drowned out in the last rows, was
lost amid the crunching of the dirt under *huaraches*, and the contact
of heels and soles against pebbles. And the reason was that Catarino Ibáñez had spread the word that the demonstration would
culminate in a feast, and that all demonstrators would be admitted
to the feast. Thus, every cry of "Long live!" and "Death to!" was
an enticement for the crowd to swell.

Once they had gone through the main streets, the vanguard
of the demonstration came to a stop before the offices of the Progressive Radical Party of the State of Mexico. The board members
and other important men entered the building, then reappeared on
the balconies. Two bands blended their chords and then went silent.
The crowd, waving signs and banners, approached at a run, broke
ranks, and congregated all at once. They filled the street and their
palm sombreros created a heavy swell that flowed from side to side.

Moments later, after Catarino, Olivier, and other leaders had
consulted briefly, Axkaná began to speak from a balcony. Since the
balcony was only half a meter above the ground, the speaker stood
on a chair so all could see and hear him. His clear and melodious
voice made the waves of the sombreros come to an immediate stop.
The disks of the demonstrator's faces drew bronze-colored fur-
rows through the field of brims and crowns of palm leaves. Leaning back slightly, the marchers oriented themselves toward the
point from which the voice came, which acted as a magnetic pole.

Axkaná did not mention General Jiménez or General Aguirre in his speech; he spoke of other things. But these matters—although apparently unrelated to the speeches made by the morning speakers—were evidently very interesting, because they immediately captured the rapt attention of the public and soon earned clamorous ovations. The mostly barefoot audience rose on tiptoe in order to hear better. It was evident, however, that Axkaná's words, although simple, did not reach the understanding of the destitute multitude that listened to him. Between his mindset and that of his audience there was an abyss—an abyss of time, class, and culture. But that did not matter. As if ideas were only a kind of inert element in human communication, the flame of what Axkaná desired and felt at that moment flew over his ideas or under them, and suddenly ignited the desires and feelings of the humble men who heard him. The ideological structure of his paragraphs was the dross that fell to the ground while the intuitive, irrational principle—begetter of enthusiasm, generator of hope—went straight to their hearts. Concepts did not live in his speech; words lived as individual, aesthetic entities revealing what was essential, solely by virtue of their immediate effect on the soul, and the orator's whole being lived in them. The light that began to dawn in the mass of Indians assembled there was generated by the mysterious warmth of Axkaná's words and the rhythm of his phrases. But it was also born from the timbre of the orator's voice, the eloquence rooted in his sincerity, the communicative charm of his gestures, and even the intensely frank and expressive glow of his eyes, which shone greener under the curls of his disheveled hair.

Shortly before the speech ended, a straggling band, making a racket, emerged from the other street. It was hissed to silence. But since the hissing, in turn, lasted longer than was necessary, it raised a long storm of protest that spread from group to group. Once calm was reestablished, Axkaná spoke again, and minutes later, when another volley of applause burst out, his figure disappeared from the chair.

Now the response was an uproarious, interminable ovation. And those who applauded were not only the democratic throngs of the demonstration, but also the same curious families at the nearby windows. At the balcony where the board of the Progressive Radical Party was, Catarino was hugging Axkaná, almost lifting him up in the air, as if he were trying to raise him for the crowd of demonstrators to see. He too had not understood very well the scope of that speech, but a strange feeling had possessed him, pulled him along. He suspected that his conduct up to then had not been that of the "humble heroes" Axkaná had just mentioned, but that of the "powerful who had no souls, whose impulse to do good had been dead since their birth." But along with that suspicion he felt an enormous capacity to forgive himself and others, a sort of affective and altruistic delirium born from contact with the noble truth that for a few minutes had been rubbing against his skin, against his flesh, touching the depths of his humanity. At that moment, Catarino wanted to convince himself, through his sudden, sincere pursuit of barely glimpsed truths, that his place was not, after all, so far from that of upstanding men, and thus he felt ready to proclaim it. That is why he raised Axkaná in his arms, to meld his own feelings, in some way, with those of the multitude.

That multitude in front of the balcony and beyond—to the end of the street—continued to applaud and to acclaim Axkaná. They no longer remembered their squalor, their hunger, their bare feet (black as mud), nor their foul-smelling rags...

Then there was a hush. A timid voice, that seemed never to have tasted enthusiasm until that day, shouted:

"*Viva el patroncito*, our little boss!"

These words, so feebly pronounced that they were intuited more than heard, hovered just above the heads covered with palm sombreros and resounded immediately in the explosion that echoed them. A "viva" burst from the multitude, but a unanimous "viva," more sincere and complete than all the others, a "viva" where the common voice of the crowd, without losing its impetus, turned strangely mournful and heartbreaking.

A tremor, not a murmur, seemed to prolong that shout.

Fifteen minutes later, in the garden of the grand, confiscated house, the demonstrators lined up before the tables that held the promised feast. Every man was given something from the piles of food on each of the three tables: a *barbacoa* taco from the first table, a guacamole taco from the second, a *taco de frijoles* from the last. Then the demonstrators were told where they could get more tortillas if they asked for them, and beyond, around some barrels, they were given drinks. All of this was neither very succulent nor plentiful, but compared to their daily privation it was a banquet.

Many among the Indians from the haciendas had walked fifteen or twenty kilometers and had not tasted food for twelve hours. Nonetheless they gave no sign of impatience or hurry, but waited their turn with meek dignity. Then, with the food in their hands, they went to sit in the shade of the trees, and there they devoted themselves to nibbling their rolled tortillas. They ate with loyal sadness—the same loyal sadness with which stray dogs eat—but also with supreme, almost ecstatic dignity. As their jaws moved, the lines of their faces remained unchanged.

IV. A Toast

For that day Catarino Ibáñez had ordered the best restaurant of Toluca to prepare a meal worthy of him, worthy of his friends, and also worthy of being remembered for its significance, among the other events of that memorable, patriotic day. Nevertheless, because Catarino liked for things to "square," well... He chose not to say anything about the banquet until the right moment came. He did not announce it until the thousand Indians from the demonstration were gnawing at their bones and their tortillas in the garden of the confiscated house. Then, turning to Olivier, to Mijares, to Axkaná, he exclaimed with splendid revolutionary simplicity:

"Food for some? Then food for all! Or don't you figure we too got a right to live?... *Ándenles, muchachos*: on to the *mole poblano!*"

And throwing his arm around Olivier's neck he started to lead all those who felt they were included in the hackneyed phrase "We got a right."

On the way, he was moved once more by the memory of Axkaná's speech, and that led him to expound on the satisfaction he then felt: that of considering himself—for many reasons—responsible for the feast prepared for the thousand half-naked Indians. He crowned his outbursts with phrases that punctuated his jubilation:

"What great pleasure, Olivier, what great pleasure to be involved in these good works! Where do our slanderers get off saying we're not pure revolutionaries? What I say is: if we wasn't, would we do the things we do?"

Olivier was in a foul mood, and answered only in monosyllables. In view of which, Catarino shifted imperceptibly from speech to an interior monologue. "Yes," he thought, with his mind on the fortune of five hundred thousand pesos he had amassed in six years of egalitarian preaching, "we have to continue making free citizens, we need to apply every little one of the postulates of the Revolution: *the economic equality of all classes*, all of them; *the distribution of production capital*, all of the capital; *the equitable distribution of the yields of labor*, all of the yields; and we have to enforce these postulates without fear of what may come, without looking back, until we achieve *total results....* What is the minimum wealth that guarantees a citizen's liberty in Mexico? At least what I have now, from five to six hundred thousand pesos, which is what every Mexican would enjoy if he were not hindered by the small group of reactionaries who exploit him. Well then, we must make sure all Mexicans *from the Bravo River to the Suchiate River...*" For a moment he imagined himself speechifying to the thousand Indians at the political demonstration: "Yes, my sons"— he would say—"when *the Revolution becomes the law in the cities and the countryside*, there won't be any more greedy rich people, any more rich exploiters of the sufferings of the poor. Instead, we will all be good rich people, useful rich revolutionaries, as some of us already are: those of us who, with God's help, and without taking anything from anyone, are slowly gathering our savings..." At this point in his reverie, Catarino could not help remembering his magnificent farm. He thought about Mimosa, the Shorthorn cow that cost him twenty thousand pesos; he thought about Kewpie, the Jersey bull for which he paid thirty thousand, and both visions, refreshing his soul, made him smile to think that he already—he at least—was one of the free citizens into which it was necessary to turn the fifteen million inhabitants of the Republic. "The same as me"—he repeated to himself—"five hundred, six hundred thousand pesos.... No"—he corrected—"six hundred and fifty thousand"—because he suddenly remembered the deal he was currently working on and which he was about to close.

To Catarino's right, on the banquet table, sat Olivier; to his left, Axkaná, and then, on either side until the end, another twenty-five or thirty guests.

All immediately noticed that the banquet was very lavish. Little flowers had been spread over the pristine whiteness of the tablecloths; exquisitely folded napkins fell like crumbling castles at the touch of their fingers. Four glasses, lined up from the largest to the smallest, announced, at each place setting, the plurality of wines. One glass was green; another, the smallest, was topaz colored. And at the foot of the glasses, placed against one of their stems, were the menu cards, printed in different colors. Crowning the list of delicacies—centered at the top of the cards, and printed in gold letters—was the following: "Banquet to celebrate the nomination of Citizen General Hilario Jiménez as the State of Mexico's P.R.P. candidate to the Presidency of the Republic." And below, at the edge, also in gold letters, was this note: "The butter is from the Great Dairy of the Citizen Governor."

Immediately, Olivier wanted to protest the alleged reason for the banquet:

"This," he said, "is a scandalous lie. There is no way I will accept this. Neither Hilario Jiménez nor anyone else is the party's official candidate yet."

But Catarino Ibáñez, with wise humility, undercut the reproach by fully accepting it:

"You're right, Olivier. Of course, you're right! I'm not a bit tickled by this either. If you want, we can have the menus removed.... They're the ones we had printed when you gave the order for General Jiménez to be nominated. Truth is that after that, when you went and changed your mind, no one remembered to correct them. But, hell, this ain't worth your gettin' upset about! Or, are you gonna spurn my invitation for such a tiny thing?"

Olivier seethed as he replied:

"No, I'm neither angry, nor do I spurn your invitation. But I demand these cards be collected and destroyed."

"That's fine. We'll destroy them, just as you order. Only thing is, if it's all right with you, let's keep them during the lunch. At least that way you all will know (I mean, those who can read) what I'm serving you."

And they began to eat.

Catarino presided over the banquet with uncouth ease. The headwaiter came often to consult him, and Catarino answered his questions without hesitation and with the greatest confidence.

"Shall we serve the *mole poblano* now, my General?"

"No, my friend, the *mole* comes later."

"Also the wine from the big boxes, Governor?"

"Of course, my friend, all the wines."

Catarino answered some of these questions, like this one about the wines, loudly enough so they could hear him at the other end of the table.

"This fellow," he said, "thinks I've bought all these wines to store them. No siree, they're for drinking! Which doesn't mean I will force anyone to drink every last drop poured. Let each drink what he wants, and as much as he wants, like me. No red or white wine for me! The more expensive they are, the less I like 'em. Toluca beer for me, and of course, later on, my cognac.... How are those pork rinds, counselor? ..."

Axkaná, Correa, and Mijares, who, due to Olivier's frown, felt increasingly less and less at ease as the meal advanced, made enormous efforts to keep the conversation away from politics. But their attempt was in vain. Behind the most anodyne word or the most unrelated observation, the political theme was stalking and reemerged suddenly and with greater force each time.

Just before the national dish, the *mole poblano*, was served, someone thought to utter a word of praise that no one could have foreseen would have a dire effect.

"Now, that was a good guacamole!" a voice said.

To which Ibáñez, without knowing exactly who had spoken, replied:

"You like it, friend? Well, just goes to show you, this guacamole is the same one the comrades we left in the garden a while ago are eating out there with their *tacos de barbacoa*."

And Catarino underscored the words with smiles of deep democratic conviction. He added immediately:

"Who will dare to say now that we don't feel the Revolution deep in our hearts? Would we be eating so happily here, if we hadn't attended the people's feast afore?"

It was a rhetorical question, and that is how everyone understood it. But Olivier, looking for a way to answer in his own way, fired, at point blank range, words that could be interpreted as advice, but really sounded more like a challenge or an insult.

"Catarino," he said, "don't be a phony."

And as Olivier pronounced these words, his face, slightly pale, contracted with a smile that underscored what he had just gotten off his chest.

Catarino at first did not know how to take it. Perplexed and surprised, he answered:

"Me, a phony, Olivier?"

But Olivier insisted:

"Yes, you, a phony. Because what you're saying is a lie, and you know it's a lie."

There was a sudden murmur that created a silence for the length of the whole table. For two or three seconds, the waiters stopped serving. Then they pretended to turn their attention to the bottles and platters, while Catarino replied with extraordinary calm:

"I haven't told a lie, Olivier. I swear the guacamole in the tacos our comrades are eating in the garden is the same as the one we are eating here."

"The guacamole may be the same," Olivier affirmed implacably. "I don't dispute that. But the lie consists in calling the poor Indians from the demonstration 'comrades' and saying we wouldn't enjoy this banquet if we hadn't seen them eat before. If they are our comrades, why do you give them bones and broken tortillas, and furthermore let them eat it all on the ground, while you treat us regally? Here we are, at most thirty, over there more than a thousand. Nevertheless, I am certain our meal is going to cost you double or triple of what you will pay for the paltry barbecue for those who came to shout your 'vivas' and 'mueras.'"

"We give them," observed Catarino, as calmly as before, "what they're able to appreciate. We eat according to what we're used to."

"What you're used to!"

Eduardo Correa intervened here. Pretending to side with Catarino, he rushed to keep the argument from escalating:

"Of course, Olivier, of course. Catarino is right."

And since Mijares noticed at once Correa's purpose, he also intervened, and so did others, until they all managed to restore harmony, or at least its semblance.

After that altercation, Catarino did not display his joviality again. Instead, he gradually stopped talking, shrinking into himself, becoming somber, sullen. And it was in vain that Correa and Mijares undertook to lead the conversation, that they strove to make people laugh or tried to elicit boisterous responses. They were unable to bring back the joy, much less get Catarino and Olivier to talk to each other. Shortly after that, Catarino stopped drinking beer; he asked for cognac and devoted himself to drinking it steadily.

It was getting dark (it was already past five in the evening when they sat down to eat) by the time they made it, painfully, to the desserts. Catarino Ibáñez was half drunk, wobbling in his chair, and most of his friends were totally drunk. As far as Axkaná, Correa, Olivier, and the rest of the politicians who had come from Mexico City, some were still of sound mind, and the rest, mostly of sound mind.

The waiters were already serving champagne. Yet two or three stuttering voices, from the opposite end of the table occupied by Catarino and Olivier, shouted for more beer:

"We don't want fizzy lemonade! You hear?"

"Roll that barrel of Toluca over here!"

"That's it. The only thing I say is, 'Long live Toluca and my General!'"

Another, when he saw his glass full of champagne, stood up with great difficulty and seemed about to make a toast, and, in effect, he said something:

"Hardly... hardly..."

And he got no further. Standing, his drunkenness grew. The dizziness generated by the beer and wine mixed in his body with the vertigo caused by the new posture and the double row of guests, which receded and changed before his drunken eyes like a plantation of agave seen from a train. He made a visor with his hand and with an effort glimpsed the end of the table as he continued to say:

"Hardly... hardly... hardly..."

Until his comrade next to him said impatiently:

"Get it out now, *compadre*, hardly what?"

"I can't hardly make you out, sons of a goat..."

And he sank in the chair, spilling the contents of his glass on himself.

Mijares and the others laughed and applauded him with gusto; which encouraged the "Long live Toluca and my General" enthusiast to give vent to his mood in more exclusive cheers than the previous one:

"Long live my General Catarino Ibáñez!" he shouted.

Mijares led the response:

"Viva!"

Catarino at that moment was wiping his lips after his twentieth glass of cognac, and when he heard he was being cheered, replied from the depth of his baleful and taciturn expression:

"Gracias. Thanks for being fair, my sons."

Immediately, he raised himself from his seat, raised his champagne glass and made signs for all to be quiet so no one would miss the least of his words. All present raised their glasses and made ready to listen. But once more, the man who cheered for "My General and beer" burst out:

"Viva General Catarino Ibáñez!"

They applauded him and got him to be quiet. Catarino spoke:

"Gentlemen... fellow citizens..."

Since his arm swayed too much, making the wine trickle down his hand, he put the glass on the tablecloth, but still held it.

He continued right away:

"My friend here, Emilio Olivier, who's a good revolutionary, like all of you..."

Olivier, with his glass raised, kept his eye on him.

"... a good revolutionary, I say, though before he used to be a fancy pants—a *catrín*—told me last week we had to get the nomination for my General Hilario Jiménez.... Fine.... Two days later, he tells me no, now the candidate has to be Citizen General Ignacio Aguirre.... Fine.... And I, comrades, ask you, as honest and responsible revolutionaries: when he goes and flip-flops like that, my friend Olivier, doesn't it show that if I'm a phony, as he said a while ago"—and at this point Catarino struck the table with his free hand—"isn't he, I wanna say, a bigger phony than me?"

There was no time for the reply to be heard. Quick and impulsive, Olivier threw the champagne in his glass at the governor's face and then hit him on the forehead with the glass itself.

Which quickly unleashed an intense battle.

Axkaná had come between them.... Catarino tried clumsily to draw his revolver.... Olivier, gun in hand, wrestled with Correa and Mijares.

"Viva General Catarino Ibáñez!" some shouted from the other end of the table.

Plates and bottles flew.... A shot rang out.... Another...

Now part of the tablecloth and everything that was on it was on the floor...

"Viva Catarino Ibáñez!"

"Viva!"

The confusion swirled immediately into two centers: one group held Catarino and pushed him, his face bathed in blood, to a corner, while on the opposite side, Axkaná, Mijares, and Correa dragged Olivier to the exit...

The fight went on like this for several minutes, the smell of wine mixing with that of tobacco and gunpowder, and the clamor of shouts with flashes and detonations.

Some of Catarino's friends, the drunkest ones, were still sitting at the table, from which they brandished their pistols, without knowing for sure on which of the groups they should fire. Others, on the floor, tried in vain to get up...

The Mexico City politicians had managed at last to get Olivier out into the street. Their cars were in front of the restaurant and the commotion now began to spread around them. Waiters and cooks ran for shelter around the street corners. Insults and curses could be heard through the restaurant's half-opened windows. The powerful voice of the governor was heard above all:

"I'll get you next time, you *catrines jijos de la tiznada!*—you fancy sons of bitches! I'll get you!"

Meantime, the uproar, far from abating in intensity, grew louder and spread, since there was no shortage of curious people approaching, even as most of the people fled.

Finally disarmed by Mijares, Olivier wrestled now with Axkaná near the cars. Correa at last managed to hold him from behind and get him into the nearest car, as he shouted to the driver:

"Get going and don't stop, even if they shoot at us!"

Meanwhile, the rest of the leaders had left the restaurant and jumped hurriedly into the other cars to flee behind the one carrying Olivier. From the balconies at the site of the banquet, the din and insults followed them in waves, as well as some bullets, but the automobiles were already making their escape through the main streets, and shortly, with gas pedals pressed to the floor, they entered the highway to Mexico City.

Book Four

The Assault

I. The Men at the Jai Alai Fronton

Within twenty-four hours, Olivier Fernández reacted to the events in Toluca by organizing the "bloc of deputies and senators for Ignacio Aguirre"—a bloc so powerful that from its birth it included two thirds of the Chamber of Deputies and an almost equal portion of the Senate.

This action poisoned spirits and caused passions to boil over. Immediately there were rumors that the Caudillo considered the new step taken by the Progressive Radicals as a challenge to his power; it was an intolerable affront to his prestige as supreme guide of the Revolution. It was also said that Hilario Jiménez, furious at the list of 180 deputies and 38 senators who supported his opponent's candidacy, was threatening to go and exterminate both legislative chambers, *en masse*.

Reports about Jiménez were particularly extensive and disquieting—disquieting, even if at times picturesque. He was described pacing his office at the Secretariat of the Interior and tirelessly uttering phrases as outrageous as they were irate. "Vile scum!"—he shouted, beside himself—"Despicable bunch of self-serving louts!... When have they ever felt the proletarian pain of the cities and the countryside? We deserve to be hanged if we let them live!..." It was also said that during those fits, only two things calmed him down: first, to speak of the most efficient methods of eliminating all his enemies at one blow, and second, to read carefully the letters from his land agent. Because, as chance would have it, the Caudillo's candidate—and no one knew how, especially considering his terrible invectives against landowners—had just acquired, precisely in those days, the largest hacienda in the north of the Republic, and there were moments when his soul was sweetened by the honeymoon of first-time buyers.

One of those nights, Axkaná, who needed to speak urgently to Eduardo Correa, went to look for him at the Iturbide Street fronton.

Someone had told him the mayor seldom missed the jai alai games and that from nine in the evening to one o'clock in the morning, the Frontón Nacional was the best place to find him.

When Axkaná entered the building, the game had already started. The lobby, which was totally empty, filled with the echoes of faraway noises: the shouts of the bookmakers and the jai alai players, the murmur of the public, the striking of the ball alternately against the wall and against the wicker of the cestas.

Axkaná went to the ticket window, bought his ticket, and headed in, but he had only taken a few steps when he remembered he had left the taxi, from which he had just emerged, waiting. Therefore, he returned to the street to dismiss it.

At the door, he now ran into five or six men whom he had not noticed when he arrived, and who, whispering in a huddle, seemed to be planning something. When one of them realized Axkaná was getting close, the whole group became silent and moved toward one side of the door to let him pass.

For a moment Axkaná had the vague sensation those men were interested in him and that what they were saying concerned him. Therefore, he tried to observe them as he dismissed the car, and later as he again passed the group, he cast a sideways glance at the six men. It was a very quick look but enough to encompass the scene. He saw that one of the five men—because now he noticed there were only five—stood out: a tall, robust man with a chestnut hat, and Axkaná fixed his glance on him, sure that it was the same man who had already stood in front of him that very day somewhere else, perhaps as he left the Chamber or maybe on the sidewalk at Sanborn's. His forehead, narrow and with eyebrows very close together, was unmistakable, as was his pale face with a bad complexion, as was his tie, with blue stripes on a gold background.... At any rate, since the whole incident was insignificant, or seemed to be, Axkaná chose not to attach any importance to it.

Despite the fact that it was Thursday, Eduardo Correa was not among the spectators at the fronton, but some friends or acquaintances of his were: Don Carlos B. Zetina, Ramón Riveroll, Guillermo Farías, and others. Several told Axkaná that the mayor, for some time now, tended not to appear at his seat until the second game, and since that was, after all, the best information they gave him, Axkaná prepared to wait as long as it was necessary for the mayor to arrive.

In the end, the wait turned out to be long and useless, although not lacking in attractions that made it more than bearable. Because that night Axkaná, who until then had never come to the fronton, discovered a new spectacle, a spectacle that struck him as magnificent for the richness of its sculptural forms, and which he thoroughly enjoyed. His eyes filled with extraordinary sights; he believed, at times, he was witnessing an event of unreal beauty. Under the glow of the electric lamps, he witnessed the unearthly grace that pervades the deeds of the *pelotari*, the jai alai players.

Two hours later, when the second game was over, Axkaná left the fronton and jumped into the first taxi he was offered, a Ford.

"To the Calle de la Magnolia," he said to the taxi driver. "If you go by Soto, turn left. When we get there, I'll tell you where to stop."

It had occurred to him at the last minute that the mayor might be visiting the house of Olivier Fernández's lady friends.

As the Ford maneuvered to get out of the line, Axkaná once again detected the presence of the group of men whom he had noticed earlier and who, no longer at the entrance of the fronton, were now standing guard at the sidewalk across the road. For a moment, his eyes met the pale man's eyes, but Axkaná took no notice. He was still relishing the memory of the climactic scenes of the jai alai games. All his senses still admired, as superhuman deeds, as phenomena alien to the laws of physics and to everyday life, the incidents of the game he had just seen. He recalled the incredible agility of Egozcue, who climbed the wall of the court as if he were going to hang from the ball with his cesta; Elola's infinite efficacy as he returned deadly serves, almost invisible serves, at three meters; Irigoyen's rabid fierceness (he threw himself head first against the wall every time he lost a point because the ball pierced his cesta); and the heroic mastery of Goenaga, who dropped to his back to catch incredible rebounds, two centimeters from the floor.

At the Calle de la Magnolia he got out of the car, called at the door, and entered. A servant with bare feet and glossy braids came to let him in and surprised him in the hall with the news that the "girls" were not home.

"What do you mean they're not home?!"

"No, sir; they ain't."

"Not one?"

"Not one, sir. Miss *Mora* called on the phone from some-where and said something, and they all took off quick as can be, been a while now."

"Surely they said where they were going."

"No, sir."

At that moment, they heard the noise of a car that approached the house and stopped in front of the door. Axkaná and the servant were silent, waiting to see who called. Outside they could hear voices—the drivers, it seemed, were arguing. A little time passed and the recently arrived car left.... Axkaná continued:

"And Doña Petra, is she in?"

"Not neither, sir. She also up and left with the girls. They said that..."

The servant stopped.

"What did they say?"

"No, sir, nothing.... Doña Petra told me, I think she too had to go to the Police Station for some reason."

"Well, Cástula," concluded Axkaná, "you're so odd tonight. Keep your secrets."

Back in the street again, and having decided to leave his con-versation with Eduardo Correa for another day, he gave the driver directions to his house.

From Magnolia, the car shot quickly onto Calle de Soto; from there into Hombres Ilustres, and then through one side of the Alameda, to Avenida Juárez.

The driver and his assistant, with scarves up to their eyes, bowed their heads to avoid being struck by the cold wind. Axkaná continued to think about the singular sculptural beauty of the art of the fronton. Nevertheless, he too wound up feeling that the cold was going through him, and, wishing to snuggle in the seat as he had done when he took the cab in Iturbide, he sought, but did not find, the ledge where he had rested his feet before. This struck him as so odd that when the car went under the street lamps of Plaza Colón, he tried to understand what was going on, and upon closer examination, quickly came to the conclusion that he was now in a Chevrolet, not in the Ford he had taken to go to the Calle de la Magnolia. He was stunned. "Could I be wrong, then?"

He doubted for a moment. But he immediately rectified. "No, I'm sure. The other car was a Ford, not a Chevrolet."

Some meters beyond, he ordered the driver to stop. The car stopped in the midst of the massive shadows of the Paseo.

"This isn't the car I took to the Calle de la Magnolia," Axkaná said.

The driver interrupted him:

"No, boss; it isn't. At the fronton, you took the Ford my brother drives. But since he had a trip to San Ángel at two-thirty and thought you were going to stay a long time at that house, when I went by he asked me to take you. If you don't like it you can dismiss me."

The explanation was perfectly plausible.

"It's all the same," replied Axkaná. "Go ahead."

The Chevrolet then went on, but at the Glorieta de Cuauhtémoc, the driver did not take Insurgentes, as the address he was given (Londres 135) required, but continued in the same direction. "He's going by Niza," thought Axkaná, who also used to take that route. But once more, when they approached Calle Niza, Axkaná was surprised to see that the car continued on Reforma instead of taking one of the side streets. This began to make Axkaná a bit uneasy.

"I told you Londres 135," he shouted at the driver. Whereupon the latter half turned to him and replied:

"Yes, boss, Londres 135. I'm going by Florencia, because the pavement is better there and won't hurt my springs."

And that's what he did. When they got to the Plaza de la Columna, the Chevrolet, skirting the circular esplanade, came out to Calle Florencia, which came up suddenly under the headlights, completely empty—a deserted spot: not a tree, not a house. Except that now the Chevrolet, in contrast with its previous speed, was going inexplicably slowly. Stranger still was the fact that although nothing was blocking the way, the driver honked the horn repeatedly.

More uneasy, Axkaná asked:

"Why are you honking?"

"Boss?"

"I said, why are you honking?"

"On account of that car, boss, he's blocking the way up front."

Axkaná could not see any car and was about to say so. But he noted, a few meters later, that the car was going more slowly and then that at the next corner the headlights of another car, which seemed to come from Calle Hamburgo, shone suddenly and came toward the Chevrolet.

That very powerful light blinded Axkaná, erasing at one blow any sense of the topography of the street. The driver, no doubt also dazzled, stopped. But that barely took some seconds; the other car had come close enough to brush the side of the car occupied by Axkaná, and immediately passing a bit beyond, permitted the Chevrolet's headlights to shine ahead again until the beam of light was lost in the parallel sidewalks.

Axkaná was then sure the mysterious car had just stopped behind the Chevrolet, and noting that his driver gave no sign of driving on, understood, finally, that he had fallen into an ambush. He stood rapidly and tried to reach for his revolver, but things happened so quickly he did not even get to unbutton his overcoat. On the left and on the right, four arms with pistols reached into the Chevrolet. Two pointed at him and two at the driver and his assistant.

"Hands up!"

Axkaná, without moving, asked:

"What is this about?"

"It's about you either raise your hands or I'll let you have one."

That voice seemed to speak in earnest. Immediately adding:

"Hands up and get outta there!"

Axkaná did not raise his hands that time either; he merely held them open at the height of his chest. That is how he got out of the car, while in front of him the docile driver and his assistant were outlined, like pitchforks made of shadows, against the luminous stream of the headlamps.

Once he was standing by the car, Axkaná saw he was surrounded by four men. Although none of the four was wearing a hat, two were hiding their faces and parts of their bodies with something white—a rag, it seemed, or a newspaper. Axkaná did not manage to see much more. Near the cars the darkness was deep, due to the surrounding luminous area. Because on one side, the headlights of the Chevrolet lit as far as the distant buildings, while on the opposite side, the headlights of the other car sent their light up to the Columna de la Independencia. And so, the island of blackness between the two cars became impenetrable.

One of the two unknown men had immediately blindfolded Axkaná, while another, after taking away his revolver, was going through his pockets. Both then grabbed him by the elbows, made him walk, and forced him, pushing him, to get into the car they brought.

"Lie down!" the same voice ordered.

A hand pressed down on his shoulder and made him fall to the floor of the car. Feet grazed him. He felt that on his face, near his mouth, they were pressing the barrel of a pistol.

The voice said:

"If you move or yell, I'll waste you, God's truth!"

II. On the Way to the Desert

B<small>LINDFOLDED AND UNABLE TO MOVE</small>, A<small>XKANÁ GAVE HIMSELF OVER</small> to his thoughts for the moment.

He was conscious, to a disproportionate degree, of the coldness of the pistol they were holding against his face. Through the blindfold, he also sensed—with almost microscopic powers—his hair, clothes, and the rough contact with the car's carpet. But more immediate than such physical evidence, more imperative, was the doubt that drove him to speculate on the source of his kidnapping, so that he could predict the possible conduct of his kidnappers.

"In whose hands am I?" he asked himself, still reeling from the surprise. "In the hands of thugs or of a group of government agents?" And his fervent wish was for the kidnappers to turn out to be thieves, the worst kind of thieves, but in any case, not government hit men. "Because in Mexico," he told himself immediately, and the concept came to him with greater clarity than ever, "there is no worse caste of born criminals than that from which the government recruits its henchmen."

Then, from an association of emotions rather than ideas, he connected the assault he had just suffered in the middle of the night with the scene of the men who had been spying on him at the entrance of the Frontón Nacional, and the chat with *La Mora*'s servant, who had been so odd, so reticent.

His reflections did not last more than a few seconds because the car's departure jolted him out of them.

Faint lights, perceptible despite the blindfold that pressed against his eyelids, led him to assume the car was passing from the Calle Florencia to the Paseo de la Reforma, and since, at the same time, his body slid in a manner that suggested a right turn, he decided then to use his imagination to follow the route by which they were taking him—his imagination, aided by his hearing and what his muscles sensed.

A change in the direction of the car, though very slight, suggested they were passing another traffic circle of the Paseo. He realized at once they were going back, and later they turned the same way they had at the beginning. For sure they were passing through Colonia Cuauhtémoc.... Another turn to the right, a turn to the left, again to the right.... They ran along several streets...

Further on, he guessed they were crossing over the rails of the Colonia Station.... "Now, we must be going by Sadi-Carnot"... "Now, by Las Artes"... "Now, by La Industria"... A new curve to the left, wider than the last ones, confirmed his hypothesis that they were going from Calle de la Industria to La Tlaxpana.... They were reaching—he realized they were ascending a slight grade— the intersection of Tlaxpana with Calzada de la Verónica.... Quick turn of the car to the south.... They were racing down the Calzada to Chapultepec: as it went over the potholes the car jumped repeatedly.

One of those jumps was so abrupt that the barrel of the pistol, still against his face, hit his cheekbone with such violence that it cut him. Axkaná felt the flowing of blood and the wet warmth dripping to his nose.

"You idiot!" he said without moving. "Don't you realize the gun could go off?"

Between his cheek and the rug, the blood was spreading. He immediately added:

"I don't see the point of..."

But the same voice he heard when he was assaulted did not let him finish:

"Shut up, *hijo de tal*!—you s.o.b.!"

And the barrel of the pistol hit him again, only this time it was not the muzzle but the side of the barrel, as they gave him a kick in the chest.

The car then stopped for a few seconds to make several maneuvers Axkaná could only half follow. Stunned as he was by the pain, he lost track of two or three of those movements. There was no doubt, however, that they were again running down La Calzada. But in what direction now? Toward San Cosme? Minutes later, after the car turned yet again, the pavement was smooth once more, it seemed like asphalt... Through the blindfold he perceived dim lights; no doubt they were street lamps. "We have come back to the city," he thought.... "A long run"... "Many twists and turns"... "Once more a long stretch"...

There was a place where the car, without slowing down, went around who knows how many times making a perfect circle, finally shooting off on a tangent. Then Axkaná was totally disoriented.... The new stretch, over wide flat surfaces, continued for a long time.... At the end of which the potholes returned, then the car shook, as if it were going over rails, and then there were even deeper potholes...

Going uphill, up.... On the one hand the sound of the motor increased as if the car were in open country, without the least obstacle. On the other, the succession of bangs seemed to rise and follow the car, as if endless walls were holding it back, were boxing it in.... The potholes stopped.... Now began a series of slopes, curves, undulations. The series repeated. Then others began.... Suddenly there was a long, slow descent, then, as if the car were turning off at the bottom of a *barranca*, a swerving to the right, followed by a brief but very steep rise, and, already at the top, a turn to the left. And then again it sped away...

That last conjunction of features was very familiar to Axkaná; he identified it at once. A little farther, he related it unmistakably to other topographical peculiarities whose appearance he predicted. "Yes," he thought, "we're on the way to the Desert," and within the darkness of the blindfold, the landscape became clear to him. Again, he knew where they were taking him.

A little later the car stopped, and, immediately, advanced slowly, as one of the front wheels dipped. Then the other front wheel dipped as the first one rose. Then the same thing happened with the rear wheels: both fell and rose alternately.

They had gone over a curb.... They were off the road.... The car now continued to advance slowly. Through the floor, Axkaná could hear the tires crunching on the clods of earth, the whipping of grass bent by the axles.

After two or three minutes of rolling along like this, the car stopped.

Then came a moment of silence and infinite stillness. The majesty of the hills imbued with the mystery of night, the majesty of darkness, the majesty of the mountains and the countryside touched the spirit.... But all that grandeur was suddenly shattered by the insignificant sound of a voice:

"Tell 'em to cut the motors."

The locks of the doors sounded. To judge from the noise and the movements, several men were getting out.

"Get outta there!"

The voice was forceful and hoarse.

As Axkaná rose, two hands grabbed him by the arm and others threw him on the seat. Now he felt the gun barrel resting on his chest.

"Gimme the tequila," said the same voice.

Axkaná sensed someone was searching near his body. He heard them move something, tear papers.

The neck of a bottle came to touch his mouth.

"Have a drink," the voice ordered.

But Axkaná, turning his face away, answered firmly and calmly:

"I don't drink."

"You don't drink."

"No, I don't drink."

"Oh, yeah?"

The waves of the voice went in a different direction:

"Hey, you, get them to give you the oil funnel.... So you don't drink?"

You could hear the noise as they rummaged through the car equipment.

"So you don't drink.... So you don't drink," the voice repeated.

"It's going to be useless to resist," thought Axkaná. "It might be wiser not to resist."

He was, nevertheless, afraid they would poison him.

"And how can I be sure," he asked, "that what you want to give me is only tequila?"

"You can't. Enough questions. If we wanted to poison or kill you any other way, who'd stop us? But you already heard me ask for tequila. Feel the bottle. It's brand new; we just opened it. Come and drink, on your own, or we'll help you. Let's have your hand.... Isn't this a bottle?"

In spite of it all, his way of speaking amused Axkaná. Touching the bottle, he said:

"Yes, it's a bottle."

"Then take a drink.... Look: I'll drink first."

Brief silence.... Smacking of lips:

"Good tequila, God's truth!... Now you."

Axkaná drank.

"Is it tequila or ain't it?"

"Seems to be."

The bottle was still partially held by Axkaná's hand.

"Drink again."

"No, that's enough."

"Drink again, I tell you.... And just don't move around so much, my gun could go off."

And so saying, the stranger made the bottle meet Axkaná's lips. Axkaná drank again.

"Ain't it good tequila?"

"Yes, it's good.... But why have you brought me to this place?"

"Come on, don't be so curious. We'll get around to telling you when you're good and liquored up. One more down the hatch. And take my advice: if you keep moving I don't answer for my gun."

With the neck of the bottle, the stranger kept hitting Axkaná's lips. He evidently did it with the intention of hurting him and keeping him docile. To get him to stop, Axkaná drank.

This time the stranger was not content for Axkaná to drink as he had before. Instead, he stuck several centimeters of the bottle between his teeth and forced him to swallow a huge amount of liquid. Axkaná started to feel warm and dizzy from the alcohol that was almost choking him. From his face the trickle of blood continued to flow; by now the front of his shirt was wet.

"Drink again."

And the voice, turning elsewhere added:

"Hold his arms, just in case he gets rowdy when he's drunk."

The voice once more turned to him:

"C'mon, Mister whosis, have another swig. You're here to obey me."

Axkaná resisted.

"Are you going to play nice and drink, or not?"

For the fourth time, Axkaná agreed. And his kidnappers again made sure the gulp he took was enormous.

Axkaná felt as if his mouth, throat, and chest were on fire. Despite all this, he was, nevertheless, beginning to be flooded by a great feeling of well-being. He hardly resisted two more swigs; they entered him as a drug that liberates, that gives relief. But that did not last long. Moments later his sensations changed suddenly. Now he quickly began to experience the symptoms of a terrible drunkenness, a strange intoxication that plunged him into a kind of drowning rather than dizziness. He was feeling strange, stranger by the second, profoundly strange, his arteries swelling with his blood pressure.

New gulps made him think that his head was the size of the car, and the wound on his cheekbone seemed even larger than his head.... The blindfold, strangling his brows, made his temples throb with beats like massive hammer blows.

"Take the blindfold off. Take it off, please!"

"Drink again."

And once more they stuck the bottle in up to his throat. And even before he had a chance to swallow what they forced in his mouth, they were already making him take another gulp.

From that moment on the operation of making him drink degenerated into a constant struggle. Axkaná would resist for a while, and then, exhausted, yielded a few seconds until he resisted again. This was repeated, five, ten, fifteen times. They had him by the legs, nose, and hair. When he seemed to be choking, they let him rest and then started again right away. They hit his face to get him to open his mouth; they stuck something like a screwdriver between his teeth.

Finally, half drunk and almost passing out, he gradually yielded. Now he had his back against the seat, and, for greater ease, they no longer forced him to drink from the bottle, but with the funnel. He distantly tasted the flavors of tequila, blood, and oil mixing in his mouth.... For a while, he meekly drank as much as they gave him; it was a long time, very long.... He no longer felt the wound, nor his head, nor his body. He was conscious only of a single sensation: that of a metal tube molded against his tongue; his scorched tongue molded to the metal tube.

Then that sensation, which for an instant seemed to fill the universe, for it was infinite, began to fade and disappear, and as it vanished, everything began to vanish with it.

III. The Check from May-Be
Petroleum Company

At one in the afternoon the next day, Ignacio Aguirre was alone in his office at the Ministry of War. He still had no knowledge of the atrocities perpetrated on Axkaná, and, at any moment, expected him to come and get him, as his friend customarily did at that time of day. Meanwhile, as he waited, he was lost in thought. He had his elbow leaning on the table that was now free of papers. There was a cigar in his mouth, and his fingers were busy caressing its fine wrapper with pleasure.

A little before, a general staff officer had come in through the antechamber's door with a list of the persons requesting an appointment. Without reading the names or changing his posture, Aguirre had said:

"Many?"

"Eighty-nine, my General."

"Fine, I'm not receiving anyone."

Minutes later, through another door, the same officer came back. He was now asking if the minister would hold the plenary session that afternoon with the department heads who had been waiting for two weeks. Impatient and ill-humored, Aguirre replied:

"I'll say when we're going to hold a plenary. Tell that to the heads who are asking... and you too, when are you going to stop bothering me?"

After which, with the denizens of the office world in flight, the minister of war was able to follow his train of thought for a considerable stretch of time.

This did not concern, as one might have expected, the interests of the Republic or the affairs of the Ministry. Aguirre was thinking only about his personal predicament. That morning he thought he had found the proper course of action for his fight with Hilario Jiménez and his conflict with the Caudillo. Since then, he had done nothing but give himself totally, with the morbid pursuit of an *idée fixe*, to the plans that he expected to put into practice very soon.

About fifteen minutes had gone by in this manner when through the hallway door—with his hat on, walking stick in hand—appeared the figure of Remigio Tarabana.

"May one enter?"

Aguirre did not move from his seat, did not even turn his face. He was content to look at his visitor from the corner of his eye, as he muttered between his teeth and cigar:

"One may enter."

Tarabana then walked to the center of the room and there he stopped. He had that half-ironic, half-cynical air, which in him meant: "done deal." Then, seeing that Aguirre did not deign to look at him, he approached the table. As he walked, he flaunted his smile and the magnitude of his good luck.

"This is no way," he exclaimed, "to receive the best of friends, or at least the most useful friend!"

And translating the emphasis from words to action, he pulled over a chair, sat down, placed his walking stick and his hat on the table, and began to drum his fingers on everything within his reach. Aguirre did not move.

"Aren't you talking today?" said Tarabana, and then added as an aside, "We'll see if he talks or not."

He took out his wallet and extracted a yellow slip of paper that he folded in half with great care, so that it made a bridge, placed it on the table, and flicked it so that it came to rest near Aguirre's hand.

"Look out!" he said as he launched his projectile.

Aguirre then came out of his abstraction. He took the piece of paper, unfolded it, gave it a glance, and read the lines written in the most visible type. The yellow slip of paper was a check that said:

Bank of Montreal. Pay to the bearer the amount of twenty-five thousand pesos. May-Be Petroleum Co. By M.D. Woodhouse.

"Not a bad deal. The land cost me nine hundred pesos."

And Aguirre set the check back on the table.

Meanwhile Tarabana filled his smile with cynicism and irony.

"So, you finally talked! So you're not mute! It took twenty-five thousand pesos for the young minister to take the cigar out of his mouth and open his lips! Yes, sir, that's what they're giving for the land, for the land and the service, or, to tell the truth, only for the service, because the land, as far as I can make out, isn't worth an old quarter penny. But, in sum, what matters is they're giving it, and do so without requiring any signed document. Would you please put that check in your wallet instead of leaving it there as if it didn't matter to you?"

Aguirre left the check where it was.

"And the service," he asked, "what is it? Spell it out for me."

"Again? I've told you in two hundred ways: for you to order that the land occupied by the Military Cooperative be returned right away to the May-Be Petroleum Co.; and this because the company (and pay close attention to this because this is what the communiqués need to say), because the company has clearly demonstrated their right to it to the satisfaction of the Secretariat of War..."

"Fine, fine. Call Cisneros and dictate the wording yourself."

"No, sir! Not Cisneros! These are not matters for your personal secretary. The communiqués must come from the department and meet all relevant requirements. That was the deal."

"But, when did you tell me that it had to come from the department?"

"I said that the order had to be by the book, which comes to the same thing. But, let's not argue. If you don't like it, we can undo the deal. I'll return the twenty-five thousand pesos to May-Be and that's that. I won't have it any other way. What the hell! These people are paying to have justice done. And on top of it we're going to cheat them? Neither as their agent nor as your friend will I put up with this.... Furthermore, it is shameful that the Secretariat of War is abetting the larceny of a group of crooked military officers who are going around organizing oil companies with other people's land."

"It was the Caudillo who gave them the idea."

"So much the worse. Still, I bet you anything that the Caudillo, though he is capable of grabbing all of Mexico for himself, never told you to authorize May-Be's dispossession."

"He never ordered me to do it in so many words, but in a veiled manner. Not once, but many times."

"In that case, stop what they're trying to do, because it's robbery. I assure you."

Aguirre was pensive for a moment. Then, taking the check from the table, observed:

"And this, Tarabana? Isn't the mere fact of my accepting this money you bring me also something like robbery?"

"That depends, Ignacio, that depends.... If I were Axkaná, for example, I would say yes, but Axkaná is an intellectual. I, who have my feet on the ground, assure you it isn't. The evaluation of human acts is not only dependent on morality, but also on physical geography and political geography. That being the case, we need to consider that Mexico, at present, enjoys a different ethic from that in force in other latitudes. Are honest and upright functionaries rewarded, or even respected among us? I mean the kind of functionaries who would be considered honest and upright in other countries. No, they're attacked, despised, shot. And instead, what happens here to functionaries who are phonies, liars, and thieves, meaning those who'd be considered as such in nations where common, ordinary ethical values are in force? Among us, they receive respect and power, and if conditions are right, the day after they die they can even be declared benefactors of the fatherland. Many believe that in Mexico judges don't mete out justice because they're lacking in probity. Nonsense. What happens here is that the protection of life and goods is in the hands of the most violent, most immoral men. Thus, the tendency of almost everyone to side with immorality and violence becomes a kind of self-preservation instinct. Take the Mexican police: in any crisis, they're on the side of the criminals or are themselves the criminals. Notice our prosecuting attorneys; the more murders go unpunished, the higher they're held in regard. Notice the lawyers who defend our accused. If they ever dare to do their duty, the powers of the Republic draw their pistols and silence them with death threats, and when that happens there's no virtue that can protect them. In sum, meting out justice, which elsewhere requires only modest and common virtues, in Mexico requires heroism or martyrdom."

Aguirre had listened to Tarabana's speech with an expression of indulgent incredulity. He smiled faintly. He made no reply. Tarabana continued:

"So now you know. Do you feel like a hero? Give May-Be their money back and mete out justice for free, *ex officio*. Because to return the check and leave them in a bind would also not be honest; it would be like siding with those who steal. Do you feel neither like a hero nor like the accomplice of highwaymen? Fine, then you need to accept the rate at which your service is valued and render it. To ask more of you would not be just. The nation pays you to be minister of war (a post you hold for reasons that have nothing to do with your salary), but it doesn't pay you to bring upon yourself all the hatred and risks of behaving in an upright manner. Things being as they are, the truly honorable thing to do is to act well in exchange for a fair honorarium. How much is the land May-Be is fighting for worth? Two or three million pesos. What will the simple act of declaring that the company's titles are legally unimpeachable cost you? You yourself don't know: the final rupture with the president, the hatred of many generals, your political career, your life.... Why then should it be considered theft for you to accept a very small sum in exchange for acts that, if not executed, place you on the side of the real scoundrels and, if executed, expose you, for sure, to give sooner or later more than what you are now receiving? Believe me when I say that by behaving like this, you or any other minister of Mexico's government is acting with greater probity than surgeons who charge five thousand pesos for an operation or lawyers who submit bills for a hundred thousand. What I mean is that, in cases such as this, ministers exploit their position less, earn their money more conscientiously."

Aguirre, with the check between his fingers, kept smiling. In the end he exclaimed:

"Want me to tell you the truth, Tarabana? You're a very talented scoundrel, and although I lack your talent, I'm another scoundrel."

"Please!"

"Yes. Except I still have a virtue you have already lost: I don't justify myself. I know I'm a scoundrel and I admit it plainly. I dare you to admit it just as plainly!"

"I'd be lying."

"You'd be telling the truth. That's when you'd be telling the truth..."

"I assure you..."

"Ah! You won't? Fine, fine. Let's skip it and go to the heart of the matter. Look, I'll pocket the twenty-five thousand pesos. I'm also going to give you the communiqués the way you ask. But since you talk about morality, don't confuse my motives. You know why I'm taking the money? Not because I think it's a good thing to do; I'm not that dumb. I take it because I need it, and this is a definitive and conclusive reason: 'because I need it.' As for your syllogisms, you'll never convince me. They're good for those who are pliable and those who are pusillanimous, and although I'm a scoundrel, I won't descend to that level. I am a scoundrel, but a scoundrel endowed with courage and will."

As he pronounced the last words, Aguirre touched one of the many buzzers on his table. Seconds later his personal secretary appeared.

"Señor Cisneros," ordered the minister, "be so good as to go in person to the office of General Olagaray and tell him to come here immediately with the May-Be file."

IV. The Last Days of a Minister

GENERAL OLAGARAY ENTERED THE MINISTER OF WAR'S OFFICE, casting suspicious glances and pressing the fat file of the May-Be Company against his chest. It was obvious from the way he clasped the papers that the matter they contained was of enormous personal importance to him. He was tall, robust, red-faced. His hair and mustache, already salt and pepper, contrasted with his youthful, ruddy complexion. His demeanor too contrasted with Ignacio Aguirre's: everything in Olagaray bespoke the old soldier, a career soldier; everything in Aguirre, youthful improvisation.

"I am at your service, my General," he said, saluting the minister with the academic stiffness of old federal officers. And then, after turning with a slight nod to Remigio Tarabana, who was pretending to look at the street from the recess of a balcony, stood at attention two meters from the table, confident that the minister, as usual, would invite him to sit. His tone was hypocritical, his manner servile.

Aguirre not only kept him standing this time, but purposely allowed several seconds to elapse before addressing him. When at last he began to talk to him, he did so with ambiguous gravity, equally solemn and ironic.

"I'm very sorry, comrade," the minister said, "to have to give you bad news. I've called you so we can be done once and for all with this mess with that May-Be oil company. I know you are the party most interested in seeing that the company's petition will be denied, and it goes without saying that if it were up to me, I would give, in a minute, the orders that would satisfy you. Unfortunately, this cannot be. I've thought the matter over carefully, studied it calmly, and my decision is contrary to your interests and those of your friends. The Military Cooperative must immediately relinquish the land it presently occupies. Furthermore, the Cooperative must not speak again about this land belonging to it in any way, nor attempt, under any circumstances, to take it again by force.

Therefore, see to it that the necessary communiqués and telegrams be drawn up immediately, and bring them right away for me to sign. Don't forget the documents must first be registered and placed in the appropriate envelopes. That way each secretariat will remit them to their destination. I want it done this way."

General Olagaray, red though he was, had gone white; he felt the business deal of a lifetime slipping between his fingers. At first he sputtered approving servile phrases, but later, partly recovered, overcoming the effect of the surprise, he hazarded phrases of a firmer nature:

"I would only like to make an observation, my General, if you permit."

"Go right ahead, comrade, go ahead."

"The land taken from May-Be is, as I'm sure you know, the only solid hope of the Military Cooperative. Once relinquished, the Cooperative must consider itself bankrupt."

"Yes, that's very likely. And?"

"The president of the Republic, and I'm sure you also know this, promised us his full support. He himself suggested the May-Be land as the most appropriate place to launch the Military Cooperative under favorable conditions."

For a moment General Olagaray was silent. From one of the drawers of his table, Aguirre had taken a sheet of paper and was rapidly writing several lines. The scratching of the pen underscored the silence that revealed Olagaray's depths of servility, his respectful and submissive insincerity. Once Aguirre had put the flourish on his signature, Olagaray decided to continue:

"I was pointing out, my General, that I'm sure you know the promises the president made to us…"

"Comrade," replied the minister, "the president couldn't have promised you that he would authorize outright plunder. Let's get this straight: to whom does the land in dispute rightfully belong, to the Cooperative or to May-Be?"

Olagaray answered with sudden firmness, with surprising firmness given his previous vacillation:

"As director of the Cooperative I declare the land is ours, my General. We occupied it by virtue of the decrees that annul, or at least call into question, the bad concessions made under Don Porfirio…"

"Yes, yes, I know the story. But let's not get our roles mixed up. I'm not speaking now to the director of the Military Cooperative, an entity unrelated to this Secretariat. I'm talking to the head of one of the departments of the ministry, a public official. Judging from the documents you have in your hand, who has a stronger claim: the Cooperative or May-Be?"

"If you only consider the legal history, I mean, if you dismiss what is most important here, all considerations of a revolutionary nature..."

"The Revolution doesn't work as an argument in your favor. Remember that in 1913 when you led Huerta's troops in Sonora, we were the ones who represented 'considerations of a revolutionary nature.' You were fighting for those who wanted to trample them. Keep to the legal considerations and answer frankly."

"Legally... the law... seems to favor May-Be..."

"Very well, comrade. That's the only thing we're interested in. If in the opinion of the Secretariat, the land belongs to May-Be then, as minister, I will neither authorize nor cover up the armed takeover of this land by a military group. Do I make myself clear?"

"Yes, my General."

Aguirre then handed General Olagaray the sheet of paper on which he had recently written.

"Here is the memorandum. I expect the documents in a half hour. All of them must bear an exact transcription of what the memorandum says: that the land is being returned to May-Be because it has proven to the satisfaction of the Secretariat of War that its claims are beyond question.... See you later, comrade."

No sooner had Olagaray closed the door than Remigio Tarabana let loose with a commentary on the scene. As he walked from the recess of the balcony to the center of the room, he said:

"That's it! That's the way to do it! Thrust the sword in to the hilt. If he hated you before, he'd kill you now. But the truth is he doesn't deserve any sympathy at all; he's despicable. A federal general who let himself be defeated ten times, always out of sheer cowardice, and who now wants to get credit because his defeats contributed, as he says, to the military glory of the Revolution! If the Caudillo weren't such a fraud, instead of protecting him, he'd have him shot."

Just then the antechamber door opened and the aide on duty came in. Tarabana stopped. The officer approached the minister's table, gave him a card and, almost at his ear, whispered some words.

After reading the card, Aguirre remarked out loud:

"It's not true; I don't even know this woman's name.... What does she look like?

"She looks very good to me, my General."

Aguirre smiled. Then he asked:

"And she said that? That as soon as I knew it was her I would see her?"

"That's what she says, my General."

Aguirre looked at the card again, as he repeated, trying to remember:

"Beatriz Delorme... Beatriz Delorme... Who is she?"

Now it was the officer who smiled. Tarabana suddenly burst out laughing:

"Beatriz Delorme? Who's Beatriz Delorme?! *La Mora*, Ignacio! Who else?"

Aguirre also laughed as he ordered:

"Have her come in immediately."

Indeed, it was *La Mora*. She was very agitated and nervous, which meant that her appearance was not what her friends were accustomed to admiring during their hours of nocturnal dissipation. A little wilted, somewhat tired, her beauty was dimmed in the daytime, as if tarnished by sunlight.

She came in speaking hurriedly:

"Forgive me, Nacho, forgive me if your orders, your instructions, as your officers say, were disobeyed because of me, but I'm..."

Aguirre and Tarabana had met her at the door and taking her by her arms led her to the sofa. Meanwhile, Aguirre said:

"Instructions! For you, *Mora*, there are no instructions. You command here, here as everywhere else. Come, sit down. Tell us what is wrong with you. How may I be of service?"

"I'm... I can't tell you how I am: I'm totally devastated..."

And she was on the verge of bursting into tears.

"What's wrong with you? Tell us."

"No, it's not me; it's Axkaná."

Aguirre's joviality clouded over at once.

"Did something happen to Axkaná?"

"Yes, something very bad, very, very bad.... You see, I've just come from the police inspector general's office, I mean, from seeing the inspector himself. Last night, around eleven, I was taken into custody for matters not worth talking about. In exchange for letting me go, the inspector tried to impose certain conditions, and since I, for whatever reason, chose not to please him, time flew by as we argued back and forth. The more tiresome he got the more I teased him. Midnight came around, then one, then two. Around three in the morning, the head of security came to talk to the inspector, the guy they call 'the Meat Hook'..."

"Zaldívar?"

"That's the one, Colonel Zaldívar. I was in one room, and they went into the next room to talk about things by themselves. At first I didn't care what they were talking about; I only heard the murmuring of their voices, but suddenly I was afraid they might want to do something to me and I went to the door to listen. Then I got really curious because twice I heard them pronounce Axkaná's name clear as a bell. Unfortunately, they were at the other end of the room and they spoke so softly it seemed they were whispering. But I heard snatches; I caught two or three phrases and many single words. Zaldívar, it seems, was telling the inspector that they had kidnapped Axkaná when he was coming out of the National Fronton, took him out to the desert, and threw him I don't know where, after they did something to him that I didn't hear well. They talked a lot about tequila, a car, a funnel, oil. The inspector said several times, so clearly I can still hear it: 'Hey, and if he dies?' And Zaldívar answered once: 'If he dies, he dies. Stranger things have happened.'"

Aguirre did not wait for *La Mora* to continue her account. He rushed to his desk, and after pressing one of the buzzers, he went to the door. Seconds later Cisneros, his personal secretary, came in.

"I want you to phone Deputy Axkaná González's residence right now," Aguirre said. "If he's there have him come to the phone immediately.... Get going, Cisneros, this is urgent."

Cisneros was not long in returning. Now he was beside himself; he couldn't bring himself to convey the message.

"What's up? Speak up!"

"Don Axkaná is home, my General, but he can't come to the phone.... They say he's dying."

"Dying!" shouted *La Mora*. "Dying! You see?"

And she dissolved into tears.

With perfect serenity—a serenity that contrasted with his nervous rush a few minutes before—Aguirre took his hat and walking stick and returned to the sofa. He placed his hand on *La Mora's* shoulder, as she shook with sobs, and caressing it, said:

"Thank you for this, Beatriz. You're an excellent friend. Now, calm down, go home. Don't let anyone know what you heard last night at the inspector's, and don't tell anyone you came to tell me. Tarabana and I are going right away to see Axkaná, and in a while we'll let you know if he is, in fact, as they say."

As he, too, went to pick up his hat and walking stick, Tarabana let Aguirre walk a few steps ahead, and before following him made a sign for Cisneros to get closer. At the door, taking him by the arm, he said:

"General Olagaray won't be long in coming with some papers. Tell him to give them to you; it's an order from the minister.... It has to do with the May-Be Company... a very important matter.... Do you understand? I'll make it worth your while. I promise!"

And he went out.

V. Zaldívar

At Deputy Axkaná González's home, everything had been in a state of agitation and turmoil since the early hours of the morning. Friends and acquaintances came in and out; three doctors gave orders; the phone rang constantly. Meanwhile, Axkaná's mother and sisters kept up a constant lamentation in the background, underscoring the extraordinary commotion.

Ignacio Aguirre arrived around three, accompanied by Tarabana, and asked to be taken immediately to the sickroom. This was done. With the French doors wide open, the room was flooded with light. The midday light, still strong, seemed to emanate from the two blinding rhombuses that the sun cut on the edge of the floor. Far away, you could hear the horns of the passing cars on Paseo de la Reforma, and farther still, toward Calzada de Chapultepec, the muffled racket of streetcars. Noise and light suddenly dissolved into a single sensation for Aguirre, a fleeting, intangible presence of his friend's spirit. For the first time, he had an inkling of that sensation that Axkaná always sought in the features of each hour of the day.

For several minutes, Aguirre stayed close to the bed, bending over so far that his face almost touched the sick man. With his sight, his hearing, his touch, he wanted to confirm the suspicions that *La Mora*'s account had awakened in him. But no matter how close he got, he could hear only hoarse rales, see only the pile of bandages that wrapped Axkaná's head, and a bare arm, with a great deal of bruising on the wrist, the black-and-blue marks contrasted with the perfect pallor of his hand.

Half an hour later, speaking alone with the family doctor, Aguirre demanded a scientific explanation of what had happened or, at least, any information they had. The doctor, who evidently lacked character, began by trying to wriggle out of it. He was alarmed by the presence of the young minister of war, his very presence was for him, a good Mexican professional, an omen of odious political complications and terrible personal inconvenience.

"General, I myself can't understand it," he said, "or if you prefer, I understand it all too well. It's a simple case of poisoning, alcohol poisoning."

Slippery, faint-hearted men like him were easy prey for Aguirre. From a weak look—opaque with fatigue—the eyes of the minister changed abruptly to another gaze, one that revealed mysterious and sinister depths, evoking the worst scenes of the Revolution.

"A simple case, you think?" The tone of Aguirre's words matched the look in his eyes.

The doctor stammered something. Then said:

"Simple in terms of the cause, in terms of the alcohol.... With regard to the effects, things get complicated. I do understand that the symptoms are so acute as to be unbelievable.... On the other hand, it's almost impossible for a habitually sober man like Axaná to manage to ingest the quantity of alcohol he seems to have drunk. This morning, when they found him in the street, he oozed tequila, literally, even through his fingernails. I don't know where they found him, nearby, they say.... Since then he has been as you see him. The most energetic but prudent treatment has not been able to pull him out of the coma.... To judge from the wounds and contusions to his head, he must have been involved in a fierce fight. He has three broken teeth, and I don't know how many loose ones…"

Aguirre, by now impatient, cut him off:

"Let's speak clearly, doctor. You know full well that Axaná did not receive those blows in any fight."

"I?... How could I know that, General?"

"Easily. Have you examined his hands?"

"Of course, and the rest of his body."

"Well then, although I've barely looked at them, I'm sure Axaná did not strike a single blow with them. What fight are you talking about then?"

The doctor's evasions took a new tack.

"I'm not a politician, General. I don't get involved in things like that."

"Of course, doctor, and I don't expect you to. But you are the family doctor and you have the obligation not to cover up what should be known. Or would you prefer the embarrassment of my calling for a person more worthy of our trust?"

As if by magic, the doctor became tractable.

"No, absolutely not! I'm totally at your service. And let there be no confusion, I'll confess to you right away that I too have my suspicions. It is possible Axkaná did not drink the tequila, but that violence was used to make him swallow it."

"That's the first thing you should've told me."

The doctor tried to backtrack:

"Of course, it's only a hypothesis."

"What do you mean a hypothesis! And his teeth? His tongue? His arms?... But now let's come to what matters: are you sure it's only alcohol?"

"General, how can I be sure? In these matters you can never be sure. But if it isn't alcohol, I can't see what it could be. The only terrible thing, unless I'm wrong, is the quantity. You notice how even from here we can smell the tequila?... It's still oozing from all his pores..."

Aguirre purposely prolonged his visit to Axkaná's house until the late afternoon, so he did not return to his office at the Secretariat of War until well past six. In the elevator he said to Tarabana, who was still with him:

"Now they've really gone too far. I won't stand it one more hour. Not a minute longer! This very night I'll have proof of this plot in my hands and tomorrow... Tomorrow one of two things will happen: either Hilario Jiménez resigns, or I'll resign after breaking with the Caudillo. They want to force us to fight? Then we'll fight; in Mexico's politics, everyone loses in the end. Let's see whose turn it is now."

The private secretary came to the minister's office bearing a stack of papers that he placed on the table. Aguirre asked curtly:

"What is it?"

"For your signature, my General."

"I'm not signing today. Connect me with the police inspector general; have the inspector general come to the phone."

Cisneros was already gathering up the papers when he noted Tarabana's wink. Then he quickly pulled out several sheets and again placed them in front of the minister.

"These documents," he said, "were handed to me by General Olagaray. He assured me they were very urgent. Shall I leave them here or shall I also take them away?"

"Yes, leave them. While I sign them, call the police."

Cisneros left and Aguirre began to sign. Tarabana helped him: using the blotter, turning the pages. Then he took the first two documents and began to read them with care. As soon as Tarabana finished reading, Aguirre asked him:

"Are you satisfied?"

"It's more than I expected. With this, even if you resign, May-Be is safe for now. If it's all right with you, I will deliver the dispatches myself. It's safer that way."

Minutes later the minister of war was speaking on the phone with the inspector general. Short and amicable, there was nothing extraordinary about the conversation. Aguirre simply requested the services of Colonel Zaldívar, chief of security, and those of two other efficient agents, for an urgent investigation at the Secretariat. In other words, his request was not very different from those he frequently made.

Once he hung up the receiver, Aguirre called the duty officer and gave him several orders, and then asked, "Is Cahuama here?"

"Yes, my General."

"And Rosas?"

"Also, my General."

"Good. Tell Cahuama that in a few minutes I'm going to his house with some people. He and Rosas will also come. They should get ready, go down to the courtyard of the Secretariat, and when they see me leave the elevator they should come over and get into the car with me. The driver should be told now where we are going, so he won't have to ask for orders.... Understood?"

"Understood, my General."

"Oh. Something else. Colonel Zaldívar and two police officers will arrive here at any moment. Have the colonel come in as soon as he arrives, but not the agents. They are to stay in the office of the chiefs of staff, and they're not to leave, for any reason, until further orders. Do you understand? For any reason, until further orders."

It was about seven-thirty in the evening when Aguirre's car left the Secretariat of War and headed for Lagunilla, the neighborhood of Captain Cahuama's house. In the car, besides the minister, were Tarabana, Colonel Zaldívar, Cahuama, and Rosas.

Cahuama's house was not really his; it was Aguirre's, but it was Cahuama—an old assistant of the minister, promoted now to aide of the chiefs of staff—who lived in the house and after whom it was called. Aguirre visited it only from time to time, for certain appointments or interviews. This had made it famous in the neighborhood because of the magnificent cars that waited at the entrance, and the praise of the neighborhood storekeepers and bartenders who were pleased by how much was consumed there. Besides Cahuama and a servant, two or three soldiers from Aguirre's guard always lived in the house.

Everything was closed up and dark when the car stopped in front of the entryway. A soldier came to open up. The servant opened doors and turned on lights.

They entered. In the living room, or what passed for it, the servant was rushing to open the shutters to the balconies when Aguirre stopped her:

"No, keep the shutters closed and leave. If I need anything, I'll call you."

Cahuama and Rosas had remained in the hallway. Inside the room were Aguirre, Tarabana, and Colonel Zaldívar. The latter was tall, robust, and his reddish hair at that moment reproduced the shape of the Stetson hat he had just taken off. His air, very tranquil but alert, was typical of men who are used to all sorts of unforeseen events. He was calmly smoking the fine cigar Aguirre gave him when they left the office and with his other hand stroked his watch chain—an observant man's habit.

"Sit down, Colonel," said Aguirre. "Sit," he added, addressing Tarabana.

And all three sat down: Zaldívar on the sofa, Tarabana and Aguirre in armchairs. Then, after a brief pause, Aguirre began to explain the reason for their meeting, which he did in such a serene tone that he almost seemed indifferent to the meaning of his words.

"As you can see, Colonel, it's a very simple matter. This is about last night's assault on a person I esteem very much—Deputy Axkaná González. What is known about that at the inspector general's?"

Zaldívar answered in a voice no less placid than the minister's: "Nothing much, my General, only rumors."

"Fine. Then between your rumors, and what I know for certain, we're going to find the perpetrators of this crime, if you don't mind... Are you carrying a gun?"

"Yes, my General."

"Allow me to see it."

Without revealing the smallest wrinkle in his smooth demeanor, Zaldívar took out his weapon and gave it to Aguirre. He looked like a friend showing something to another.

"Cahuama!" shouted Aguirre taking the pistol.

Cahuama came in.

"Have the colonel give you his other weapons, if he has any," ordered the minister.

"I never carry more than a pistol, my General," said Zaldívar.

"Just in case, we will make sure."

Cahuama began to frisk the colonel.

"He's not carrying anything else, my General."

"Good.... Rosas!"

Rosas came in. The minister handed him Zaldívar's pistol:

"Take this and remain here.... You, Cahuama, bring writing paper, a bottle of cognac, another of tequila and three glasses."

Cahuama went out.

"If my General permits," observed Zaldívar, still totally calm, "I'd like to explain it wasn't necessary to disarm me. I'm a man you can trust."

Instead of answering him, Aguirre stood, and began to pace the room from one end to the other. Silent in his chair, Tarabana looked on.

Not long after, Cahuama came in with one of the bottles and the paper. A soldier brought the other bottle and the tray with the glasses. They placed everything on the small table in the center. The soldier went out.

Aguirre took the cognac bottle and filled two glasses, then poured tequila into the remaining glass.

"For you," he said to Zaldívar, handing him the glass he had served last. Without speaking, he gave Tarabana a glass of cognac. He took another for himself.

"*Salud!*"

All three drank.

"Now, Colonel, you are going to sit at this table and set down here on this paper, in your own hand, what you and the other police officers did last night to Deputy Axkaná González on the way to the desert. And it'll be good for you to know from the start there's no point in lying. I know the story as if I'd lived it myself."

Zaldívar answered impassibly:

"My General, I protest, I don't understand a word you're saying."

"Well, I say the contrary, Colonel; I say you're lying."

"No, my General, I'm not lying..."

"Fine. Then, if you don't know what I'm asking about, you will allow me to enlighten you.... Rosas!"

"My General."

"Go out to the street and ask the driver to send me the oil funnel."

Then, all at once, Zaldívar lost his composure. Perhaps unwittingly, his eyes turned to the bottles that were on the table. And his agitation increased considerably when Captain Rosas returned holding the funnel.

"Do you insist you know nothing?" asked Aguirre, whose voice remained unchanged.

"I already said I don't know anything, my General."

"All right. Now you're going to undergo the same torture that the police inflicted on Axkaná. Colonel Zaldívar, I ask no one to forgive me, and therefore I also do not forgive. By confessing in writing, you would have avoided the treatment you deserve, but since you won't confess, there's no reason for me to spare you. With the funnel, you'll be forced to swallow all the tequila that'll fit inside your body."

Zaldívar's face turned pale.

"You won't do that, my General."

"No? Let's see... Cahuama!"

"My General."

"Is there any more tequila in the house?"

"Two more bottles, my General."

"Bring them."

By now Colonel Zaldívar's red hair contrasted with his skin like a flame to a white candle. A slight tremor shook the hand that was busily caressing the chain on his vest; the cigar in his other hand was going out. The change that was coming over him was palpable, obvious. Suddenly he cried out in a tone of voice that revealed his lack of control:

"A written confession would be my ruin, my General!"

"I don't know that and I don't care. Are you writing, yes or no?"

"A deal, my General, I'll write if you promise to protect me. Put yourself in my place; it was a direct order from my General Hilario Jiménez.... What stake did I have in it?... I had never exchanged a word with Don Axkaná."

Aguirre hesitated for moment, a barely perceptible moment, and finally said:

"Agreed. I'll protect you as far as I can. But the account must be detailed and complete."

A minute went by, Zaldívar sat at the table, and, very slowly, took his fountain pen out his pocket, although he did not write immediately. Before doing so, he served himself a glass of cognac and drank it, drank it anxiously. He savored it as if he didn't want the least aftertaste of the tequila he had just drunk to remain in his mouth.

VI. Fruits of a Resignation

T HE NEXT MORNING, ARMED WITH COLONEL ZALDÍVAR'S HANDwritten confession, Ignacio Aguirre set off to Chapultepec Castle.

The Caudillo took the three sheets of paper given to him by his minister. He read them very slowly, put them away, and then said, with the aplomb of his best moments, an ironic aplomb over which his flashing smile held sway:

"Unquestionably a very interesting tale. But I reject its veracity. Hilario, as a functionary and as a man, is above such trifles."

"And if I were to assure you that everything described there is true?"

In this manner Aguirre sought to close off all exits at one blow.

"Then I would think," replied the president, "that you are blinded by passion and would recommend you pursue the matter in court."

Aguirre, enraged, forgot his habitual respect.

"In that case, I would reply, my General, that for a man of Jiménez's political rank, the courts are also trifles!"

"No, Aguirre, you would not answer that. Because, when I govern, such things are not said in my presence."

And the Caudillo had taken off his glasses and, above the gray line of his unkempt mustache, allowed his expression—at once laughing and domineering—to emphasize his words. From his eyes, like those of a tiger, shone golden gleams, magnificent gleams.

Hours after that interview, Aguirre resigned his post as secretary of war, and, four days later, when he accepted the resignation, the Caudillo answered in cordial and highly favorable terms. In his reply the president mentioned the young general's wartime service, his strength in any crisis, his administrative dedication, and even his faith in the people's cause.

That epistolary sweetness had very little impact in the face of another simultaneous occurrence: the new surge of political agitation set off by the mere announcement of Aguirre's resignation. The whole nation, curious about the struggle of the groups trying to wrest power from each other, felt then that the spectacle was entering the decisive phase. The word on the street had been that Aguirre and Jiménez would face each other, and that clash was now coming. Olivier Fernández and his Progressive Radicals had striven in vain to take hold of their candidate: now they had him in their claws. General Jiménez and his supporters—Ricalde and his "Laborites," López Nieto and his "peasants"—had talked about Aguirre's two-facedness: now they could shout that their predictions were not mistaken. And on both sides, whether in public or in private, they tallied and made lists of governors and generals: those who would do their duty by supporting them, those who would betray the fatherland by supporting the opposing group.

In such an environment, it took only two or three weeks for passion alone to assert itself, with no guide but its own frenetic impulses. The Caudillo appointed General Martín Aispuro—of all the revolutionary generals, the one who most hated Ignacio Aguirre—as the new minister of war. For head of operations in the Valley and military commander of the capital, he chose General Protasio Leyva, already notoriously committed to Hilario Jiménez's candidacy. And soon enough these excellent plans yielded excellent results.

Two weeks after assuming his post, General Aispuro presented to the Caudillo a report on the state of the Secretariat of War. According to the report, Aguirre had done nothing during his tenure but deceive the president, misappropriate public funds, and sow corruption and disorder in all the branches of the Secretariat and the various military institutions. Was it true? Was it false? It did not matter. What mattered was that Aguirre, almost simultaneously, had accepted the candidacy offered by his friends. In view of which, the president, a great lover of *coups de théâtre*, gave Aispuro's report to the press, along with a wealth of his own commentaries, interlarded here and there—because the Caudillo was a great coiner of vulgar phrases—with very terse and sarcastic opinions about the incompetence and immorality of his former favorite.

The ex-minister defended himself in few words; he dismissed the report as false and malicious and said that the irregularities, if any, were done on the Caudillo's express orders. But, as could be expected, the public revelations did not stop there. The Caudillo responded, Aispuro spoke, and that, in turn, led to the lurid front-page newspaper headlines announcing Colonel Zaldívar's confession about the attempted assassination of Axkaná. The police then provided the press with declarations in which Zaldívar affirmed the alleged confession was a fraud. Aguirre, as evidence to refute this, published the photographs of the handwritten confession. Zaldívar then declared the handwriting was his but not the confession. They had forced him, on pain of death, to copy and sign a text that had been prepared beforehand by Aguirre himself. The latter, faced with this accusation, brought forth witnesses. Zaldívar impugned them as biased, declared them worthless. Then someone, in an anonymous letter, revealed what *La Mora* had seen and heard at the inspector general's on the night of the event. In a newspaper interview, she expanded on and bravely confirmed what she knew to be true, but the police rushed to discredit her. They described her as a hopeless cocaine addict, with a long police record of scandal and vice, and certified that on the night of the alleged crime *La Mora* had been locked up in a cell at the police station where she suffered one terrible hallucination after another.

Naturally, all those accusations were actionable under the penal code, but there was something that effectively nullified the code and excluded the magistrates from the debate: the accused did not seek redress from the judges nor did the courts perform their duty. A kind of tacit agreement—political and national—seemed to place crimes of that order beyond the law, or at least in the gray area where reprisals by both sides were the only law.

The bitter fanaticism then found another channel, overflowing principally into the Chamber of Deputies. Many interminable sessions—five, six, seven—each stormier and more riotous than the former, followed in succession after General Aispuro's report saw the light of day. These sessions all began with massive brawls on the staircase or in the lobby, as Olivier's "Aguirrista gang" attacked Ricalde's "Hilarista gang," or vice versa. And shortly afterward, unbridled speeches in galleries and rostrums—a frenzy of words, rampant ideas, raw vehemence—matched the onslaught of the gangs, bringing violence and the pistol to the fore.

Being in the majority and having a quorum, the Progressive Radicals called General Aispuro to testify; they wanted to punish him, to flog him for the content of his report. Olivier took on Aispuro in one of his formidable speeches and ground him into dust. Ricalde, the "Laborite," and López, the "peasant," defended him with eloquence—eloquence tinged frequently with the cruelest derision for Aguirre. It was as if the insolence of one side ricocheted off the other, while the galleries above exploded with outrage and insults.

But eventually even this came to be considered a playful debate, a mild introduction. Because in subsequent sessions the vigorous, masculine oratory—slanderous revilement below, vulgar interjections above—was no longer poured on the private and political honor of the candidates; it spread even to their supporters and friends. Olivier denounced Ricalde as an impostor, as an exploiter of workers who was getting rich in the name of revolutionary ideals. Ricalde, for his part, told the story of the handling of funds in the state Olivier had governed. The latter then delved deeper, making an inventory of Ricalde's property before and after his rise as a labor leader. He listed Ricalde's bank accounts, described his life—sybaritic, orgiastic—and demonstrated, finally, that Ricalde had sold to the government, for two hundred or three hundred pesos, goods that cost barely seventy or eighty in the factories he managed.

And so, on the afternoon of the Hilarista counterattack, the acrimony reached even greater extremes. On that occasion, López Nieto, the "peasant," pounced with fury on Aguirre's reputation. He spoke of the candidate's life as a libertine, his venality, his five homes, of Paquita Arévalo, of his conniving with Remigio Tarabana, and finished his speech with a terrible forecast of the evils that would befall the fatherland because of Aguirre's corrupt work with the army. On hearing López Nieto, the Hilarista gang, larger than usual, deafened with their cheers and insults the air of the hallowed halls, and since this encouraged the Hilarista phalanxes, the other side decided that an action equal in force to their foes' was required. Juan Manuel Mijares rushed to the rostrum; if there was anything left of the presidential image of Hilario Jiménez, he

was going to tear it to shreds. He told of violent deeds, embezzlement, sinister exploits, and a whole history of public insincerity in
which Jiménez's false support for agrarian reform was translated
into the mysterious acquisition of farms and landed estates; Jiménez's "love of the masses" led to self-enrichment.

The vehemence of such an attack, effective as few could be—
full of data, figures, dates, and names—dragged the partisan controversy to its ultimate consequences: the name of the Caudillo
rang out, invoked as a shield by the Hilaristas. But then rose the
voice of Emilio Olivier, who, far from mitigating what Mijares
had said, left nothing standing. Amid the frenzied exclamations
of some and the dull murmurs of others, Olivier dared to do what
nobody had done until then. He implacably stripped of all its radiance, all its pomp, all its aura of unquestioned supreme leadership,
the figure of the man no one dared to touch: the Caudillo.

Olivier's speech, which all the newspapers of the Republic
would print the next day, produced a brief truce in the debate,
but it did so with tragic forebodings. The session broke down into
violence; in the hallways deputies killed each other; in the lobby
and in the streets the clashes of the political gangs left a wake of
wounded and dead.

Book Five
Protasio Leyva

I. The Plot

Shortly after those memorable sessions, General Protasio Leyva, chief of operations in the Valley and military commander of the city, brought Deputies Ricalde and López Nieto to his office. They were the leaders of the Hilarista movement in their respective chambers. Leyva wanted to ask their opinion on how the fight was going there.

"For now," declared Ricalde, in his eternally oratorical manner, "we are lost." And he explained why.

His explanations were clear and precise. As the general understood, they came down to the following: "Since the Aguirristas now have the majority and the quorum, they will later have the Permanent Committee and the Transition Committee, and as long as they have those, they will be the masters of the electoral battle, that is to say, the future congress, which is to say, the future presidency."

"Therefore," observed General Leyva, "everything depends on our ending the Aguirrista quorum and majority. Isn't that right?"

Yes, it was. But Ricalde and López Nieto then explained why that task, which seemed easy, in actuality would be very slow and difficult.

"Fine," concluded the general. "That only means we need to think on a large scale. I'll think about it, gentlemen, I'll think about it."

And he arranged to meet General Jiménez's two supporters on the evening of the following day.

General Leyva did not need many hours of reflection to come up with the quick and vigorous means to put an end to the Aguirrista majority in the Chamber of Deputies. In Leyva, one trait—so great he himself was in awe of it—eclipsed all others: that of always quickly and directly attacking any problem, situation, or enemy that might bother him. Regarding the present case, Deputies Ricalde and López Nieto had said to him:

"If we could manage to dominate now in the Chamber of Deputies, we'd also rule, not only in the Chamber but in the whole Congress, when the next legislature meets; and once we control Congress, no one could challenge us for the presidency of the Republic. Therefore, our present efforts must aim at the destruction of the Aguirrista majority. Everything else—programs, propaganda, votes, elections—is nothing but lip service, mere backdrops to give things an air of democracy for the newspapers, or, at most, it's the means or the pretext that justifies the rise to power. Do you understand, my General?"

Leyva, of course, understood, and eliminating useless words and transitions, rephrased their lecture thus:

"So, all we have to do is get nine or ten pathetic, speechifying deputies out of the way, and nothing will keep Hilario from being the next president of the Republic.... Easy!"

In the new interview with Ricalde and López Nieto, Leyva set out the details of his plan. Judging by the tranquil objectivity with which the general expressed himself, the plan was, or seemed, very simple:

"The lives of a handful of rebellious deputies," said Leyva, in a tone similar to a financier explaining an exchange rate mechanism or an architect recommending a house renovation, "are too small an obstacle for us. Will we allow the good of the Republic and the hopes of our proletarian and peasant masses to be dashed by them? No, gentlemen, let's not complicate matters. Let's act with the simplicity that the present historical moment requires. Direct action is within our reach; let's use it, let's use it with courage, I mean, let's make use of it, deaf to those scruples that always make the conduct of reactionaries contemptible.... Isn't it true the salvation of the Republic and the revolutionary cause hangs on the complete transfer of that power personified by the Caudillo to General Hilario Jiménez? Yes, it is true. Isn't it true the Aguirrista reactionary movement, embodied by two dozen traitors, is the only barrier we're facing? This is also true. Then, gentlemen, let's crush the reactionaries once more. With one blow, let's eliminate these two dozen traitors, since acts such as these are the unavoidable responsibility of those of us who bear on our shoulders the enormous burden of revolutionary purity. It can't be helped! Every two, three, four years, we make the necessary sacrifice of beheading two or three dozen traitors in order to prevent the interruption of revolutionary continuity. We're ready to do it again, and our duty commands us, as before, to act rapidly and with extreme rigor. Tomorrow, or the day after tomorrow at the latest, I'll put you in touch with Major Manuel Segura, my nephew and a man I trust completely. You'll give him a list of the ten or twelve enemy deputies who bother us most and work out with him the best way to identify them easily at a given point. After receiving my detailed instructions, he'll go to the Chamber, position his men, and take advantage of the first brawl between the gangs, or some such incident, to make sure that not one of the Aguirrista leaders is left standing."

Deputies Ricalde and López Nieto left that interview with General Leyva heartily convinced of their candidate's victory. Ricalde, giving free rein to his dishonest and oratorical temperament, remarked:

"We are witnessing solemn moments, moments of transcendental historical importance!"

And López Nieto, who saw everything through the lens of his glorious action in the Zapatista ranks, replied:

"He really is a first-class revolutionary, a true revolutionary: sincere, strong. What couldn't Emiliano Zapata have accomplished with four men like him!"

The list that Major Manuel Segura received from the hands of the Hilarista leaders was topped by Emilio Olivier Fernández, president of the Progressive Radical Party, and included up to nine more names, all of them Aguirrista deputies whose elimination was considered essential. After Olivier's name came Axkaná's, then López de la Garza's, then Mijares'. Three red crosses next to Olivier's name indicated that his disappearance was essential for the success of Hilario Jiménez's candidacy. Other names, like that of López de la Garza—who, besides being a deputy and supporter of Ignacio Aguirre, was General Encarnación Reyes' chief of staff—were marked with a double cross, and others, finally, like Axkaná's and Mijares', had only one cross.

Major Manuel Segura, following the instructions he was given, made his calculations with that implacable precision that raises those who are masters in a particular trade above the rest of mortals. He estimated that, to be on the safe side, the hunt for Olivier would require no fewer than five men; in the case of others, he thought four or five would do; others two; and yet others one. And so, in total, he thought he would require the services of twenty-five collaborators experienced in the execution of "important assignments."

Well then, men such as these were not lacking in General Protasio Leyva's large entourage. They had always been needed and they had always been available. But since the current project outstripped all previous ones, no matter how Segura tried, he was not able to select, from among his comrades in arms, more than five or six proven auxiliaries, and this included Major Canuto Arenas, notorious for his sinister history and for being chief of Leyva's bodyguard. Leyva, as was typical for him, solved the problem without much hesitation; he resolved to use officers from the regiments and the battalions of the garrison (for which he issued precise orders) to fill out the group of twenty-five assistants his nephew needed. On such and such a day, at such and such a time, the designated officers were to present themselves at the Operations Headquarters ready to carry out an assignment whose nature would be revealed to them later. They were to come dressed as civilians, without any identification in their pockets and armed with their service pistols.

At eleven in the morning on the day appointed for the execution of the plan, Major Segura and all his men were gathered at the offices of the National Laborite Party.

Suggestive and mysterious, Segura had greeted each of his henchmen with a demeanor befitting great occasions, and then, in order to steep the event in a solemn and justificatory atmosphere, he had introduced them one by one to Deputies Ricalde, López Nieto, and Cayo Horacio Quintana, who shook hands with a profusion of partisan declarations. Because neither Ricalde nor López Nieto sought to avoid these moments of such grave responsibility, there they both stood—their deputy's pins on their lapels—ready to face all risks and to make sure the plot would not fail. Their flesh trembled with the nervous excitement of those about to make a heroic sacrifice.

For the time being, however, there was nothing to do. Segura and his men dispersed through the rooms, forming various small groups, and stayed there until one o'clock, when all of them, without much ado, went to eat at nearby restaurants. Around two, they were already back at the offices of the party, and minutes later Segura began the pertinent explanations, after which Ricalde gave a brief speech in order to raise their spirits.

Ricalde was an intelligent, unpleasant, and monstrous man. There was no light in his asymmetrical eyes. His head seemed to have suffered the endless torture of a double twisting. The crooked deformation of his skull, above, exacerbated the equally crooked deformation of an enormous, fleshy wart, next to his chin, below; and between the first deformity and the second, the heaviness of his eyelids, of an almost paralytic limpness, added another touch to the dynamics of ugliness that stretched and spread to his feet, encompassing a body of massive volume.

"You are not unaware," he said to the officers, as his enormous double chin trembled with rhetorical emotion, "that General Protasio Leyva is always motivated by the deepest patriotism. You could say, without hyperbole, that wherever General Leyva is, there too are the supreme ideals of the Revolution and the fatherland. Well then, my friends, once more, hidden forces—those dark powers we men of the Revolution have not managed to put an end to, because, like the Hydra, they are able to reproduce eternally—have once more returned, marching in step, and again threaten to destroy, with a wily and underhanded blow, the redemptive triumphs dearest to our hearts. For you must know, I will speak to you with frankness, that until recently, in the loftiest places of the Revolution, shone a man to whom we all attributed incorruptible civic virtues and a strong faith in the historic role the fatherland assigns its best sons. But it has happened that that man (you all know him, I am referring to General Ignacio Aguirre, until very recently minister of war and now presidential candidate of the so-called Progressive Radical Party), it has happened that that man, I say, heeding the allures of his ambition more than the voice of his patriotic duty, is now already involved in cozy deals with the reactionary movement, whose loathsome interests he is preparing to serve without any scruples. Thus, surprisingly transformed from comrade to rival, from friend to enemy, from patriot to traitor, his defection seriously compromises revolutionary continuity and power, since all those who champion him—some of them endowed with great energy, some whose ability is far from negligible—join in his betrayal. Fortunately, General Protasio Leyva, always alert, has not failed to observe the danger in time and has resolved with speed, with the speed of thought and deed that are so characteristically his, to destroy with one blow the shoots of that fatal plant, by attacking its roots…"

Ricalde made a brief pause to allow his audience to plumb the meaning of the words he had spoken, and then concluded as follows:

"In order to carry out such an endeavor, an endeavor great and noble as few are, an endeavor that aims to save our supreme revolutionary ideals, the ideas of the masses, that is to say, the ideals of the fatherland, General Leyva has thought of his most valued collaborators, he has thought of us, he has thought of you, and he expects that you will not disappoint his hopes, which are, at this hour of a new national crisis and collective danger, the hopes of Mexico."

Several officers who had drunk plenty of beer at lunch applauded; otherwise, the speech was generally given a chilly, suspicious reception. And it was then that Major Segura got down to the concrete instructions.

What he said was more or less as follows: "This afternoon, the Aguirristas have hatched a plot against the supporters of my General Hilario Jiménez; they aim to kill the principal chiefs of the Hilarista group by provoking a clash between gangs. But my General Leyva, fully cognizant of the plot, has given orders for us to go and protect the Hilarista deputies, and, if it becomes necessary, he orders that we do to the Aguirrista leaders what they hope to do to their rivals, in short, we're not to show any mercy. This is the mission I've been given and the one you now officially receive through me."

There were signs of surprise in the circle of officers around Major Segura. But the latter, without stopping to consider the first impression made by his words, continued:

"It's very simple. We're going to leave here now, in groups. Some of us will approach the Chamber by one street, others by another; some of us will remain for a while in front of the main entrance, the one with the steps; others will wait in front of the Factor Street entrance. This way we can see who comes in and out. Then, little by little, all of us will enter the building; we'll go up to the balconies, we'll take our positions in the one on the right (take note: all of us in the right balcony), and we'll stay there on guard until the free-for-all starts."

"Do you have that order in writing, my Major?" said one officer.

Segura replied:

"Are you afraid, Captain?"

"No, my Major."

"You seem to be."

The officer drew back as if embarrassed, as Segura continued:

"Major Canuto Arenas, Major Licona, Captain Fentanes, and Special Agents Márquez, Lomas, and Abat here already know who the most dangerous Aguirrista leaders are. Their task is to identify them for each group as each leader enters the Chamber or takes his seat. Outside of those leaders we're not to attack anyone, unless at a given moment Deputies Ricalde, López Nieto, or Quintana decide otherwise. Do you understand? We'll all take our positions in the right balcony. When the shouting starts and they cry, 'Long live Ignacio Aguirre!' we'll shout, 'Death to Aguirre!' and cheer my General Hilario Jiménez. With our guns and fists, we'll intimidate and drive out any Aguirristas who are in the gallery with us.... If more instructions are needed, I'll give them as we go along."

No officer had dared to make any observation after Segura had reproached the one who asked for a written order for being afraid. Now all, after listening in silence, seemed ready to obey. One of them walked by Ricalde when the groups were being organized. He was short, dark-complexioned, with prominent cheekbones, slanted eyes, and thick lips. Ricalde held him by the arm and said:

"Major Segura has a special assignment for you."

"Yes, Deputy Ricalde."

"But I'm going to tell you what that assignment is so that you will understand how important it is to me."

"Yes, Deputy Ricalde."

Ricalde hesitated a moment.

"Let us see," he said, "if you deserve the high opinion General Leyva has of you.... It comes to this: if Deputy Olivier Fernández manages to escape from the Chamber, you are to kill him in the street. Do you understand?"

That officer's name was Adelaido Cruz and he had the appearance of a peaceful, good man. He looked at Ricalde sadly as he said:

"My General Leyva gave that order in writing? Because, sir, I..."

Ricalde interrupted him:

"Oh, you too are afraid!"

"No, sir, I'm not afraid."

"Well, if you're not, then don't act as if you were."

Captain Cruz joined his group. They all went out to the street.

II. The Hunt for Deputy Olivier

WHEN THEY REACHED THE STREET, GENERAL LEYVA'S NEPHEW asked Captain Adelaido Cruz:

"Do you know Deputy Emilio Olivier Fernández?"

"No, my Major."

"And Deputy López de la Garza?"

"Not either, my Major."

"Then what deputies do you know?"

"None, I think, my Major. This is the first time I've come near the Chamber."

Segura seemed to be thinking for a few seconds. Then he said:

"Right. You stay with the officers under Major Canuto Arenas, so that he can show you, at the right time, who Deputy Olivier Fernández is. And when the time comes to carry out the orders, just remember what I told you: the instructions we all have come from my General Protasio Leyva. All of us, do you understand?"

"Yes, my Major."

The officers had formed three groups. One headed by Major Licona and Captain Fentanes, another by Canuto Arenas, another by Special Agents Márquez, Lomas, and Abat. Arenas' group was the largest one; the agents' was the most menacing. The three groups spread out enough so as not to arouse curiosity in the streets, and thus, each by a different route, they made their way to the Chamber. They did so in such a manner that Canuto Arenas' men came out in front of the Palace of the Legislative Assembly looking like groups that had formed spontaneously at the corner of Donceles and Allende; Licona and Fentanes' troop came out of Manrique Street, and that of Márquez and the other agents by way of Belisario Domínguez Street. That is also where Major Segura was supposed to arrive, although later and by himself.

Outside the Chamber there was a large, restless crowd. Aside from genuine onlookers, who were not few, there were the contingents of the two enemy political gangs, the Aguirristas and the Hilaristas, who had taken over both streets as they waited for the public to be allowed into the building. The deputies also began to arrive: some went up the steps, protected by a double row of policemen who had already been there for two hours; others entered by the Factor Street entrance. Their drivers—in the case of those deputies who had their own cars—angle-parked their cars by the sidewalk, on either of the two facades, and they immediately joined the clusters of people nearby. These drivers had a certain political look about them; these chauffeurs were enthusiastic about their employers' factions and were almost always armed with a pistol. Some drove with loaded carbines and cartridge belts full of bullets under their seats.

Canuto Arenas positioned himself with his people just opposite the corner of the Chamber, so that he could communicate, from there, whatever his most dependable aides needed to know. He began by informing them, in a low voice, of the names of the principal Aguirrista leaders as they passed. Then, after a few seconds of preparatory smiles, in an even lower voice, he went into detail, sharing with each one, sometimes concretely, sometimes by hints, the orders issued by General Leyva that they all needed to execute.

Licona and Fentanes, meanwhile, were similarly occupied across from the Factor Street entrance, and Márquez, Lomas, and Abat did likewise on the Donceles Street sidewalk.

"That one, that's Axkaná!"

"That one over there is Juan Manuel Mijares!"

"Over there is General López de la Garza!"

And that is how General Leyva's henchmen saw for the first time the politicians whose lives were, from that moment, in their hands.

When Olivier's olive green Lincoln was spotted in the distance, Canuto Arenas held Captain Cruz's arm and whispered in his ear:

"Here comes your man, my friend."

In a few seconds, as he watched the car approach, Cruz saw, behind its windows, three smiling young men pass in front of him.

"The one on the left," Arenas said then, "is this guy Olivier."

"The one with the gray hat?"

"That's the one.... Just don't chicken out on me."

The Lincoln stopped next to the steps. For a fleeting moment, as Olivier said something to his companions, he looked absent-mindedly in the direction where Arenas, Cruz, and the other officers were. Captain Cruz then felt the weight of Canuto Arenas' hand on his arm—as if his eyes and those of the political leader, as their glances crossed, had met precisely there, where Arenas' peremptory hand pressed.

"Now you won't confuse him, friend?"

"No, my Major."

Other deputies arrived. On the steps the most quarrelsome members of the gangs threatened to fight. The doormen made ready to let the public in.

Cruz, who had seen Olivier's gray hat disappear into the shadow of the vestibule, said to his chief:

"With your permission, my Major, I'm going to drink a shot of tequila."

Canuto replied:

"Tequila at this time of day?"

"I need it, my Major."

"Well, since you need it, go, but just don't be long about it."

Captain Cruz walked some steps, entered the nearest cantina, and ordered the drink he wanted, but before they even brought it, he changed his mind.

"No, not tequila," he said quickly, "better have a glass of beer."

At the other end of the bar, three men whispered and drank. The bartender brought the glass of beer, next to which he left the cash register receipt. Cruz mechanically picked up the slip of paper as if he only wanted to see the price and then placed it, also mechanically, where it had been.... He drank down to the middle of the glass.... He seemed lost in thought.... As his left hand got wet holding the glass, an image persisted in his memory, an image that was almost a sensation; he saw the brim of a gray hat, and under it a pair of intelligent eyes looking at him, and, farther down, lips that moved, always repeating the same movement.... He drank again.

Unthinkingly, his right hand came to rest on one of his vest's upper pockets. There was a pencil; the hand took it, and, as if he were only guided by reflexes, the hand again descended to the slip of paper and began to write on it slowly. It was a clumsy hand, barely used to handling a pencil.

One or two minutes went by like this. Cruz drank a third time and, as he left the now empty glass on the bar, was surprised to find the pencil between his fingers. He put it in his pocket, called the bartender, paid. And it was then, while the bartender took the coin and turned around to open the cash register and count the change, that Captain Cruz's eyes consciously read what he had written before with his pencil; it was nine words that said:

"Be careful this afternoon because you are being hunted."

Cruz hurriedly picked up the slip and could not repress the urge to crumple it up feverishly. He took his change from the bar. He went out.

In the street, the political crowd had diminished. Now the doors of the Chamber were opened wide, and the people ascending the steps, between the double row of policemen, were free to enter.

Cruz approached the corner. Canuto Arenas still stood there, no longer with the group of officers but by himself. He looked at everything with an indifferent air, trying to make sure that no one would notice him, which, perhaps to observant eyes, would have made him more noticeable. His athletic figure, that of a horseman in repose, revealed extraordinary vigor. His flat, dark face was hard to see in the shade, barely lit by the reflection of the sun on the shimmering asphalt sheet.

"I was afraid I wouldn't see you again," he said to Cruz as soon as the captain was near. "Seems like a long time for a shot of tequila. Are you afraid? Tell me."

"I'm not afraid, my Major."

"Feel strong now?"

"Yes, my Major."

"Well, then, let's not waste time. You go in now; they're all inside already. I'll meet you there in the gallery on the right."

The first sensation Captain Cruz had when he found himself in the lobby of the Chamber was akin to dizziness. Deputies, women, police officers, members of the political gangs filled the premises. It was difficult to walk.

In order to get his bearings a little, the captain asked an usher how to get to the gallery on the right.

"That way," he was told.

Cruz began to move in the direction he was shown. But he hadn't gone more than a few steps when he chanced to see, a short distance away, over several heads, the eyes and mouth of Emilio Olivier. The young leader was hatless, with a bunch of papers in his left hand and surrounded by several persons to whom he was talking with animated eloquence.

For a moment that scene had a spellbinding effect on Captain Cruz, a kind of magnetic pull. He stopped to watch it. And then, almost immediately, not knowing why, he walked in that direction. Meanwhile, in his mind, a strange emotional and volitional process played out, an indefinable process involving, all confused into one, the shape of the receipt he had been given in the cantina—which he still had not stopped crushing with his fingers inside his pants pocket—the liveliness of Olivier's face, and the words, "I'm not afraid, my Major," which he had said not five minutes before to Canuto Arenas.

As he drew near, Cruz noted that Olivier's voice was already associated in his mind, for him a nascent development, with the person from which it came.

"That doesn't matter to us," the Aguirrista leader was saying, "as long as no one is insubordinate. Tomorrow we will all go together. I expect you at nine..."

Cruz walked by and at last reached the foot of the staircase, but even there he was again seized by an impulse to walk over to the cluster where Olivier was speaking. Then he thought distinctly about the words written on the little slip of paper; an idea was forming.... He hesitated, wavered... looked around... raised his eyes.... Then he discovered that from above, leaning on the guardrails and balustrades, many people were looking down to the lower part of the lobby. He started to go up...

At the head of the stairs, Captain Fentanes and Agent Abat were watching and waiting.

"Through that door," said Fentanes to Cruz as the latter passed by him.

Cruz went in as he was told: the door led to the right balcony. Cruz immediately observed that all the men whom Segura had summoned to the offices of the National Laborite Party were already positioned there. There were also men of a different type; there were no women. Cruz went down the steps to look for a place to sit, but as he did not see a single empty seat, he went to lean on a column, from where he set to looking at the parliamentary hall.

The deputies' chairs were arranged in concentric semi-circles. There were many deputies. Some of them were speaking in low voices; others were reading or writing; others were dozing. Up front, the rich mahogany and gilt structure, consisting of an ensemble of tables, railings, and a dais, contrasted sharply with the white color of the walls in the background. On them, in large capital letters, shone, row upon row, the names of many heroes and patriots.

After reading some of these names, Captain Cruz turned his eyes to the center of the hall. Now he paid close attention to the deputies in their seats; he recognized some whose names he had first heard half an hour before; he recognized Axkaná, Mijares, López de la Garza. Almost below his feet he saw Ricalde and López Nieto together. Ricalde was then speaking with the same gestures he had employed when he told Cruz at the offices of the party:

"If Deputy Olivier escapes with his life from the Chamber, you are to kill him in the street."

And later when he said this:

"Well, if you aren't, then don't act as if you were."

In vain did Cruz search for Olivier; he did not see him anywhere.

III. The Death of Cañizo

HALF OBLIVIOUS AND APATHETIC, ALTHOUGH FAVORED WITH strange insights, Captain Cruz continued thus to contemplate for a long time the scenes that the assembly hall of the Chamber of Deputies offered to his eyes below. His mind at that point was reduced to only two activities. On the one hand, it functioned as a mirror endowed with enormous reflective powers; on the other, it attempted to harness a bundle of feelings to an immense task. He needed to familiarize himself quickly with the premises, to understand the nature of this place where he had never been. Cruz, nonetheless, already sensed that it was the theater where he might play the leading role.

Meanwhile, Canuto Arenas and, a little farther away, the other lieutenants of Major Segura were preparing to put into action the plan of attack prescribed by their chief. It was true that Segura had ordered that nothing should be attempted until his arrival, and he still had not come. But as Arenas saw a section of the Aguirrista gang becoming stronger in the center of the gallery, where it was already giving signs of attempting to take over, he thought it appropriate to deviate from his orders. He invoked his right to take the initiative, a right they never denied him in cases like this, and decided to force the small nucleus of enemies out of their positions.

The Aguirristas' offensive, in fact, barely exceeded the bounds of what might be called feeble. It didn't go beyond laughter, whispers, and isolated cries, because Aguirre's supporters were merely listening, with feigned attention, to the names called out at the foot of the table by the secretary in charge of the roll call. Meanwhile, one of the Aguirristas—their chief, it seemed—made comments after each name was called, provoking mildly suggestive murmurs from the rest of the group. It was true that since the secretary purposely read the list slowly—to allow the presence of a quorum—and there were often long delays between the litany of names, silences favorable to expressions of Aguirrismo, that, for a moment, hovered triumphantly over the public in the gallery.

Twice Canuto Arenas turned in the direction from which those voices seemed to come. But neither his fierce appearance, nor the intention in his look (somewhere between aggressive and haughty) had the least effect on the Aguirristas' tactics. Their chief—a thin man, with curly hair and a light brown suit—was content to respond to Canuto's provocations with ironic smiles.

In this way, an already hostile environment was becoming steadily worse. Thus, when the secretary pronounced the name of Axkaná González, one of the members of the Aguirrista gang could not resist the impulse to exclaim in a stifled cry:

"Viva Ignacio Aguirre!"

The rest, in a dense, dull murmur replied:

"Viva!!"

Upon which, Canuto, more openly than before, assumed the fiercest of his poses, and shouted the challenge:

"Death to Ignacio Aguirre!"

Black and snub-nosed, his ugly face, parted in two by the white line of his teeth, then shone horribly, and his expression already implied the threat of going for his pistol. But instead of shrinking back, the chief of the Aguirristas replied by addressing one of his men, the closest to Canuto Arenas:

"Look out, Cañizo, that one will scare anyone just with his ugly face!"

And he underscored his words by imitating Arenas' face so effectively that several of the latter's comrades joined in their rivals' laughter—a slightly hysterical laughter, a tense, nervous laughter, the laughter of those who are working themselves up to go into battle.

Canuto was cut to the quick by the mockery. His complexion, which had been shiny until then, with a varnish-like sheen, dulled suddenly and turned the deadliest, ashiest black. Instead of confronting the chief of the Aguirristas, he went after Cañizo, who, still laughing and grasping tightly the walking stick he carried, repelled Canuto's attack by stealthily moving his free hand to the area of his hip.

The conflict, for the time being, went no further. It caused only a kind of wave-like motion that rippled from one end of the gallery to the other as the right shoulders of all those present, moved. If not their hands, their thoughts were adjusting the weapons at their hips.

A little later, the reading of the name of Hilarista deputy López Nieto accelerated the build-up to the clash, although now for the opposite reason. Arenas' people wanted to greet that name with demonstrations of approval, but one of the Aguirristas, with great speed, opposed them in his own way. While the deputy below answered, "Present!" the Aguirrista said, with a vulgar gesture and in a voice, perfectly audible from the gallery:

"Death to Hilario Jiménez and his flunkies!"

The Chamber was shaken out of its drowsiness; the balconies and galleries broke out in exclamations and laughter. The secretary, who was an Aguirrista, stopped to smile.

One of Canuto's subordinates shouted with booming resonance:

"Long live my General Hilario Jiménez!"

And this second cheer did not go unnoticed. Together with the protests of the entire Aguirrista gang, scattered throughout the audience, the Hilarista cheers were also heard, shouted by their gang, among the cries and applause of some deputies. Foremost among the latter, and a major contributor to the furor, was the obese, twisted, deformed figure of Ricalde, and next to him López Nieto.

Drawn by these exclamations, the many deputies still in the corridors came back into the hall. There were maneuvers from both gangs in the balcony across and in the upper galleries. At the back door, the members of the executive board appeared, coming from the Yellow Hall.

Meanwhile, the conflict was growing between Canuto's followers and the Aguirristas on the right balcony. The special agents, under the command of Márquez and Lomas, had managed to intimidate the Aguirre supporters near Cañizo, keeping them almost motionless in their seats, and now they were trying to bully Cañizo himself, who held firm against all of them. On both sides they hurled threats and insults, and while Cañizo, fired up by his own words, made ready to use his walking stick, although only his enemies on the side could notice, Márquez's and Lomas' hands were ready to draw their guns.

It would have been very easy to put an end to these intimations of armed violence, but since the session had not yet begun—the executive table was deserted—no one was in charge. Another circumstance favored the incipient conflict, perhaps a crucial one: the fact that neither of the two principal groups of deputies would have agreed to deprive themselves of the support of their collaborators in the galleries and balconies.

A new cheer from Canuto, with unanimous support from all the Hilaristas—those in the gang and those in the deputies' seats, without a reply from the enemy side—brought a transitory restoration of the peace. The voice of the secretary was heard once more in the chamber; the stifled, playful murmurs of the Aguirristas began to recur in the balcony. But just then something happened that finally ignited the battle they had all foreseen and expected.

For a while now, the schemes of Canuto Arenas and his troops had been the object of scrutiny from the left balcony. They were observed by a short man of indefinable appearance who at the moment held in his hands a hat—between Mexican and Texan, judging by its shape, coffee-colored, with a high nap, a black cord, and a yellow braid trim. The same individual, accompanied by three or four others, soon appeared, unnoticed, at the top of the right balcony. He silently observed Canuto's men for a few brief moments—his eyes and Canuto's met fleetingly—and then, approaching the Aguirrista leader, whispered in his ear. The noise in the Chamber allowed the leader, after listening to the man in the coffee-colored hat, to ask in an undertone:

"All of them, Don Casimiro?"

"Yes, it goes for all of them," answered Don Casimiro, who once more ascended the steps and left, this time alone.

Canuto, Lomas, and several of their comrades had not failed to hear Don Casimiro's last phrase, nor the previous muttering. It also did not escape them that as soon as Don Casimiro left, the gang's leader spoke to the comrade beside him, and he to another one farther on, and so on, until all of them had been made aware of something that in a certain way was expressed in the furtive looks that the Aguirristas began to cast right and left. All of them, it was plain to see, were now aware of the identity of Canuto Arenas and his men.

At this point, something else happened: a name rose from the Chamber, all the way up to the great central lamp, a name that had an extraordinary impact in the galleries and balconies and caused slight movements in the deputies' seats:

"Olivier Fernández, Emilio," the secretary said.

Captain Cruz who, until then, had been standing motionless against a column, was shaken out of his trance. Olivier—he saw him now—was sitting in a chair on the dais, almost hidden by a table and a group of deputies to whom he was speaking.

"Present!" the leader signaled with a gesture, without interrupting his conversation.

After which, the leader of the Aguirrista gang, far from making veiled observations, as he had on other occasions, proclaimed at the top of his lungs:

"Viva Olivier Fernández!"

And this set off the fight. The Hilarista deputies below, and Arenas and his band in the balcony, spoiling for a fight, almost simultaneously raised a cheer for General Jiménez.

"Viva Hilario Jiménez!"

"Viva!"

Among the deputies, López Nieto was the one who shouted most, and as he shouted he stood facing the place occupied by Arenas' men, his arms outstretched in order to show them the cartridge belt under his vest. Near him, Deputies Ricalde and Cayo Horacio Quintana seconded his cheer no less vigorously.

"Viva Hilario Jiménez, you sons of ——!"

"Viva!"

Cheers of "Long life to!" and "Death to!" shook the interior of the legislative palace with the same ardor and disorder as if it were a stage at a party rally, and most of all in the right balcony, where the scene truly began to resemble a choppy sea. There Cañizo, wielding high his walking stick, vented thunderously:

"Viva Ignacio Aguirre!... Viva Ignacio Aguirre!"

"Long live!... Death to!... Long live!"

To which Canuto, over the swelling tide of opposing cheers, wanted to give the answer that was burning his lips. Illustrating his words with a brutal smile in which the whiteness of his teeth and the darkness of his deformed features took on a symphonic value, he said to Cañizo, as he leaned toward him:

"We shall see, Mr. What's Your Face, who will really live and who will die."

Cañizo snapped.

"It's not hard to guess," he answered. "I only have to look at the murderers' faces."

The impatience to reach for their weapons grew amid the general uproar. The Hilarista closest to Cañizo almost jumped on him, insulting him in a voice made dense and dull by rage:

"The only murderer here is you, you bastard!"

And he held Cañizo's walking stick as he continued:

"And don't chicken out on me. Let's go out to the street, just the two of us."

"I won't chicken out; let's go."

Meanwhile, pandemonium swirled through the galleries and balconies. Though they couldn't hear anything, the deputies in the galleries below insulted and vilified each other. Some had already drawn their guns.

Cañizo and his enemy looked for the door. Cañizo was ahead, the latter two or three meters behind. As he left the balcony, Cañizo turned to face the Hilarista, who already had his right hand on his hip. In this manner, walking backwards, Cañizo took a few steps in the hallway, making sure his enemy would not get the jump on him. He too had already placed the palm of his hand on the grip of his revolver.

And it all took place in less than a second. As the Hilarista passed the doorway, he went for his weapon, intending to shoot. Cañizo had the slightest of leads on him—enough for his bullet to hit first; his gun was out of the holster and rising to aim at the target; his index finger, having become one with the trigger, felt the slackening that precedes firing, a feeling that is only perceptible to the shooter at the culminating moment when his life seems to lengthen a hundredfold; the barrel of the gun was about to aim, the bullet about to shoot out.... But in that fraction of a second, Cañizo felt someone grab him by the elbow, another hand twisted his wrist, and his revolver, after firing at the ground, fell to the floor. Facing him, the Hilarista's automatic pistol was staring at him with its only eye.

With a jolt, Cañizo freed himself from those holding him—it was Captain Fentanes and Agent Abat who had grabbed him from behind—and, failing to recover his weapon from the floor, rushed to the stairs. He jumped once, twice, three times, and was in the midst of a fourth leap when the Hilarista fired from above. The wounded body described a scrawl in midair and fell to the tile floor of the lobby. It fell as if the pistol had fired not the bullet but the corpse itself.

IV. Parliamentary Battle

Emilio Olivier had the doors of the Chamber shut and gave orders that no one was to enter or leave until the assassin had been caught. Thus two violent, compact mobs were locked in a terrible, heartless struggle in the parliamentary building: the Aguirrista mob was trying to identify Cañizo's killer and arrest him, and the Hilarista mob wanted to save the murderer and also take advantage of the confusion to carry out its other plans.

In the lobby, both mobs buzzed and swirled around the place where Cañizo's corpse lay face down. As soon as the gunshots were heard, a great number of deputies, journalists, and scattered members of both political gangs had gathered there. The occupants of the galleries and balconies plunged like a river from all the staircases.

Referring to the murderer, an anonymous voice had said from the start:

"It's a tall man in a blue suit!"

Those words, now repeated from mouth to mouth, spurred the Aguirristas to find the person, hidden in the crowd, who matched that description.

The din grew by the second. The number of people streaming in from the chambers and corridors below grew with every passing moment; the influx of those from above, who were abandoning the higher locations, added to the pressure.

Near Emilio Olivier, a police captain and several policemen listened in bewilderment to the orders the young leader was giving them:

"While half your force guards the exits of the Chamber," the chief of the Aguirrista majority said furiously, "you, yourself, at the head of the other half, will go up that staircase and arrest the assassin, who is crouching over there, near that tall man with a black, deformed face."

And Olivier pointed with his finger to the part of the staircase where Canuto and his people were fighting to get through.

But the captain resisted:

"As I said, Deputy Olivier, I have only twenty men here. Let me send for backup from the police inspector's."

Olivier was becoming more furious:

"Yes, backup so the assassin can slip between our fingers, while we wait for backup!... Are you afraid?"

"No, Deputy Olivier, I'm not afraid; but what's impossible is still impossible, even with all the courage in the world. To guard the entrances to the Chamber I need no less than fifteen men; to go up where you want me to, I would need another twenty men and room to maneuver, and in order to protect you in the middle of this disorder I need the five policemen who are here.... Which of these three tasks do you want me to carry out?"

Without relenting the least bit, Olivier answered:

"I haven't asked for your protection, and I don't need it. I order you to go after the assassin and capture him, and keep guarding the doors."

The captain and the five policemen then moved toward the staircase.

At first, their progress was not difficult; the lower part of the lobby was full of Aguirristas who not only let the policemen through, but were ready to follow them and come to their aid. But once they reached the foot of the stairs, things changed. There, with a mix of Aguirristas and Hilaristas, and more of the latter than the former, the mass of humanity became impenetrable. The policemen—all from the mounted police—used their carbines to push apart those in their way and then tried to go up the stairs. Thus, they went up, two, three, four steps. But at that level, their hard-won progress came to a halt, because the slightest surge of the crowd above them was enough to make them lose their footing and plunge back to the first step.

At the top, Canuto Arenas, Fentanes, Abat, and all their comrades acted as if they had nothing to do with the origin of the disturbance; they sought to give the impression that they were like the few curious onlookers who wandered into the Chamber that afternoon to suddenly find themselves involved in unexpected events. They were no longer shouting, "Long live!" or "Death to!"; they showed no signs of their recent belligerence. They made their way without cheering, like the other Aguirrista and Hilarista groups that were crammed the length of the corridors or squeezed up to the ceiling, along the curves of the stairs.

Cañizo's assassination had produced a change of tactics on both sides. The original plan to intimidate, so as to have control of the parliamentary hall, was now replaced by the intention to employ violence opportunely in order to derive the greatest benefits from it. Only the physical confines of the space kept the political gangs from going for their guns and killing each other: the very narrowness of the place paralyzed them. Although they yearned to kill each other, they were so close together they actually protected each other.

One of the surges of the crowd, jostled below by the struggle of the policemen, brought Captain Cruz and Don Casimiro elbow-to-elbow at the top of the stairs. Intent on the scenes on the lobby's floor, Cruz's gaze alternated between two spots: in one, Olivier was gesticulating and giving orders; in the other—an island of quiet in a sea of intense agitation—stretched the body of Cañizo, face-down with his head in a halo of bloody stains. As he looked from one scene to the other, Cruz's eye spotted Olivier communicating by signs with Don Casimiro, and then noticed that the latter, together with the men around him, was making efforts to mix with Canuto Arenas' men. In order to do this, Don Casimiro and his men ably used the pressure of other groups, those higher up, who were either trying to descend or were trying to get those up front to descend.

A new element had been added to the turmoil and struggle in the corridors and stairs. Now that they knew the doors to the Chamber would remain closed until the assassin was captured, the Hilaristas, on one hand, could not agree on what was the better plan—to stay there, or to go down to the lobby. The Aguirristas, on the other hand, were increasingly determined to push their enemies down the stairs and then take them on below.

In the meantime, no one could find, anywhere, the "tall man in the blue suit," identified by many as the perpetrator. And meanwhile, the real killer—who was a short man in a gray-green gabardine suit—was cowering near Canuto, protected by the three special agents, Márquez, Lomas, and Abat, within whose huddle he did everything possible not to be noticed. Nevertheless, there were some, particularly among the Aguirristas, who had just been in the right balcony, who began to identify him as the sole perpetrator of the assassination. Others mistakenly accused Fentanes; others Abat.

The weak file of policemen had been battling for about five minutes to make their way to the foot of the stairs when Canuto began to fear a larger force would come to support that attack; this fear led him to precipitate the crisis in order to control it. First, he wanted to bring Cañizo's killer to safety, and then be free to execute the plan against the Aguirrista leaders.

"Truth is," he thought, "we could give this Olivier what he's been thirstin' for, right here and now."

This idea, as a follow-up to the previous one, seemed excellent to him. With a discreet gesture, he called Captain Cruz, who, not without some effort, was able to approach little by little, helped by his comrades, who made way for him and then closed ranks to keep Don Casimiro and his people from advancing.

When Cruz was near enough, Canuto said in a low voice:

"Listen, my friend. You can see for yourself, things are going fine; we only need to keep an eagle eye out so we don't mess up.... We're gonna let the policemen climb for a bit; then, when the moment's ripe, we fall on them, roll them down to the very bottom; then we scatter them, grab their weapons, we add to the ruckus, and then, while I take over the door and get our comrade outta the tight spot he's in, you, with two guys for backup, get near this Olivier, and I want you to eliminate him on the sly for me. Get it? On the sly. And then you come to the door so I can cover your retreat.... Your hand isn't shaking?"

"No, my Major."

"Good, then stay here, behind me, ready to carry out orders."

The first part of Canuto's plan was fulfilled with mathematical precision. The Hilarista phalanx on the stairs organized quickly; it let the policemen and the captain climb eight or nine steps, and then made the mass of humanity in front of the policemen collapse on them, while they cleared the space behind, leaving them without support. And all of a sudden it was like a landslide: breaking up into bunches that clashed and pushed each other, the crowd on the stairs slid, uncontrollably, overwhelmingly, dragging down even the Hilarista groups above who could not check their own momentum in time.[1]

Losing their balance, the captain and one of the policemen disappeared under the human flood. The remaining policemen—two of them now without weapons or kepis—were trampled and scattered. They were later seen swept along at the mercy of the currents that the stormy surf of the new mass of people stirred up in the crowd at the lower part of the lobby, as it ebbed like water in an inlet. Only Canuto's group came down compact and intact. Nothing disorganized or affected it, not even the formidable pressure Don Casimiro's band continued to exert, as his band was dragged like others in the general collapse, although it managed not to lose contact with the enemy and to keep its balance once on solid ground.

This is why Arenas' escape plan failed right from the start. The policemen and the doormen guarding the entrance, insignificant in the face of the overwhelming attack of the Hilaristas, unexpectedly received considerable reinforcements from Don Casimiro and his men and from the Aguirrista gang in the right balcony. Reinforced in this manner, they were able to resist. Canuto was not only unable to take possession of the door, but also found himself and his group isolated from the other Hilarista factions. Now the enemy was both before and behind him.

For the first time, Canuto considered that his situation was dire: the Aguirristas would have time to organize and attack him in force until they could wrest Cañizo's killer from his hands. Now the only hope was for Captain Cruz to accomplish his mission with respect to Olivier: if fulfilled, this plan would sow panic and create new opportunities.

Canuto looked for Cruz. The latter, followed by Agent Lomas and Captain Thivol, was then skirting the area where the corpse was and getting close to Olivier; he moved as if dragged by one of the currents in which all those men were tossed. At that moment Canuto also saw, at the entrance of the assembly hall, Deputies López Nieto and Ricalde; both were shouting and gesticulating

---

1. The Spanish text says "Aguirristas," but since the Hilaristas are the ones pushing, it must be an error.

wildly together with other Hilarista deputies. That raised his spirits.

"Hang on like men," he whispered to his people. "If no one chickens out on me, one more minute and the afternoon is ours."

Cruz, Lomas, and Thivol were already two steps away from Olivier, who, his eyes fixed on Canuto's crew, was saying something to several individuals beside him.... Cruz was getting even closer.... Now there was only one head between his and Olivier's...

"God's truth, Cruz is quite a man!" thought Canuto, quick to admire the mastery of another professional. He held his breath for several seconds and stood slightly on the balls of his feet.

Thus, a minute passed, a minute in which Don Casimiro reinforced his troops and improved their deployment for the attack. Canuto was unaware of this; his whole being was intent on following the slightest movements made by Captain Cruz's head and the demeanor of Olivier, who was still speaking and giving orders.

Another half a minute... Canuto Arenas held his breath.... A shot was heard... then another... and another.... Olivier's face turned left, his eyes riveted on the entrance to the assembly hall, from which López Nieto and Ricalde vanished in a leap. And still in that posture, Olivier kept looking over there—not with the expression of someone who had been dealt his death blow, but a look revealing just the faintest curiosity or a little disquiet. For an instant, which seemed to last a century, Canuto waited for that face to be covered by mortal shadows and to see it drop and disappear immediately. But that did not happen nor did Captain Cruz move from where he was.... All that Canuto saw then was, first, the whirlwind of many heads turning toward the place where Olivier's eyes were fixed (that is, where the shots had come from, not where Canuto thought), and immediately afterward, a mass of people who, coming down on him, pushed him back several meters, throwing his whole troop into disarray and snatching the assassin.

His excessive confidence that Cruz would kill Olivier had, for two minutes, clouded his sense of reality.... Wanting to recoup what he had lost, he reached for his pistol. But before it had come out of the holster, Canuto stopped; Don Casimiro put a knife to his belly and threatened him in a whisper:

"If you but move your tongue, I'll nail you, count on it."

Canuto looked down. He was tall; Don Casimiro, squat. He looked and fell silent; he barely replied by flashing his teeth.

That night it became known that Cañizo's killer was a driver from the Secretariat of the Interior. First thing the next day, Emilio Olivier received a visit from Captain Adelaido Cruz. The captain came to tell the political leader how, the night before, he'd had the opportunity to kill Olivier—and how, in the end, instead of committing the crime, he had resolved to wait and tell Olivier, in great detail, just what the chief of operations in the Valley and commander of the city garrison were plotting against the lives of the principal Aguirrista deputies.

Book Six

Julián Elizondo

I. Symptoms of Rebellion

THE PLOT TO ASSASSINATE THE AGUIRRISTA LEADERS OF THE Chamber of Deputies failed in its purpose, but there were significant consequences nonetheless. Immediately there was sharper division along partisan lines. Many of Aguirre's supporters—those who had only been faithful to him until then because they thought him capable of the greatest violence—convinced that they had been wrong, went over to Hilario Jiménez's side. On the other hand, the loyal, steadfast Aguirristas—those who aspired to win under their own flag, not the enemy's—reaffirmed in their endeavor, prepared for all the excesses of the struggle they foresaw.

The so-called public opinion then manifested its influence on events. Secretly, it supported Aguirre—whom the public considered to be the brave champion of the opposition to the Caudillo—and public opinion was, also secretly, against Jiménez, whom it saw as the personification of imposed *continuismo*. But in the end, since public opinion was really just the voice of the cowardly classes (classes whose civic duty was corrupted), it did not dare to choose courageously, or openly take sides in the struggle between the groups. Instead, it restricted itself to participating in the struggle as the public does in boxing matches: by egging on the contenders. Outlandish and unsubstantiated, the rumors ran from mouth to mouth: "Encarnación Reyes will rebel in Puebla," "Figueroa will rebel in Jalisco," "Ortiz will rebel in Oaxaca," "Elizondo will rebel in Toluca."... It was as if a mirror were reflecting a reality that was not yet there, but that reflection was eventually taken to be real, simply because it had been reflected.

Those who had the opportunity to address more than a couple of words to Aguirre would say, with varying degrees of sincerity, "Your only choice is the rifle." Sociologists raised this piece of advice to the category of a law, saying: "In Mexico all presidents are elected with bullets." And likewise, on the other side, rumors of the imminent Aguirrista rebellion swarmed around Jiménez and the Caudillo.

Faced with such insinuations, Aguirre hinted that he knew what to expect—though he did so with a skeptical smile. Meanwhile the Caudillo, unable to entertain the idea that anyone would dare to rebel against him, increased his largesse to the most suspect generals, opening wide the great coffers of the Treasury for them.

In other words: the characters in this profound and ever-evolving drama did not act of their own volition: they did not obey their own impulses or inner voices. It was as if they were simply actors, cast in roles sketched out for them by an anonymous and irresistible force that compelled them to learn, rehearse, and perform their parts.

Determined to take extreme measures, Emilio Olivier met one night with the principal representatives of the generals and governors who supported Aguirre's candidacy.

The meeting was held at the home of General Alfonso Sandoval—ex–head of operations, ex-governor, ex–right-hand man of the Caudillo, who had been his comrade in the first stages of the Revolution, and was now an enemy of his former comrade and chief due to the incompatibility of their identical ambitions. This circumstance, fortuitous up to a point, reflected the true nature of the meeting. Because Sandoval was not an Aguirrista. He merely pretended to be one in order to further his own aspirations: for years, he had toiled to become president. Many others like him—Ortiz, Figueroa, Carrasco—all wanted the presidency, not for Ignacio Aguirre, but rather for themselves. If they now joined forces to bring down the reigning president, it was only with the secret aim to later fight over what currently unified them. Among the generals at that point there were only two true Aguirristas: Julián Elizondo, head of military operations in the State of Mexico, and Encarnación Reyes, his counterpart in Puebla.

Of the generals who commanded troops, the only one who came in person to the meeting was Elizondo; the others sent representatives. Consequently, since he was a divisional general, Elizondo's opinions prevailed from the start. This meant that the final agreement was quite different from what the most impatient or malicious among those present would have wished. The secret meeting, in fact, was reduced to a confrontation of two points of view: one—which included López de la Garza, representing Encarnación Reyes, Olivier Fernández, and the generals who were no longer on active duty, like Sandoval and Carrasco—advocated an immediate recourse to arms. The other—defended above all by Elizondo—preferred not to rush things yet, but to continue recruiting among uncommitted generals and colonels.

Both sides seemed to have good points.

"Either we strike the Caudillo at dawn with all we've got or the Caudillo will strike *us* at dawn," said Olivier. "In these cases, those who take the initiative always win. What happens when two good shots face each other, pistols in hand? Whoever shoots first, kills first. Well then, Mexican politics, the politics of the pistol, has only one axiom: strike at dawn."

López de la Garza argued along the same lines, although not with the axiomatic flair of the Progressive Radicals' leader, but with concrete facts.

"My General Reyes," he said, "is reluctant to wait more. He's afraid that any moment now, he'll lose his most loyal units. He knows for a fact that government agents are trying to turn some battalions against him. And then, like all of us, he remembers well the evil arts of the Caudillo: he fears that if he is careless, he'll be raided at dawn."

But General Elizondo had suitable responses for one and all. He was one of those guys from the North—he had a face without curves; straight mustache; light, spotless complexion; white, dry lips—guys who seem very frank and very loyal until they're not. Northern brusqueness in his case took on a peremptory tone, a tone that became more forceful, more incontrovertible owing to the notable role he had played in several of the Caudillo's most important military victories.

He said to Olivier:

"Yes, dawn strikes are good, counselor, but we must ensure we don't run the risk of being laid to rest too early. We have to strike at dawn, but we need to keep an eye on the clock. Otherwise, what good is it?"

To López de la Garza he replied:

"Good generals never present a flank where they can be hit, and Encarnación Reyes is a really good general. So, they want to take away his best units? He should refuse to hand them over. And if they're trying to turn his people against him, he should coddle them, take care of them, and they'll remain true to him. The thing is not to rush into a revolt any which way, but to wait until we're confident of its success, and we can't be confident yet. What garrisons can we count on? Those in the State of Mexico, those in Puebla, those in Jalisco, those in Tamaulipas, those in Oaxaca. Well, all that is still not enough."

"We count on the whole nation," argued Olivier.

"Yes, counselor, but let's be clear about this. In cases like this, the nation doesn't fight, the army fights, and there's no question that the greater part of the army is not yet with us. Therefore, we need to keep working to win them over."

It was at moments like this that Sandoval and Carrasco usually spoke up; as generals in disgrace they were the most active proponents of the uprising.

"We've spoken to all the commanders who can be approached," they said, "only it's the same as always: most of them won't commit, won't come over, until others take the first step. But then they will. Once we get going, the fear of losing drives them on. That's what happened four years ago. Once the forces in Sonora had rebelled, we were all with the Caudillo. Grain by grain, the army crumbled in the government's hands like a rotten ear of corn."

One last remark by Elizondo came to show that the junta, strictly speaking, was not in a position to decide one way or the other. The head of operations of the State of Mexico said:

"Above all, we're missing the most important thing: a thorough knowledge of General Aguirre's thoughts. We know that he's ready to rebel, but when? Judging from what he's said to me, I don't think that he'll agree to do it soon. And frankly, if he's our standard-bearer, it would be unfair for us to fail to recognize that it's up to him rather than us to choose the time for bullets to fly."

Olivier Fernández and Sandoval turned furiously against this argument. In the first place, they denied, although without ignoring Aguirre's rights, that the decision to take up arms wasn't incumbent on them all, because this was a matter of life or death and all of them were equally at risk. Secondly, they affirmed that Ignacio Aguirre, who had hardly demonstrated enthusiasm himself, not only needed to be pushed, compelled, in the present situation, but if left to his own devices, would expose everyone to a disaster. He had done enough harm by failing to accept his candidacy quickly.

But neither the efforts of Sandoval and Olivier, nor those of some of the others, managed to overcome Elizondo's opinion. In the end, they agreed that the latter, accompanied by López de la Garza, Olivier Fernández, and Sandoval, would consult with the candidate on the matter, and that, at least for the time being, they would agree to everything that the candidate decided.

Ignacio Aguirre decided in the manner Olivier feared. To the frank observation—made by Olivier himself—that it was high time to think seriously about rebelling, he answered with greater frankness:

"I *have* resolved to rebel. That is something I neither gloss over nor ignore, because I know that in the end it'll come to that. I believe, nevertheless, that we should not take up arms until we have the legal justification to support us. What grounds have we, now, to rebel against the government? The imposition of a candidate that has not yet taken place? The violation of an election that has not yet been announced? I agree that we might win, and it would all depend on the army's seeing us as their best bet and joining us in time, as in May of 1920. But the truth is that such movements always start out weak, weak in terms of popular support, and that puts us at the mercy of the contingency of the number of troops that rise up. Now, since we're gambling on winning or losing everything, I don't want to proceed in this manner, neither for my sake nor that of my supporters and friends. Because it would not be right for us to expose ourselves to losing like ambitious incompetents, deserving of public scorn.... And to this I can still add something else: the importance of certain personal considerations. As you know perfectly well, I did not want to be a candidate. A series of hardly believable events have gradually forced me into a contest that was not mine. Today the die is cast; I don't regret it; I will gladly continue to the end. But while this is true, it's also true that I don't want to seize the presidency at any cost, and not because I claim to be moral, pure, and incorruptible—to a greater or lesser degree, we have all made mistakes in the Revolution and in politics, I perhaps more than many others—but because I think that despite the lies and mud in which we're drowning, there are roles that demand dignity, moments of decorum that must not be forgotten. We know that the vote doesn't exist in Mexico: what exists is the violent struggle of groups that covet power, sometimes with public support. That is the real Mexican Constitution; the rest is nothing but a farce. But since even our quarrels have their rules and are, despite everything, subject to certain standards of decency, I am resolved not to fire the first shot until the Caudillo and Jiménez have pushed matters to the point that the whole nation will applaud us if we do the same. Yes, I do want to win, but to win the right way, and if that is not possible, I prefer to lose the right way, that is to say, leaving criminal and ignoble means to others. At this point, winning is not the most important thing, what matters is the decision of the intimate plebiscite that the nation is always holding. And if that decision favors us, it's all the same if we win the presidency or are assassinated. How many times haven't we risked our lives even for the most stupid and base whims?"

General Elizondo was quite satisfied by Aguirre's reasoning, either because he agreed, or because he saw that it confirmed his thesis that the rebellion was inopportune. Likewise, this curbed López de la Garza's and Sandoval's impatience. But the candidate's eloquence did not penetrate the deeply rooted political ideas of the leader of the Progressive Radicals. Nevertheless, Olivier did not want to contradict Aguirre then—he understood it was useless—although he still observed:

"Everything you have said to us sounds fine to me; I neither refute nor question it. But there is a point that deserves further consideration: the existing rules for our public disputes. There's only one rule and I'll state it now: in Mexico if you don't strike your rival at dawn, your rival will strike *you* at dawn."

II. Candidates and Generals

FOR SEVERAL DAYS, THE ELECTORAL CAMPAIGN STILL DISPLAYED ALL the trappings of a democratic event: there was talk of political parties, platforms, tours, and meetings. But the truth is, behind these simulations, the sole aim of both contending groups—the goal at which they directed all of their efforts—was to cause, and repel, acts of violence whenever possible. The Caudillo and Jiménez spared no means to destroy the seeds of the inevitable revolt. Afraid that the government would hit them before they were ready to resist, the Aguirristas spied, plotted, and distributed their seditious and defensive propaganda to the army.

Things having reached this point, there were signs of a final clash on the evening when the Group of Pro–Ignacio Aguirre Deputies held a special rally to welcome the candidate on his first visit to their offices.

The headquarters of the Group were located at the corner of Avenida Madero and Calle Bolívar. There were always people there. That evening the headquarters filled with Aguirristas an hour earlier than usual, and at six-thirty, when the guest arrived, the crowd did not fit in the building. Spilling out of the corridors, the courtyard, and the vestibule, the people crowded the street. Olivier had, of course, summoned his parliamentary gang, Eduardo Correa, his municipal forces, and—with the addition of the public's enthusiastic support for Aguirre—the rally was decked out with the glittering trappings of authentic democracy.

Well into the ceremony, the candidate received a phone message that he was urgently needed at home. Messages like this, at such solemn moments—Olivier was about to eulogize the future president of the Republic; the candidate in turn was about to respond with praise for the platform of the Progressive Radical Party—were unheard of. Thus there had to be a very serious reason. Nonetheless, Aguirre only said that he would go home as soon as possible, and continued to follow the speech Juan Manuel Mijares was giving at that moment.

Half an hour later—Olivier was already at the rostrum—the summons was repeated, more urgently than the first time. Aguirre then called Remigio Tarabana and asked him to go quickly to find out what was going on.

Twenty or thirty minutes went by. Olivier finished. Aguirre stood and began the lengthy speech he had prepared. Presently Tarabana returned, Aguirre saw him speak with López de la Garza—who, in turn, left a few moments later—but he did not detect signs of great concern in either's face. Therefore, he devoted himself to the delivery of his address to its conclusion. He reached the end, having spoken for close to an hour. And he did so with such consistent eloquence that, after every so many sentences, there was an ovation.

When the speech was done, the cheers in the hall ignited the corridors; from there they spread to the stairs, to the courtyard, to the vestibule and, from there, to the street. There, the Aguirrista gang and the people congregated on the corner cheered the candidate, and, joined by a crowd of curious bystanders, they shouted for him to appear. Olivier had the balconies opened and Aguirre and the most notable leaders appeared there, while below the brilliant nocturnal bustle in the avenue came to a halt. It was then, in the interval provided by the brief words Olivier addressed to the crowd on the street, that Aguirre and Tarabana were able to speak in a hush:

"Anything urgent?"

"Too urgent, it's suspicious. It's Jáuregui, the chief of the sixteenth battalion; he's waiting at your house, desperate to talk to you. It seems that there's a groundswell of opposition…"

"Spare me the melodrama! What does the colonel say?"

"Little and a lot; that it's a matter of life or death; that you have to speak to him right away."

"But, concretely, what's it about?"

"Oh, that I don't know! He insists that he can only tell you. He also said that if he was here, López de la Garza should come to him immediately. He's already on his way."

The crowd greeted Olivier's last words with frenzied applause. They began to shout. The crowd wanted the candidate to address them in person. At the end of the street, car horns honked in unison, protesting the blocking of traffic. Aguirre, who sensed the gravity of what the chief of the sixteenth battalion might want to say to him, used that as a reason to barely say a couple of words, bringing the meeting to an end in a few minutes.

At about nine-thirty, Aguirre entered his house accompanied by Axkaná González, Olivier, Correa, and a few other supporters and close friends, among them the governor of Jalisco, Agustín J. Domínguez, who had come from Guadalajara for the special meeting. His companions stayed in the living room; Aguirre went to the room where Colonel Jáuregui was still waiting for him.

After a quick salute, the colonel said:

"You don't have to believe me if you don't want to, my General, but what I've come to tell you is as true as the fact that I'm looking at your face and you're looking at mine. Once, they came to you with some gossip about me. You believed them, passed me over, I resented it, and since then, it seems, we haven't been friends. It's what people say and I figure even you yourself think that. Luckily, for my good name, that's not true right now, because I'm not the type to forget all your past favors when I hit the first stumbling block. We are friends. What I mean is, I'm your friend, and my conduct is proof that I'm not lying to you. While others you've protected before have betrayed you, I've come here to tell you about the coup your enemies are preparing against you. The thing is this: my General Leyva has asked three colonels (from the forty-fourth, the twenty-first, and me) to denounce, as if we ourselves had been approached, the proposals that, so the story goes, the generals who favor your candidacy are making to win over all troop commanders. The chiefs of the forty-fourth and the twenty-first—for the same reason they turned their backs on you since you resigned from the ministry—were glad to plot with Leyva in exchange for some benefits. Caught in the crossfire, what could I do? I agreed in order to fool them. But that's not the worst part. After the interview with Leyva, which took place early this evening, I learned that this very night they'll apprehend you when you least expect it. They plan to justify their actions by using our denunciations as well as a disturbance that Colonel Siqueiros, chief of the nineteenth, is going to create in Puebla against my General

Encarnación Reyes. They'll also apprehend my Generals Sandoval and Carrasco, along with the principal civilian leaders who work for your candidacy. And I know from a good source that all of you will be subjected to a summary trial that will sentence you to death. My General, I've kept faith with you by warning you in time. I ask only two things in return for warning you: don't hurt me by letting people know that I'm the one who came to you and ratted, and forgive me for bearing false witness. If I had refused to denounce you, I would have sacrificed myself, and what good would it have done me? It wouldn't have benefited you or anyone.... General López de la Garza, who was here a while ago, already knows of the plot against my General Reyes, and, by now, I guess, is on his way to Puebla."

Back in the living room, Aguirre quickly decided on a course of action with his friends. Clearly it was urgent to leave Mexico City as soon as possible. But where should they go? The governor of Jalisco wanted them to go to Guadalajara. There the troops under General Figueroa were Aguirristas. But traveling there was impossible, or nearly so. Then they thought of Puebla since it offered the best protection: Encarnación. But if the news about Colonel Siqueiros' disturbance was true, it wasn't prudent to take that route. They reached the conclusion that the quickest and surest course, perhaps the only feasible one, was to go to Toluca where they could count on the protection of General Elizondo, also an Aguirrista.

Aguirre gave a few commands as they prepared to leave. He ordered that two of the cars they had left in front of the house should rush to find Carrasco and Sandoval, with instructions to return immediately if they did not find them at home. He notified Cisneros, his secretary, and Cahuama and Rosas, the aides he still retained, about his trip. And, last of all, he thought about money.

As usual, he did not have more than three hundred pesos on him; in his house he probably had barely a thousand. He called Tarabana aside to ask him how much money they could get ahold of at that late hour:

"At home," Tarabana replied, "I have six thousand pesos that belong to me and fourteen thousand from the paving company."

"Would you risk lending them to me?"

Tarabana only said:

"I'll run and get them."

Ten minutes later Generals Carrasco and Sandoval showed up, and Tarabana returned at almost the same time.

The latter accompanied Aguirre to his study; behind the closed door he said to his friend:

"Do you want to take the money, or shall I?"

"I'll take it."

Tarabana then pulled out his wallet and took from it, with the deft and indifferent gesture of someone used to frequently handling large sums, a wad of bills. All were new; all identical. Holding them with his fingers, between which he still held the wallet, he pressed the edge of the package with the thumb of the other hand, as if he were counting the bills at a glance and said to Aguirre as he handed him the money:

"Exactly twenty thousand pesos. Forty five-hundred-peso bills."

Almost without looking, Aguirre placed the bills in the left inside pocket of his vest, and then the two friends returned to the living room.

Minutes later, they all went out to the street.

At the door, unexpectedly, a reporter from *El Gran Diario* accosted the candidate with youthful aplomb:

"Good evening, General. What luck to run into you so quickly! I came to interview you and to get the most sensational statement of our time from you, so maybe I'll get a raise."

He was almost an adolescent; judging by the innocence of his face, a child. Aguirre, who knew him well, answered sweetly:

"No, my young friend. I'm not up to making statements today."

The reporter noticed that Rosas and Cahuama were placing two carbines and several bundles of blankets into one of the cars. That made him exclaim:

"Big news! You're going on a trip!"

"No, young man," Aguirre replied, "I'm just going for a ride, and since you are a good friend, you'll do me the favor of not breathing a word about it."

"Only on one condition, my General."

"I'm sure you'll tell us..."

"Take me along."

For a moment pity, optimism, and self-interest vied in Aguirre's mind. Then he said:

"And if I ask you not to come along?"

"I'll run to the paper and will be doubly happy to give them the news."

"Well, in that case, come along."

Apart from the drivers, thirteen men got into the cars. Those who got into Aguirre's Cadillac, besides the candidate, were Axkaná, Domínguez, Tarabana, and Correa. Mijares, Carrasco, and Sandoval went with Olivier; in the remaining car, Cisneros, Cahuama, Rosas, and the reporter from *El Gran Diario*.

As they were leaving, Aguirre asked that the cars take a detour to the Calle de Rosas Moreno. The Cadillac stopped there in front of Rosario's house. The ex-minister got out; entered, and a few minutes later came out again. The shadow of a hand drew a net curtain; a head pressed against the pane of a balcony window...

It was eleven-thirty when the three cars left the Calzada de Tacubaya and headed for the highway.

III. The Plan of Toluca

AT MIDNIGHT TOLUCA'S STREETS WERE LIKE DESERTS BETWEEN THE houses. Glowing streetlights floated silently in the shadows; the dark, motionless outlines of the night watchmen seemed as if attached to the walls by the diagonal rays of their flashlights. Every now and then, a bark, a cry.

Aguirre and his twelve companions got out of the cars at the hotel entrance. They asked for many rooms; it would take a while to get them ready. Since they also had to wait for General Elizondo, for whom Aguirre sent Cahuama and Rosas, and since it was cold, Olivier asked for the bar to be opened.

Once there, they all settled according to their custom in such places and at such hours. There were three little tables; they chose seats around them in order to eat and drink. Aguirre asked for his daily drink: Hennessy Extra, a whole bottle; the others followed suit. The budding excitement generated by their having to leave Mexico City unexpectedly now became a firm and noisy optimism. They were now under Elizondo's military protection; they felt secure.

Sandoval and Carrasco did nothing but talk about the need to rise up in arms immediately. Elizondo's troops from the State of Mexico and those of Encarnación Reyes from Puebla could soon pounce on the capital, while Figueroa, maneuvering from Jalisco, could cut off the northern states from the Caudillo and Jiménez, and thereby deprive them of any possible help from the North American government. Then, when their magnificent strategic position became known, the "generals' strike" would come, just as it had in 1920. Whereupon, the rebellion would triumph in a month.

"Isn't it a good plan?" Sandoval asked the candidate. Between sips of cognac Aguirre replied:

"From a military standpoint it's not bad, but we have to study the political ramifications. The first thing we need to know is what course public opinion will take when the plot against us is revealed."

Olivier, who was sharing the bottle of Hennessy with Aguirre and Tarabana, had taken out his notebook and was jotting down—with the same enthusiasm as if they were motions to table and temporary motions at the Chamber—the points that, in his judgment, should be included in the plan of their movement. Made voluble by a surge of optimism, he recited aloud what he wrote:

"Considering, in the first place... Considering, in the second place..."

Between jottings, he observed several times:

"We shall see how history treats the Plan of Toluca."

Mijares, Axkaná, and Correa were speaking with Domínguez about General Figueroa's military resources in Jalisco; they considered the state of popular sentiment in the West. And so it was with all of them. Even the young correspondent from *El Gran Diario* unexpectedly engaged Cisneros in conversation, sketching out plans for political and military action. The journalist felt waves of euphoria flowing in his veins, activated by the mysterious virtue of the wine, in tandem with a new emotion: he felt raised, as if by magic, from his humble task as a reporter of great events to the rank of protagonist, or at least co-protagonist, of an important drama.

Aguirre was now fully committed, but he felt the need to rein in so much enthusiasm. On the table, next to him, there was a chessboard with pieces. He asked for it, and partly to rest from the political obsession, said to Olivier Fernández:

"Let's see who wins: the Hilaristas or the Radicals."

As if on springs, the rest of them jumped from their seats. Although they were not superstitious, the atavistic allure of the horoscope, the omen, the portent—heightened by the growing effects of the wine—took them over immediately. They all approached to see the match.

Although it was going Aguirre's way from the beginning, the match barely advanced, because minutes later General Elizondo entered the bar in the company of Cahuama and Rosas.

When they saw him appear, some were very effusive. And why not, since in the course of two hours, the chief of operations in the State of Mexico and his four thousand men had become

all-important in the minds of that small number of already perse-
cuted Aguirristas? Furthermore, it was understandable that not all
of them were able to control their feelings.

Perhaps on the basis of their high prerogative as generals,
Sandoval and Carrasco claimed the right, together with Aguirre,
to inform Elizondo of the facts and then decide with him on the
course of action. But Aguirre, displaying the firmness he adopted
whenever he felt like it, said, precluding any reply:

"No, gentlemen. First, General Elizondo and I will speak
alone. Then I will ask Olivier and General Domínguez to please
study the matter with Elizondo and me, and when we are finished,
I will tell you what needs to be done."

In a corner of the room facing the bar, the candidate and the
commander of the troops conversed. The conversation was long,
but in essence there was little to it. Aguirre began with categorical
declarations.

"Don't think," he said, "that I've come to implicate you, taking advantage of your repeated offers of help when the moment of
truth came. The Caudillo and Jiménez were preparing to seize me
and my friends tonight, to subject us to a summary court martial
under the pretext that I'm heading a rebellion. That's why we are
here. I've come, therefore, not to invite you to join an uprising but
to ask for your protection. You have four thousand men and we're
old friends, comrades in arms. You can, therefore, without the least
affront to the strictest military obedience, keep the Caudillo from
perpetrating an infamous attack on us. Since he won't order you to
arrest me as long as he suspects that you might disobey, my friends
and I run no risk by waiting in Toluca until matters are cleared up.
I already know the governor here is our enemy, but that doesn't
matter. It doesn't matter as long as it's understood that your forces
protect us. Does my request implicate you beyond what you were
prepared to do? If that is the case, tell me right now, give me (or let
me procure) horses and a few men, and within two hours we'll go
elsewhere.... Now, having said this, I also say that if you want, of
your own free will, to join your fate to mine and recommend that
we rise up in arms, because you think that's the only thing we can
do, then I am ready to reach a different type of agreement with
you. Without the least duplicity, however, I can tell you that I'm
not looking to start a rebellion."

With brief, northern precision, which in his case gave the impression of a deep and unshakable penchant for loyalty, Elizondo, his words given force by quiet emphasis, repeated several times:

"Justice is on your side and you are my friend, a friend to whom I owe many favors. I'm at your disposal; my troops are yours."

It was then agreed, in the presence of Olivier and Domínguez, that any decision would be postponed until they had news of what might happen to Encarnación Reyes that night in Puebla, and how he would react. And in order to deprive Catarino Ibáñez (the governor) of any pretexts—given his Hilarista hatred of Aguirristas—it was agreed that the Aguirristas' visit to Toluca should be disguised as part of a campaign tour. In the meantime, that would also allow Domínguez to find a way to warn General Figueroa in Jalisco to be on the alert for suspicious people and to be ready to act.

When the rest of the military officers and the politicians learned about Elizondo's favorable stance, the lights of the bar seemed to shine with a purer light. There were many rounds of drinks. General Elizondo chatted frankly and cheerfully, although only for a few moments, with Aguirre, with Tarabana, with Axkaná, with Carrasco. He drank with all of them. Finally, as he said goodbye, he made an important recommendation: the next day, the Aguirristas should approach him as little as possible. It was a crucial precaution.

On his way to the door he stopped for a moment to say to Aguirre:

"Catarino Ibáñez is more dangerous than you think. As a sign of good faith, I'm going to send you a bodyguard."

When Elizondo left, despite the late hour, no one thought anymore about going to bed. How could they, when nights spent like this—always the best for most of them—were irresistible for these veterans of revolutionary and political struggles? For now, they were all invaded by, and in the thrall of, the rare dynamic elation, the restless euphoria, that encourages hope in the face of chance. That feeling multiplied by a hundredfold their sense that every minute was special, and that they should partake of all the pleasures now available to them.

They called the bartender, ordered more bottles, and went back to the seats they had occupied a few minutes before.

"The Hilaristas lose!" exclaimed Olivier, throwing the chess pieces into the box.

In that state of mind, they reveled in their excesses for a long time, well into the pre-dawn hours.

Around four-thirty, when even the toughest of them was overtaken by exhaustion and wine, a captain, followed by two other officers, several sergeants, and some soldiers, appeared at the door. At that moment, the reporter of *El Gran Diario* was holding forth, for the hundredth time, with barely intelligible words, on his current theme: his lot was to be the official chronicler of the rebellion.

Several voices sounded a welcome to the soldiers:

"Now we have a bodyguard!"

"Well done, Elizondo!"

"Let's get to know each other!"

The three officers and the three sergeants approached Aguirre's table; the rest of the contingent was deployed, as if by design, between the exit door and the counter, between the counter and the tables, and among the tables.

"Have some cognac, Captain!" shouted Olivier, without even waiting for the head of the bodyguard to greet the ex–minister of war.

The captain took the glass and drank it in a gulp. Immediately, leaning over Aguirre, he said:

"My General, excuse me for interrupting you at this late hour..."

"You're not interrupting at all!" exclaimed Olivier, swaying in his chair.

At the same time, Aguirre said, as firmly as he could (although his words were noticeably slurred):

"Don't worry, comrade.... Just a few hours of happiness with my friends.... Do sit down."

The captain went on speaking without sitting:

"My General Elizondo orders me to ask you and your friends to come over and speak with him immediately. Would you be so kind as to come with me?"

In a total but fleeting flash of lucidity, Aguirre attempted to rise. But the captain and his aides had already seized him, as well as all those around the table. Meanwhile, beyond, the soldiers apprehended and disarmed the other men in the room. The assault was so sudden, so unimaginable, it was accomplished in ten seconds. When Aguirre had moved the glass from his lips, his friends were free; when he laid it on the coaster, they were prisoners. Truth is that in the whole group, no one, or almost no one, was in any condition to resist. Axkaná, Cahuama, and Rosas, the only ones who were moderately sober, rose in vain. Before their fingers reached their revolvers, they were already feeling the bayonets of Mausers against their bellies.

The captain ordered the escort and prisoners to leave the bar immediately. Aguirre, though still drunk, recovered his dignity. It did not look as if the two lieutenants who were helping him to leave were arresting him. Each holding an arm, they merely seemed to be accompanying him. On the other hand, Olivier, Mijares, Correa, and the journalist were practically carried out. Carrasco, Domínguez, and Sandoval put up a weak resistance; Tarabana slept. Axkaná, Cahuama, and Rosas walked, held by many hands and with the barrels of the pistols pointed at their faces. But the capture of the whole group had been silent: without a shot, without a cry.

There were more soldiers on the street. The three cars that came from Mexico were still there, by the sidewalk. The drivers, half-awake, sat up behind their steering wheels without realizing what was happening.

The captain had all the prisoners and their escorts get into the cars. He himself got into the one that would take Aguirre and Olivier, and immediately ordered the cars and the escort to get under way. In the first car, next to the driver, one of the sergeants gave directions.

Little by little Ignacio shook off his torpor. The image of Elizondo, the scenes at the bar, the vague forms of the soldiers keeping step alongside the car, were arranging themselves in his consciousness. Eventually, he had an almost clear idea of what had happened.

With a voice that was now less insecure, he asked the captain:

"Where did you say we're going?"

"To regimental headquarters, my General, which is where my General Elizondo is waiting for you, sir."

Aguirre kept silent and looked out the partially opened window. It was beginning to get light; brushstrokes of milky light rose to the sky beyond the farthest end of a street. A single phrase came to his mind, and he heard it syllable by syllable. His lips then took it and repeated it in a whisper, "strike at dawn," after which his mind, taking the phrase anew, strung it together into an idea: "Mexican politics has only one axiom: strike at dawn." Aguirre was reciting, to himself, Olivier Fernández's supreme political aphorism.

IV. El Gran Diario

IN A ROOM OF THE BARRACKS WHERE HE HAD BEEN DETAINED, Aguirre awoke hours later. He had no sense of alarm. Instead, he woke in the usual fashion, slowly becoming aware of faraway noises and basic bodily sensations. As his memory was restored, he suddenly understood the precariousness of his situation. But even that—a smile rose to his lips as he realized it—did not produce in him any deep anxiety, beyond what was reasonable. He understood, but in a distant sort of way, that his was a desperate case. Which is why what bothered him most at the moment was a practically negligible incoherence that arose from the unconscious but undeniable certainty that he had slept only a few hours, and the physiological illusion that a whole night had passed since the time of his arrest.

Lying on his back in the cot, he spent quite a while patching together his memories. He saw again the dim forms of his twelve friends in the light of dawn at the moment they crossed the courtyard of the barracks, as he, meanwhile, walked diagonally in relation to them. He recalled a pale and useless lantern held by a soldier leading the way; then a door opening; then, in the almost totally dark room, this dialogue with the captain:

"Why did you say General Elizondo was waiting for me here?"

"I was ordered to do so, my General."

"Well," he said, after a brief pause, "then, listen to me."

And taking from his pocket the five gold *aztecas* he had there, gave them to the captain and said:

"Please take this in case I need something."

Now he thought, "perhaps those will turn out to be the best spent one hundred pesos of my life."

The room in which he was being held had no opening except the door. The darkness was almost total. The light of day shone, in a bright, thin horizontal line, between the door and the floor.

He had not taken off his clothes. He stood and, almost feeling his way, walked toward the line of light. He held his watch to the very edge of the luminous angle, to see what time it was. The watch had stopped at ten.... From the other side of the door he heard steps; further away, military sounds.... Aguirre wound his watch, which he set at twelve, calculating that it must be noon, and he returned to the cot. Soon after a bugle sounded: his calculation was off only by a few minutes.

One, two, three hours went by. Not hours of uncertainty and unease, but of serene awareness of what it all meant. Elizondo's betrayal had been unthinkable when the captain and the escort came to the hotel. But now that it had taken place, it all seemed perfectly logical to Aguirre. For Elizondo, supporting him would have meant gambling everything; betraying him was risk-free and secured the victory of Aguirre's rivals, a victory that would also be Elizondo's.

Aguirre whispered, "Elizondo will be minister of war in Hilario Jiménez's administration."

From these reflections, into which he fell again as soon as he left them, he went on to others and others. For a few seconds, he evoked Rosario's hand, drawing the balcony curtain by way of farewell; he saw her outline against the windowpanes. He thought at times about his wife, and about Axkaná. Several times he remembered the latter's words on the evening of his final interview with the Caudillo. From Axkaná, his mind jumped to *La Mora*, then to Olivier, then to the image of Colonel Zaldívar getting rid of the taste of tequila by drinking cognac. Since his thoughts did not feel an urgent need to become clear, they drifted in a leisurely manner. Profound, unmoved, his fatalism made him feel that the die of his destiny was no longer in the cup.

Inside and outside his room, time ran with a uniform rhythm that was finally broken when, for the first time, voices and steps stopped behind the door. Then bits and pieces of shadows danced in the line of light. Something rustled between the board and the floor, something that first struck the door on the outside and then slid into the room. Aguirre got up slowly to see.

They had slipped him a newspaper.

"The first fruit of my hundred pesos," the candidate murmured.

By the light of the crack he read, character by character, the name of the newspaper and the headlines. As if by magic, the mystery of each syllable was solved. But that magic suddenly turned to amazement. *El Gran Diario* said that Aguirre and his supporters had risen up in arms. "In arms!" Kneeling, bent over, and with his face almost touching the ground, the candidate began to feel his identity melting away; he laughed at himself for a few moments.

The weak light under the door was insufficient to read the smaller print: the captions and the articles themselves. Aguirre returned to the bed; he sat on it and spread out the paper by the light of the matches he still had in his pocket.

Strictly speaking, *El Gran Diario* itself did not assert anything: it offered only three lines, and then an official statement followed by two very long press releases with all the paragraphs in quotation marks. It was therefore evident that the newspaper was not reporting what it knew to be true, but rather what it was forced to report. The first lines of the text were eloquent in their brevity. The article read as follows:

"After midnight yesterday, rumors of military uprisings in Puebla and Toluca reached this paper. We immediately turned to the president's chief of staff to request an official confirmation. There General Carlos Torres, chief of the aides of the president of the Republic, said to us: 'Several units garrisoned in Mexico City were on the verge of abandoning their barracks this evening, lured deceitfully by the rebellion that certain disloyal parties had been preparing. Fortunately, the commanders of the sixteenth, twenty-first, and forty-fourth battalions, in accordance with their duty, informed their superiors in time about the rebels' plans, and made it possible for those plans to be almost totally destroyed thanks to the most efficacious intervention of General Protasio Leyva, Head of Military Operations in the Valley. Regarding the events that took place in Puebla and Toluca, this office will make available to the press, within two hours, detailed press releases.' 'What connection is there between these events and the presidential candidates?' we asked General Torres. 'Regarding this,' he answered, 'I will also give you an official report soon.'"

The press releases, without any commentary by the paper, followed. The first was signed by the Caudillo and it said:

"From the beginning of the electoral contest I was aware of the seditious acts carried out by General Ignacio Aguirre and some of his supporters. I learned that military leaders had been invited to rebel against the government. Several Aguirrista agents traveled throughout the Republic for the purpose of bribing the commanders of different units. Furthermore, it is common knowledge that in declarations to the press and in speeches, Aguirre as well as his backers had constantly announced, in more or less covert language, their firm intention to resort to arms. Despite all this, this government always maintained a serene attitude; never interfering with the man who had himself declared the Progressive Radical candidate; allowing ample freedom of action; providing an example of patriotism; and promising that public suffrage would be respected. In this regard, the conduct of the government was so clear that General Aguirre was never able to level any justified charges of partiality. All this, unfortunately, has been to no avail. General Aguirre managed to corrupt the greater part of the forces commanded by General Encarnación Reyes; yesterday evening these forces were in open rebellion in Puebla, and Aguirre was on the verge of achieving similar results with several battalions in the capital. In fact, he planned matters so the movement would erupt at the same time here, in Puebla, and in Toluca. Thanks to the energetic intervention of General Leyva and the loyal service of Colonels Jáuregui, Acosta, and Hernández, the uprising in the capital completely failed. In Puebla, the traitorous General Encarnación Reyes has taken possession of the state after disarming and cowardly executing the honorable Colonel Siqueiros and almost all the officers of the nineteenth regiment, who refused to abet their treasonous plans. Finally, in Toluca—where Aguirre and the movement's principal leaders were headed shortly before they expected the military uprising to start—the attempted coup had almost no success at all. The upright General Julián Elizondo was quickly able to persuade the officers and the troops, who were about to forget their duty, of the error of their ways, leaving Aguirre with no choice but to escape with a small number of military and civilian followers. The government I preside over has, without delay, taken energetic measures to fight and destroy these traitors. At one o'clock this afternoon General Aispuro, with five thousand men, will set out, together with forces from Tlaxcala and Veracruz, to begin the advance on Puebla, and within forty-eight hours, I assure the nation, Aguirre and all those with him will have fallen into the hands of loyal troops; he is already being closely pursued. Finally, I make a solemn promise to the nation: if this government was indulgent at the beginning, to the point of overlooking many offenses that were being committed, now at the hour of the crime it will know how to impose a rigorous punishment, without preference or compassion, on all the military and civilians who have disrupted public order, threatened our fundamental institutions, and been responsible for the shedding of innocent blood."

This is what the Caudillo's official bulletin said. Right below, in the same column came the statement, also official, that Hilario Jiménez, as a presidential candidate, addressed to the people of the Republic:

"I am the first," he asserted, "to regret the painful events that are occurring. During my whole campaign, I have declared emphatically the duty of all concerned to seek victory through the ballot box, not through violence. But, in any case, my personal impression is that the coup plotted by Aguirre and his associates is bound to total failure, despite the fact that the traitorous General Encarnación Reyes controls the state of Puebla at present. So that he could not be accused of partiality in the elections, the president endured in silence the seditious propaganda Aguirre and his followers disseminated among the military; thus he holds the moral high ground. He can also count on the support of almost the entire army who will back him unanimously in punishing the traitors. And, finally, he can count on the nation's great yearning for peace, anxious as it is to see its rulers gain power by legal, rather than violent, means. The final result, therefore, is not difficult to foresee: within a matter of days, total order will reign in the country, further demonstrating the lack of intellectual and moral worth of those whose ambition was to govern without just claim. Should it turn out that I have been deceived in my assessment, I offer to suspend my political work—since all must be sacrificed in the interest of patriotism—and ask the supreme government to accept my service as a soldier to the extent of my modest ability. Then, also, I will invite the masses of peasants and workers who support my candidacy to cooperate with the loyal Army Operations Headquarters in the total destruction of the parties who seek to betray our fatherland."

Aguirre reread, until the last flicker of the last match, the false official reports of his uprising. His indignation was so great that it seemed to have made him numb, ruled by only one imperative: to keep before his eyes the proof that *El Gran Diario* had really printed what he was reading. He had seen, committed, and helped to commit many atrocities during the Revolution, but all of them—robberies, looting, abductions, rapes, murders, mass executions, the blackest treasons—taken altogether, paled by comparison to this single one.

He remained stunned for a long time, stupefied by an inexpressive and mute rage that rendered him as motionless as an object and seemed to last forever. An image shook him for a moment, Pancho Villa's. "Monstrous as his assassination was," he thought, "this one, mine, is going to be even more monstrous, more cowardly and ignoble."

Suddenly the locks and the bolt of the door creaked; one of the leaves of the door opened; the same captain who came at dawn entered, along with several other soldiers.

"I have orders for you to come with me, my General."

Aguirre looked out from the shadow, hiding his rage behind the most remote indifference:

"Are you going to execute me here?"

"No, my General. It seems they're taking you to Mexico City."

His indifference stopped for a few seconds:

"You say 'They're taking *you!*' What about my comrades?"

"I think all of you are going, my General."

Aguirre prepared himself and left the cell, surrounded by guards. When he reached the courtyard, he saw his Cadillac, and beyond that, two military trucks, all ringed by many soldiers. A colonel and several officers of the regiment—he knew the colonel well—were waiting by the car door. The colonel, when he saw the ex–minister of war, approached to salute him and said:

"I'm ordered to take you to Mexico City, my General. You're to go in your own car."

Mute, Aguirre nodded, he approached the car; the driver at the steering wheel was not his. He got in. And then, through the windshield—the other windows had drawn curtains—he saw that the two trucks were occupied by his comrades and by a great number of soldiers.

The colonel and three officers sat in the Cadillac with Aguirre; next to the driver were two sergeants.

The two trucks and the car started out. It must have been around five in the afternoon. Outside, the blue of the sky of an absolute purity—a December sky—was turning the faintest violet hues.

V. Manuel Segura

A BEAUTIFUL PACKARD, STOPPED BY A CAVALRY PICKET, BLOCKED THE entrance to the highway for a few minutes. Then the vehicles carrying the prisoners set off.

Aguirre noticed immediately that the smooth progress of the three vehicles was swift and uniform, almost noiseless, and they drove along without using their horns. This unimpeded progress was perhaps explained by the fact that the road was clear as far as the eye could see; no one and nothing was on it. Such solitude seemed somewhat suspicious to him, and he could not help relating it to the traces of the argument he thought he had witnessed during the scene with the Packard and the horsemen.

His guards, facing him and on either side, kept silent. He amused himself by observing, his pupils motionless, the parallel displacement of the two small white columns of dust made by the trucks ahead. A soft breeze was blowing; and the two lines, at an angle with respect to the road, rose in an odd manner: while the upper halves spread across the deep blue of the sky, the lower halves, fine, thin, cut energetically across the green mass of the mountains. Never until this hour had Aguirre discovered that the harmony of forms and colors could hold such interest. He momentarily regretted the slight nearsightedness of one of his eyes.

In a flash, they passed through Lerma and the villages by the side of the road. They soon came to a series of curves and steep grades that the three vehicles negotiated and scaled, again without blowing their horns or taking any other precautions. There—and further on, when they reached the valleys—the solitude of the road, suffused by the dusk, seemed even greater than in the straight stretches of the plain. There was not a cart on the road; not a horse; not even one of those Indians, bent over under enormous burdens, who move to the side of the road with sad resignation when a car passes. Evidently, orders had been given to suspend all traffic.

Far up the mountain, between two curves in the road, the first truck stopped suddenly; the other one stopped immediately behind it. The colonel ordered the Cadillac's driver to slow down, and the officers and sergeants to have their weapons ready. But Aguirre soon saw there was no cause for concern, at least not for those escorting the prisoners. A group of soldiers on foot now came into view; they calmly approached the two trucks they had stopped. Three more trucks—these seemed to come from the opposite direction—appeared, followed by two cars.

One of the officers said to the colonel, "It seems that some troops are waiting for us there."

When the Cadillac arrived, several officers emerged from the other cars and walked over. The colonel also got out to meet them. Aguirre recognized them instantly: one was General Leyva; the other, his nephew Major Manuel Segura; and the rest, aides of the Valley of Mexico's Operations Headquarters. Following them was Canuto Arenas, the chief of Leyva's bodyguard, with other officers.

Fifty meters from the Cadillac, Leyva and the colonel saluted each other and began to talk. Leyva must have said something very funny at the beginning, because his aides seemed to laugh a lot, and the colonel, to judge from the movement of his back, also seemed to be laughing. Then the aides moved a few steps away, just as the colonel and the general, already deep into a serious conversation, walked to one side of the road. Leyva seemed to be explaining something that the colonel, to judge from his gestures, did not understand or agree with. But Leyva seemed to insist with greater eloquence; he drew closer to the colonel, placed a hand on his shoulder. And the colonel then unbuttoned his tunic, took out a sheet of paper from his pocket and handed it, unfolded, to Leyva so that he could read it. Aguirre was sure they were discussing the handover of the prisoners. Leyva, without a doubt, demanded them immediately; the colonel, resisting the handover, showed his orders.

Just then, far away, coming from the direction of Toluca, they heard the sound of a car horn. Leyva, perhaps surprised, called Segura, to whom he said something very peremptory and brief, after which Segura got into one of the cars and dashed down the mountain. Aguirre did not see him when he passed—the curtains on the side windows, fully drawn, prevented him from doing so—but he felt the buzzing of the motor half a meter away.

Turning his eyes back to where Leyva and the colonel were speaking, Aguirre thought:

"If they hand me over here, they'll kill me here."

And his thought spurred on the deeds, because soon it seemed it was settled that the handover would take place there. Leyva was already putting away the folded sheet that the colonel had shown him before, smiled a lot at the colonel, shook his hand, approached his car, and the colonel, once the farewell was complete, joined the group of Canuto Arenas and the aides, and with them walked over to the prisoners' trucks.

One of Leyva's officers came to line up the soldiers standing along the side of the road. He and two others then formed the troops into a narrow barrier, placing the prisoners' trucks between two files of soldiers. The colonel gave orders out loud; his officers obeyed them. And then the prisoners got out, one by one: Axkaná, Sandoval, Tarabana, Olivier, the reporter from *El Gran Diario*, Correa, Cahuama, Cisneros, Rosas, Domínguez, Carrasco, and Mijares.

Seeing them thus, in individual succession and from a distance, Aguirre felt as though he was discovering, for the first time, the most characteristic physical features of his friends. He mouthed the names of each one; his eyes took in all twelve. Pale, hungry, and dirty, they all looked intensely nervous—but only one appeared to be depressed: Carrasco. Aguirre then felt a deep emotion, inspired by those twelve men whom Leyva would surely slaughter together with him. Though he managed not to reveal the least sign of what he felt, he did not feel it less strongly. As his body calmly rested on the cushions of the car, his soul surrendered to the most agonizing surge of compassion. Then he was tormented by Axkaná's placid air and the childish restlessness of the young journalist, curious in the midst of danger.

"They," he thought, "are the ones who least deserve it."

Just then, the chief of the soldiers who had accompanied the prisoners in the trucks came over to the Cadillac to convey orders to the colonel: Aguirre's guards were to lead him over to join his comrades.

Aguirre got out. He got out without even grabbing his coat, which he had found on the seat when he got into the car in Toluca. Then he walked until he was within the barrier, where he was met with mute questions: Olivier gave him a strange look, and the journalist smiled at him. Softness and rigidity vied on the young man's lips as he attempted an affectionate greeting.

Canuto Arenas had gone over to make arrangements with several aides; he and they spoke by the other trucks. A soldier came over to show them something—ropes, it seemed—which Canuto looked at and passed to the others. After a cursory look, the aides returned the ropes to Canuto, and then, with Canuto holding the ropes, they all approached the place where the prisoners were under guard. As he saw the chief of Leyva's escort approach—fierce face, muscular body—Emilio Olivier turned to Aguirre and said:

"Now are you convinced I was right?"

Without answering him, Aguirre leaned toward the journalist, who was also speaking to him:

"General," he said, "don't think I regret not following the advice you gave me last night at your house. Come what may, I'm not a coward. You have my word of honor!"

The others were silent.

Canuto and the aides had already reached the prisoners when the sound of two cars coming up the slope gave way to the appearance of the cars themselves. The prisoners—all but Aguirre—turned anxious, eager looks in that direction. Canuto and his men—the latter a bit uneasy—also looked and interrupted the preparations they had begun. The first of the cars was the one in which Major Segura had left just minutes before; it stopped about fifty meters down the road. The other car stopped right behind, since the first one was placed so as to prevent its going further.

A little later, Segura and a tall, blond, and apparently foreign man walked by the prisoners and did not stop until they reached Leyva's car. They spoke a bit there—surely with Leyva—after which, on the way back, they passed along the barrier made by the soldiers. They were arguing heatedly. The foreigner—a Yankee, to judge by his accent—was saying:

"In any case: it goes against the most basic diplomatic courtesy. To do this to an ambassador!"

And Segura replied:

"You don't have to tell me. The general is the first to regret this. But as I already said, in Toluca you'll be able..."

Aguirre then recognized the foreigner as one of the occupants of the Packard he had seen as they left Toluca. He turned to look at the cars; the beautiful Packard was there. The other prisoners had also identified the tall, blond man, and this started them whispering. Olivier made a move to go beyond the barrier, evidently with the intention of addressing the Yankee, but two soldiers held him back, and Canuto gave Olivier's head such a strong blow that it knocked him to the ground. The prisoners became agitated; aides and soldiers restored order by pistol-whipping and hitting them with rifle butts. Aguirre wound up between Tarabana, Cahuama, and Rosas. Tarabana whispered to him, as he looked at the foreigner:

"It's Winter.... I know him... first secretary..."

But Arenas, who noticed that Tarabana was talking, silenced him in mid-speech with a threatening look.

The foreigner got into the Packard, which at once did a U-turn and left, immediately followed by the two trucks that had come from Toluca. In the trucks were the colonel, the officers, and the soldiers who, until then, had escorted the prisoners. Only the prisoners and Leyva's men remained in that corner of the mountain.

By the time Segura left the foreigner in his car and rejoined Canuto and the aides, they had already resumed the task that had been interrupted. Standing behind the man who, at that moment, was still a candidate to the presidency of the Republic, Canuto said:

"Hands behind your back, Mr. Whatshisname. I'm gonna tie them up for you."

Aguirre didn't answer him; he didn't even turn to look at him. Addressing the soldiers, he said:

"Boys, I won't stand in the way of your carrying out whatever orders you've been given regarding me. If necessary, you can kill me right now. But what is the point of humiliating me with degrading precautions? It dishonors you, as well as me, to tie my hands at this point. I am a divisional general, I was minister of war, I still consider myself a candidate to the presidency of the Republic. Since all this is true, and I am ready to die, will you let me be treated like a bandit?"

His eloquence was so natural—for his manner even more than his words—that a wave of guilt made the soldiers hesitate and look at each other. Segura perceived this unexpected effect and rushed to quash it. Confronting Aguirre, he said with a base arrogance that underscored the coarseness of the phrase and the vulgarity of the gesture:

"You may have been a general and a minister, but here you're nothing but a *puro jijo de la tiznada*—a dirty son of a bitch."

Standing beside Aguirre, Cahuama, whose eyes were still moist from the tears his chief's words had elicited, lost control. Segura's insult made him automatically raise his arm, move his hand, and strike General Leyva's nephew. Segura only became aware of Cahuama's blow and the fact that his face was bleeding when he regained his balance, thanks to two soldiers.

Two of the aides leapt upon the attacker. But Segura, now back on his feet with his pistol out of the holster, and totally out of his mind, shouted:

"Leave him… leave him alone…!"

And he went to Cahuama and, placing the barrel of the revolver against his belly, Segura made him walk backwards to the rhythm of the same phrase:

"*Son of a bitch… Son of a bitch… Son of a bitch…*"

And in this manner Segura forced Cahuama back up against the road's guardrail, and there, after repeating the insult two more times, shot him twice.

Cahuama doubled over and fell into the ditch.

VI. Death at Twilight

THEY ALL WITNESSED THE SCENE IN ABSOLUTE SILENCE. NOW TWO officers held Ignacio Aguirre by the shoulders while Canuto tied his hands behind his back; other officers and soldiers did the same with the remaining prisoners. But they'd run out of rope by the time they came to Axkaná and the reporter from *El Gran Diario*.

"Tell the man in charge of the trucks to give you something else to tie them with," Segura ordered a sergeant.

Two minutes later, the sergeant returned saying that the only things that could be used for tying were what he had in his hands—a piece of copper wire and a piece of electric wire about a meter long.

"They'll do," said Arenas.

So, they used the wires to tie the hands of the last two prisoners: the almost inflexible copper wire for the journalist; the coated, flexible wire for Axkaná. They tied the wire so tightly on the young reporter that one of his wrists started to bleed a few seconds later.

Once this was done, they made the group of prisoners walk about eighty meters up the road. From his car Leyva saw them pass. Most turned back to look at him. Resisting the soldiers' shoves and rifle butts, Carrasco even tried to stop for a moment, and shouted at him:

"Please, Leyva, just one word!"

But others, like Aguirre and Axkaná, who now walked side by side, simply pretended that the instrument of Hilario Jiménez and the Caudillo was not there, just ten paces away. Certain they were going to be killed, life mattered less to them now than their determination not to display any weakness. Some had already chosen the phrase their mouth would pronounce when the bullets hit them: "¡Viva México!" In the cruelest hours of the Revolution that is what Bauche Alcalde, Berlanga, and Bolaños had said, and the marvelous vanishing twilight that now enveloped them inspired them to say it.

Beyond the bend of the road, on the left, was a hollow that ran down one side until it faded into the nearby valley; on the other side of the road the hollow spread upward until it broke against the escarpments of the mountain. That is where the soldiers led the captives, making them walk three hundred or four hundred meters, until the road was hidden by the mass of the hill.

Segura ordered a halt. He arranged the soldiers into three groups: one on the right, in an oblique line toward the sheer side of the mountain; another group arranged in the same way on the left; and the last group placed in the center behind the prisoners, so as to block access to the hollow on the side of the valley. In this manner, with the mountain as the background and the hill as the foreground, the prisoners were enclosed by a quadrilateral without exit. On the hill was an almost perfectly vertical natural declivity: that is where the executions would take place.

But before the soldiers could take their places, an unexpected event altered the course of the execution. When he heard the orders Segura was giving, Aguirre could no longer contain himself. He said:

"You and Leyva are murderers, but you don't even know how to kill."

This short phrase, spoken with such deep disdain—with such offensive, derogatory, and lordly haughtiness—was at that moment guaranteed to provoke a man like Major Manuel Segura, whose face was still bleeding.

General Leyva's nephew did not so much as open his lips. He took out his revolver and with a coldness matching that of Aguirre's words, without betraying the least emotion, and without further preparation than motioning to the soldiers to get out of the way, he shot Aguirre in the chest.

"See, I *do* know how to kill!" he said in a tone that was terribly calm and strange, as if he were explaining, through the execution of that act, that although the art of killing was difficult, it was easy for him.

Aguirre had not budged; he'd waited for the bullet with absolute calm. And he was so conscious of his self-control that in that fraction of an instant—as the panorama of his revolutionary and political life flashed through his mind—he admired himself and felt cleansed of his faults. He chose to fall with the dignity with which others rise.

As Aguirre hit the ground, the other prisoners, acting on an irresistible impulse, broke through the guards and ran toward the mountain where there were fewer soldiers. They ran, and at first no one attempted to stop them. The contrast between the two scenes and what motivated them was so abrupt—Segura's cold-blooded killing of Aguirre, who fell majestically; and the prisoners, overcome by sudden panic—that the soldiers stood perplexed, listless, detached. Reacting instantly, Segura threatened them with his pistol and shouted:

"After them, you idiots! After them! Kill them all!"

Only Axkaná had not fled. He remained there, motionless, his gaze fixed on Aguirre's body. A space of two meters and the criminal Segura stood between the corpse of one friend and the sorrow of the other.

For several seconds Segura watched Arenas, the aides, and the soldiers begin their hunt of the fugitives. Then, turning to Axkaná, he raised his pistol and fired. Axkaná felt the bullet enter his body between his left nipple and shoulder, and fell. It was not unbearable pain that brought him down; nor was it a real physical collapse. It was the irresistible need to also succumb, to succumb beside his friend because it was some consolation to be killed by the same hand.

When Aguirre fell, he'd bowed his head in such a way that his hat came off and rolled to his feet. Axkaná still had his hat on; his head rested on a bush. In his mind, his desire to die stumbled for an instant on that immediate difference; he'd thought that his death would replicate his friend's, detail by detail, gesture by gesture.

His eyes were open and motionless, but he sensed—he sensed without thinking—that he could have moved them at will. Before his eyes, his field of vision limited above by the brim of his hat, were the legs of Segura who had approached Aguirre's corpse. Between Segura's legs Axkaná saw an arm reach down, and a hand that was feeling for the dead man's chest wound. There the hand ran into something; it unbuttoned the vest, flipped one side of it over, and immediately took out a wad of bills, the fingers stained with blood. The fingers wiped the blood off on the dead man's shirt, and the arm and hand rose once more out of view. Then the other arm reached down, this one armed with the pistol; the barrel stopped above the ear—Axkaná closed his eyes—the shot was heard…

When Axkaná raised his eyelids again, Segura's legs had disappeared. Far off, beyond Aguirre's corpse, he could see soldiers running and shooting. Now, Axkaná could not only see, he could hear: he heard distant screams and shots being fired; he also felt the lukewarm moistness of the blood soaking his chest. His eyes scanned the facing mountain. Though twilight had fallen, and it was almost dark now, he could easily make out the ways in which his comrades were dying some four hundred meters away. He thought he saw the journalist rolling down from a rock, and Olivier, who'd climbed with incredible effort, also fell.

His inclination to die disappeared in a mounting horror, a sense of terror, of panic, of ungovernable fear.

He tried to move his arms and legs, and discovered that he could.

He sat up.

He stood.

He ran.

He ran down toward the valley, along the hills that separated the hollow from the road. The pain in his chest soon tired him, and having his arms tied behind his back increased the pain as well as hampered his ability to run. He stumbled; every ten steps he lost his balance; he was about to fall. He had traveled barely a hundred meters when the whistle of bullets announced that he was being pursued. For an instant, he turned to see: six or seven soldiers ran after him, although they were still far away. He resumed his flight; they kept shooting at him.

In this manner, he ran for three or four more minutes, pursued by the bullets. He reached a spot where a trail opened between two hills; to protect himself from the bullets he went there. The trail led him suddenly to the edge of a small cliff, it ended so abruptly that at first he had mistaken the rising tops of the distant trees below for weeds and bushes sprouting from the ground. He lay down to keep from falling into the gorge. Almost exhausted, he rose again and ran, panting, another few steps along the rising precipice to the slope of the second hill. For now, the soldiers could not see or fire at him.

Once on the other slope he advanced fifty or sixty meters, on an incline almost parallel to the previous one. The end of this slope overlooked the edge of a craggy hillside that at that spot made a violent fold and plummeted like the bed of a dried arroyo. Axkaná stopped. There were only two choices: either go over the edge, or hide among the boulders. If he chose the former, the soldiers would reach him in less than ten minutes; if he chose the latter, they would find him in five or six. He looked around. To his left, about fifty paces away, he could see the treetops poking over the edge of the cliff; the trees were so close they almost grazed the edge of the drop-off. In a flash, he knew what he had to do: he shook his head between his knees to make his hat fall off, and then, without hesitation, immediately ran to the cliff and jumped. He jumped with such fury that it didn't look as if he were trying to save himself but rather trying to commit suicide, ending it once and for all.

The leaves and branches of a tree opened up; Axkaná fell between them for an indefinite, seemingly infinite, time. Head-first, eyes closed, his hands and arms still bound, he fell, giving himself over entirely to the forces of chance. Sharp ends scratched him; he slammed into hard surfaces and rebounded; rough edges seemed to strip all the skin off of his face. Something stabbed his back and then ripped his flesh through his clothes before wedging itself between his wrists, which creaked and twisted. And there he stayed: legs above, neck against the fork of a tree, and hooked, hanging from the electric cord that a second ago had rendered his hands useless. He opened his eyes. The last glimmers of the afternoon were fading among the branches above. He remained motionless. Soon he heard running and the voices of the soldiers. He sensed the moment when his pursuers stopped to look at his hat. Then he heard them run on, shouting. They fired their rifles. He heard other shots much farther away.

Part of Axkaná's back rested on a branch; part hung in the void. Aware that one of his legs had found secure support, he moved the other there, in order to relieve the pain in his shoulder, which was becoming unbearable. He then noticed that the weight of his body was stretching the wire around his wrists and loosening the knots. So, he alternated relief and pain until his hands managed to reach the spot where the electric cord had become stuck.

Making a supreme effort—and being careful to ensure he didn't lose the support of the branch under his back—he pushed with his feet until his body had passed between his arms (his shoulder felt as if it were tearing!), and he was able to sit astride the fork in the tree that had previously cradled his head. Then he rested, light-headed from the pain of the gunshot wound and the bruising from the fall, and tormented by vertigo.

Night was falling. A white line, now barely perceptible about two hundred meters away, cut across the downward slope of the cliff's base: it was the road. Axkaná gazed at it remotely. A strong dizziness and the sudden accumulation of a lifetime's worth of dramatic events were unhinging him. A little later, he again heard voices and running. He held his breath; it seemed the soldiers were leaving.

A period of silence, of solitude followed. Early stars appeared in the darkest part of the sky. Only the whispering of the wind could be heard. Placing all his weight on the right arm, and pushing with his feet, Axkaná was able to raise himself with his hands and finally managed to free himself and stand up. The last residue of light allowed him to assume the posture he found least uncomfortable.

He did not have the least idea what he could do. He examined his wound. The bullet had entered below the shoulder joint, also wounding the arm; he was still bleeding profusely. His shoulder, finally at rest, was paralyzed by an acute piercing pain that spread across his chest and down into his elbow. From what he had seen at first, and from what he saw now, he figured it would not be impossible for him to get down from the tree. The trunk, which was not very tall, had outgrowths. He waited.

A while later, the solitude of the mountain, now inhabited by nocturnal sounds, was shaken by the faraway, harsh grinding of car engines: no doubt, the trucks and cars of Leyva's men, leaving. For several minutes these noises echoed across the valleys. The clutches of the trucks engaged and disengaged as they descended the grades. All of that gradually moved away; vanished.

Axkaná then faced deadly moments of indecision. Should he get down from the tree? If so, why? But he was no longer guided by his conscious will; he was guided by instinct and, above all, by pain. With one arm immobilized, and the other blindly feeling for support among the branches, he descended slowly. Clinging to the trunk, he slid down until he found a foothold. Somehow keeping his balance, he managed to slide his hand over the bark and stretch out his foot until he found another toehold farther down. Thus, little by little, he reached the ground. There he felt so faint that he had to lean against the tree for several minutes to avoid falling over. Then he oriented himself toward the road and began to walk slowly, between stones, between plants. He had not eaten for almost twenty-four hours, and he had lived centuries since then.

He had advanced about a hundred meters when he was assailed by the fear that he was not walking toward, but parallel to the road. His vertigo returned, and he staggered. He sat down for a moment. After a while, confident he was headed in the right direction, he stood up and with great effort resumed his march.

When he at last reached the edge of the road, he was overwhelmed by a single, overwhelming desire: to lie down, to stretch out. He let himself fall. But he did not remain thus for long. Soon, beams of light broke the monolithic darkness of the mountain above him; he then heard the faraway honking of a car horn, quickly drawing near; and finally, he saw the round and enormous headlights of a car coming around a curve.

Axkaná then half-crawled toward the middle of the road. There, with his face distorted and tragically lengthened in the beams of the headlights, he knelt, stood, and again fell to his knees, his hand raised. The gesture was one of despair, not weakness or entreaty: it was all the same to him if that car came to his aid or crushed him.

Five or six meters away the headlights came to a stop. A door opened and closed; the silhouette of a driver was outlined against the light; then, behind it, another shape. Stretched on the ground, Axkaná saw in the light two faces above his, observing him. He heard another person from the car asking something in English. One of the men near him, whom he vaguely recognized as Winter— the foreigner who'd been in the Packard stopped by Leyva's soldiers—also answered in English.

The person who had spoken from beyond the headlights said something else and then Winter and the driver took Axkaná in their arms and brought him to the car.

VII. A Pair of Earrings

THE DAY AFTER IGNACIO AGUIRRE'S DEATH, THE NEWSPAPERS IN Mexico City did not speak in much detail about the uprising in Toluca. Once again, a force greater than them kept them from saying what they knew. *El Gran Diario* ran only an official bulletin under this revealingly vague headline: "Court Martial in the State of Mexico." The bulletin read:

"In the early hours of the morning, the president's chief of staff made the following bulletin available to us:

'General Ignacio Aguirre, the principal perpetrator of the uprising that began last night, was captured, along with a group of his followers, by the loyal forces of the State of Mexico under the command of the honorable Divisional General Julián Elizondo. The prisoners were brought before a summary court martial and executed by firing squad. Relatives may pick up their corpses at the capital's *Hospital Militar*. The corpses are those of the following persons: Divisional General Ignacio Aguirre; Brigadier General Agustín J. Domínguez, governor of Jalisco; Señor Eduardo Correa, mayor of the City of Mexico; attorneys Emilio Olivier Fernández and Juan Manuel Mijares, deputies to the National Congress; ex-Generals Alfonso Sandoval and Manuel D. Carrasco; Captains Felipe Cahuama and Sebastián Rosas; and *señores* Remigio Tarabana, Alberto Cisneros, and Guillermo Ruiz de Velasco.'"

On an inside page of Section Two, *El Gran Diario* also published, in different sizes, the twelve death notices. Aguirre's took up an eighth of a page and said briefly:

"On the fifth day of this month, Divisional General Ignacio Aguirre passed away. It is with deep sorrow that his grieving wife and other relatives make this known to you. Mexico, December 6."

And the others were similar.

But the laconic style of the newspapers ironically did nothing but exacerbate the surprise and consternation of the public, even as it silenced them. The city went on living as always, but only in appearance. It bore its shame and sorrow on the inside.

Close to noon, the Cadillac that had once belonged to General Aguirre came to a stop on Avenida Madero, at the door of *La Esmeralda*. The slouching driver—dirty, badly dressed—did not move from his seat. A man opened the door and got out: it was Major Manuel Segura. The car drove on, and Segura, adjusting the revolver in his belt, entered the jewelry store.

The clerk who came to the counter looked Segura up and down a bit, made the client repeat (twice) what he wanted, went to the rear of the store, and soon returned with several pairs of diamond earrings wrapped in velvet cloth.

Segura selected the pair that had the largest stones, and, after looking them over, asked how much they cost.

"Six thousand, five hundred pesos."

Segura looked at them again. He said almost immediately:

"I don't like them. I want them larger."

The same scene was repeated with a pair of earrings that cost eleven thousand, five hundred pesos, and later with another worth seventeen thousand. Finally, the clerk showed Segura what he wanted:

"Twenty thousand pesos. In this size, there are no better diamonds."

Segura received the box and paid. He paid with a wad of forty five-hundred peso bills. All forty bills had the same tear—it was almost a perforation—and all forty had the same dark stain that extended almost a centimeter from the tear to the center.

As he counted the bills, the clerk noticed the stain and hesitated for a moment. He raised his eyes; Segura's eyes made him lower them again. Then the clerk pretended to count again and accepted the bills without any objection.

Segura went out to the street. Ignacio Aguirre's Cadillac was waiting for him next to La Profesa Church.

Historical and Literary Context of
The Shadow of the Strongman

The Mexican Revolution

My purpose here is not to give a nuanced, detailed account of the Mexican Revolution. Many historians have done this and I include several useful works in the list of recommended historical readings that follows this introduction. My aim, rather, is to provide those readers unfamiliar with the confusing military and political process known as the Mexican Revolution with an orientation sufficient for understanding many of the events and historical figures mentioned in Guzmán's novel. In this regard the glossary should also be of help. It is also useful to contextualize the action depicted in the novel *The Shadow of the Strongman* within the larger canvas of the Revolution and the period following the armed phase of the Revolution.

Porfirio Díaz (1830–1915) entered Mexican history as the hero of the Cinco de Mayo. As a young general in President Benito Juárez's army, his decisive action helped inflict the first defeat on the invading French army on May 5, 1862, during the defense of the city of Puebla. A mestizo of humble origin, Díaz was associated originally with President Benito Juárez's liberal reforms. Although Díaz first ran for the presidency with a "No Reelection" slogan, he served as president of Mexico from 1876 to 1880 and then from 1884 to 1911, being reelected again and again without real opposition. His long regime ushered in an era of modernization and foreign investment that brought prosperity to the upper and middle classes but left the masses of the people in grinding poverty. Any protests were crushed by the federal army and the *rurales*. In 1906, for example, when the miners at the Cananea Consolidated Copper Company went on strike, the American owner of the mine was allowed to bring U.S. troops from Arizona, who brought the strike to a bloody end. The Díaz regime favored the rich over the poor and foreigners over Mexicans.

The challenge to Porfirio Díaz's dictatorship came from an unexpected source, not from a peasant or a factory worker, but from the scion of one of Mexico's richest families, the liberal and idealistic Francisco Madero. The initial form that challenge took was also unusual: not conspiracy or armed revolt, but the publication of a book. In *The Presidential Succession of 1910*, published in January 1909, Francisco Madero bluntly described Mexico's ills and proposed a solution. As Mexican historian Enrique Krauze puts it:

> For Madero, the Mexican sickness—a natural consequence of the militarism that had devastated the country throughout the nineteenth century—was absolute power in the hands of one man. Such power could not support any genuine progress, nor was there any infallible man who could wield it with balance. [...] [T]he balance sheet on his [Díaz's] thirty years of administration—in the ways that most mattered—placed the Porfiriato solidly in the red.
>
> On the slim credit side, Madero acknowledged material progress, at the cost of freedom; and advance in agriculture, though not without importing grains; buoyant industry, though monopolistic and subsidiary; and unquestionably peace—at the price of sacrificing all political life. The liabilities, on the other hand, were "terrifying": the slavery of the Yaqui people, the repression of workers in Cananea and Río Blanco, illiteracy, excessive concessions to the United States, and a ferocious centralization of politics. Economic, social, and political wounds translated into something worse. For Madero, absolute power had corrupted the Mexican soul, inciting "a disinterest in public life, disdain for the law, and a tendency toward cunning, cynicism, and fear."[1]

The solution Madero proposed was a return to democracy without reelections, and he sent a copy of his book to President Díaz. The response of the Díaz regime was to harass the Madero family, to attempt to thwart Madero's growing anti-reelectionist movement, and eventually to jail him. In July, Díaz was reelected and Madero escaped from prison in San Luis Potosí.

In October 1910, Francisco Madero initiated the revolution against Porfirio Díaz's unconstitutional government with the proclamation of the Plan de San Luis Potosí that called on all Mexicans to rise up in arms against Díaz on November 20. There were popular uprisings throughout the country, and with the help of many local leaders (among them Pancho Villa and Pascual Orozco in the north and Emiliano Zapata in the south),

---

1. Enrique Krauze, *Mexico: Biography of Power* (New York: HarperCollins, 1997), 252.

the revolutionaries won many victories. On May 25, 1911, Díaz went into exile.

On November 6, 1911, Madero was elected president. Madero's inexperience in politics, his desire to avoid the authoritarianism of Porfirio Díaz, and, paradoxically, his restoration of democracy all helped to undermine his administration. He unwisely kept many of Díaz's appointees in power, and the new political freedom was employed by labor and peasant groups to demand reforms. Madero did not have a clear political plan beyond opposing Díaz's dictatorship and a firm stance against presidential reelection. Madero's revolution was political rather than social, but his Plan de San Luis Potosí talked about tyranny and oppression and criticized the Díaz regime for promoting the prosperity of a small group rather than that of the country.[2]

Although Madero had no plan for labor or agrarian reform, his vague statements were interpreted by many among the bourgeoisie and the peasantry to promise far more than he probably intended. This misunderstanding contributed to Madero's downfall, because the very sectors of society that helped defeat Díaz felt betrayed when the economic and social reforms they expected did not materialize. First among these former supporters to rebel was Emiliano Zapata, whose November 1911 Plan de Ayala called for the immediate restitution of communal lands that had been usurped over the years by landowners in southern Mexico. Zapata's rebellion was put down by Madero's army. In the north, Madero's army also had to quell uprisings by General Bernardo Reyes and by Emilio Vásquez Gómez in Chihuahua. In March 1912, Pascual Orozco, who had put down the Vásquez Gómez revolt, in turn rebelled against Madero. The Orozquistas were a serious threat to the government until they were contained by General Victoriano Huerta in May 1912.

The resultant disorders and apparent danger to the lives and property of foreigners caused American ambassador Henry Lane Wilson to become an enemy of the Madero administration.[3] In February 1913, part of the army rebelled against President Madero in Mexico City. On February 18, Victoriano Huerta, commanding general of the Madero government troops, joined the rebels and with the aid of Ambassador Wilson forced Madero's resignation and assumed the presidency. On February 22, as they were being taken to prison, President Madero and

---

2. Michael C. Meyer and William L. Sherman, *The Course of Mexican History*, Seventh Edition (New York: Oxford University Press, 2003), 498.
3. Meyer and Sherman, *The Course of Mexican History*, 520.

Vice President Pino Suárez were shot, either on Huerta's orders or those of his co-conspirators.

The army coup and Madero's assassination set off uprisings to restore constitutional government in three northern states: by Venustiano Carranza in Coahuila, Pancho Villa in Chihuahua, and Álvaro Obregón in Sonora. Meanwhile in the south, Emiliano Zapata continued to lead an Indian peasant rebellion for agrarian reform.

The Constitutionalists, as those who opposed Huerta were called, gained the support of Woodrow Wilson, the new president of the United States. Wilson allowed the Constitutionalists to buy munitions in the United States and imposed an embargo on Huerta. In April 1914, the United States Navy seized Veracruz to keep Huerta from receiving German arms. A series of Constitutionalist victories, culminating in Pancho Villa's capture of the city of Zacatecas, forced Huerta to go into exile in July 1914.

In November 1914, the Aguascalientes convention failed to resolve differences between the Constitutionalist factions. Once Huerta was gone, divisions sharpened between the Constitutionalists regarding the direction the Revolution should take. In the discussions at the Convention, a rift became clear between Villistas and Zapatistas, who favored immediate agrarian reform, and Carrancistas who favored a more gradual approach. In December 1914, civil war broke out, with Villa and Zapata forming an alliance and Obregón supporting Carranza.

The turning point of this civil war came on April 15 at the battle of Celaya where General Obregón, who had been studying reports from the war in Europe, employed new tactics that defeated Pancho Villa's cavalry with well-placed machine guns, barbed wire, and devastating artillery. By the end of 1915, Carranza controlled most of Mexico and served as president until 1920. Carranza did not carry out the promised land and labor reforms. Zapata resisted until he was assassinated at the behest of Carranza in 1919. In 1920, Obregón overthrew Carranza, who was assassinated on May 23. Pancho Villa came to terms with President Obregón, agreeing to stay out of politics in exchange for a large ranch. In Parral, Chihuahua, Villa was murdered under mysterious circumstances on July 20, 1923, most likely on orders from Obregón.

Although the Cristero Rebellion—a conservative Catholic revolt against the Revolutionary government's anticlerical measures enforced by President Plutarco Elías Calles—again rocked Mexico with civil war from 1926 to 1929, the armed phase of the Mexican Revolution can be said to have come to an end with the assassination of Carranza and the rise to power of Álvaro Obregón, the general whose modern tactics had defeated Villa at the battle of Celaya. In Mexican historiography, however, the term "Mexican Revolution" also applies to the political process that continued, according to some, until the 1940s. The name of the political party that monopolized political power for seventy-one years, Partido Revolucionario Institucional (Institutional Revolutionary Party), founded in 1929 by Plutarco Elías Calles, is an example of the concept that the Revolution continued by political means once the armed phase was over.

This does not mean, however, that Mexico was free from politically motivated violence and significant armed conflict in the post-Carranza period. As we have seen, Carranza was overthrown by Obregón in a conflict where opposing armies were mobilized, and the same mobilization occurred in two military uprisings that challenged Obregón. The decade from 1920 to 1930 was characterized by the power struggles of generals who had been comrades-in-arms during the Revolution, but who now vied for the presidency. This is the historical context of *The Shadow of the Strongman*, the first political novel of the Revolution.

If Mariano Azuela's *The Underdogs* (1915) and Martín Luis Guzmán's *The Eagle and the Serpent* (1928) are famous for their depiction of the armed conflict during that period of the Revolution, *The Shadow of the Strongman* has been hailed for its accurate depiction of the complex dynamics of the period where the generals of the Revolution fought for political power as they simultaneously sought to establish an elective and representative government where power would be transferred without bloodshed and with at least the appearance of constitutional procedure.

This transitional period started in 1920, when Carranza's presidential term was coming to an end and he tried to impose an almost unknown civilian politician, Ignacio Bonillas, as his successor.[4] Adolfo de la Huerta, governor of the state of Sonora, and several Sonoran generals, chief among them Álvaro Obregón, led the Revolution of Agua Prieta, which had widespread national support and led to the flight and assassination of Carranza. De la Huerta was then chosen as interim president, until November when Obregón was elected.

As president, Obregón brought stability to the government of the revolutionaries. He secured the diplomatic recognition of the United States for his new government and advanced some revolutionary goals: modest land reform, labor laws, and public education. His appointment of José de Vasconcelos, rector of the National Autonomous University of Mexico,

---

4. This tendency of Mexican presidents to impose their successors became known as *imposicionismo*.

as secretary of public education led to the advancement of Mexican public education, with the building of rural schools and public libraries. It was Vasconcelos too who began commissioning Diego Rivera, José Clemente Orozco, David Alfaro Siqueiros, and others to paint murals for public buildings.

As his presidential term was ending, Obregón, following ominously in the steps of his predecessor Carranza, sought to impose Plutarco Elías Calles as his successor. Adolfo de la Huerta, who had helped overthrow Carranza and served as interim president to facilitate Obregón's election, objected to the president's plan. Historians of the Mexican Revolution Joseph and Buchenau explain the chain of events that led to this first rift between the Sonoran generals:

> Over the previous few years, relations between Obregón and de la Huerta—never as amicable as those of Calles with either one—had become increasingly strained. In 1922 de la Huerta, who served as Mexico's finance minister, had unsuccessfully attempted to obtain new loans from a group of U.S. bankers. Obregón believed that de la Huerta had offered wide-ranging concessions in exchange for the loans. He claimed that these concessions exceeded those authorized by him and charged that the treasury secretary had become too chummy with the bankers. This attack stung de la Huerta, especially as he watched Obregón make even greater concessions in the Bucareli agreements. Moreover, he correctly suspected that Obregón and Calles were behind the assassination of Pancho Villa. Incensed when his Sonoran colleagues intervened in an electoral dispute over gubernatorial elections in the state of San Luis Potosí on behalf of a politician who opposed one of his allies, de la Huerta finally resigned his cabinet post in September 1923. As the rift among the Sonorans became public, Obregón added insult to injury by appointing de la Huerta's archenemy, Alberto Pani, as his successor. The new finance minister alleged that his predecessor had embezzled funds from the national treasury. These fabricated charges forced de la Huerta to take a stand against the government in order to salvage his personal honor. On December 7, 1923, he proclaimed the Plan of Veracruz, calling Mexicans to arms against the imposition of Calles as Obregón's successor. Almost two-thirds of all military officers joined the revolt, including some of the country's most influential divisional

generals, most notably Enrique Estrada of Jalisco and Guadalupe Sánchez of Veracruz.[5]

By February 9, 1924, when Obregón's troops defeated de la Huerta's in the battle of Ocotlán in Jalisco, seven thousand more Mexicans had died.[6] Some historians consider this the last battle of the Mexican Revolution.

More importantly, it was a victory for *imposicionismo* and a setback for the principle of peaceful democratic succession. After the Revolution had again devoured more of its own, elections were held and Calles became president. Although Obregón retired to his farm, he remained an important influence in the affairs of state, and it was during this period that people began to call him the "Caudillo."[7] Calles sat in the presidential chair, but he owed his turn at power to Obregón. Many Mexicans were prepared for a repetition of the pattern established by Porfirio Díaz, the dictator whom the Revolution had helped to overthrow, with Obregón wielding the real power, but with Calles filling in as president to give an appearance of democracy.[8] What actually transpired during Calles' term and its aftermath was more complicated and had unexpected consequences. As Mexican historian Enrique Krauze explains:

> Calles's extremely complex presidential term (1924–1928) had many political protagonists: the generals, the union leaders of the CROM, the *agraristas*, the cabinets. There were eight thousand political parties in the country. The verbal and physical battles between them spun an almost insoluble tangle at national, state, and local levels. Pacts, ruptures, threats, confrontations,

---

5. Gilbert M. Joseph and Jürgen Buchenau, *Mexico's Once and Future Revolution* (Durham, North Carolina: Duke University Press, 2013), 96.
6. Krauze, *Mexico: Biography of Power*, 398.
7. A title given in Spain and Spanish America to military and political leaders who hold power through force of arms.
8. In *The Last Caudillo: Álvaro Obregón and the Mexican Revolution*, Buchenau explains:
"With good reason, many observers considered Obregón the true power in Mexico despite Calles's election. In the absence of a formal political title, Mexicans knew him simply as *el caudillo*. The caudillo still held a commanding position in the army—a position demonstrated in his leadership during the de la Huerta rebellion. Most Mexicans regarded the incoming president as Obregón's creation, the head of an interregnum during which the caudillo's influence would remain unabated.... In the eyes of most Mexicans, Obregón had imposed Calles with the force of arms, and the new president remained beholden to him."

campaigns, embezzlement, light-handed theft, bravado, shoot-outs, riots. The political life of Mexico turbulently overflowed the formal boundaries of legislatures, cabinet meetings, or the press and spilled into bars, brothels, and casinos.[9]

As we shall see when we discuss the historical context of *The Shadow of the Strongman*, Calles' presidency provides the model for the political environment of Guzmán's novel.

During his term (1924–1928), Calles was to a degree successful in coming out of the "Shadow of the Strongman," by pursuing a reform program that favored industrial and agrarian workers more vigorously than his predecessor. Thus, while the army remained Obregón's power base, Calles could now counter with the support of the unions. Calles also enforced the agrarian reform mandated by the Revolutionary Constitution of 1917 to a greater degree than the previous administration, distributing eight million acres of land to indigenous villages versus the five million under that of Obregón.[10] Likewise Calles also sought to enforce the Constitution's anticlerical provisions (Articles 3 and 130) that had been pragmatically ignored by Carranza and Obregón. The result of the Calles Law of July 2, 1926, among whose measures were the barring of priests from teaching and the banning of outdoor religious ceremonies, was the outbreak of a Catholic revolt that became known as the Cristero Rebellion. Seventy thousand people died in the fighting and crops were destroyed with a consequent forty percent drop in Mexico's production of grain between 1926 and 1929.[11]

As Calles' term was winding down, several revolutionary generals began to eye the presidential chair, chief among them Arnulfo R. Gómez and Francisco R. Serrano. The latter, who was Obregón's long-time associate and protégé, counted on the support of the Caudillo. General Serrano, who had attended to Obregón when he lost his arm in a battle during the Revolution, was sorely disappointed to learn that Obregón planned to return to the presidency. Although Obregón was barred from being president by the Constitution that had embodied the paramount Revolutionary principle of anti-reelectionism, Calles was successful in getting Congress to pass an amendment that permitted nonconsecutive reelection. As was the case with de la Huerta in 1923, Gómez and Serrano, this

9. Krauze, *Mexico: Biography of Power*, 424.
10. Joseph and Buchenau, *Mexico's Once and Future Revolution*, 98.
11. Jürgen Buchenau, *Plutarco Elías Calles and the Mexican Revolution* (New York: Rowan & Littlefield, 2007), 130.

time under the banner of anti-reelectionism, challenged Obregón's bid for power. Buchenau describes the predictable consequences of standing in the way of the Caudillo's wishes:

> When attempts at persuasion did not work in subduing the caudillo's rivals, Calles and Obregón turned to repressive tactics and finally adopted the ultimate solution to political conflicts. On October 3, 1927, Calles ordered the arrest of Gómez and Serrano after he received word that the two generals had designed a coup d'état. Later that day, an army contingent under the direction of General Claudio Fox—a general known for his blood-thirsty cruelty—detained Serrano and twelve of his men and machine-gunned them unceremoniously.[12]

This time Obregón's and Calles' repression cost the lives of five hundred anti-reelectionists.[13] Obregón was reelected on July 10, 1928, but never assumed the presidency because he was assassinated seven days later by José de León Toral, a member of the Catholic National League for the Defense of Religious Freedom, an organization that opposed the anti-clerical measures of the Calles Law.[14]

What Calles did after Obregón's assassination changed Mexico from a "country ruled by one man" to a "nation of institutions and laws" as he himself put it in his final state of the nation address.[15] To the surprise of many, Calles did not assume the presidency in the midst of this national emergency. Instead he appointed Emilio Portes Gil to serve as interim president from 1928 to 1930. Subsequently, although Calles exerted so much power that the period from 1928 to 1934 came to be known as the "Maximato" since he was known as "El Jefe Máximo," the presidential successions were free of bloodshed. Calles achieved this largely through the marginalization of the military, made possible by the founding in 1928 of the Partido Nacional Revolucionario, which under different names (Partido de la Revolución Mexicana [1938–1946] and Partido Revolucionario Institucional [1946 to the present]) had the monopoly of power in Mexico until 2000 with the election of the PAN candidate Vicente Fox.

---

12. Jürgen Buchenau, *The Last Caudillo: Álvaro Obregón and the Mexican Revolution* (Chichester, England: Wiley-Blackwell, 2011), 157–58.
13. Buchenau, *The Last Caudillo: Álvaro Obregón and the Mexican Revolution*, 158.
14. Historians have not been able to confirm rumors that Calles was behind the assassination of Obregón.
15. Joseph and Buchenau, *Mexico's Once and Future Revolution*, 105.

In the "Informe" of September 1, 1928, his final report to the legislature, Plutarco Elías Calles spoke of the useful role caudillos had played in the Revolutionary process, but he also dwelt on the harm they had done:

> I do not need to remind you how the caudillos—perhaps not always intentionally but always naturally and logically enough— have hampered the appearance, formation and development of other national power options, to which the country could resort in moments of internal and external crisis, and how they some- times delayed or blocked, even against the will of the caudillo himself—in that same natural and logical way—the peaceful evo- lutionary development of Mexico as an institutional country, in which men may become, as they should be, mere accidents with no real importance beside the perpetual and august serenity of institutions and laws.[16]

Calles thereby announced the end of the era of the caudillo in Mexican politics as he ushered in the beginning of seventy years of one-party rule.

The Shadow of the Strongman in the Context of the Revolution

The Shadow of the Strongman vibrantly captures in its pages the tumultuous period of political intrigue following the armed phase of the Revolution, and it does so thanks to the privileged viewpoint of Martín Luis Guzmán, a man who was a close observer and participant in many of the events. Faithful as he is in his depiction of historical incidents and the intrica- cies of political intrigue, there is a sense in which the novel is funda- mentally ahistorical, because it fuses two historical moments of what was then recent Mexican history into one event. For his novel, Guzmán chose to blend the rebellion of Adolfo de la Huerta (1923–1924) with that of Generals Arnulfo R. Gómez and Francisco R. Serrano in 1927. Guzmán was not only a witness of the events in 1923 but also a participant, since he backed de la Huerta. In December 1923, Guzmán, who was serving in Obregón's government, was warned by his boss, Finance Minister Alberto Pani,[17] to leave Mexico because his life was in peril for supporting

---

16. Krauze, *Mexico: Biography of Power*, 427.
17. Pani was also secretary of foreign affairs.

the candidacy of Adolfo de la Huerta to the presidency. Guzmán wisely went into exile, and his newspaper, *El Mundo,* was confiscated. By the time the second event took place in 1927, Guzmán was already living in Madrid. It was his reading of newspaper reports of the rebellion and the subsequent assassination of General Francisco R. Serrano on October 4 that impelled Guzmán to write what eventually would become the novel *La sombra del Caudillo (The Shadow of the Strongman).* As Guzmán explains:

> I was writing the first part of a trilogy of novels that would depict the Revolution as it becomes a government regime. The first part would deal with the Carranza phase, the second with Obregón and the last one with Calles. About that time, Mexican newspapers giving an account of General Serrano's death reached Madrid. These papers included the twelve or thirteen—I can't recall—death notices of the men slaughtered in Huitzilac. Suddenly I had a vision of how those events could become the climax of the second novel. I dropped what I was doing and feverishly began to write *The Shadow of the Strongman,* swept up by the emotion. I wrote the four last chapters in one day.[18]

This first version of the novel was serialized in newspapers from May 20, 1928,[19] until November 10, 1929,[20] in the United States (in San Antonio's *La Prensa* and Los Angeles' *La Opinión*) and in *El Universal* in Mexico.

Guzmán's novelistic departure from a strict chronology of Mexican history paradoxically has the result of making *The Shadow of the Strongman* more historically significant. Instead of just producing an interesting roman à clef about political intrigue, by melding two crucial moments in the evolution of the post-Revolutionary government, Guzmán turns the novel into a critique of caudillismo, the blight that affected post-Revolutionary Mexico beginning with Carranza's presidency. The rebellion of 1923 and the rebellion of 1927 had very different protagonists and

---

18. Interview in *Diecinueve protagonistas de la literatura mexicana del siglo XX,* edited by Emmanuel Carballo, 73–74. Mexico City: Empresas Editoriales, 1965.
19. Antonio Lorente Medina, *La sombra del Caudillo* (Madrid: Clásicos Castalia, 2002), 46.
20. Bruce-Novoa, Introduction to his *Martín Luis Guzmán La sombra del Caudillo: Versión periodística* (Mexico: Universidad Nacional Autónoma de México, 1987), p. xliv.

motivations, but they both slammed into the harsh political reality of caudillismo—the primary predominance of a man over the institutions of government. The de la Huerta rebellion fought against *imposicionismo*—the president's imposing a candidate as his successor, while Gómez and Serrano rebelled against a former president's attempt to be reelected. Everywhere Guzmán looked, however, he saw generals vying for their turn at the presidential chair. In every case, the choice was among caudillos.

Of course, *The Shadow of the Strongman* is also a roman à clef and the "Strongman," the "Caudillo" of the title, is Álvaro Obregón.

As Guzmán explained in a 1958 interview with Emmanuel Carballo:

> All the characters that appear there are replicas of real persons, except for one, Axkaná González, who as his name suggests has blood from the two races: indigenous and Spanish. Axkaná represents the revolutionary conscience in the novel. In the novel, he plays the role reserved for the chorus in Greek tragedy: he strives to have the ideal world cure the wounds of the real world.[21]

In the interview, Guzmán goes on to identify each of the major characters in the novel:

> The Caudillo is Obregón, I describe him physically. Ignacio Aguirre—Minister of War—is the sum of Adolfo de la Huerta and General Serrano; in his external appearance, he does not resemble either of them. Hilario Jiménez—Minister of the Interior—is Plutarco Elías Calles. General Protasio Leyva—named Head of Operations in the Valley by the Caudillo after Aguirre's resignation, and a supporter of Jiménez—is General Arnulfo Gómez.[22] Emilio Olivier Fernández—the most extraordinary of the political agitators at that moment, was the leader of the Progressive Radical Bloc of the Chamber of Deputies, founder and leader of his party, ex-mayor of Mexico City and ex-governor"—

---

21. Carballo, "Interview with Guzmán," 73–74.
22. Here Guzmán's blending of the two rebellions creates some confusion. The character Protasio Leyva represents the historical General Arnulfo R. Gómez, as he acted in 1923, not in 1927. In 1923 he supported Obregón against Adolfo de la Huerta, in 1927 he and Serrano opposed Obregón's attempt at reelection.

is Jorge Prieto Laurens. Encarnación Reyes—Divisional General and Chief of Military Operations in the State of Puebla—is General Guadalupe Sánchez. Eduardo Correa—mayor of the city—is Jorge Carregha. Jacinto López de la Garza—intellectual advisor of Encarnación Reyes and his chief of staff—is General José Villanueva Garza. Ricalde—leader of the workers who support Jiménez—is Luis N. Morones. López Nieto—leader of the peasants; and like the former a supporter of the Minister of the Interior—is Antonio Díaz Soto y Gama. (Carballo 74)

Guzmán's decision to combine elements of the de la Huerta rebellion with the Serrano rebellion was probably also based on aesthetic considerations. Adolfo de la Huerta went into exile and, like Guzmán, returned to Mexico during Cárdenas' presidency, dying of natural causes in 1955. On the other hand, Serrano and his entourage met a tragic end in the massacre at Huitzilac, the event that inspired Guzmán to write *The Shadow of the Strongman*. In *The Last Caudillo: Álvaro Obregón and the Mexican Revolution*, Jürgen Buchenau describes the events of 1927:

Despite Gómez' and Serrano's shortcomings, the government took their political challenge seriously. [...] On October 3, 1927, Calles ordered the arrest of Gómez and Serrano after he received word that the two generals had designed a coup d'état. Later that day, an army contingent under the direction of General Claudio Fox [...] detained Serrano and twelve of his men and machine-gunned them unceremoniously. Thus the caudillo's protégé, a man who had once tended to the caudillo as he lay bleeding from the loss of his arm, died as a result of his mentor's ambitions. Also among the dead was Chiapas governor Carlos Vidal, one of the men who had helped Calles build a power base of his own. (157–58)

Although Guzmán deeply admired Adolfo de la Huerta, he was not attracted by General Francisco Serrano who, despite his distinguished military service, had less admirable traits:

Many Mexicans knew Serrano as an alcoholic, and he held a well-deserved reputation for violence, as well as notoriety for his pursuit of unmarried women, especially while drunk. Although many among the political elite participated in alcoholic orgies, Serrano's excesses embarrassed his friends as much as did those of Morones, whose character inspired the protagonist in Katherine Anne Porter's noted short story *Flowering Judas*. (Buchenau 157)

Although General Ignacio Aguirre in *The Shadow of the Strongman* shares some of Serrano's reprehensible traits, Guzmán's protagonist is redeemed by his courage and dignity in the face of his tragic death. It is not hard to grasp how Guzmán suddenly "had a vision of how those events could become the climax of" *The Shadow of the Strongman*.[23]

Other events depicted in the novel were also inspired by historical events. Some contemporaries of Guzmán who read the novel also noted that the assassination of Cañizo in Book Five, Chapter Three, is a fictionalized version of the assassination of Senator Francisco Field Jurado. While the character Cañizo is murdered in the Chamber of Deputies, the real-life Senator Field Jurado was gunned down in the streets of Mexico City in January 1924. For his novel, Guzmán likely changed the site of the assassination from the streets to the Chamber of Deputies in order to underscore symbolically the flagrant violation of democracy, but the account of the systematic murder of several leaders of the opposition by the *Obregonistas* led by Deputy Luis N. Morones (Ricalde in the novel) is accepted by many historians. Another possible inspiration for the killing of the fictional Cañizo is given by Martínez Assad: "Episodes like the one organized by Leyva in the Chamber of Deputies in order to eliminate Olivier in the novel are almost a replica of the assassination of Guillermo Landeche Zetina in the political context of 1923."[24] Note, once more, that Guzmán's decision to combine the events of 1923 with those of 1927 means that his novel serves more as a condemnation of caudillismo rather than as a faithful representation of a specific historical moment.

Finally, the circumstances surrounding the publication of *La sombra del Caudillo* (*The Shadow of the Strongman*) in Mexico furnish another example of how Guzmán's career is inseparable from the history and politics of the Mexican Revolution. Although Calles was no longer president of Mexico in 1929, when *La sombra del Caudillo*—published by the Spanish publisher Espasa Calpe—appeared in Mexican bookstores, he tried to stop the distribution of the novel. Guzmán himself describes what happened:

---

23. The trilogy Guzmán describes was never written.
24. Martínez Assad, "*Entretelones de La sombra del caudillo*," *Confabulario*, suplemento cultural de *El Universal* (October 13, 2007): 7.

When the first copies of *La sombra del Caudillo* reached Mexico, General Calles was fuming and wanted to order a ban on the distribution of the novel in our country. Genaro Estrada intervened immediately on his own initiative and made the *Jefe Máximo de la Revolution* [The Supreme Leader of the Revolution] see that it would be an atrocity and an error. The former because of what it meant in terms of constitutional rights, the latter because banning the novel would increase its circulation. The government and the representatives of Espasa Calpe—the publisher—who were threatened with having their Mexican branch shut down, came to an agreement: the representatives of the publisher would not be expelled from the country, but Espasa Calpe promised not to publish, in future, any book of mine that dealt with events after 1910. (Carballo 74)

Guzmán adds that his contract with Espasa Calpe was altered in accordance with Calles' demands and that he was obliged to set his subsequent books in the nineteenth century or earlier. The Espasa Calpe–Calles agreement probably explains why Guzmán never wrote the other two novels of the projected trilogy.

In 1960, Mexican director Julio Bracho filmed an adaptation of Guzmán's novel. Although he had the support of President Adolfo López Mateo, and the film, *La sombra del Caudillo*, received an award at the Karlovy Vary International Film Festival in Czechoslovakia, the Mexican Secretariat of National Defense objected to its being shown because it "denigrated Mexico and its institutions" and "offers a false vision of history and of the Mexican Army."[25] The copy of the film disappeared without explanation and the film was banned for thirty years. Thanks to the copy that remained in Czechoslovakia, the film was shown there and in Poland, Bulgaria, the Soviet Union, Romania, and China. Julio Bracho appealed unsuccessfully to subsequent administrations to release his film and died in 1978. Clandestine videos of the banned film began to circulate in the seventies, but the film adaptation of Guzmán's novel was not shown commercially in Mexico until 1990. In November 2010, the film featured in the centenary celebration of the Mexican Revolution as part of a series on cinematic adaptations of novels of the Revolution. Poignantly, the film was shown in the Palacio de Bellas Artes where the

---

25. Lucero Solórzano, "¿Qué diría don Julio Bracho?" *Excelsior*, November 21, 2011, http://www.excelsior.com.mx/node/785709.

funeral vigil for Martín Luis Guzmán had been held thirty-four years before.[26] The film is now easily available.

Literary Considerations

One valid way to read *The Shadow of the Strongman* is as a political thriller, but it is also a novel written by a cultured and cosmopolitan intellectual who is keenly aware of international artistic tendencies in the first quarter of the twentieth century. From 1913 to 1915 he spent his time in the company of men of action, the leaders of the Revolution: Venustiano Carranza, Álvaro Obregón, Pancho Villa, but his formative years were spent receiving a privileged and progressive education. In his youth, he made friends with two young men who would become two of the most famous Mexican intellectuals of the twentieth century, Alfonso Reyes and José de Vasconcelos. Around 1910, they were all members of the Ateneo de la Juventud Mexicana (Mexican Youth Atheneum), later known as the Ateneo de México (Atheneum of Mexico). Impatient with the restrictive intellectual climate of the declining years of Porfirio Díaz's reign, the Ateneo de la Juventud was an organization that sought to expand Mexican education by promoting intellectual and artistic culture. They championed freedom of thought and rejected the dominant scientific determinism of the Porfirian regime. An important influence on the members of the Ateneo was the thinking of the Uruguayan José Enrique Rodó, who in his 1900 essay "Ariel" argued for the need to resist the cultural influence of the United States. Instead, Rodó argued in favor of cultivating the culture of classical Greece and Rome, which he saw as the historical inheritance of Latin Americans. Rodó felt that each culture had its particular genius, and by imitating another culture they would deprive the world of an important tradition. While the Porfirian regime valued the foreign over the national, the young members of the Ateneo looked to define the national. Guzmán's concept of Aguirre as a tragic hero and Axkaná as the Greek chorus reveal his Ateneo roots. The trenchant and lucid analysis of contemporary Mexico that he presents in *The Shadow of the Strongman*

---

26. "La sombra del caudillo: Del hecho histórico al lenguaje literario y su adaptación al cine," *Coordinación Nacional de Literatura*, November 23, 2010, http://www.literatura.bellasartes.gob.mx/index.php?option=com_content&view=article&id=618:la-sombra-del-caudillo-del-hecho-historico-al-lenguaje-literario-y-su-adaptacion-al-cine&catid=121:boletines.

is woven from the social reality of the nation, but the insights of Greek tragedy are enlisted in the task.

Language itself was a lifelong fascination for Guzmán. Although he is not made a Corresponding Member of the Spanish Academy of Language until 1940 and a full member until 1952, readers of *The Shadow of the Strongman* are aware at every moment of how important word choice is to the author. From the first page of the novel, it is clear that what matters is not just the story being told, but how it is being told:

> General Ignacio Aguirre's Cadillac crossed the streetcar rails of the Calzada de Chapultepec, and, making a sharp turn, came to a stop next to the sidewalk, a short distance from the Insurgentes stop.
>
> The chauffeur's assistant jumped from his place to open the passenger door. Bright reflections of the early afternoon cityscape—the outlines of houses, trees on the avenue, blue sky covered at intervals by large, white cumulus clouds—slid across the dark bluish window as the door opened. (p. 3)

The first paragraph uses the simple, factual language that we would expect in a hard-boiled detective novel, right down to the details of the name of the street and the make of the car.[27] But then, in the second paragraph, in what seems like a cinematic zoom, our attention is focused not on the novel's protagonist, who has just been introduced, but on the effect of the afternoon light on the car window as the door is opened. The business-like first paragraph yields to Guzmán's aesthetic imperative and the result is a short poem, a sequence of images.

In *The Shadow of the Strongman*, Guzmán harnesses the stark power of descriptions reminiscent of hard-boiled detective fiction (appropriate to a political thriller) to passages of great poetic beauty. The effect is ultimately heartbreaking because he makes readers see repeatedly that in the world his characters inhabit, brutality and cruelty coexist with exquisite beauty. The persistent attraction of the beauty in this world paradoxically makes the effect of the violence harder to take.

Another example of this juxtaposition of the momentary and unexpected manifestation of beauty, akin to Joycean epiphanies, with episodes of harrowing savagery occurs in Chapter One of the Fourth Book, when Axkaná goes to the jai alai fronton to speak to a politician. He does not

---

27. Dashiell Hammett published *The Maltese Falcon* in 1930.

find Eduardo Correa, but as he waits he is visited by a powerful aesthetic experience:

> In the end, the wait turned out to be long and useless, although not lacking in attractions that made it more than bearable. Because that night Axkaná, who until then had never come to the fronton, discovered a new spectacle, a spectacle that struck him as magnificent for the richness of its sculptural forms, and which he thoroughly enjoyed. His eyes filled with extraordinary sights; he believed, at times, he was witnessing an event of unreal beauty. Under the glow of the electric lamps, he witnessed the unearthly grace that pervades the deeds of the *pelotari*, the jai alai players. (p. 93)

In fact, when he leaves the fronton, because he is thinking about the unexpected beauty he just witnessed, Axkaná fails to focus on the fact that he is being stalked:

> As the Ford maneuvered to get out of the line, Axkaná once again detected the presence of the group of men whom he had noticed earlier and who, no longer at the entrance of the fronton, were now standing guard at the sidewalk across the road. For a moment, his eyes met the pale man's eyes, but Axkaná took no notice. He was still relishing the memory of the climactic scenes of the jai alai games. All his senses still admired, as superhuman deeds, as phenomena alien to the laws of physics and to everyday life, the incidents of the game he had just seen. He recalled the incredible agility of Egozcue, who climbed the wall of the court as if he were going to hang from the ball with his cesta; Elola's infinite efficacy as he returned deadly serves, almost invisible serves, at three meters; Irigoyen's rabid fierceness (he threw himself head first against the wall every time he lost a point because the ball pierced his cesta); and the heroic mastery of Goenaga, who dropped to his back to catch incredible rebounds, two centimeters from the floor. (p. 93)

Soon after this unlooked-for manifestation of beauty, Axkaná is kidnapped by thugs in the employ of Aguirre's foes. Seeking to intimidate Aguirre, they make Axkaná, his best friend and political confidant, drink enough tequila to almost kill him. With a jolt, Guzmán takes his readers back to the world and the language of the hard-boiled novel:

With the neck of the bottle, the stranger kept hitting Axkaná's lips. He evidently did it with the intention of hurting him and keeping him docile. To get him to stop, Axkaná drank.

This time the stranger was not content for Axkaná to drink as he had before. Instead, he stuck several centimeters of the bottle between his teeth and forced him to swallow a huge amount of liquid. Axkaná started to feel warm and dizzy from the alcohol that was almost choking him. From his face the trickle of blood continued to flow; by now the front of his shirt was wet.

"Drink again."

And the voice, turning elsewhere added:

"Hold his arms, just in case he gets rowdy when he's drunk."

The voice once more turned to him:

"C'mon, Mister whosis, have another swig. You're here to obey me."

Axkaná resisted.

"Are you going to play nice and drink, or not?"

For the fourth time, Axkaná agreed. And his kidnappers again made sure the gulp he took was enormous.

Axkaná felt as if his mouth, throat, and chest were on fire. (p. 102)

Throughout *The Shadow of the Strongman*, the prose fluctuates between what seem to be two irreconcilable worlds, one full of the dazzling beauty of life and another where violence destroys that beauty. The terrible insight is that they coexist in the same world.

Another feature of Guzmán's writing that critics have identified is how his description of many scenes seems to have a cinematic quality and power. Guzmán's interest in the cinema dates at least to 1915 when he wrote articles about film.[28] Many examples can be found in *The Shadow of the Strongman*, but two are remarkable: the assassination of the delegate Cañizo (Book Five, Chapter Three) and Axkaná's escape (Book Six, Chapter Six). At the end of the chapter titled "The Death of Cañizo," Guzmán describes the melee at the Chamber of Deputies. When Cañizo realizes the Hilaristas intend to kill him he tries to leave the Congress:

28. Antonio Lorente Medina, introduction to his critical edition of *La sombra del Caudillo* (Madrid: Clásicos Castalia, 2002), 60.

And it all took place in less than a second. As the Hilarista passed the doorway, he went for his weapon, intending to shoot. Cañizo had the slightest of leads on him—enough for his bullet to hit first; his gun was out of the holster and rising to aim at the target; his index finger, having become one with the trigger, felt the slackening that precedes firing, a feeling that is only perceptible to the shooter at the culminating moment when his life seems to lengthen a hundredfold; the barrel of the gun was about to aim, the bullet about to shoot out.... But in that fraction of a second, Cañizo felt someone grab him by the elbow, another hand twisted his wrist, and his revolver, after firing at the ground, fell to the floor. Facing him, the Hilarista's automatic pistol was staring at him with its only eye.

With a jolt, Cañizo freed himself from those holding him— it was Captain Fentanes and Agent Abat who had grabbed him from behind—and, failing to recover his weapon from the floor, rushed to the stairs. He jumped once, twice, three times, and was in the midst of a fourth leap when the Hilarista fired from above. The wounded body described a scrawl in midair and fell to the tile floor of the lobby. It fell as if the pistol had fired not the bullet but the corpse itself. (pp. 150–51)

The entire scene seems taken from the screenplay of a noir film. When Axkaná escapes his captors, he takes a desperate leap off a cliff:

The leaves and branches of a tree opened up; Axkaná fell between them for an indefinite, seemingly infinite, time. Head-first, eyes closed, his hands and arms still bound, he fell, giving himself over entirely to the forces of chance. Sharp ends scratched him; he slammed into hard surfaces and rebounded; rough edges seemed to strip all the skin off of his face. Something stabbed his back and then ripped his flesh through his clothes before wedging itself between his wrists, which creaked and twisted. And there he stayed: legs above, neck against the fork of a tree, and hooked, hanging from the electric cord that a second ago had rendered his hands useless. He opened his eyes. The last glimmers of the afternoon were fading among the branches above. He remained motionless. Soon he heard running and the voices of the soldiers. He sensed the moment when his pursuers stopped to look at his hat. Then he heard them run on, shouting. They fired their rifles. He heard other shots much farther away. (p. 197)

We follow Axkaná's fall as if we were with him, very much the way we would experience it in a film.

While the cinematic scenes in the novel adopt an objective, exterior perspective, the novel relies heavily on the omniscient narration to give readers access to the interiority of the characters. Guzmán's interest in psychology is evident throughout the novel and contributes greatly to his nuanced characterizations, making us privy to the fears and motivations of the protagonists of this political thriller. While every page of the novel could furnish examples, perhaps the most outstanding one is Aguirre's fateful interview with the Caudillo at Chapultepec Castle in the first chapter of the second book. Here Guzmán reveals the depth of the personal relationship between Aguirre and his chief of many years. The emotional ascendancy that the Caudillo has over his Minister becomes clear. In this scene, as we assume Aguirre's point of view, and as we read, we note how attentively he interprets the smallest sign on his chief's face, the smallest change of intonation in his voice:

> The Caudillo had the imperious eyes of a tiger, eyes whose golden glints matched the somewhat fiery disorder of his gray mustache. But when they looked at Aguirre, they never lacked (not even during critical moments in combat) the soft expression of affection. Aguirre was well used to having the Caudillo look at him in that manner, and it moved him so deeply that perhaps it was the root, more than anything else, of the feelings of unswerving devotion that bound him to his chief. However, this time he noticed that just as soon as he mentioned the topic of the election, his words arrested the Caudillo's customary look. Now, when the Caudillo answered, only spurious, ironic glimmers remained in his eyes; he became opaque, impenetrable.
>
> "I'm listening," he said.
>
> But even these seemingly neutral words did not leave the president's lips without being accompanied by the nervous gesture—a trace of old wounds—that revealed he was more than merely willing to listen; he was ready to defend and attack.
>
> "I just want to make one or two things clear," continued the young minister, "to make sure both you and I are on guard against insidious gossip."

"All right, all right, let's see."

As he spoke Aguirre felt that for the first time in ten years an invisible curtain was being drawn between his voice and the Caudillo. With each passing second, the Caudillo seemed to become more severe, more hermetic, more distant.

[...]

"Yes, that's it. What do *you* think?"

"... I answered, as you can imagine, that I don't consider myself worthy, nor is it my ambition..."

"Fine.... And that is what you believe? That's what matters."

The question was wrapped in the deeply ironic tone that Aguirre had often heard the Caudillo use when addressing others, but never when talking to him. So now the tone of the Caudillo's voice disconcerted and wounded him, just as his chief's look and expression had. Something inside him broke as he replied:

"If I didn't believe it, my General, I wouldn't say it." (pp. 39–40)

From a novelistic point of view, this scene is gripping and readers understand that it marks a turning point in the plot of the novel. At the same time, however, in the interview between Aguirre and the Caudillo, Guzmán captures an important historical truth about caudillismo, how the power of the leader springs from the intense personal relationship with his aides and followers. The scene is a novelistic tour de force, but it is also a historical lesson, and a portrait of the model of the Caudillo, Álvaro Obregón.

Martín Luis Guzmán is known primarily as a novelist, but all his important works, *The Eagle and the Serpent*, *The Shadow of the Strongman*, and *The Memoirs of Pancho Villa* are extra-generic. They live in the hazy boundary between history, novel, and memoir. Critics and Guzmán himself have pointed this out. In his 1958 interview with Emmanuel Carballo, Guzmán addresses this subject in an enlightening manner:

I consider [*The Eagle and the Serpent*] a novel, the novel of a young man who goes from the halls of a university to an armed movement in full swing. He recounts what he saw in the Revolution, just as he saw it, with the eyes of a university student. It is not a work of history as some affirm; it is, I repeat, a novel. *The Shadow of the Strongman*—it may surprise you—is at the same time a novel and a historical work, in the same sense as the

Memoirs of Pancho Villa. No feature, no event, acquires its full dimension until literary form confers it by elevating them. It is then that it becomes true, and not when any historian looks at it using his ordinary senses. He sees, but does not know how to grasp—to express—what his eyes have seen. Mexican truths are there, by virtue of the literary force with which they are seen, recreated. (73)

Guzmán's observation about *The Shadow of the Strongman* and *The Memoirs of Pancho Villa* illustrates a fundamental approach in his work. His fascination with history is constant, but he feels that historical truth, Mexican truths, will not emerge from a conventional historical work. It is only when the historical material is viewed through the novelist's eye and re-created in a work of fiction that it will reveal its truth to the reader. This, for example, is why it made sense to Guzmán to collapse two historical moments in order to gain access to a deeper understanding of caudillismo.

Guzmán's View of the Revolution

Martín Luis Guzmán's life and career are inextricably woven into the process of the Mexican Revolution and our understanding of it. From the time Francisco Madero is assassinated, through his participation in the armed struggle against the usurper Victoriano Huerta, through a first exile, his participation in Obregón's administration, a second longer exile, his triumphal return in 1936, and then until his own peaceful death forty years later, Guzmán was an eyewitness and active participant in the historical process that produced the modern Mexican state. In essays, speeches, and through his steady literary output, Guzmán commented on, interpreted, and helped shape how Mexicans came to understand their history in the twentieth century.

It is dizzying to trace Guzmán's itinerary and surprising to see how this young, highly cultured intellectual who lacked any political or military experience came, at different times, to serve in the staff of three of the most important protagonists of the Revolution: Venustiano Carranza, Álvaro Obregón, and Francisco Villa.

In February 1913, after Madero's assassination, Guzmán joined other Maderistas in founding the newspaper *El Honor Nacional* to denounce the plots of the supporters of Victoriano Huerta. After an earlier abortive attempt, he successfully left Mexico City and joined revolutionary forces in Sonora in September 1913. In November, Guzmán joined the general staff of General Ramón F. Iturbe in Culiacán, Sinaloa. By February 1914, Guzmán joined the general staff of General Álvaro Obregón in Nogales, Sonora. In March, Guzmán was sent by Venustiano Carranza on a mission to Ciudad Juárez, Chihuahua, and there he joined the general staff of General Francisco Villa. In August, Villa sent Guzmán to accompany Constitutionalist troops as they entered Mexico City and ordered him to remain there as the envoy of the Division of the North. In September, however, Carranza ordered his arrest, together with that of other Villistas, in reprisal for Villa's imprisonment of Obregón in Chihuahua. In October, Guzmán was freed with other Villistas by order of the Military Convention of Aguascalientes, and he traveled there. In November, Villa sent him to Mexico City to serve as advisor to General José Isabel Robles, secretary of war and the navy. At that time, Guzmán was also appointed secretary of the National University and director of the National Library, and Generals Villa and Lucio Blanco confirmed his rank as a colonel in the Revolutionary Army.

When the Aguascalientes Convention failed to settle the differences between the Constitutionalist factions, civil war broke out with Carranza and Obregón on one side and Villa and Zapata on the other. In January 1915, not wishing to take sides in the conflict, Guzmán chose exile with his family, first in Spain and then New York.

Guzmán returned to Mexico in 1919 and was appointed chief of the editorial section of *El Heraldo de México*, a daily newspaper founded by General Salvador Alvarado. In May 1920, Guzmán went to Mazatlán, Sinaloa, to meet with General Ramón F. Iturbe, who had not joined the uprising led by Obregón against Carranza's government. In May, when the rebellion triumphed and Carranza was assassinated, Guzmán boarded a U.S. ship to San Diego with Iturbe. The next month, Guzmán returned to Mexico and negotiated the safe return and reinstatement of General Iturbe with the leaders of the rebellion, General Adolfo de la Huerta and Obregón. By December 1920, Guzmán was serving in President Obregón's administration, having been appointed private secretary of Alberto Pani, secretary of foreign affairs. At this time Guzmán's friend José de Vasconcelos was also serving in Obregón's government as minister of education. Representing the Secretariat of Foreign Affairs, Guzmán was appointed to the Organizing Committee for the Celebration of the Centenary of Mexican Independence in 1921. On March 29, in the presence of President Obregón, he delivered the funeral oration at the burial of Jesús Urueta at the Rotunda of Illustrious Men at the Dolores Cemetery. In September 1922, Guzmán was elected deputy for the Sixth District of the City of Mexico, in the Thirtieth Legislature of the Congress of the Union. Referring to this period in Guzmán's life, Juan Bruce-Novoa remarks: "He is part of the inner circle of power during the brief but defining moment of the great cultural drive, in the early years of the Obregón administration" (xviii). As the end of Obregón's presidential term approached, Guzmán supported Adolfo de la Huerta instead of Obregón's chosen successor, Plutarco Elías Calles. Warned by Pani that his life was in danger, Guzmán fled the country in December 1923. This second exile was much longer. He did not return to Mexico until April 1936, on the invitation of President Lázaro Cárdenas, who had just deported Calles.

For Guzmán, who had feared for the fate of the Revolution as he saw caudillos succeed one another, the presidency of Cárdenas represented a righting of the course of the ship of state. For the four decades from his return to Mexico until his death, Guzmán devoted his energy and his talents as a writer, speaker, and publisher to the Revolution as represented by the Partido Revolucionario Institucional (Institutional Revolutionary Party). Guzmán was a public figure who often accompanied presidential candidates on campaign tours.

Martín Luis Guzmán's persistent advocacy is chiefly responsible for the reinstatement of Francisco Villa in the Mexican national imagination as one of the major figures of the Revolution. Villa, who had lost the power struggle to Carranza, Obregón, and Calles, had been largely left out of the national narrative by the winners. From 1938 to 1951, Guzmán's writing and publication of the five volumes of *The Memoirs of Pancho Villa* helped to restore the prestige of Villa. In November 25, 1966, Guzmán attended the unveiling of the inscription honoring General Francisco Villa on the wall of the Chamber of Deputies and received a standing ovation from the deputies in recognition of his tireless efforts to have Villa recognized as one of Mexico's heroes.

Even as many members of the Mexican intelligentsia increasingly expressed their disenchantment with the Mexican Revolution under decades of one-party rule, Guzmán continued to support the PRI. In addition to winning many literary awards throughout the years, Guzmán's achievements were recognized by the Mexican government. In 1965, he was awarded the Medal for Revolutionary Merit, and he was awarded the Medal for Military Merit in 1968. He was elected and served as senator for the Federal District from 1970 to 1976. When Guzmán died on

December 22, 1976, in Mexico City at the age of eighty-nine, a public vigil headed by President José López Portillo was held at the Palacio de Bellas Artes.

Martín Luis Guzmán holds a unique place in the history of the Mexican Revolution as its chronicler in works such as *The Eagle and the Serpent, The Shadow of the Strongman,* and *The Memoirs of Pancho Villa,* and as an active participant in its belligerent phase and later in its institutional phase through his journalism, influential work as a publisher, and his governmental work, for example, as president of the Comisión Nacional de los Libros de Texto Gratuitos (National Commission for Free Textbooks) established in 1959.

As the two most famous writers of the Mexican Revolution, comparisons of Mariano Azuela and Martín Luis Guzmán are natural and inevitable. Guzmán's relationship with the Mexican state stands in stark contrast with that of Mariano Azuela. Although Azuela also participated in the armed phase of the Revolution and, like Guzmán, went into exile in 1915 when the revolutionaries started to fight each other for power after Huerta's defeat, upon his return to Mexico in 1916, Azuela resumed his medical practice, continued to publish novels, and withdrew from politics. Like Guzmán, Azuela received awards and honors. In 1941, he received the literary award of the Ateneo Nacional de Ciencias y Artes (the National Atheneum of Arts and Sciences). In 1942, he was admitted to the Seminario de Cultura Mexicana (Seminary of Mexican Culture), and, like Guzmán, was also invited to join the Academia Mexicana de la Lengua (Mexican Academy of Language), but unlike Guzmán, Azuela declined. In 1943, the Mexican government named Azuela one of the twenty founding members of the Colegio Nacional. From 1916 to his death in 1952, Mariano Azuela chose to remain a private citizen aloof from party politics. The role of the Revolution in the lives of its two most famous chroniclers could not be more different. The Revolution, for Azuela, was a key episode in his life that he captured with memorable vibrancy and ambivalence in his novel *The Underdogs*; for Guzmán, the Revolution became inseparable from his political life and his literary career.

Gustavo Pellón
University of Virginia

Recommended Readings

About the Mexican Revolution

Beezley, William H. *Mexico in World History*. New York: Oxford University Press, 2011. See especially chapter 6, "Revolution 1910–1946."

Brenner, Anita. *The Wind That Swept Mexico: The History of the Mexican Revolution of 1910–1942*. Austin: University of Texas Press, 2003. First published 1943. One hundred eighty-four photographs assembled by George R. Leighton.

Buchenau, Jürgen. *Plutarco Elías Calles and the Mexican Revolution*. New York: Rowman & Littlefield, 2007.

Buchenau, Jürgen. *The Last Caudillo: Álvaro Obregón and the Mexican Revolution*. Chichester, England: Wiley-Blackwell, 2011.

Hall, Linda B. *Álvaro Obregón: Power and Revolution in Mexico, 1911–1920*. College Station: Texas A&M University Press, 1981.

Joseph, Gilbert M., and Jürgen Buchenau. *Mexico's Once and Future Revolution: Social Upheaval and the Challenge of Rule since the Late Nineteenth Century*. Durham, North Carolina: Duke University Press, 2013.

Knight, Alan. *The Mexican Revolution*. 2 vols. Cambridge, UK: Cambridge University Press, 1986.

Krauze, Enrique. *Mexico: Biography of Power: A History of Modern Mexico, 1810–1996*. New York: HarperCollins, 1997. Translated by Hank Heifetz. See especially chapters 13–15 on Carranza, Obregón, and Calles.

Meyer, Michael C., William L. Sherman, and Susan M. Deeds. *The Course of Mexican History*. New York: Oxford University Press, 2003. See especially chapter 9, "The Revolution: The Constructive Phase, 1920–1940."

About Martín Luis Guzmán and His Novel

Cifuentes-Goodbody, Nicholas. *The Man Who Wrote Pancho Villa: Martín Luis Guzmán and the Politics of Life Writing*. Nashville, Tennessee: Vanderbilt University Press, 2016.

Grimes, Larry M. *The Revolutionary Cycle in the Literary Production of Martín Luis Guzmán*. Cuernavaca, Mexico: Centro Intercultural de Documentación, 1969.

Glossary

Ándenles, muchachos: Let's go, boys.

aztecas: Gold coins, each worth twenty Mexican pesos.

Bravo River to the Suchiate River: the rivers that mark respectively the northern and southern borders of Mexico.

cambaya: Common cotton fabric used to make the clothing of workers and peasants.

catrín: Roughly, a fancy city slicker.

catrines jijos de la tiznada: City slicker sons of bitches. Tiznada, *the soiled one*, is a euphemism for the even more offensive *chingada*, a woman who has been taken sexually, usually violently.

caudillo: A military or political leader. The fact that the term can be translated as *leader* and *chief*, but also as *warlord*, *dictator*, or *strongman* attests to its evolution in Spain and Latin America. Originally considered a positive title, in the nineteenth and twentieth centuries, *caudillos* and the political tendency, caudillismo, came to be seen as a bane to democratic government.

cesta: A wicker basket used in jai alai to throw and catch the ball.

compadre: Strictly speaking a father and the godfather of his child are *compadres*. In common use it is the equivalent of "friend" or "buddy."

continuismo: The practice of incumbents keeping themselves in office.

fronton: The building where jai alai is played.

hijo de tal: S.O.B., euphemism for son of a bitch (*hijo de puta*).

imposicionistas: Those who want to impose a candidate in an undemocratic manner.

jai alai: A game of Basque origin played in a walled court with a ball (*pelota*) and wicker baskets (cestas).

jijo: A dialectical version of *hijo*, meaning *son*. Short for *son of a bitch*.

La Mora: The Mooress, the nickname given to one of the characters, Beatriz Delorme.

manta: Rough cotton cloth, usually white, and typically used for clothing worn by Mexican peasants.

mole: Mexican sauce. For example, "guacamole" is an avocado sauce.

mole poblano: Mexican sauce served with meat. Literally "Puebla sauce," after the city of its origin. It contains many ingredients including chilies and chocolate. It is considered by many to be the national dish of Mexico.

paseo: The custom of taking a stroll. Also the time at which it takes place.

patroncito: *Patrón* means *boss*, *patroncito* means *little boss*. The use of the diminutive—*cito*—denotes affection.

pelotari: Jai alai players.

puro jijo de la tiznada: Nothing but a son of a bitch.

salud: Cheers, literally health.

taco de barbacoa: Grilled meat tacos.

taco de frijoles: Bean tacos.

viva, muera: Respectively the equivalents of "Long live" and "Down with." For example, "¡*Viva Zapata!*" (Long live Zapata!); "¡*Muera el traidor!*" (Down with the traitor! Literally, "Death to the traitor!")

Related Texts

The texts included in this section give contemporary views of the novel and of General Álvaro Obregón, the real-life model for the Caudillo. The first text is by Carleton Beals (1893–1979), the noted American journalist, author, and historian of Latin America. His review of *La sombra del Caudillo* was published on March 8, 1930, by the *Saturday Review of Literature*. The second text titled "Citizen Obregón" is chapter three from the book *Mexico in Revolution* (1920) by the famous Spanish novelist Vicente Blasco Ibáñez (1867–1928), author of the novels *The Four Horsemen of the Apocalypse* and *Blood and Sand*. Both were bestsellers in the United States and were made into Hollywood movies. The chapter gives an account of Blasco Ibáñez's interview with Álvaro Obregón and sketches a revealing portrait of the general at a crucial point in his political career, when he is about to rebel against Venustiano Carranza and become president of Mexico.

Mexican Militarism[1]

La Sombra del Caudillo. By Martín Luís Guzmán. Madrid: Espasa-Calpe. 1929.
De Mi Vida. By Rodolfo Reyes. Madrid: Biblioteca Nueva. 1929.
La Revolucion Mejicana. By Luís Ariquistain. Madrid: Biblioteca del Hombre Modern. 1929.
En el Vertigo de la Revolucion Mexicana. By Alfonso Taracena. Mexico: Editorial Bolívar. 1929.
Voces de Combate. By Alessio Robles. Mexico: Manuel León Sanchez. 1929.

Already, the centenary of the birth of the great Mexican dictator, Porfírio Díaz—to be celebrated this year—has stimulated numerous books, pamphlets, and articles in Mexico and abroad, both on Díaz and the revolution which has rattled over the land since his tumble from power. After twenty years of civil strife, the figure of the half-Indian *caudillo*, who imposed his will upon the destinies of Mexico for thirty odd years of enforced peace, begins to take on truer dimensions. When the dictator embarked for Vera

---

1. Beals, Carleton. "Mexican Militarism." Foreign Literature reviews, *The Saturday Review of Literature* 6, no. 33 (March 8, 1930): 802.

Cruz, never to return, he is reported to have said: "They have unleashed the wild beasts. We shall see who will tame them again."

During these past two decades many have tried lion-taming, but nearly all have gone down to tragic graves: Madero, Huerta, Carranza, Villa, Zapata, Obregón, to mention only the supermen. Leader after leader has been swept on the crest of the revolution tidal wave; the outlines of Mexican society have been considerably altered; the Indian and the peasant have been honored with fulsome words, magnificent laws, and occasionally helped by deeds. Yet political and military practices, in most respects, have remained as debased as in the days of Santa Anna: among most of the revolutionary *caudillos*, the same loot and egomaniacal spirit has reigned supreme. Most of the military ringmasters, in the name of "Land and Liberty," have imitated without equaling, the tyrannical practices of Díaz, including the timely use of the firing squad. Had any single one of them possessed the ruthless will, the unflagging cleverness, or the enlightenment of Díaz, they might have held the storm-tossed ship of state to the course demanded by their pretended ideals. Many important and even beneficent things have been accomplished in Mexico, but with the exception of Calles and a few others, these accomplishments occurred more in spite of those in power and the existing system than because of true leadership or the methods in vogue.

Increasingly, however, the Mexican students of contemporary affairs are beginning to husk off the chaff and get down to the kernel of events. Revolutionary sophistry is being pierced. The more capable writers are sloughing off their sentimentalism and their fear, and are freeing themselves from dependence on political favors which long made it impossible for them to analyze the situation of their country accurately. A courageous impartiality begins to emerge. It takes stamina to put the blade to one's own throat as some recent writers have done. But in so doing they have discovered also a clear, unaffected prose, completely divorced from the colonial Góngora influence and from the rococo French writing of the Díaz epoch.

The outstanding chronicler of contemporary military and political Mexico is Martín Luís Guzmán. He has created a new school of writing, his principal follower being Rafael Muñoz. Guzmán's latest book, "La Sombra del Caudillo," lacks some of the intimate biographical touch that animated his earlier "El Aguila y la Serpiente" (to be brought out in English by Knopf), which recounted his campaign episodes by the side of the fantastic Pancho Villa; but nevertheless this semi-fictionalized account in "La Sombra," from the standpoint of objectivity, literary construction, and conciseness, is far superior. Don Martín's present book is a synthetic, swiftly moving description of a futile Mexican revolt, probably that of Serrano in 1927. Guzmán's own revolutionary experiences, his activities as a member of the agitated national Chamber of Deputies, have been tempered by his quiet methodical life in Madrid, where he frequents the memorable *tertulia* of Valle Inclán in the Hotel Regina. His new work has unbroken texture, sureness of touch. In relentless, sculptured Mexican prose, he throws the cruel spotlight on all the treachery, the sycophancy, and corruption of generals, politicians, and labor leaders; here is oil graft, murder, plotting, the vileness of the local political and military scenes pinned down by the dagger of truth. He takes the wheels out of the clock; he passes from the façade gilded with fine words regarding the freeing of the peasants to the grimy back stairs of Mexico's political edifice.

Across his pages stride Olivier, leader of the euphoniously but inconsistently named Radical Progressive Party, an oratorical demagogue ever ready to double-cross his best friends; Axkaná, the devoted confident of the Secretary of War, capable of superior and objective understanding, but obliged, because of the revolutionary turmoil, to drift like jetsam on the fast torrent of greedy politics; Jiménez, the tricky, cold-blooded official candidate, who "no one knew how, and in spite of his terrific indictments of the landed proprietors, had just acquired the largest hacienda in the north of the Republic,"—a paradox that might be laid at the door of almost any of the actual revolutionary leaders; Protasio Leyva, the murderous Commandant of the Valley of Mexico, who gloats in killing; the puffy assassin labor leader, Ricalde, with his sumptuous residence and scandalous orgies; La Mora, the prostitute whose fierce loyalty toward the group by which she is favored shames loftier treacheries.

The power of Guzmán's delineation lies in its complete lack of moralizing. Here is a simple narration of a relentless chain of circumstances. The characters, on the whole so despicable, are illuminated with occasional searching gleams into their recondite nobler possibilities, choked from ordinary sight by their helpless enslavement to their sordid environment. Some of them are powerful men, clever men, fearless men, yet they never overleap the wall of treacherous Mexican politics. They are puppets of their debased theatre. "Mexican politics is conjugated with only one verb," declares the cynical Olivier, "rise early." Get the drop on the other fellow, be your weapon a Colt '48, a regiment of troops, or a political convention.

Ever in the background of this ignoble picture towers the majestic yet caressing landscape of Mexico, brooding sadly, wistfully, over the debasement of the children of sin who tread the land so haughtily and so stupidly. Every once in a while the glory of the gigantic volcanic setting impinges upon the blurred consciousness of the protagonists, imparting to them a fleeting, lost-soul stirring, some weak, distant beauty, harshly thrust aside from lives ill-spent.

Thus Guzmán has quite passed beyond the romanticism of the earlier raconteurs of banditry, such as Manuel Payno in his "Los Bandidos del Río Frío." "La Sombra" is charged with a grieving consciousness of some lost, yet potential, Mexican greatness, some tremendous hope undivined, a realization of social forces twisting out of mire into light. The book will easily hold its own with Valle Inclán's "Tirano Banderas," with "Facundo," and several other type novels in Latin America. Cruel as "El Militarismo Mexicano," by Blasco Ibáñez, it is free from the flamboyance and maliciousness of the Spaniard, and it is better written. I doubt if Guzmán achieves the classic simplicity of Azuela's "Los de Abajo" (translated as the "Underdogs"), by E. Munguía, Jr., but he is more sophisticated, more conscious of the entire range of contemporary Mexico. His canvas is broader. The gang-war scene in the Chamber of Deputies, the final execution of Aguirre, and the fantastic tragic excape of Axkaná, are unforgettably vivid, palpitating with suspense, touched with the sanguinary majesty of d'Annunzio.

From the pitying above-the-battle position of Guzmán, in "De Mi Vida" we descend to partisan conflict of a bygone day. Rodolfo Reyes, the loyal son of General Bernardo Reyes (dictator of Coahuila under Díaz, who subsequently became a plotter against his master and against Madero), revives an old feud which has now lost much of its savor. "De Mi Vida" elevates the Caudillo Reyes much above his real capacities. His disloyal activities toward the Dictator were prompted not by deep convictions or patriotism, but by personal ambition. Reyes merely sought to capitalize the stirring sentiments of the close of the Díaz epoch for his own ends. But the book contributes first-hand knowledge to a little clarified moment in Mexican history. Its attacks upon Reyes's rival, the notable finance Minister, José Ives Limantour,—even more than the earlier Menckenesque critiques of the brilliant Díaz journalist, Francisco Bulnes—have served to stir up extended and informative controversy in the Mexican press.

Ariquistaín, the genial Socialist writer of Spain, who on a minor scale has often imitated the propaganda activities of Blasco Ibáñez, has written a typical apologia for the Calles régime and its one-time labor adherents. Ariquistaín reveals lack of preparation and limited contact with the native scene. It is blurred by just that sentimental optimism which clearer sighted Mexican writers are abandoning. It is reminiscent of the less capable pro-Carranza propaganda of González Blanco.

Taracena's little volume is a mine of information regarding the end of the Díaz administration and the revolution, through 1920. Written in diary form, recording only significant incidents, it gives a running-fire account, terse, unadorned, but throbbing with actuality. In these pages one quick-steps to the whole revolutionary movement; the remote is vividly contemporary; the reader scans the headlines of each day. From the years of his youth in tropical Tabasco, the author follows the Díaz persecutions down to the whirling events of the Madero revolution. Madero, Huerta, de la Barra, Carranza, Obregón, De la Huerta, Serrano, gallop past in the tragedy of their meteoric achievements. Unexpected lights flash upon their obscure antecedents. Madero, though an ineffectual temporizer, emerges as the finest character of all. Stubborn Carranza is shown as originally wavering from camp to camp, at the outbreak of the revolution. Secretly Carranza hates the revolution, is opposed to most of the reforms of the 1917 Constitution he himself established. On the other hand, the author is duly pleased with Carranza's firmness during the Pershing expedition and the Marine occupation of Veracruz.

The volume is not only a mine of information, but it is also stored with valuable anecdotes. Too much stress is laid upon purely military events, but Taracena's title—"En el Vértigo" is apt, for his laconic references to writers—Rubén Darío and Chocano deported from the country, the imprisonments of the free spirits of the day, not merely under Díaz but during the revolution, the insincere enunciation by Carranza of his 1915 agrarian law to attract adherents—show that all the art and literature and legal reform were but straws whirled on the full torrent of the military tempest. A book refreshingly free from cant.

In Alessio Robles's "Voces de Combate," we again pass to one of the camps of battle, right to the firing line. Alessio Robles, sincerely interested in political purification, belongs to the Rousseauan and Maderist tradition of democracy. He is less conscious of the economic and social upheaval. But sadly enough, as one of the leaders of the anti-Reelection Party, he was forced to collaborate with types having nothing in common with his own staunch idealism and far less worthy than those whom he opposed largely because they landed sure-footed on the platform of power. Alessio, for all of his honesty, has not caught the true pulse of the Giant, Revolution. Yet in his liberalism, so apart from the smashing militarism of the epoch, one feels that he would ever have been less ready to betray the cause he espoused than those extremists who have enriched themselves at the point of the gun, shouting creeds of freedom, for which they sacrificed only as gamblers and not as persistent strugglers in the interludes of peace. For peace, they have found it easiest cynically to put themselves under the wing of the United States against whose "predatory imperialism" but a few years ago they constantly railed in order to hoist themselves to power.

III. "Citizen" Obregón[2]

I met Obregón two days before he fled from Mexico City, declaring himself in open rebellion against the authority of President Carranza.

At the time of my arrival in Mexico Obregón was campaigning for his election in distant States of the republic. Several friends of mine, who are enthusiastic followers of the General, were anxious to have me meet and hear their idol. "As soon as Obregón comes back," they said, "we'll arrange a luncheon or dinner so that you two men may meet and know each other."

As a matter of fact, Obregón did not return; he was forcibly brought back to the capital by Carranza, who decided to try him for complicity with the rebels who had been in arms for some time against the Government. This was an effective means of putting an end to the campaign of insults and threats that Obregón had been conducting in various States.

The forcible return of Obregón to Mexico City caused great excitement among the people of the capital and stirred their curiosity even more.

"What next?" they asked. "Will the old man have courage enough to send Obregón to jail and put him out of the running in that way? Will Obregón start a revolution to preserve his personal liberty?"

And when many were asking themselves these questions with a certain anxiety, fearing the consequences of a final break between the master Carranza and his old pupil Obregón, my Obregonista friends came to notify me that they had arranged my interview with their hero.

"The General expects you to take luncheon with him to-morrow," they told me.

---

2. Blasco Ibáñez, Vicente, "III. Citizen Obregón," in *Mexico in Revolution*. Translated by Arthur Livingston and José Padin (New York: E. O. Dutton, 1920), 49–73.

Luncheon with the National Hero

I had insisted that the luncheon take place in a public restaurant, in full view of everybody, to avoid the possibility of false interpretations. If the luncheon were given in a private house to many people it might seem that I had a certain predilection for Obregón. There was no reason whatever why I should figure as a Carranzista or an Obregonista. My wishes were more than amply fulfilled. The luncheon was held in the Bac, the most centrally located restaurant in the capital. To make it even less secret, it was decided to have it in the main dining room, near the orchestra platform, rather than in a private room.

Obregón was at that time a personage in disgrace. It was true that he might rise again at any moment, but it was equally possible that he might be down for the full count. He had enthusiastic friends, but he had also against him "old man" Carranza, an enemy of tenacious hatreds and indomitable energy. The mysterious hour when public opinion shakes off its inertia and swings unexpectedly to one side or the other had not yet struck. The timid were still holding aloof; the crafty were making their calculations, but had not yet succeeded in dispelling their own doubts.

Obregón was still an unknown quantity. If you sided with him you might climb to a position in the Cabinet, but you also might walk to a place in front of the firing squad. The shrewd ones were waiting for the atmosphere to clear a little, and Obregón could count only on his personal following, the friends who had been faithful to him through thick and thin. The men who watch the trend of events from a point of vantage and eagerly await the psychological moment to rush to the succor of the sure winner had not yet heard the call.

The Disconcerting Obregón

When I entered the restaurant I saw Obregón sitting at a table with a friend to whom he was explaining the fine points of a cocktail which the General himself had invented. The reader must not jump at conclusions and infer that Obregón is a drunkard because I found him so engaged. I believe he drinks very little. During luncheon he took beer in preference to wine, and on several occasions he called for water. But as a warrior who has lived in the open air, suffering the rigor of inclement weather and spending whole nights without sleep, he likes to take a casual drink from time to time to tune up his nervous system.

It would be equally erroneous to imagine him as a Mexican chieftain of the type which we so frequently see in the movies and vaudevilles—a copper-colored personage with slanting eyes and thick, stiff hair, sharp as an awl; in short, an Indian dressed up like a comic-opera General. Obregón is nothing of the sort; he is white, so positively white that it is difficult to conceive his having a single drop of Indian blood in his veins. He is so distinctively Spanish that he could walk in the streets of Madrid without any one guessing that he hailed from the American hemisphere.

"My grandparents came from Spain," he told me. "I don't know from which province. Other people bother their heads a great deal about their ancestors. They imagine they come from noble stock and claim descent from Spanish Dukes and Marquises. I know only that my people came from Spain. They must have been poor folk driven to emigrate by sheer hunger."

The personage began to reveal himself. Obregón is a man who is always trying to amaze his hearer, now with explosions of pride, now with strokes of unexpected humility. The important thing for him is to be disconcerting, to say something that his listeners are not expecting to hear.

Close-Up of the Idol

He is still young—not quite 40. He has a strong and exuberant constitution. You can see at once that the man is brimming over with vitality. A slight varicosis has colored his cheeks with a number of slender, red veins, which give a reddish tint to his complexion. His enemy Don Venustiano suffers also from varicosis of the face, but his nose is the only feature that shows it prominently. It is furrowed by a series of red, blue and green veins that remind you of the wavy lines on a hydrographic map. All aggressive men have a more or less close resemblance to birds and animals of prey. Some are thin and sharp beaked, like hawks. Others have the mane and the arrogance of the lion. A few are lithe and mysterious, like the tiger. Obregón, with his short, thick neck, broad shoulders and small, sharp eyes, which on occasion emit fierce glints, reminds you of a wild boar.

Obregón is single and lives the life of a soldier, attended by one aid, an ex-ranchman who is even rougher than he. As Obregón has only one arm, and, consequently, cannot devote more than one hand to the care of his person, the "hero of Celaya"—as he is frequently called—is rather slovenly in appearance. In his military uniform he may look better. The man I met wore a dirty and much-worn Panama hat, baggy trousers and a shabby coat, one of whose sleeves hung empty, showing that the arm had been amputated near the shoulder.

Obregón's apparent contempt for all personal adornment is character-istic of the man. Another reason for his carelessness in matters of dress is his desire to flatter the Mexican populace, who consider that his slovenly garb brings him closer to them.

The missing arm enables the people to recognize Obregón at a dis-tance. They greet him enthusiastically whenever they see him. Obregón is the conqueror of Pancho Villa; he is the man who broke up the military power that came near placing that old cattle rustler in the Presidential chair of the republic.

Villa, Defeated, Almost Forgotten

Villa is almost forgotten in Mexico. He is talked about more in the United States than in his own country. A few years ago he was "The General" among all Generals, and many even spoke enthusiastically of his military talent, seeing in him the man who would take it upon himself to exter-minate any foreigner daring to invade the soil of the nation. Now he is nothing but a bandit and people avoid all reference to him. He will continue to make trouble, but his star has surely set. Obregón defeated him in ten bloody skirmishes, misnamed battles, and this was sufficient to make Obregón the hero of the hour. Moreover, Pancho Villa has escaped bodily injury; he has all his limbs. With insolent good luck he has kept out of the way of bullets. Obregón, on the contrary, has only one arm, thus adding to his heroic record the sympathy that the martyr arouses.

I sat down and the luncheon began, a luncheon that started at noon and lasted until 4.

Don Venustiano, always suspicious, as is natural in the head of a nation where every one is likely to *darse la vuelta*—to betray—and no one knows with certainty who is his friend and who is his enemy, spoke to me a few days later about this luncheon. I was the one to broach the subject. I told him frankly that I had lunched with one of his enemies.

"I know," he replied. "But what the devil did you have to talk about that it took you four whole hours?"

And he scrutinized my eyes as though he were trying to read my thoughts.

Obregón's Debut in Chick-peas

In reality Obregón had nothing interesting to tell me. But he is such a character! It is so agreeable to sit and listen hours and hours to his animated, lively and picturesque conversation, which is more Spanish than Mexican.

He had selected the table near the orchestra so that he could give orders to the musicians. He was anxious to show me that he was not an ignorant soldier and that he loved music—Mexican music, of course, for other kinds of music mean little to him. And while the orchestra played the "Jarabe," the "Cielito" and the "Mañanitas"—Mexican national airs— Obregón talked and talked, swallowing meanwhile pieces of food that he had an attendant cut for him, as he can use only one hand. The General is invincible in conversation. I can talk a great deal myself, but I was forced to withdraw before his onslaught, as thoroughly defeated as Pancho Villa himself. I listened.

He told me the story of his youth. He is sure that he was born to be the first everywhere. He does not say so himself, but he helps you to suspect it with modest insinuations. In Sonora he was a trader in *garbanzos*—chick-peas—and although he made rather small profits, he is sure that he would have become eventually the first merchant in Mexico—a great millionaire.

"You see, the revolution spoiled all that for me. I then became a soldier and I rose to be a General."

What he neglected to add was that, in spite of his General's commission, he remained in business just the same, and his enemies affirm that he has realized his ambition to become a millionaire. He has a monopoly at present of all the chick-pea trade in Mexico. The peas are exported to Spain, where *garbanzos*, as they are called, are an article of common consumption. The same enemies assert that all the farmers in Mexico are obliged to sell their *garbanzos* to Obregón, at a price which he himself fixes. That is the advantage of being a hero and of losing an arm in defense of the Constitution.

"All of Us Thieves, More or Less"

However, I shall not dwell on what Obregón's enemies say about him. The General went on talking about himself. He has a line of *risqué* stories which he tells with a brutal frankness smacking of the camp and the bivouac. They helped me to understand the popularity of the man. He talks that way with everybody, with the women of the street, with the workingmen he meets, with the peasants in the country, and those simple people swell with pride at being treated with such familiarity and at hearing such amusing stories from a national hero, the conqueror of Celaya, a former Minister of War, and a man who has only one arm!

"They have probably told you that I am a bit of a thief."

Taken somewhat aback, I looked around in surprise to make sure it was really Obregón who had said that, and that he had said it to me. I hesitated, not knowing really what answer to make.

"Yes," he insisted. "You have heard that story without a doubt. All of us are thieves, more or less, down here."

"Why, General," I said, with a gesture of protest, "I never pay any attention to gossip! All lies, I am sure."

But Obregón ignored what I was saying, and continued:

"The point is, however, I have only one hand, while the others have two. That's why people prefer me. I can't steal so much or so fast."

A burst of laughter! Obregón saluted his own witticism with the reserved hilarity of a cynical boy, while his two friends who were with us paid tribute to the hero's jest with endless boisterousness.

Joke of the Itching Palm

This oratorical success made the General still more talkative. He insisted on treating me to more stories, perhaps to show me that he held the gossip about him in contempt, perhaps to enjoy the pleasure of surprising and embarrassing me by the spectacle of a man depreciating himself.

"You probably don't know how they found the hand I lost!"

In reality, I did know, just as, for that matter, I had already heard the joke about his being more honest than the others because he had only one hand. But in order not to spoil the General's delight in his own brilliancy I assured him I did not know the story.

"You know I lost my arm in battle. It was carried off by a shell which exploded near me while I was talking with my staff. After giving me the first treatments, my men set out to find my arm on the ground. They looked about in all directions, but couldn't find it anywhere. Where could the hand and its fragment of arm have gone to?

"'I'll find it for you,' said one of my aides, an old friend of mine. 'It will come back by itself. Watch me!'

"He took out of his purse a ten-dollar gold piece, an aztec, as we call it, and raised it above his head. At once a sort of bird, with five wings, rose from the ground. It was my missing hand, which had not been able to resist the temptation to fly from its hiding place and seize a gold coin."

A second ovation from the guests! And the man with the one arm exploded with laughter at the naughty prank of his missing hand, and, not to be discourteous to its former owner, I laughed as well.

The Ambassador's Missing Watch

"And you never heard how the Spanish Ambassador lost his watch?"

I could see what Obregón was driving at. This story was to be not at his own expense, but against "that other fellow," his enemy and persecutor. However, I pretended to be quite innocent, so that the General could have the pleasure of telling the story.

"A new Minister from Spain had just presented his credentials, and President Carranza was anxious to welcome him with a great official banquet. The thing had to be done well. Spain had been the first European nation to recognize Don Venustiano's Government after the revolution."

As I listened to the hero I thought of the grand dining hall of the palace at Chapultepec, which recalls the tragic days of Maximilian, the Austrian Emperor of Mexico. I could see Don Venustiano in evening dress, with his white beard and red-white-and-green nose, seated opposite the Spanish Ambassador, and beside the latter, Obregón, Minister of War; Cándido Aguilar, Minister of Foreign Relations; the elegant Barragán, in a new uniform bought for the occasion, and all the other dignitaries created by the First Chief.

"Suddenly," continued Obregón, "the Spanish diplomat raised his hand to his vest, and grew pale. 'Caramba!' he exclaimed. 'My watch is gone!' It was an antique timepiece, gold and inset with diamonds, an heirloom in the Ambassador's family.

"Complete silence! First he looks at me, for I am sitting next to him. But I have an arm missing, and, as it happens, on the side nearest the Ambassador. I cannot have taken his watch! Then he looks at Cándido Aguilar, Don Venustiano's son-in-law, who is sitting on the other side. Aguilar still has both his arms, but one of his hands, and by chance the one next to the Ambassador, is almost paralyzed. Neither can he be the pick-pocket! Convinced that he must say good-by forever to his lost jewelry, the Spanish Minister sat out the rest of the meal cursing desperately under his breath.

"'They have stolen my watch. This is not a Government. This is a den of thieves!'

"When they got up from the table Don Venustiano, with his usual dignified and venerable bearing, stepped up to the Ambassador and whispered, 'Here you are, but say nothing more about it.'

"The diplomat could not contain his astonishment and admiration! 'It was not the man on my right! It was not the man on my left! It was the man across the table in front of me! Oh, my dear Mr. President, quite rightly do they call you the First Chief.'"

If the laughter at a joke on Obregón had been noisy, that for a joke on Carranza resembled a cannonade.

There is no doubt about it. Obregón is an excellent table companion. His amusing chatter is inexhaustible.

Leaving his stories, he went on to the subject of his election campaign. He is as proud of his speeches as he is of his triumphant battles. The General is a born orator, and like all self-educated men who take up reading late in life, he noticeably prefers the sonorous, theatrical sentence which never says anything.

He invited me to attend one of his election meetings to hear him speak to a crowd. At the moment he had on his mind a great parade which the laborers of the capital were preparing in his honor. It was to be headed by 1,500 Mexican women—all the dressmakers in the city. The women of Mexico feel a purely spiritual inclination toward this plain-speaking soldier, who treats every one as his equal.

He expounded his platform to me volubly: democracy—enforcement of the law—realization of the promises made by the revolution, and which the "old chief" had forgotten—distribution of lands to the poor. The real reason for his candidacy, the argument that has greatest weight with him, he never mentioned, but I could read it in his eyes.

"Besides," Obregón undoubtedly says to himself, "besides, I made Don Venustiano President. I took him in triumph from Veracruz to the Presidential chair in Mexico City. He became President through my efforts. Now it is my turn. Isn't that fair?"

He Is an Author, Too

Since the General had already forgotten his jokes and stories and had now to speak with the seriousness befitting a Chief Executive, he gradually and imperceptibly passed from oratory to literature. The General became a "colleague" of mine, a man of letters. He has written a book telling the story of his campaigns. That has been the custom of all victorious warriors since the time of Julius Caesar. Why should he not also indulge in a set of "Commentaries"?

He promised to send me a copy of his book. But to forestall the chance that his difficulties with Carranza might prevent him from keeping the promise, he went on to give me an idea of the book in advance.

He said that he expressed himself simply and with modesty. Of course his battles could not be compared with those of the European war. . . . "I also realize that I am only an amateur in the military business, a civilian forced to take up arms—Citizen Obregón promoted to be a General: and doubtless I had strokes of sheer luck!"

I was listening to Obregón with real affection. I was regarding him as the most attractive and most able man among all the Mexican Generals made by the national upheaval. But suddenly the wind changed. Men never get really to know each other. Obregón began to twirl his sharp-pointed, upturning mustache, and smiling in pride at his own modesty, he lay back on his divan.

"When I was Minister of War, at a banquet at the President's house one day, the Dutch representative, who was a military man, came up to me and said, 'General, from what branch of the service did you come—artillery, cavalry?' In view of my victories he thought I must be a professional soldier. Imagine his astonishment when I told him I had been a chick-pea dealer in Sonora! He refused to believe it."

More About His Great Book

The General stopped a moment to enjoy the impression his words were making on us.

"Another time the German Minister came to see me. You doubtless know him by reputation, Mr. Ibañez."

"Very well indeed," I replied. "He was the fellow who during the late war suggested to the Mexican Government the possibility of recovering California and Arizona. He used to appear at public ceremonies in a great Prussian uniform with decorations, to receive the applause of a paid claque or an ignorant crowd which was always hissing the plain black evening dress of the diplomatic representative of the United States."

"Well," said Obregón, "the German came to see me, and in his short abrupt accent said to me: 'General, I have read your book, and I need two copies of it, one for my Emperor and the other for the archives of the German General Staff. The people back in Berlin are much interested in you. They are astounded that a plain civilian, without military training, has been able to conduct such noteworthy and original campaigns.'"

"I suppose you gave him the books?"

"No, I don't care for honors like that. I told him he could find them in the bookstores if he wanted them. And I suppose he bought them and sent them on home."

What a farceur that shrewd German was!

The hero doubtless remembered my hatred of German militarism, so to emphasize his impartiality he jumped to the Far East.

"The Japanese Minister also asked my permission to translate the book into Japanese. My campaigns seem to have aroused a good deal of interest over there."

"Has the translation appeared yet?" I inquired.

"I don't know. I don't bother about such matters."

Popular Appeal of a "Bad Man"

A long silence. I sat looking somewhat disconcertedly at this man, so complex for all of his primitive simplicity, who alarms you at one moment by his craftiness and at the next astonishes you by his complete ingenuousness.

Nevertheless, he is the most popular and the most feared man in Mexico, the man everywhere most talked about. Some people love him to the extent that they would die for him. Others hate him and would like to kill him, as they remember the barbarous outrages he ordered in the early days of the triumphant revolution, actuated by some perverse whim of his very original character.

He appeals to the multitude for his somewhat rustic frankness, his good-natured wickedness and his rather brutal gayety. He has, besides, the prestige of a courage which no one questions, and of an aggressiveness, in a pinch, like that of a wild boar at bay. To cap the climax, he has lost an arm.

My readers must pardon me for emphasizing this latter point. In Mexico such things are more important than elsewhere. The people in Mexico, who are ready to take up guns and kill each other at a moment's notice and most of the time without knowing why, are very sentimental and easily moved to tears. Mexicans give up their lives with the greatest indifference and for anybody at all. At the same time they will weep at the slightest annoyance occasioned to one of their loved heroes. The Mexican populace descends from the Aztecs, those magnificent gardeners who lovingly cultivated flowers and, at the same time, tore the hearts out of a thousand living prisoners at each of their religious festivals. Poetry and blood, sentimentality and death! It is a pity that Obregón's lost arm did not actually leave its hiding place to seize the gold "aztec" which the General's aide held out to it, in the story! It would have been worshiped by the people with national honors.

Value of an Amputated Leg

There are precedents for this. General Santa Anna was an Obregón in his day. Though the latter has never been President yet, the former reached the Presidency several times through uprisings or manipulated elections. The Mexican people hated Santa Anna after his unsuccessful campaign against the secessionists, who had established a republic in Texas. The Texans defeated his army and made him prisoner. However, at that moment, it occurred to the French Government of Louis Philippe to send a military expedition into Mexico to enforce some diplomatic demands, and French soldiers disembarked in Veracruz. Santa Anna rushed to oppose them, and the last shot the invaders fired hit him in the leg, and the surgeons had to amputate it.

Never did a popularity rise to such pure and exalted heights. Santa Anna's leg, properly pickled, was taken from Veracruz to Mexico City with a great guard of honor. The Government bestowed on the amputated limb the honors of a Captain General killed in battle, and in the midst of triumphal pageantry, the booming of cannon and the music of bands, it was buried in the center of the city under a great monument.

However, reversals of opinion and sudden waves of anger must be looked for in sentimental peoples. Years later Santa Anna went to war with the United States over the Texas affair. The campaign went against him and the Americans took Mexico City. The people needed to vent its wrath on somebody, and since it could not get its hands on Santa Anna, it tore down the monument to his heroic leg, paraded the unfortunate bone through the streets of the city and finally threw it into a dung heap.

His Threats Not "Celestial Music"

Obregón spoke to me about a friend of his, a newspaper man, some of whose articles were worthy of admiration. "He is ill," said the General, "and practically dying. He has been in bed for several months. He would be delighted if you would pay him a visit."

The General and I agreed to go together. "I am going to see the silver mines at Pachuca to-morrow," I said. "I shall be away two days."

"When you come back I shall still be here," said the General. "All that talk about the old man's prosecuting me and putting me in jail is just celestial music (Mexican for 'hot air'). We shall see each other. I'll give you my book and we'll go and see my friend."

When I got back the General had disappeared. He had fled from the city not to return till just now, when he comes back as a conqueror.

Obregón did well to get away when he did. The threats of "the old man" were not music. A few hours later Carranza would have had him locked up.

Carranza told me so himself the last time I saw him.